Praise for STRIKE THE ZITHER

'Joan He takes no prisoners, and *Strike the Zither* is her latest triumph.
An intricate, expansive epic that poses difficult questions and eschews
easy answers, this book is as ambitious as its scheming, ruthless cast—
and just like its narrator, delivers above and beyond.'
MARGARET OWEN, author of The Merciful Crow duology

'This soaring, masterful retelling becomes an epic all of its own as He's
heroine outsmarts and outmaneuvers a vibrant cast of military geniuses.
With its startling twists and constant intrigue, readers will get lost in this
rich, gorgeous, and dangerous world.'
EMILY SUVADA, author of This Mortal Coil series

'A twisty, body-snatching, gender-flipped retelling of
The Romance of the Three Kingdoms. Prepare to be transported.'
REBECCA LIM, author of *Tiger Daughter*

'Filled with twists and turns, *Strike the Zither* is a meticulously plotted,
supremely satisfying story that explores identity, legacy, and loyalty in
unexpected ways. This is Joan He's best yet.'
HANNAH WHITTEN, author of *For the Wolf*

'[A]n ode to loyalty, family, destiny, and the complicated ways each of
these elements bind or free the cunning strategist at the center of the
tale. This riveting read is full of twists and surprises that shock and
delight, building up to the epic conclusion that left me gasping.'
JUDY I. LIN, author of The Book of Tea duology

'Rich with intrigue and epic in scale. *Strike the Zither* grows tall on the
heroic classics it draws from, yet beats powerfully with a heart of its own.
Joan He aims ambitiously and lands true each time.'
CHLOE GONG, author of the These Violent Delights Duet

Praise for THE ONES WE'RE MEANT TO FIND

'A perfect synthesis of high-tech futurism and dreamlike imagery.
Gripping, heartfelt, and joyously cerebral, this is a story
to dive into and let its twisting currents pull you into
a strange, clever, and startlingly original world.'
EMILY SUVADA, author of This Mortal Coil series

'I fell in love with this haunting, futuristic world and
the sisters searching for each other in it. He's words will
stay with you long after the final page.'
MARIE LU, bestselling author of the Skyhunter series

'In a climate-ravaged future, the love between two sisters is the only
hope for humanity's future. This is sci-fi at its best:
floating cities, kindness and desert islands.'
LAUREN JAMES, author of *The Reckless Afterlife of Harriet Stoker*

'Smart, twisty and electrifying, this is the work of an astonishing mind.'
DAVINA BELL, author of *The End of the World Is Bigger Than Love*

'This book doesn't hold your hand. It shoves you into the abyss, and
trusts that you will find your way back, and every step is worth it.
Joan He is charting an ambitious new course in fiction,
and I will follow her anywhere she goes.'
V. E. SCHWAB, author of the Shades of Magic series

'An expansive near-future narrative that centers Asian sisterhood
and family...He crafts an intricate, well-paced rumination
on human nature, choice, and consequence.'
PUBLISHERS WEEKLY (starred review)

'One of the strongest sci-fi novels I've ever read.
Action-packed and philosophical, ambitious, melancholic,
and mind-blowing...sings with sublime ache.'
TOR.COM

Joan He is a Chinese-American writer. At a young age, she received classical instruction in oil painting before discovering that storytelling was her favourite form of expression. She studied Psychology and East Asian Languages and Cultures at the University of Pennsylvania and currently splits her time between Philadelphia and Chicago. She is the *New York Times* bestselling author of *Descendant of the Crane* and *The Ones We're Meant to Find*. *Strike the Zither* is the first in a fantasy duology.

joanhewrites.com

@joanhewrites

STRIKE THE ZITHER

JOAN HE

TEXT PUBLISHING MELBOURNE AUSTRALIA

The Text Publishing Company acknowledges the Traditional Owners of the country on which we work, the Wurundjeri people of the Kulin Nation, and pays respect to their Elders past and present.

textpublishing.com.au

The Text Publishing Company
Wurundjeri Country, Level 6, Royal Bank Chambers, 287 Collins Street, Melbourne Victoria 3000 Australia

The Text Publishing Company (UK) Ltd
130 Wood Street, London EC2V 6DL, United Kingdom

First published in the United States of America by Roaring Brook Press, a division of Holtzbrinck Publishing Holdings, New York, 2022
Published by The Text Publishing Company, 2022

Cover design by Aurora Parlagreco
Cover illustration by Kuri Huang
Book design by Aurora Parlagreco
Illustrations by Tida Kietsungden
Typeset in Garamond Premier Pro
Map by Anna Frohmam

Printed and bound by CPI Group (UK) Ltd, Croydon, CR0 4YY

ISBN: 9781911231417 (paperback)
ISBN: 9 9781922791115 (ebook)

A catalogue record for this book is available from the National Library of Australia.

To Heather, my 孔明

MAJOR FIGURES

North / Capital of the Xin Empire / Kingdom of Miracles
  Empress: Xin Bao*
  Prime Ministress: Miasma
  Strategist: Crow
  Advisor: Plum
  Notable Generals: Viper, Talon, Leopard

Southlands / Kingdom of Knowledge
  Lordess: Cicada
  Strategist: November

Westlands
  Governor: Xin Gong*
  Advisor: Sikou Hai
  Notable Generals: Sikou Dun, Aster, Bracken

Without Land
  Lordess: Xin Ren*
  Swornsisters: Cloud, Lotus
  Strategist: Zephyr
  Notable Generals: Tourmaline

*Surname precedes given name. For example, Xin Bao and Xin Ren both
  share the surname "Xin."

CONTENTS

辛仁

Xin Ren, Xin clan member and first of the three swornsisters

高云

Cloud (Gao Yun), second swornsister

黄蓮子

Lotus (Huang Lianzi), third swornsister

潘奇林

Zephyr (Pan Qilin), strategist to Xin Ren

Please note that this is a work of fantasy. The Xin Dynasty does not exist in history, and the story is neither set in China nor a true-to-times portrayal of social orders and demographics. Furthermore, Strike the Zither *should not be used as an educational reference for Chinese philosophy and spirituality; the metaphysics of qì; the mythology of gods; or the playing techniques of the gǔqín, to name just a few areas in which artistic liberties have been taken.*

STRIKE
THE
ZITHER

STANZA ONE

To the north, a miasma
descended over the capital,
trapping the young empress in its thrall.

To the south, a cicada
sang a song of vengeance
as the people mourned their late queen.

Between lands, a lordess
with nothing
sought to change her fate.

And in the skies above,
the heavens were one god short.

SOMETHING FROM NOTHING

Some say the heavens dictate the rise and fall of empires.

Clearly, those peasants have never met me.

My abilities as a strategist have earned me many sobriquets, from the Dragon's Shadow to the Tactician of Thistlegate. Rising Zephyr is my personal favorite. "Zephyr" will do, if you please.

"Peacock!"

Unless you're Lotus. Then it's too much to ask for.

I struggle to steer my mare around; horses don't appreciate genius.

Neither does Lotus. "Hey, Peacock!" she hollers over the creaking wagons, crying babies, and cracking whips. She urges her stallion up along the other side until we're somewhat eye to eye, the heads of people and oxen coursing between us. "They're catching up!"

Consider me unsurprised. Miasma, prime ministress of the Xin Empire in name, acting empress in reality, was bound to close in on our soldiers and peasants, who now—thanks to Lotus—realize they're about to die. A child bursts into tears, an auntie trips, a young couple spurs their mule faster. No luck. The steep forest path is doughy from last night's rainfall, kneaded to mush by the hundreds we've evacuated.

Still hundreds more to go.

"Do something!" Lotus shouts at me. "Use your brain!" Her hair has frizzed into an impressive mane around her face, and she waves her ax as if she's itching to use it.

Wouldn't help us. It's not just Miasma we're up against: Our own numbers are bogging us down. *We must evacuate everyone,* Ren said sternly when I suggested it was time we flee our current town for the next. *Miasma will slaughter the commonfolk just for harboring us.*

Miasma may still yet, at this rate, but there's no arguing with our warlordess Xin Ren's benevolence. Most strategists wouldn't be able to cope with it.

I can.

"Think of a plan!" Lotus bellows.

Thanks for the confidence, Lotus. I already have—three, in fact. Plan one (ditch the commoners) might be off the table, but there's plan two (cut down trees and pray for rain), and plan three (send a trustworthy general to the bridge at the mountain's base to hold off Miasma).

Plan two is in motion, if the humidity is any indication. I've set General Tourmaline and her forces on felling trees behind us. The trunks will wash down in the coming storm, and the resulting dam should delay Miasma's cavalry by a couple of hours.

As for sending a trustworthy general to the bridge . . .

My gaze cuts from Lotus to Cloud, Ren's other swornsister.

She's helping evacuees farther up the muddy slope, her ultramarine cloak rich against the muted greens of the firs.

Cloud thinks better than Lotus under pressure. A shame, because I don't know if I can harness her. Last month, she released Miasma from one of my traps because *Sage Master Shencius forbids killing by way of snare.* That's all very nice, Cloud, but was Sage Master Shencius ever on the run from the empire? I don't think so.

"You." I point my fan at Lotus. "Ride down to the bridge with a hundred of your best and employ Beget Something from Nothing."

Lotus gives me a blank look.

"Just . . . make it look like we have more forces across the river than we actually do. Stir up dust. Roar. Intimidate them." Shouldn't be too hard for Lotus, whose sobriquet only suits her if you visualize the root, not the flower. Her war cry can shake birds out of trees within the radius of a li. She forged her own ax and wears the pelt of a tiger she killed as a skirt. She's as warrior as warriors come, the opposite of everything I stand for. At least Cloud knows her classical poems.

But Lotus has something Cloud doesn't: the ability to take an order.

"Intimidate," she repeats under her breath. "Got it." Then she's galloping down the mountain on her beastly stallion and referring to herself by name in that gauche way some warriors do before riding into battle. "Lotus won't disappoint!"

Thunder swallows the rumble of her departure. Clouds brew in the sky, and leaves drift around me in a breeze more stench than air. Pressure builds in my chest; I breathe through it and focus on my hair, still clasped back in its high ponytail. My fan, still in my hand.

This won't be the first time I've delivered the impossible for Ren.

And deliver it I will. Miasma isn't reckless; the impending rains combined with Lotus's intimidation will make her think twice before pursuing us up the mountain. I *can* slow her down.

But I'll also need to speed us up.

I jerk on the reins; my mare balks. The insubordination! "Turnips and figs later!" I hiss.

Jerking harder, I trot us down the slope.

"Forget the pack animals!" I bark to the sluggish stream of people. "Leave the wagons! This is a command from Xin Ren's military strategist!"

They do as they're told, scowling all the while. They love Ren for her honor, Cloud for her righteousness, Lotus for her spirit. My job is not to be lovable but to get every peasant off the mountain and into the town over, where Ren should already be waiting with the first wave of evacuees, the other half of our troops, and—hopefully—a boat passage south so that I can secure us some much-needed allies.

"Hurry!" I snap. People plod a little faster. I order someone to help a man with a broken leg, but then there's a pregnant woman who looks seconds away from labor, children without shoes, toddlers without parents. The humid air thickens to soup, and the pressure in my chest climbs to my throat. Harbinger of a breathing attack, if there ever was one.

Don't you dare, I think to my body as I ride farther down the line, shouting until I'm hoarse. I pass a girl shrieking for her sister.

Ten people later, I cross a younger girl in a matching vest, bawling for hers.

"Follow me," I wheeze. I barely see the sisters reunited before lightning strips the forest bare. The animals whine in chorus—my horse among them.

"Turnips—"

Thunder claps and my horse rears, and the reins—

They slip through my fingers.

‡ ‡ ‡

Death and I have met before. In this regard, I'm no different from hundreds if not thousands of orphans. Our parents died to famine or plague or some rampaging warlord, rising up in droves under the empire's waning power. Death may have spared me then, but I know it's there, a lingering shadow. Some people have the physical abilities to outrun it. I don't bother. My mind is my light, my candle. The shadow flees *me*, not the other way around.

So I'm not scared, when I dream of heaven. It's familiar. A white wicker gazebo. Nested limestone terraces. Magnolia-bloom skies. Wind chimes and birdsong and always, always this melody.

This melody of a zither.

I follow the familiar music, over lakes of pink clouds. But the pink fades, and the dream becomes a nightmare of a memory.

Clash of steel. Steeds thundering down the street. A spearhead erupts through a torso, red. I grab your hand and we run. I don't know if these warriors are friend or foe, which warlord has seceded from the empire now and named themselves king, if they're empire forces come to relieve us or kill us. We're just orphans. Less than people, to these warriors. All we can do is run from them. Run. Your hand tears from mine; I scream your name.

Ku!

The fleeing tide is too thick. I can't find you. Finally, the dust settles. The warriors leave.

You've left me too.

I bolt upright, panting.

"Steady." Hands, closed around my upper arms. A face: hawk-beak brows, nose bridge scarred. It's Tourmaline, Xin Ren's third general—the *only* general of Ren's with a fitting sobriquet, seeing as Tourmaline's disposition is as solid as the gemstone. We tolerate each other, as far as warriors and strategists go. But right now, Tourmaline isn't the person I want to see.

She's not the sister from my dream.

"Steady, Zephyr," she coaches as I lunge against her grip.

Gasp by gasp, I release my disappointment. Tourmaline, in turn, releases me. She hands me a waterskin. I clutch it, hesitating. Water will wash the name from my tongue, the name I haven't spoken in six years.

Ku.

But the dream wasn't real, and when Tourmaline says, "Drink," I do.

Tourmaline sits back. Dried mud cakes her silver armor. "You, Zephyr, are god-blessed," she says, and I cough on a mouthful of water. "That, or you did something good in a previous life."

Reincarnation and gods are both the stuff of peasant myths.

"I reached you seconds before the wheels of a wagon did," Tourmaline continues, stoic. I could have done without the image, but if anyone had to find me on the ground, better it be Tourmaline than Lotus or Cloud. Those two would have squawked about it to everyone and their mothers. On the subject of everyone—

My gaze darts to my surroundings. We're in a tent; it's night; something gamey is roasting outside. All good signs we weren't decimated by Miasma.

Still, I need to hear it to be sure. "We made it to Hewan?"

Tourmaline nods. "Exactly ten li, a mountain, and a river away from Miasma's forces. The rain came just as you said it would. It'll take them at least a day to clear a path, four to go around."

"Lotus?"

"Will be the talk of the empire. Think lots of drums and bellowing. Miasma's generals ran so fast, you'd think we had a hidden force of ten thousand."

I choke down some more water. Good. Miasma is the paranoid type. She'll hear the war sounds, see the difficult terrain, and think *ambush*. A maneuver like that requires more forces than we actually have, but as long as Miasma believes in Lotus's illusion, we've bought ourselves however long it'll take for her to gather reinforcements—a day, by my estimates.

Then I remember the limping man, the groaning woman, the crying sisters. If they're alive—"They are," Tourmaline confirms—they owe it to the ideals of one person. "And Ren?"

"She was meeting with the Hewan governor, last I checked," says Tourmaline.

She steadies me as I rise. Hands braced against my lower back, I eye the scant pile of belongings that survived the journey with me. My white robes are muddied beyond salvaging, and I wrinkle my nose at the replacement set. Beige. Blech.

Tourmaline breaks the quiet. "You shouldn't ride off on your own like that."

"I can *ride* fine. It's the horse. Your turnip-and-fig trick didn't work." Or I was the fool, for taking a warrior's advice.

Tourmaline blinks, once and slow. "I found no turnips or figs on your person."

"I promised them as rewards." Obviously, the horse did not earn them.

Another drawn-out blink.

"I'll let you dress," Tourmaline finally says.

She leaves the tent. Alone, I groan and put on the beige robes. I fasten my broadbelt, reach down—hand hovering over the wrapped bundle that is my zither—and pick up my fan. I beat the crane feathers clean and smooth out the kinks, fingers slowing to trace over the single kingfisher feather. A gift from my last mentor, who'd lived longer than the rest. *One star cannot light a galaxy*, he'd said as he'd sewn on the feather.

I'm not a star, I'd countered. *I am the universe itself.*

But even the universe is subject to unseen forces. The next night, a meteorite punched my mentor and his outhouse clean into the ground.

I can predict meteors now. Trace the paths of all stars, foretell weather patterns nine times out of ten. The environment, as it stands, is our only ally. Using it to our advantage has earned me the sobriquet of Fate Changer. But the work I do isn't magic. It's memorization and analysis and application. It's limiting the factors I can't control, and reducing our reliance on miracles.

Today, without a doubt, was a miracle. It pains me to admit it, but unless a meteorite kills Miasma next time, even *I* can't save us, not if we keep on traveling with so many commoners.

It's time I had a talk with Ren.

I slip my fan's bamboo handle between the broadbelt and my waist, clasp my hair back into its ponytail, and head out of the tent, into the night.

Braziers raised on cross staves line the road to Hewan's town square. Suckling pigs roast over fire pits. Under a pavilion canopied with drying laundry and hemp quilts, the townspeople and our troops raise wine dishes in Ren's name. Our popularity has never been an issue. Towns welcome us. Governors who detest Miasma give us refuge. Commoners practically line up to follow us over rivers and mountains.

That needs to stop here.

I spy Ren at a table under the pavilion, sitting with the Hewan governor and townsfolk. With her threadbare gray robes, patched broadbelt, and modest topknot, she's almost indistinguishable from the rabble. Almost. Her voice carries a weight to it. A sadness, I sometimes think, that doesn't match her easy grin. She's grinning now at something a soldier says to her.

I make my way over.

"Hey, Peacock!"

Heavens spare me. Not this again.

"Peacock!"

Ignore her. But then I hear the voice of my third mentor, the chess master. *You can't push people around like chess pieces. You have to inspire trust.*

To inspiring trust, then.

"What are you calling her here for?" Cloud asks Lotus as I face their table. Her blue cloak spills over her broad, armored shoulders; her hair hangs in a thick braid down her back. "Haven't you had enough of being ordered around for a day?"

"I want to see her up close!" Lotus explains, face lighting up when I am *up close.* "You *did* change colors."

Peacock or chameleon, Lotus. Make up your mind.

"Huh," says Cloud, glancing over me. "What happened to the white? Let me guess: You tired of the dung stains."

The soldiers around her snicker. I sniff. *They* wouldn't understand the significance. White is the color of sages, of purity and wisdom and—

"Rumor is that you had a little spill today." Cloud's not done. "Ren asked me to search for a carpenter in this town. It's just too bad there's no one skilled enough to fix your carriage."

Chariot. The contraption I rode before it too fell victim to the mud. I level my gaze at Cloud and she stares back, arch. No doubt she dislikes me because I have Ren's ear, despite not being one of her two swornsisters. Pity for her. I have little interest in fraternizing with either Lotus or Cloud, a nineteen-year-old and twentysomething who act like they're ten. I start to leave—and yelp as Lotus grabs my arm.

"Wait! A toast to the peacock!" Wine spills from the dish she raises. "She saved everyone today!"

I extricate myself. "Carry on without me."

Lotus's expression falls.

"Oh, don't look so down," says Cloud. Her proud voice carries over the din as I make my escape. "You know what they say about strategists."

Walk away.

"They can't hold their liquor."

Walk away.

"One drink, and they're barfing—"

I march back, snatch the dish from Lotus, and down it.

Lotus slaps the table. "Another round!"

Suddenly I'm boxed in by warriors, everyone crowding for their fill. Dishes go bottom-up. Lotus pours more from the jug.

"Who here thinks Skull-face is a god?" Skull-face must be Lotus's nickname for Miasma. Hands rise and Lotus roars, "Cowards! *Ren* is the god!"

"Quit yapping," says Cloud. "Ren doesn't want you spreading that." Then she pounds her chest with a fist and declares to the table, "I'm the god!"

"No, *I'm* the god!"

"I'm the god!"

"I'm the god!"

Peasants, all of you, I think darkly as more wine is sloshed onto me instead of into mouths. Someone belches. Lotus farts. I wiggle free the second I see an opening, squeezing out of the crush.

I barely make it to a bush before throwing up.

That was three, *Cloud.* I frown at the mess I've deposited in the bush—yew bush, to be precise. Scaly brown bark. Needles spiraling around the stem. Berries round and red. Toxic to humans, who I'd hope are smart enough not to graze on wild bushes, and horses, who probably aren't. I should warn the cavalry—

I retch again.

"Aiya, my swornsisters got you, didn't they?"

Ren.

I wipe my mouth and hurry to face her, bowing low from the waist.

"At ease, at ease." Ren waits for me to straighten. "I'll have a word with them."

And make them even more recalcitrant? "It wasn't—"

"Who said they were the god this time?"

"Cloud." *Ugh.* "But all of them, eventually."

"Heavens forgive their sedition," Ren says, but she's smiling. "Shall we escape them for a while? Survey the town?" She turns, then glances back to me, concern softening her smile. "If you're up for it."

As if I'd let some warriors get the better of me.

I wipe my mouth again, and accompany Ren through our temporary camp. She checks in with our troops, helps a soldier fix a pair of boots, asks the mother-to-be when she's due. I stand off to the side—this isn't quite the "surveying" I had in mind— and at last, our path brings us to Hewan's western watchtower. Ren goes up the bamboo stairs first. I climb behind her, lungs smarting. We reach the top and gaze at the town. The night is clear, the sky dashed with stars.

"Tell me, Qilin." Only Ren still calls me by my birth name. It's too late to tell her that I loathe it. "On a scale of one to ten, how close are you to quitting?"

I rush to bow again. "If I've done anything to disappoint—"

"You saved us today," Ren interrupts, firm. "But this can't be what you signed up for."

She can't know. Of all the times I've washed my robes, trying to rid them of grime and filth, or the nights I've lain awake, sleepless, feeling more like a shepherd of peasants than a strategist.

But in the end, those are all small inconveniences. Even the peasants. Our most pressing problem is my lack of a boat passage south. *Bring it up—*

"I won't fail you," I blurt.

"I know," says Ren. "I just worry that I'll fail you. And maybe . . ." She looks up at the sky. "I'll fail her."

There are hundreds of stars in the night, but I know exactly which one she's looking at. It's small and dull, our Empress Xin Bao's star.

Ren beholds it as if it's the sun.

To my knowledge, Ren has only met our prepubescent sovereign once—which is one more occasion than most. Empresses since antiquity have lived cloistered within the palace, their power vested not in who they are, but in the ancient tradition they symbolize and their courts. Xin Bao's court has belonged to a long line of regents.

Miasma is simply the latest.

When Xin Bao asked Ren to liberate her from Miasma's clutches, Ren heard a child's cry for help. She abandoned her post in the empire army, took up arms against her old colleagues. Miasma has been hell-bent on exterminating Ren ever since, for the same reason so many peasants follow her: of all the warlords who've challenged the empire in the last decade, Ren has the most legitimate cause. The most legitimate *claim*, should she covet the throne one day. As members of the Xin clan, she and Xin Bao share blood. And while Miasma is professing to be heavens-sent, I know some think it's Ren. Because next to Empress Xin Bao's star is another star. It appeared in the sky eight years ago. Miasma may have all the imperial cosmologists wrapped around her finger, but even she can't kill rumors. New stars are said to represent gods.

That rogue star could belong to anyone.

I know my stars, but I don't believe in gods. Even if I did, I don't believe they care one bit about us. As we stare at the sky, Ren's hand drifts to the pendant at her throat, engraved with the Xin surname. I wonder which is more burdensome: chaining your fate to a higher power or to your family.

I'm lucky to have neither.

Eventually, Ren snaps out of her spell. "Get some sleep, Qilin." Her hand starts for my back, then rests on my head instead. My bruises still ache in response, for some reason. "We'll depart early tomorrow. We'll keep the commoners here—"

My heart lifts.

"—and supply the town with some of our forces."

No loss, I tell myself. "Forces" don't mean much when you're constantly on the retreat.

"Lordess—" I call out before she descends the tower. "My boat passage south?"

Ren grimaces. "I'm sorry, Qilin. Every river within a hundred lǐ from here is empire-controlled."

"I'll find a way." I always do.

I watch Ren from above as she goes, people bowing in her path. I close my eyes, weary suddenly. But I haven't lost what's most important: my role in this world.

I am a strategist. Ren's only one. Three times she came to my Thistlegate hut, beseeching me to serve her. I'd heard of warlords like her. Toss them a bone of wisdom, and they'd be on their way. So I told her the Rising Zephyr Objective: *Ally with the South. Establish a stronghold in the West. March on the North too soon, and you'll be crushed. But claim the South and West first, and the empire is as good as yours.*

Ren had held firm. *The empire belongs to Empress Xin Bao. I am but her protector.*

And though Prime Ministress Miasma also called herself a protector, something about Ren's words rang through me. They compelled me to leave with her that day. At the time, I didn't know why. Now, after a year in her service, I do. Surnames and god rumors be damned—it was her sincerity. Her charisma. Traits I've never personally valued, but if Ren could get *me* to leave my hut, then what power might she hold over the common people? I saw the thousands of Xin loyalists who would rally around her cause. I saw my future. Help Ren restore power to Xin Bao, and I'd be the greatest strategist of the land. I'd erase the girl I was, a girl I see as I nod off.

A lone figure in dirty beige robes on the roadside.

My sister, lost to the fleeing tide.

Blood and dust. That's all the warriors have left behind. Their war cries, distant. The smell of fire is closer . . .

Fire.

My eyes fly open.

Smoke. It plumes from the helm of the mountain, feathering gray into the night. Scarlet webs through the forest we just cleared, bleeding from tree to tree. There's no beat of the drum, no rallying cry for war, but the smog of burning wood—much too damp to kindle naturally—tells me all I need to know:

Miasma is coming.

A KNIFED SMILE

Miasma is coming.

She shouldn't be. We should have had hours before she returned with reinforcements at dawn. Now I have minutes at most before the town guards sound the alarm and send everyone into a brainless frenzy.

I stumble down the watchtower steps and run to the pavilion, where Lotus is snoring, sprawled flat on the bench, an empty wine jug in one hand. I nudge her with a foot; she throws an arm over her face. I kick the arm aside and she's up on her feet, swinging her ax.

I step in as soon as the danger of evisceration passes. "What did you *do*?"

"Do what?" mumbles Lotus, pawing at her face.

"At the bridge." I white-knuckle my fan; it's all I can do not to shout. "Report everything. Spare no detail."

"I scared off Skull-face and broke down the bridge, just like you ordered."

"You *what*?"

"I scared them off and broke down the bridge—"

"You. Touched. The. Bridge."

Lotus nods.

No. No, no, *no*. The whole *point* of Beget Something from Nothing is to create an *illusion* of strength, and Lotus broke the illusion when she broke the bridge. A lordess with ten thousand strong would never do such a thing. A lordess with ten thousand strong would leave the bridge be, to *beckon* the enemy into an ambush.

Like the cunning vulture she is, Miasma must have circled back, seen the torn-down bridge, and called the bluff. We could have bought ourselves days by appearing formidable enough to warrant reinforcements. Instead, we bought ourselves however many hours it took for the empire's best engineers to construct a temporary crossing.

"Was I not supposed to?" Lotus is asking, but my mind has already raced on to the burning trees. Another smart move. The fire smokes out any concealed troops, clears the path of felled logs, and announces Miasma's intentions. She *wants* us to panic and run. It's all downhill from Hewan. We'll be easy targets for enemy archers. Like deer in a royal hunt, we can't flee. Can't fight. We're at the disadvantage—and dead if we pretend otherwise.

As I pace back and forth, Lotus lifts her head and snorts the air. "Is that . . . fire?"

"Brava! Right on the first guess. And who do you think set it?"

"Who?"

"Give it another guess."

Lotus works her jaw. It shouldn't be that hard—there's only

one person in this entire empire who wants our heads badly enough to torch a forest—and slowly, her eyes grow round as cymbals.

She lopes for the stables.

Brilliant. Just what I needed. "Lotus! Stop!" I trip into a run after her. "Stop right there! I order you!"

I reach the stables just as she bursts out, already mounted. Her stallion rears, and I scramble backward.

"Get Ren to safety!" she shouts, as if *she's* the strategist. Then she gallops off with a rallying cry. Her underlings stream out from their tents and leap onto their mounts. I narrowly avoid death by horse again.

"*Lotus!*" *Rat-livers.* Futile as it is, I give chase. As I run past the granary huts, the guards on the watchtowers come to their senses. Bronze bells clang up and down the tamped-earth walls, and Ren's troops pour out, grabbing polearms and Ren's tattered banners. The evacuees and people of Hewan follow some sleepy minutes later, grabbing plows and meat mallets.

I shove past them all. Civilian or soldier, everyone's a peasant, so hasty to die.

Lotus is no exception. I reach the town gate too late; I'm not built to race warriors. Doubled over and wheezing, I glower at her stallion's massive hoofprints while her underlings tear past right and left of me. Then I straighten. Tighten my ponytail.

I'm still in control. I still have my stratagems.

When I find Ren by the stables, she's already saddled, double swords—fittingly named Virtue and Integrity—strapped across her back. My face falls in disapproval, and Ren's hardens.

"It's me she wants," she says, as if that's an acceptable reason to ride into Miasma's five thousand strong.

"So you'll just hand yourself over."

"Lotus is out there."

"Without your orders." And against mine.

"Qilin—"

"Allow me." I fist one hand, slant the other over my knuckles, and bow over both in deference. "Allow me to ride out after them with twenty troops."

"To do what?" Cloud trots up beside Ren on her massive mare and gives me a cold once-over. "Die?"

That may be Lotus's plan, but it's not mine. "To stop Miasma," I say politely. We can't all be the lesser person.

"With twenty soldiers." Cloud's gaze sharpens on my knobby wrists. I know what she's thinking. I've encountered so many like her: stronger children in the orphanage. Soldiers in the cities. She thinks my strategies are for weaklings and cowards who can't face their enemies head-on. That I want to ride out with twenty soldiers is a trick or bluff, never mind that Lotus rode out with half that number. Defeat is unthinkable to a warrior. They die before they see it coming.

I've fought death all my life. "If I fail, I'll accept the martial punishment for lying to my lordess."

"If you fail, your head will be on an empire spike alongside ours." Cloud leans forward, looming over me from her mount. "Just what are you going to do? Kill her with your sweet tongue?"

"Cloud," says Ren, her voice a warning.

Truthfully? *Yes, Cloud, and that stratagem has a name: Hide a Knife Behind a Smile.* But why enlighten a warrior? "Whatever I have planned, it's our only option." Then, before I can help myself: "I'd take you with me, Cloud, but I just can't risk having Miasma set free a second time."

"*You—*"

"*Enough.*" Ren holds out a hand; reluctantly, Cloud removes hers from the pole of her crescent-bladed glaive. To me, Ren says, "Twenty troops. Against Miasma."

"Yes."

A beat of silence. "I trust you, Qilin."

Then humor me.

"You may have your twenty."

"Thank you." I bow again. When I raise my gaze to Ren's, her eyes swim with worry. *For Lotus.* But when I vow to bring her swornsister back unharmed, Ren's brow furrows, and the uncomfortable thought crosses my mind that maybe, just maybe, Ren is worried for *me.*

Well, why wouldn't she be? I'm this camp's lone strategist. Ren can't afford to lose me. But she shouldn't worry. I haven't failed us yet, and I don't plan on starting now.

Quickly, I gather my twenty. They're neither the strongest nor the smartest. They blanch when I tell them our objective. But they don't dawdle, and in minutes we're ready to ride.

I seek out Tourmaline before we leave. "By the pavilion," I say under my breath, "you'll find yew shrubs. First chance you get, feed the leaves to the horses. Make sure no one catches you, and make sure the blame goes to me."

Tourmaline doesn't respond at once. Perhaps she also knows

what yew leaves can do to a grown horse. If so, she doesn't call me out for sabotage either. Her eyes flick to the stallion beside me. "Where are you going?"

First? To Miasma. Then? To wherever Miasma takes me. But ultimately?

"South." I say it with conviction. I pray she won't ask me *how*. That's for me to work out.

"When will you be back?"

"I don't know." Too truthful. It's the wine—has to be the wine, I think, as I grab Tourmaline by the arm. "No matter what happens, I'm on your side. Do you understand?"

Tourmaline stares at my hand like it's sprouted from her wrist-guard. My grip tightens. "Do you understand?"

"I understand."

"When the time is right, I'll return. Until then, forget we ever had this conversation. If Ren probes, say nothing. Keep her here. She's safest in Hewan." Once I divert Miasma, that is.

"I understand," repeats Tourmaline. "But one thing."

She leaves—and returns with her horse, a mare of pure white. She holds out the reins.

"Pearl behaves, with or without turnips or figs."

It takes me a moment to understand her intentions. Suspicion sets in. *Rumor is that you had a little spill,* Cloud said earlier. Was it Tourmaline who told her? What if this kindness is an insult? My mind spins—and recoils when Tourmaline offers me her arm. "I can do it myself."

Three attempts later, I successfully mount. Huffing, I stare down at Tourmaline.

If I could replicate myself, I would. I would carry out my own final instructions. But as it is, I have to trust that Tourmaline will execute my plans better than Cloud or Lotus. She passes me the reins and steps back.

"Ride safe."

I nod stiffly, and cast a final glance to Ren.

Orphaned at thirteen. Unsupported by her clan. Fighting for Xin Bao's empire, but against empire troops commandeered by Miasma. Others might see a lost cause, but I see a saga that will live on for generations.

I won't return empty-handed. Next time I see everyone, it'll be with a Southlands alliance.

I dig in my heels. The gate thunders up for me and my twenty; the watchtower bells ring loud, then soft as we plunge into the open night. Our mounts eat up the muddy, rutted path, bringing us back the way we came, the mountain rising like a dark-haired head on the horizon. Moonlight pours into the hoofprints left by Lotus and her underlings, minting the trail with silver coins. Then the trees close in—ten lǐ passes by incredibly quickly when you're riding in the wrong direction—and the trail is no more. The darkness closes us in its fist. I can't even see the firs, only feel their needled fingers on my cheeks as we slow from gallop to trot.

The smoke strengthens. My eyes tear as I fight the urge to cough. The first torches appear, small like fireflies. Pearl whickers; I coax her forward. A whimper comes from behind me. To my right, a bowstring hums as someone nocks an arrow.

"Put that away," I snap. To the rest: "You are to do *nothing* without my orders."

No one makes a sound after that. It's just the rustle of under-growth beneath our hooves and the drumming of my heart. The reins in my hand slicken, and I'm thankful my soldiers can't see me flinch at the percussion of steel against steel in the distance.

Any moment now. Anticipation is a wolf, hunting my thoughts. *Any moment—*

"Halt!"

Miasma's soldiers emerge from the trees. Their faces and bodies are smeared with soot, but behind all the black, their laminar glows. Only the best for the empire's minions.

One rides up to me. Her leopard-skin cloak elevates her above a rank-and-file soldier. She's a general.

A warrior.

My heart pounds faster.

I dismount, sending thanks to the heavens when my foot doesn't catch in the stirrup and Pearl doesn't spook and I don't otherwise make a fool of myself. My soldiers try to close around me but are stopped by Miasma's. A spear is shoved under my chin, forcing it up. A torch is thrust before my face.

Leopard Cloak motions for another minion. Together they consider my ragtag group of twenty.

"Ren's," says the minion.

Leopard nods, then raises a hand. Bowstrings moan from the surrounding trees in which Miasma's archers are perched.

I bite my cheek, triggering saliva flow. My voice is full and round when I say, "I'm here to speak with your lordess."

Bated breaths. Quivering strings.

"She's expecting me. And"—I lower my voice—"you know how she is when she doesn't get what she wants."

Leopard is silent.

"Kill the rest," she finally says.

"They come with me," I say over the whine of bowstrings. Then I command my soldiers to dismount and discard their weapons.

The extent of our helplessness is glaring once our weapons lie in the undergrowth. Twenty versus at least two hundred. Unarmed versus swords and bows, fitted with arrows, in the trees. We're not just weak. We're pathetic. Crushing us would be like using a hammer on an ant. Overkill.

Leopard lowers her signaling hand, and empire soldiers stream in. Rope goes around my wrists while what feels suspiciously like the tip of a polearm prods my spine, goading me into a forward walk.

My calves strain as the ground slopes upward. What feels like hours later, we're led into a mist-laden clearing at the mountain's base. My eyes struggle to adjust to the ruddy torchlight and moonbeams shafting through, but once they do, I immediately make out Lotus and her underlings.

They're trussed up like ducks for the plucking, their faces bruised, mouths bleeding, eyes swollen shut. Unlike them, I know better than to act rashly. Because standing before them, with a head half-shaved and a single, red lacquer bell hanging from her earlobe like a blood droplet, is the one and only Miasma.

She doesn't see us, not with her back turned, but she must hear our approach. She definitely does when Lotus croaks, "Peacock?"

It's a good thing my anonymity isn't a requisite for my stratagem.

Leopard slips up to Miasma and whispers into her pierced ear. In reply, the prime ministress of the Xin Empire reaches for her sword. The twisted blade grows out of its sheath, mirror bright. "I'll be with my guest in a moment."

Then she swings.

Bells should tinkle. Heads should thud. But my senses are all mixed up, and the head tinkles as it falls into the ferns and Miasma's bell thuds and thuds, swinging violently from her ear as she uncoils and returns to her center while the underling keels over in a headless bow.

Roosting birds roost no more at Lotus's howl.

"There. Now you have my undivided attention." Miasma runs a thumb along the soaked blade and licks the pad, then holds the sword out to me in offering. "Care for a taste?"

The tang of iron taints the air. My own neck throbs.

"I'm afraid my stomach isn't as strong as yours." Or anything of me, for that matter. Miasma may be less than five chǐ tall, but her arms are corded, shown off by her sleeveless laminar vest. Her face is chiseled like an arrowhead, the bare minimum of skin stretched thin over bone and vein. At twenty-five, she's only two years Ren's senior, but she appears ten years older and has inspired a thousand rumors. Miasma can kill assassins in her sleep. Miasma pickles the livers of her enemies. Miasma is like a worm: cut her in half, and she'll grow back.

The latest rumor is that Miasma is a god, sent by the heavens to save the crumbling empire. I prefer fact to rumor, but fact isn't much better. When a group of radical peasants called the Red Phoenixes marched against the empire capital seven years ago, Miasma put down the rebellion and rose to the rank of cavalry general. When the Ten Eunuch Cabal plotted to assassinate Empress Xin Bao six years ago, Miasma exterminated them and all their living ancestors, "rescuing" Xin Bao while consolidating power in the military and court. So naturally, when humble Xin Ren, a fellow veteran of the Red Phoenix Rebellion hailing from some no-name town, decried her as a usurper, Miasma was not pleased, to say the least.

Now I stand face-to-face with the enemy. Many call her evil. I'd call her opportunistic—which is far more dangerous, in my opinion.

Miasma shrugs at my refusal, wipes down the blade, and sheathes it. Lotus sobs. I gird my nerves and take a step forward.

"I wouldn't," says Miasma. The torchlight flares, allowing me a fleeting glimpse of the hundreds of mounted troops encircling the clearing. "Unless you want more of your friends' heads to roll."

I force myself to take another step. "They're not my friends." Another. "I've been waiting for this opportunity for a long time." Kneeling is a challenge with bound hands, but I manage, bowing over a patch of white toadstools. "My lordess."

Silence.

Miasma's laugh is more of a caw, starting and ending in her throat. "Not bad—for your first speech of defection. Practice will do you good."

"I speak with actions, not words. Let me show you my loyalty."

"Loyalty coming from one who betrays her own lordess."

"I never swore an oath of fealty to Xin Ren. I took up her cause only because she came to my hut and *begged*."

Lotus stops sobbing. "Y-y-you . . . *traitor*!"

Miasma gives a lazy wave of her hand, and Lotus is gagged. "Begged," she says, savoring it.

"Yes, begged," I say. "On her knees. Three times."

"She would, wouldn't she?" Miasma muses. "Always desperate, Charity Ren. And you." Her voice suddenly booms. "You, *Rising Zephyr*, always crafty." The sobriquet sends a shiver of delight through me; Miasma has to be thinking of every occasion we've eluded her. "You speak with actions?" She nods at Lotus. "Well, go on. Prove your loyalty by killing this one."

"And cause you to lose this war? I think not."

"Oh?" Miasma raises a brow. "Elaborate."

I should be too terrified for words. My head might end up severed from my neck before this night is over. And I *am* terrified—until I touch my fan. This is what I do best: reading my opponent's attacks, playing the information I've already accrued as counterattack.

I am in control of the board.

"You know Ren as well as I do," I start. "Better, perhaps, considering your shared history." Miasma chuckles at the reminder of a bygone time, when two nobodies—Miasma, the foster child of a eunuch, and Ren, the powerless offspring of a powerful clan—served the dynasty side by side. "Xin Ren is a lordess without a territorial stronghold to train or supply her troops. Leave her be, and the elements will take care of her. But kill any of her swornsisters, and you'll end up with a rabid dog on your hands."

"Then what are we waiting for?" cries Miasma. "We'll crush her right here, right now. I'll even save you the honors of claiming her head."

"Why bother? Just before coming here, I poisoned two thirds of their steeds with yew." Lotus screams against her gag. I ignore her and continue, "Xin Ren and her troops won't be leaving Hewan anytime soon."

That gives Miasma pause. Clearly, she didn't think I had it in me to cull a cavalry. She'll probably send a scout to check. It's in her nature to be suspicious. "You didn't come alone," she notes.

"*Me*, riding to meet you on my own? Even a fool like Ren would have suspected something. These soldiers are but a cover for my defection. And now they're sacrifices for a deserving lordess. Kill them. Interrogate them. Twenty may not be much use against your five thousand, but twenty talking mouths? That's information."

An acrid scent stings my nose—the scent of urine, coming from my own ranks. To them, I must sound utilitarian, heartless, cruel. If only I could tell them that there's a three in four chance Miasma will spare their lives; she has a weakness for talent, regardless of its source.

"A camp full of traitors." Miasma rubs her hands together. "Oh, Ren. It'd break her heart if she knew. So the horses—"

"Dead by dawn," I assure her.

"Excellent." But I still haven't won her over. Not quite. When it comes down to it, dead horses and sacrificial troops could just be strategy, tightly wielded in my hand. I need to show Miasma that I have something real to lose. Show her that I've made an enemy out of my previous camp.

The ground finally starts to tremble.

About time.

Come on. My fingers curl around my fan's handle. I set the bait, I planted the distrust, but what happens next is out of my control. *Come on.*

I know you can go faster.

Two of Miasma's elite generals, Talon and Viper, immediately appear at their lordess's side, reaching for their swords. The rest of Miasma's troops take formation around us. In the dark, a shout is cut short. Mist ghosts over the ferns, reaching for our feet. Miasma looks pale. Some say the prime ministress believes in ghosts. I suppose it's only natural; ghosts and gods are one and the same.

But no ghost could barrel through both bracken and soldiers the way Cloud does.

She's a riot of blue cloak and bronze armor atop that monstrous mare, her glaive raised high above her head before it comes down. The bladed end sinks into the chest of one of Miasma's minions while the poled end smashes into a helmed head. Bronze and bone cave, and it's my turn to pale, as I'm reminded of the warriors from my nightmare. But this is all a part of my plan.

Cloud is too, even if she doesn't know it.

Her tawny gaze sweeps the clearing, taking in my soldiers, Miasma's soldiers, Miasma herself, before finally landing on me.

I see the exact moment she pieces together my defection.

By the time Lotus works through her gag and screams traitor, Cloud's already cut through a whole line of Miasma's infantry. Her crescent blade is oiled with their blood as she whirls down to one knee. Arrows release at her signal, flying over her head. One hits Leopard in the eye. Another nicks my shoulder. I hiss, grip the bleeding wound as Miasma's troops return fire.

Cloud's archers drop from their mounts like plums from a tree.

But Cloud—she spins her glaive until it's a blur, a maw of blade that devours everything in its path—a path leading to me. Me, the trickster. The traitor. The one who taunted Cloud about letting Miasma go right before riding out to swear myself to her.

She never reaches me, of course. One Cloud could feasibly kill thirty minions, but not hundreds. Foot soldiers surround her, their pikes pointed like a ring of teeth. A lesser warrior would panic.

Cloud's eyes remain pinned on me.

"Want us to take care of her?" asks Viper.

Miasma doesn't answer. She eyes Cloud with a glassy sort of rapture. "What a marvel to behold." She says it so softly that I wonder if Viper even hears.

"My lordess?"

With a running start, she mounts a stallion twice her height. "Let her go alive."

"But Prime Minis—"

"Hand over the horse."

Cloud's voice, not Miasma's. "The horse," she repeats as we stare at her. "Pearl."

Pearl whinnies at her name. I come to my senses and look to Miasma.

The prime ministress waves a hand. "Granted. Viper."

Viper walks Pearl over to Cloud. Cloud takes the reins.

I breathe out. *Thank you, Tourmaline, for getting me this far. You too, Cloud. Thank you for trying to kill me so . . .* convincingly, *and for leading Pearl home.*

Take care of Ren while I'm gone.

"We're really just letting her go?" asks Talon as Cloud remounts her own mare.

"For now, Talon. Just for now. One of these days, she'll realize her talents are wasted on Charity Ren, just like this one did." Miasma smiles down at me. I cling tighter to my arrow wound. It convinced Miasma of my desertion, and now it justifies my wince as she says, "Welcome to the empire, Rising Zephyr." Her smile widens to a toothy, skull-like grin. "Or, as I like to say, welcome to the Kingdom of Miracles."

KINGDOM OF MIRACLES

elcome to the Kingdom of Miracles.
      The North. The capital. The Kingdom of Miracles.
They all refer to the empress's empire. Only in a kingdom can
Miasma herald herself as a queen without renouncing her loyalty
to Xin Bao.

She just did, the tricky fiend.

We're a hundred-some lǐ ride to the empire's nearest military
base, giving Miasma plenty of time to play hostess. She has her
personal physician see to the arrow wound in my arm. When she
notices I'm having trouble with my new horse, she offers me the
"gentlest mare in the empire."

True to her word, the mare doesn't startle once the whole
way, not when Lotus chews through her gag to scream "Traitor,"
or when she nearly takes off Talon's finger as he tries to re-gag
her. His blows rain down. I don't try to block out the sounds.
Thwack goes his fist into her cheek, and I think, *That could be
me. Crunch* go his knuckles against her nose, and I think, *That*

could be all of Hewan. I'm the only thing standing between the town and Miasma's five thousand strong.

I'd better start laying on the flattery now.

"Milordess Miasma is as generous as the rumors claim," I say as we splash over a small creek and head into another stand of trees.

"Call me Mi-Mi," Miasma says. "Unlike Charity Ren, my reputation lives up to itself. Wouldn't you say, Crow?"

At first, it seems like she's talking to herself; there's no one around us who could possibly be "Crow." But then a noncommittal grunt floats out of the murky dark.

"Crow, Zephyr. Zephyr, Crow." Miasma introduces the rider to her right. He's a shapeless, faceless heap of feathered black cloak topped off with a conical hat woven from yellow straw.

"Crow is one of my strategists," says Miasma while he breaks into a phlegmy coughing fit. I hold my breath. "He'll show you the reins around camp. You might even learn a thing or two from the old bird."

"Eager to," I lie through my teeth.

Crow stops coughing long enough to grunt. I shudder gratefully as he falls behind us.

We crest several knolls, each bigger than the last. I clutch the saddle's horn as we ride up the steepest incline yet. My breath grows scratchy in my chest, then stops altogether.

Below us sprawls one of the empire's many military bases, huge like a city, its gridded pattern glowing as if it'd been stamped into the indigo landscape by a hot iron.

I knew Miasma had the financial backing of the empire, but my heart still sinks as we ride past the palisaded gates and into a warmonger's paradise. The stallions practically gleam. The soldiers look stronger, older, better fed than Ren's. The very air is alive: Hammers ring against anvils, generals bark out orders, and a crowd of soldiers scream around a wrestling pit. As we ride past the sand-sacked arena, the victor thrusts up a fist. I don't think much of the gesture, but when Miasma slows her horse and circles back, I look again and make out something dark tufting from his clenched hand. It's a clump of human hair and scalp.

Bile burns up my throat.

Miasma, meanwhile, is busy groping his sweaty arm like she's at the butcher's buying a boar. "Strengthening up nicely, I see." She pats his bicep. "Keep up the good work."

"Yes, my lordess!"

"This way," Miasma instructs as the soldiers we were riding with break off and stream through various pathways to their barracks, leaving us with Talon, Viper, and Crow. We pass burlap tents for miniature pavilions decked in lacquer and gilt. Guards in red coral laminar snap to attention as we ride through lines of them, and a reedy eunuch draped in empire scarlet scurries alongside Miasma, announcing as she goes:

"Prime ministress of the Xin Empire, commander in chief of the Xin armies, heavens-sent protector of Empress Xin Bao—"

"Enough already," says Miasma. "Can't you see we have a guest?"

If only I had my white robes, or a eunuch to trumpet all my sobriquets. Instead, I'm stuck with beige and Lotus for an announcer, once she chews through her third gag.

"*Traitor!*" It might be the wind, but I swear I can feel the blast of her words. "*Traitor!*"

"Muzzle her and keep her with the animals," Miasma says. Soldiers rush to carry out the order.

"*You traitor!*" Lotus screams as they drag her away. "*You filthy, dirty traitor! Ren should never have trusted you! I hope you choke on a fish bone and die!*"

How uninspired. Lotus, Cloud, and all the peasants can hate me for all I care. Ren too; a strategist detested is a strategist doing something right.

But even as I tell myself that, the thought of Ren's resentment saps my strength, and when we reach the largest of the pavilions, my half-hearted dismount ends with my cloak tangling in the tack.

A hand closes around my arm before I can bite the dust. My gaze shoots to my savior's face. Or where his face should be.

Still shielded by his conical hat, Crow breaks off into another coughing fit. I pull free, skin crawling, and step aside to let him go first before surreptitiously dusting off my arm.

We climb up a set of stairs lacquered to a liquid shine and step over a gilded threshold, through black velvet drapes smoked with incense, and into the pavilion that somehow appears larger than it did from outside. Servants glide around with tripod pitchers of wine, their numbers reflected and multiplied by the polished bronze partitions. Scarlet silks emblazoned with the Xin Empire's phoenix insignia unfurl from the rafters, and candlesticks pool red wax in golden dishes.

A peasant might be dazzled by the opulence, but my gaze arrows to the group of generals, advisors, and strategists. They're huddled around a large table spread with a map of the empire. A few years ago, the map would have been a lot more colorful with dissident warlords, especially in the North. Now I make out only four broad swatches: sage ink for the semitropical lake valleys of the Southlands; tan ink for the Westlands, wheat basket of the continent and a Xin clan stronghold; a lighter tan for the Marshlands, wedged between South and West; and gray ink for the arid, mountainous North, home to the empire capital and birthplace of many rivers, rendered as lines of black ink that converge down South before emptying into the Sanzuwu Sea.

When I'm closer, I pinpoint our current military base by the flag sprouting above the triple intersection point of the Northern, Southern, and Western regions. It's surrounded by tiny clay soldiers, the kind my sister loved but we could never afford. These look even more intricate. Artisan-made. But they're not art, just numbers represented. *Expendable*, Ren would say, *like the commoners who die when the empire goes to war.*

I wrench my thoughts away from Ren as a voice rises from the head of the table.

"The Southlands may appear strong," says the middle-aged speaker. "But our sources report that it's rife with internal discord. I say we let them tear themselves apart and end Xin Ren tonight!"

Not if I can help it. As resounding agreement meets the speaker's words, I work myself through the back end of the crowd and rise to the balls of my feet for a better view of the map.

The Southlands also have lines of clay soldiers. Fewer than the North, but enough to blanket an entire river valley. Their recently coronated lordess, Cicada, is represented by a jade cicada—not very original—and their new strategist, a mysterious figure who goes by the sobriquet November, stands beside the cicada as an ivory figurine.

"They won't know what's coming for them until they're ashes in the wind!" cries a general to my right, setting off a slew of insults to Ren.

My eye twitches. It cuts to where Hewan is located.

Nothing. No clay troops, no Ren, much less a figurine for me, her strategist. Not even a derogatory "Charity Ren" as a placeholder on the land, which is achingly empty compared to the Westlands, governed by Ren's uncle, Xin Gong. Spineless worm. He's ignored Ren—and my letters requesting support—probably because he's too afraid to side with us against Miasma. I doubt the empire worries about him seceding, but at least he's represented on the map.

We, on the other hand, don't even exist. We're like all the warlords that Miasma has built a career out of putting down. Most recently it was Xuan Cao. But unlike Xuan Cao, we're still here. We have *me*. I *will* secure us allies. Cicada of Southlands has no great love for the empire. If I could just convince her that Miasma is our common enemy . . .

. . . Right after I convince Miasma that her greatest enemy is Cicada, not Ren.

The applause is still going strong when I say, "You're wrong."

Voices fall around the table, starting with the ones closest to me. Heads turn in my direction, clearing a view to the speaker at the head.

Plum, senior registrar of the empire. Her grandfather served the twelfth empress, Xin Diao; her mother served Xin Chan. Her ancestors must be rolling in their graves to know that Plum serves not Xin Bao, Xin Chan's daughter, but Miasma. Once a young talent herself, Plum is now in her late thirties. Overbearing, wine-colored robes drape over her slightly hunched form. At the sight of me, her face sours.

"This is no place for children," she snaps as I march through.

Older doesn't always mean brighter, as evidenced by Ren's swornsisters.

"Cicada of the Southlands may lack experience," I say upon reaching the table. "But she's not as weak as you take her for. She and her new strategist, November—"

"A farce!" cries the general to Plum's right.

"—demolished the Fen pirates," I finish.

"Pirates?" someone snorts. "More like degenerates!"

Degenerates who raided and looted the Southern marshes and waterways for years on end. They killed Cricket, heir to the Southlands, a warrior respected for her brains *and* brawn. Now her younger sister Cicada has managed to rout the Fen, burn their ships, and slaughter their leaders just months after her ascension. She's done what the empire has failed to do. I don't think I need to belabor my point.

I tap my fan to the green portion of the map. "The Southlands use peacetime to stockpile surpluses and self-strengthen. The empire would be doing Cicada a favor by going after the easy prey."

"And just who do you think you are?" snaps Plum.

"My newest talent."

The hubbub quiets as Miasma sweeps through the crowd, bell tinkling at her ear. "Plum, please welcome Rising Zephyr. You are to show her the same respect you show me."

"Please." I hold my arms out in a circle and bow over them. "The honor is mine."

Plum doesn't say a thing. Her cheeks are swarthy when I straighten. "You're *Ren's*."

"Thereby also *the* expert on Ren's situation." I leave Plum to her spluttering and turn to my audience. "Xin Ren is weak. She'll need years to build up her base. But the South has armies and silver. Their ranks of strategists and generals grow by the day. Give them a month and they'll pose a more serious threat than Ren ever could."

"So what would you do?" an advisor asks.

Me? I'm trying to shoot two pheasants with one crossbow bolt. If I can divert Miasma's troops from Ren *and* secure myself a boat passage to Cicada, then I'll be living up to every single one of my sobriquets.

Reaching across the map, I lift a clay soldier and place it at the junction of the Mica and Gypsum Rivers. "Obvious, isn't it? Bring the war to the Southlands.

"While the South is nowhere near as weak as Ren, their victory over the Fen pirates came at a high cost. And as Senior Registrar Plum was saying, Cicada's court is not without strife. She has yet to solidify support for her claim to sovereignty. The empire, meanwhile, is at the peak of its strength, and our prime ministress had the foresight to expand the navy." I cup a handful of model ships and push them down the inky line of the Siming River. "Sail down to the escarpment and bring the might of the empire to the South's threshold. Make them swear fealty and tribute to Empress Xin Bao. If they refuse . . ." I sweep my fan over the table, toppling the Southern fleet and soldiers. "You'll be perfectly positioned to send a message."

I look up, into the hardened, weathered faces of Miasma's retinue. One day they'll think back to this moment, realize our ascension started right under their noses. One day, the sound of my name will haunt them. One day—

Miasma prowls toward me. *She knows.* There's no way. *She knows that everything you've risked is for your one true lordess, Ren.*

She stops a single reed length away from me, and I remind myself that I'm not defenseless. Not weak. Her hand moves—

Will there still be blood on the blade?

—to gesture for a serving maid.

A girl in empire red glides to her side with a tray full of tripod goblets. Miasma selects a goblet and holds it aloft.

"To the Rising Zephyr."

Generals rush to copy her, toasting my name.

"To the Rising Zephyr!"

"To the Rising Zephyr!"

"To the Rising Zephyr!"

Miasma orders her generals to see to the logistics of sending a delegation south. This is my moment; I should volunteer. Instead I excuse myself, pleading fatigue. I float into the dark galleries scalloping the pavilion, clutching at the gilded colonnades as I go.

Why am I so light-headed? I had nothing to fear. I fooled Miasma, prime ministress of the empire.

I deceived a roomful of warriors.

I come to the end of the gallery and gaze into the open air. The moon glows in the night sky, and I take note of its phase. In less than a month, I'll return to Ren as a hero. Lotus will have no choice but to call me by my proper sobriquet. Cloud will apologize for trying to shoot me dead. Ren will earn a mark on that map, and I'll be there beside her, as her strategist.

To the Rising Zephyr.

It sounds all the sweeter on the enemy's tongue. I chuckle, shakily at first, then with more ease. My fan rises to my mouth, concealing my smile. I compose myself and begin to turn—

A hand clamps around my upper arm. "I know what you're planning."

GLISSANDO

I know what you're planning.

My assailant spins me around. A blade of moonlight cuts between us, illuminating the lower half of his face. His mouth slants with a smirk as I raise my fan. "Nice weapon."

"Bet you've never been fan-slapped." *Don't panic.* I don't reveal that I do, in fact, have a weapon. I wasn't keen on compromising my accessories, but Ren insisted on it. Now, how to knife him without ruining my robes . . .

"Do you mean 'fan-stabbed'?" In one motion he grabs my other wrist, pins it to the colonnade above my head, and flips up my fan's bamboo handle. The silver switchblade glints in the corner of my right eye, wicked sharp.

"Don't worry," he says as I struggle. "I'm looking to spill secrets, not blood."

"What secrets?" He must have been following me. The question is for how long.

I squint at his face for answers. He helps me out by bending into the moonlight. He's lean, bordering on underfed, graced with a pair of sharp cheekbones and heavy-lidded eyes. His complexion is somehow more anemic than mine, his pale temples a startling contrast against his long, raven-black hair. It's tied in a half-up, half-down style. Strands of it tickle my face as he puts his lips to my ear. "Why don't we start with the real reason why you're here?"

He pulls back, out of the moonlight. His face falls under shadow again, and I stiffen. Something about him seems familiar. He's young like me, which should have made him stand out against all those puffy adults crowded around the map table. But I don't recognize him. Don't remember seeing him in the pavilion. How could I have missed him? Could he be a servant?

He's not dressed like one, a detail that becomes apparent when a real servant appears around the corner. The gilded tray balanced upon her arms clatters as she stops in her tracks. She stares, and I stare right back over my captor's shoulder. I don't know how we look, but judging by the flush on the servant's face, I doubt it's appropriate.

That won't do. I didn't become the Rising Zephyr just so strange boys could flatten me against colonnades. My fan might be inaccessible, but his pelvis certainly isn't. My knee is halfway there when the servant recovers her voice. It warbles like a bird's.

"M-master Crow, do you need the physician?"

"Master Crow" is suddenly overcome by a coughing fit. He buckles and collapses—onto none other than me.

I've been thrown off horses. I've stepped in ox crap. I've been thrown off horses and landed *in* ox crap. Life on the run from Miasma is far from glamorous. But I've never suffered the humiliation of becoming a human cushion. My cheeks flame, and I try to shove him off me, but he's heavy for a sack of bones. The full weight of his body pins me as he rasps something that sounds like "fine" and "run along" to the servant.

She's all too glad to obey.

The moment she turns the corner, I wrench my wrist free and smack him with my fan.

"My apologies," I say as he staggers back, clutching his face. "Muscle spasms."

"It's quite all right." He pats his cheek, winces, and lowers his hand. "I'm sorry too. For what happened just now." He gestures at his chest. "Lung spasms."

He thinks he's being smart. He thinks that I don't notice the snick of a grin at the corner of his lip, disappearing as he ducks his head and readjusts his robes.

This is why I didn't recognize him. Cloakless and hatless, he's not the overgrown, half-dead Crow I thought I'd met. For one, he's a lot younger—he can't be many years over my eighteen—and given his antics, a lot healthier too.

"Does *Mi-Mi* know you're faking your illness?" I ask as he tugs his collar back over a milky clavicle.

"Faking it?" His eyes widen innocently. "I wish. No, still dying of consumption."

My nose wrinkles. Others might think I'm the walking stereotype of a strategist, fan and all, but at least I don't have consumption or some other disease of overwork. "You should be wearing a mask."

"Why? My cough is *my* secret weapon." I start to inch away; he blocks my escape. "But I'll spare you from it, if you tell me why you defected."

"Because I'm loyal to the empire. Always have been."

"Try again." He steps in and catches my sleeve. His eyes glitter, dangerous. His irises are onyx, but when the moonlight hits them just so, I see steel, cold and hard.

I can be colder and harder. "Because I'm sick and tired of scraps for victories. Ren will never give me the greatness I deserve."

A cloud passes over the moon, and the gallery darkens.

"Let's put your words to the test," Crow finally says. He releases my sleeve, and for a brainless second, I consider bolting. But there's nowhere to run. Beyond Crow is more enemy ground. Showing fear here is the same as showing my true colors.

"Test me, then." I fold my arms—and nearly jump out of my skin as he places a hand on the small of my back.

"Relax," says Crow, sounding wounded. "I'm just leading the way."

"And I'm just trying to stay uninfected." A scalding bath is in order, after I burn these robes.

"If it makes you feel any better, the physician says I'm not actively contagious."

"For now."

"Yes. It appears that my condition worsens with my perspective. You're lucky I'm such an optimist."

I clamp down on a retort and let him lead me down the gallery. We pass by tearooms and courtyards. I memorize what I can, for when I make my eventual escape.

Escape. My heart skids with sudden apprehension. If I want to escape, I need to steer clear of people who can see through my plans.

People like Crow.

He's the first strategist I've come face-to-face with in a while. A true opponent. My fingertips tingle in anticipation of his tests. Then they chill. Strategist or not, he's from the North. If he's anything like his lordess, he may not be above torture. How many nails can I stand to lose before I bleed a confession?

Calm yourself and stop assuming. I touch my fan as Crow continues to guide me, past latticework doors, into an unlit room.

It appears empty, at first. Then I see the zither, the gleam of its seven silken strings stretched taut across an oblong body crafted from paulownia wood. One zither—no, two. Raised on tables and facing each other like the banks of opposite shores, a lake of hardwood floor between them.

I know just how Crow plans on testing me.

He crosses the room and sits behind one of the zithers.

I do the same after a second.

"I take it that you know how to play?" he asks, sliding up his wide sleeves.

"Don't insult me."

"I don't recall seeing your zither on the ride over here."

"It's broken." A string *did* snap, last month. Even so, leaving it behind was an oversight I try to deflect from. "Ren never fixed it."

"Ah." Crow's smile is light. "No wonder you defected."

A harmless joke. Or is it? I hate that I can't tell, hate how petulant I sound when I say, "Point is, I know how to play." Any self-respecting strategist would. Through zither duets, truces have been negotiated, alliances cemented, battles decided. Zihua, strategist of the Luo Dynasty, once played the zither to end a war. My own zither had been gathering dust long before the string broke. Ren's camp isn't exactly filled with people who'd appreciate the intricacies of the music, and to play for a warrior like Cloud or Lotus would debase the instrument.

Crow, though . . .

He knows that zither music is a language shared between strategists. He thinks my playing will reveal what my words don't.

But I'm not that easy to decipher. When he opens with a common phrasing, I cut to the chase and strike the zither, fingers slashing across the strings. The dissonant notes surge upward like a flock of hunted pheasants, then plummet to dead silence.

My right hand plucks out a rapid staccato, faster and faster, until every string quivers with sound and after sound. But before the notes can ring out, I cut them short.

I infuse the music with my frustration. Ren's camp is limited in resources. I strum out my weariness. Lotus and Cloud don't respect me. I fold my hurt into the crescendo. My efforts are squandered, misunderstood. The melody quickens. With knife-sharp technique, I craft wings for my caged emotions. I lift my hands from the strings and let the notes take flight.

There. Crow wanted the truth? I played every reason why I'd *dream* of being on Miasma's side.

Breathing hard, I look to him. The room is dark, barely lit by the moon beyond the round lattice window. I can't see his face or read it. I can only hear his voice:

"How strange."

"Excuse me?" But as soon as the words leave my mouth, a bitter memory floods in and another voice rings through my head: *Wrong! Play it again!*

Music interrupts the memory—music from Crow. He's bent over his zither, a lock of hair spilled over his shoulder. Moonlight gleams over his knuckles as his hands circle around and around the strings. Notes tumble like water over rocks.

A classic mountain melody, albeit improvised. Peasant song, really. I don't know what he's trying to do with it, but after a while, I forget the other voice. My shoulders settle. My sleeves ride up to my elbows as I raise my hands, fingertips to the strings.

I join him in his improvisation.

This time, I don't think about strategies or lordesses or empires. I don't play my emotions either. My eyes fall shut; I try to evoke mist and moss. Our songs cast wider and wider ripples until the music transcends this room and moment. Images fill my brain. I'm with Ku; we're in the marketplace crowd. She stops by a spun-sugar stall; I know which one she wants. The orphanage doesn't give us an allowance. When the vendor is distracted, I steal the most misshapen creation, and Ku smiles, and it's worth it. It's worth—

My melody collides with Crow's; he seamlessly harmonizes

with it. My throat twinges at the simple gesture—then closes. Crow wasn't looking to understand my intentions; he was looking to understand *me*. I've played my heart into the music, a heart that not even my lordess knows. Ren has only ever seen me as the tactician, the strategist.

She's never seen the girl who failed her sister.

Applause kills the music before I can. Flame flares into the braziers, ripping away the cover of darkness.

A small crowd stands by the entrance to the room.

Crow rises to bow to them. I can't move. The zither strings dig into my fingertips. Miasma strides forward.

I force myself to my feet.

"Marvelous!" she cries as I bow, my bones feeling like they've been replaced with cartilage. "What artistry! What taste!" Her minions parrot her praise. "You are a person of many talents, Rising Zephyr. Tell me, where did you learn how to play?"

"Yao Mengqi mentored her for several years," Crow beats me to answering. I glare at him and he lifts his shoulder, as if to say, *What did you expect?*

And what did I expect? First lesson a strategist learns is to keep their enemies close, and there's no greater enemy than a rival. So we memorize their every trait, from their mentors to the tea they favor. Newcomers, like Cicada's November, are dangerous because they're harder to read. The same goes for Miasma's strategists, who are executed as frequently as they're inducted. Compared to what I know about Plum, Miasma's longest-living advisor, I know next to nothing about Crow. He's either a newer initiate or extremely secretive.

I hope it's the former but suspect it's the latter.

"There will never be another Yao Mengqi in our lifetime," Miasma affirms, and it might be the first thing we agree on. Master Yao was hardly kind like my second mentor (the poet), or elegant like my third (the chess master), or funny like my last (the ex-imperial cosmologist). Yet when he played the zither, I could forgive his fiery temper. His music kept me by his side when the dementia set in. He forgot the Thirty-Six Stratagems, he forgot my name, but he never forgot his chords. We spent many of his final afternoons on his porch, me fanning away the flies while he massaged pearls of song from the zither strings.

But Master Yao's face has begun to fade from my mind, just like the rest of my mentors'. We're all so transient. We live and we die; we forget and we're forgotten. The earth claims our bodies and strangers claim our names. Only empresses are remembered—and the ones who kill them. The ones who break empires, or restore them to their rightful rulers.

Ren is my path to being remembered.

The thought draws me back into the present.

"...tomorrow at the wǔ hour," Miasma is saying. "Zephyr, you will be joining us."

I blink, and Miasma chuckles. "Look at her," she says to her posse. "She thinks I'm inviting her to hell!" To me she says, "Banish your worries. Heathen as the Southlands are, you'll know nothing but the finest. Food, entertainment—whatever you desire during the voyage you shall have. My word is steel."

Inviting. Voyage. Southlands.

Miasma is inviting me to be a part of the delegation south.

It's exactly what I was hoping for, but my gaze flickers to Crow. As much as it hurts my pride, I don't believe I convinced him that I'm on Miasma's side. If I'm heading south, will he—

"You will share a junk with Crow," says Miasma, putting the question to rest. "The two of you will represent the empire's interests in the Southern Court."

Then she gestures for me and me alone.

Carefully, I approach. She lays a hand on my arm, like she did for the wrestler. I have no brawn to squeeze, thankfully, and Miasma leaves it as a light pat.

"You're probably used to running a one-strategist show," she says, voice low. She's so close that I can smell the wine laced through her breath, see the delta of veins running under her translucent skin. *Human*, I think. Not god. It wouldn't take very much to kill her. Cloud could do it. Lotus too. Strategists aren't supposed to sully their hands, but can I ridicule Cloud for letting Miasma go, out of some warrior code, if I abide my own?

"But when it comes to the interests of the empire," Miasma continues, unaware of my hand's slow descent, "I want you to defer to Crow."

"Yes, lordess." My pinkie finger grazes the feathers of my fan, and Miasma frowns.

"Mi-Mi," she reproaches, then steps back.

The opportunity dissipates. I tuck my clammy hand under my elbow. Crow comes up beside me, and Miasma glances between us. She smiles.

"You two seem to be getting along. Just be careful," she says to me. "We wouldn't want you catching anything."

I've already caught Crow's attention, and I don't need a physician to tell me I'd be better off without it. As we depart from the room—then from each other—his words echo in my head.

How strange.

I stop in my step.

Wrong! Play it again! The switch flies down in the memory, and I flinch. My playing was never to Master Yao's liking. It was always missing *something* beyond my perception. The broken string, Ren's camp—they're excuses. Truth is, I stopped playing years ago. The bitter taste returns to my mouth, and I scowl.

Every other skill that's befitting of a strategist, I've perfected. I earned my sobriquet, my fan.

But the zither? According to Yao Mengqi, I never mastered it.

Perhaps a part of me left it behind on purpose.

‡ ‡ ‡

Ren's horses are dead by dawn. I find out from the maidservants who deliver a bronze washbasin at the sixth gong. They don't speak to me as I splash my face and rinse my mouth with hot tea, and they whisk away my used sleeping robes without so much as a glance. But the moment they're outside the paper-screened door, their heads come together, their voices soft but not soft enough.

They whisper about me, the "backwater strategist" who thinks she's better than everyone (they're not wrong). They whisper about "Master Crow," who's fallen for my foxy charms (I could barf). But mostly, they whisper about the complete and utter destruction of Ren's cavalry. The news is all over camp.

That overnight, fifty of Ren's stallions keeled over, foaming from the mouth. That *I*, her trusted strategist, was the one who orchestrated it.

Perfect. As long as they blame me, it means no one caught Tourmaline mixing yew leaves into the feed. I pull my ponytail high and tight. Warriors may fight together, but strategists work alone. The element of surprise cannot be overstated; plans must be kept a secret.

They'll worship me when it's all said and done.

The seventh gong sounds as I'm putting on fresh beige robes. Only hours remain until the delegation leaves. I shove my feet into my not-so-fresh shoes, open the doors, and freeze.

A folded set of white robes rests just beyond the raised threshold. The fabric is cool to the touch. Silk. I glance up and down the corridor. Not a soul. The maids could have left it, but why outside? And why white?

Coincidences are like deities: everyone wants to believe in them. But I'm not everyone.

Ever so slowly, I lift the robes.

A single feather falls out. Midnight black. Raven—or crow.

My heart races, just like it did when he pinned me to the colonnade. My upper arm burns with the memory of his grip; my ear tingles with the ghost of his words.

I know what you're planning.

I throw the robes back onto the ground and tread over them on my way out.

The sun is not yet up, but most of Miasma's camp is. Packs of infantry march with their regiment leaders while servants, porters, and tattooed convict-laborers run afoot loading trea-sures and curios onto wagons, to be shipped south with our delegation. One convict-laborer drops a chest, the lid banging open to a sea of green jade. His overseer comes at him with a whip.

Gaze lowered, I hurry in the direction of the prisoner barracks. Miasma might be showering the South with valuables, but they're far from gifts. *Behold our wealth*, she means to say. *Whatever you think you have, the empire has more.* She's sending a message, just as the white robes were a message from Crow. He'll be monitor-ing me on the journey.

He's monitoring me now.

Visiting Lotus is therefore a risk. But I have no choice. She's Ren's swornsister. If left to her own devices, she'll perish like last night's underling. The others are tied up along with the twenty strong I set out with. They're all nursing bruises and lacerations when I crouch down outside the barracks' wooden bars. Lotus herself is snoring some ways apart from the rest. When one of Ren's foot soldiers sees me and starts whimpering, Lotus's yellow eyes roll open. She stares at me, bleary. The sleep wears off.

She launches herself at the bars.

I fall back onto my bottom, eliciting chuckles from the guards. Their superiors glare at them and they hush just in time for Lotus's roar.

"I'll wring your neck!"

The war prisoners in the other barracks stir.

"Silence!" orders one of the guards.

Lotus roars louder.

I crawl back to her. "Shut up," I hiss under my breath. "*I'm on your side.*" More roaring. "*Lotus*, listen."

I grab the bars, and her mouth snaps shut—on my left hand. Her canines break skin. Blood streams hot down my wrist.

The indignities I put up with.

"*Lotus.*" I grip the other bar with my good hand; I must be two seconds away from fainting. "*I'm. On. Your. Side.*"

The two seconds pass. I start to see black.

Finally, Lotus releases me. She spits out a mouthful of blood, gagging.

Serves her right. "Listen closely." I could cry, but we're out of time. "The wrestling pit is your best chance. Miasma appreciates talent. You won't be freed, but if you prove yourself in the pit, your conditions here will improve and you'll be showered with rewards."

"Lotus doesn't need gifts."

"You might not, but *they*"—my gaze skips to the rest of Ren's people—"do. They won't survive the interrogations, not unless you can protect them."

"Protect them," Lotus repeats to herself.

I nod. "They're your new underlings. Train them as if your life depended on it, because it will. Now wring my neck."

"What?"

"Quickly now." I shuffle closer to the bars. "You said you would." Ten times at least, since last night. "Make good on your word."

After a moment's hesitation, she clamps her two hands

around my neck and *squeezes*, like a farmer would a chicken. The sound that comes out of my mouth sounds nothing like "Help," but it summons the guards. They pry Lotus off me. I lurch to my feet, leave the barracks choking on my own spit. No one will suspect that I visited Lotus for her own good after *that* spectacle.

You'd better follow my instructions this time, Lotus. I won't have my stratagem marred by her death. I will recoup her for Ren, just like I will secure this alliance.

Later, in the carriage to the Siming River, I inspect my hand. The bleeding has stopped, but blood is crusted on my sleeve, and Crow's eyes narrow in on it when he meets me along the bank.

"Were the robes not to your liking?" he calls after me as I stroll up the ramp to our junk. Other carriages arrive at the bank, and people pour out. Generals, registrars, naval officers—pretty much everyone important is coming down South with us, all but Miasma, who will be following with the other half of the fleet in three days. Once they board, the porters remove the ramps.

And so it begins. Me and Crow, sharing a junk for the next two weeks.

He tails me as I walk down the deck. "My failure, then. I thought white was your favorite color."

Persistent, I'll give him that. "They were dirty."

"But not bloody."

I march onward. We haven't even set sail, and the Northern ship hands I pass already appear queasy.

Crow, however, strides the deck with the confidence of a Southlander. He joins me at the stern, leaning lazily on one elbow. "You're awfully pale, and you're frequently short of breath. Now you show up with blood on your sleeve. Could it be that you have consumption too?"

He'd be the first I'd infect if I did. But he's not getting anything from me. No consumption, no laughter, no words. Just silence that I make as dry as possible by staring at the misty river ahead of us.

"Fine," he sighs, plopping both elbows onto the junk's lacquered gunwale and crossing his wrists in my exact same pose. "Be taciturn. Since we're spending the foreseeable future in each other's company, will you at least tell me your name?"

A heron swoops down from the sky and claws a fish out of the water. I wait for predator and prey to disappear into the mist before answering. "Zephyr."

"Your real name."

"That is my real name."

"I don't like it," says Crow.

He sounds like a pouting child. It's very unbecoming. "I don't like the name 'Crow.'"

"It's a fitting sobriquet. Admit it."

"Fitting, because it's a lie like you?" I turn, and Crow copies me, bringing us face-to-face. I jab a finger into his chest. "When you're not coughing your lungs out, you're more of a peacock."

"So are you." He catches my outstretched wrist. "Shall I call you 'Peacock'?"

His grip is neither warm nor cold. Just pleasantly dry, and teasing like his manner. He doesn't intone *Peacock* the way Lotus would, and he's not like Cloud, who doesn't address me by anything at all. Why would she, or any warrior? I can't fight. Can't hold my liquor. We're on the same side, but we're not of the same kind.

Crow is the opposite. We understand each other by nature of our trade. Our weapons of choice are our words and wits. I've poisoned Ren's horses, run to Miasma, brewed up strategy for the empire, but it's now—bantering with the enemy as if he were a friend—that I feel the dirtiest.

I pull my hand free and pointedly scrub it against my robes. "You don't have to call me anything at all."

The junks pull away from the dock. A southern wind puffs the sails. As we glide down the waterway, servants crowd around me, offering ginseng extracts and essence of pearl.

I wave them off. The empire is my enemy. Crow is my enemy. Every soldier on these ships, every ship in this fleet, every arrow and lance and pike in the armories belowdecks will deliver death to Ren's camp if given the chance.

Well, I won't give it to them.

‡ ‡ ‡

I spend the majority of my first week investigating the soldiers aboard. Some are native Northerners, but a good number are from the mountains beyond. Still others are prisoners of war from fallen warlords, liberated when they agreed to fight for the empire.

They have inquiries for me too. Some want to know if I really predicted a flood that swept away a fifth of Miasma's cavalry. "A fourth," I correct. Others ask if I can compose a poem in the time it takes to walk the width of the deck. I make one in seven steps. Nothing trips me up, until one ship hand stops me on my way belowdecks for supper. "Did you really defect from Ren?"

She's young, with a face full of zits and a voice full of fire. "I did," I say, and scorn ignites her eyes. She thinks I'm the scoundrel, siding with Miasma.

She's as naïve as Lotus and Cloud and all the warriors who fail to distinguish the battle from the war.

Belowdecks has been transformed to look like a palace. Miasma wasn't lying when she said I'd have everything I could desire on this voyage. Every day has brought new food and entertainment. The generals who've finally recovered from their seasickness toast each other into tipsiness. The servants are more at ease in Miasma's absence. Even pale, sickly "Master Crow" has benefitted from the pomp and cheer. Tonight, he obliges a naval officer's request for a zither song. His prerogative. *I* wouldn't play for the pleasure of others. But I find myself listening as his notes float through the raucous laughter. Pure as a songbird's call.

Innocent as the girl's question.

Did you really defect from Ren?

I push up from my table and escape to one level up-deck.

The nights have grown ever more humid, a clear sign that we're approaching our destination. The heat in my cabin keeps me up even after I strip to my under-robes, and I lie awake, thinking about Ren. As we feast on drunken duck and chilled scallops, what is she eating? As we sing and dance, what is she doing? Burning the dead horses and gazing at Xin Bao's star in the sky? Cloud surely reported my every word and action to her. Does she believe her swornsister? Does she think of me as a traitor?

She does, if I executed my stratagem without flaw.

That's all I want. All I care about.

I roll onto my back. The planked ceiling above my head trembles from the revelry. I shouldn't be thinking of Ren. I close my eyes—and see her instead. My sister. She's in that wretched violet vest. Once mine. I'd outgrown it. It'd been in the orphanage's burn pile with all our clothes that winter, after the typhoid epidemic. By the time I caught Ku snuggling with the vest a whole season later, there was no point to flying into a rage. She was unharmed. Safe.

She was wearing that vest when the warriors ransacked the town that day, causing a tide of fleeing innocents that would ultimately sweep her away.

Parents, sister, mentors—they all left me first. But Ren is different. She's not a sister, blood or sworn or otherwise. She's my lordess, and I her strategist. I serve her for personal glory.

I won't lose her.

The music finally dies. There's the hustle and bustle of servants cleaning up, then the shuffle of people heading off to their beds.

I rise from mine.

I pad out of the cabin and into the emptied galley. I take a seat behind one of the zithers and play, my fingers sliding up and down the strings in glissando, the notes changing with ease. Major to minor, minor to major. Like a human voice, laughing and crying all at once.

I hear Master Yao again.

Stupid girl! Connect with the music! With the qì! Qì, the building block of the universe. It gives energy to everything, music included, if philosophers of old are to be believed. I wouldn't know. I never felt whatever it was that I was supposed to feel.

Wrong! Play it again! You're not getting it!

I play louder, banish the voice from my head.

Someone else enters the galley, takes a seat at a different zither, and plays too.

I know who it is from the music alone. He'll note that I'm up at this hour. He might even deduce my troubled thoughts and report me to Miasma.

Leave, before he senses your shortcomings.

But his music holds me still. Crow may not trust me, but he also doesn't misunderstand me. We haven't spoken since that first day on the deck, and it doesn't matter.

We speak now.

‡ ‡ ‡

Horns herald us as we drift among the lotus flowers. Ship hands drop the anchors; the empire fleet forms a red, lacquer-shiny scab over the riverway.

A cluster of Southern courtiers meets us at the docks to escort us to the Nightingale Pavilion, where Cicada holds court. Civilians line the white limestone streets we pass by. Children who don't know any better shriek in excitement. The adults are grimmer, their eyes on the empire flags we carry.

We're led over a bridge, through a garden, and into the court.

A eunuch announces us as we travel down the center walk, fields of advisors sitting on cushions to our left and right.

Whereas Miasma's camp is populated by both young and old, Cicada's court is mostly old. They're all gray whiskered and bickering with each other, pausing only to acknowledge our presence before resuming. The atmosphere is suffocating, and I don't blame Cicada when she doesn't show up. Crow coughs, and shrugs when I glare at him. *I can't help it*, his eyes say. *I'm sick.* Then he coughs some more. The Southern courtiers nearest to us edge away.

Finally, the lordess herself makes her appearance. She's dressed in white, but unlike the robes I prefer, hers are rough-hewn. Mourning clothes. The already-grimy hem drags along the floor as she plops into her dais at the head of the room, uncorks a jug of wine, and takes a healthy glug.

So much for mourning.

"Well?" she asks, wiping her mouth with the back of her hand.

I wait for Crow to say something, but he's silent for once. Too scared to make the first move? Or does he want to put me on the spot?

Whatever it is, I make a better first impression anyway.

"Lordess of the Southlands," I greet, bowing.

"Queen," she corrects.

Her advisors wince. Claiming the title for oneself, without empire approval, is treason.

"Well, what does Miasma want now?" Cicada asks, as if *we're* here to pay tribute. "A donation of grain? Or does the prime ministress want to build another palace and lack the iron ore? Save the gifts," she says as our porters carry in chests of jade. "We all know who's really the weak one here."

Advisors appear green in the face.

I'm not feeling so well myself. It's too hot, too humid—how Crow isn't melting under all that feathered cloak is beyond me—and Cicada is . . . surprising. I've read many reports on the sixteen-year-old queen who grew up in the shadow of her older sister, and they all characterized her as learned yet demure.

But I've dealt with difficult people before. My lips part—and stay parted as a person comes out from behind one of the screens winging the dais. She squirrels herself onto the arm of Cicada's seat and pops a stick of browned sugar into her mouth, and all I can think is that I must have hurt my head after falling from my horse during the evacuation.

Because it's my sister, last seen a November six years ago.

THE FIRST OF NOVEMBER

Pan Ku, last seen a November six years ago.

In the first few weeks after I lost her, I dreaded finding her.

I simply couldn't imagine what could be left of a girl who barely survived by my side.

Now, six years later, she stands before me in the flesh. She's taller than I remember, but with the same unevenly cropped hair and wide-set eyes.

Ku. A roomful of advisors and courtiers are waiting on me but I can't breathe, let alone speak. *Ku, is that really you?*

I wait for her to look up. To notice me. It won't matter that we're in the middle of a foreign court, some thousand lǐ from the chaos that broke us apart. We're sisters by blood. She'll recognize me in the same way I recognized her. I'll tell her how I searched for her, how I traveled from town to town for months with nothing more than a string of pewters and our mother's praying beads. I spent those pewters. I pawned the beads. I searched until I ran out of money and ideas, my body so tired, so heavy.

I'll apologize for stopping too soon.

But I'm the fool. Because when Ku finally raises her gaze, it lingers on Crow, then lands on me. Recognition, so faint I almost miss it, flickers through her eyes, before hatred fills them.

It's been this way for most of my existence.

Advisors start to mutter. Cicada yawns. A feathery brush on the back of my hand—it's Crow, stepping forward.

"On behalf of the prime ministress," he says, "my fellow delegate and I have come to obtain your oath of fealty to the empire."

"Again?" asks Cicada.

"Lordess Cicada," a whiskered advisor begins, "if I may—"

"You may," she interrupts, chewing on a fingernail. "If you address me as 'Queen.'"

The advisor darts a glance at me, but I could care less. He could call her Queen Mother of the Heavens and I'd stay as I am, still as ice and just as brittle, all the feeling gone from my limbs as I stare at Ku, who's gone back to sucking on her stick of sugar.

Six years, but nothing has changed. Time just made me sentimental. Forgetful. I have fuzzy memories of Ku smiling at me, hand in mine. But the sharper memories are from during the famine, two years before I lost her. We were ten and seven. Half of the orphans starved. We didn't. Ku had been cold toward me ever since, refusing whatever I touched, even candy, and running away from me at every given moment. To this day, I don't know why.

I don't know what happened.

A throat is cleared, shunting my mind back to the court.

"Q-queen Cicada," squeaks the advisor who spoke previously.

"The cosmos themselves recognize Xin Bao as empress of the realm. Her star grows brighter by the day. The North is a great protector, and without them—"

"Oh, just spit it out," says Cicada. "You believe Miasma is a god and will smite us if we don't bow down."

My lordess—

"Xin Bao is a puppet. We defeated the Fen pirates without empire help." Cicada lifts another jug of wine, uncorks it with her teeth, spits. She props a foot onto the carved table before the dais. "Where was the empire when the Fen sacked our granaries and massacred our people? When the Pirate King killed Cricket? If you think the North is our protector, you are more senile than I thought."

The advisor falls to his knees and knocks his head against the floor before Cicada is even finished. "Her Magnanimous Empress! Long live Her Highness! Long live the Xin Dynasty!" He drags himself before my feet. "Our lordess is still in mourning. The death of her older sister has addled her judgment. Forgive her insolence. Spare her life."

Cicada snorts. But the rest of her court follow the old advisor's lead, prostrating themselves in supplication.

Only Ku sits silent.

Focus. You're on a mission. I tear my eyes from Ku and look for something else, anything else to steal my attention. My gaze lands on Cicada's foot.

Bare and planted firmly on the table, nails trimmed. The details remind me of my training. I've come here as Zephyr the strategist, not Qilin the orphan. Thanks to the ride I caught on Miasma's fleet, I am two moves away from realizing a Ren-Cicada alliance. The opportunity is mine.

I just need to seize it.

So I home in on that foot. It's clean. Cicada must have shucked her shoes right before entering the court. When she pulls the wine jug away from her lips, a droplet falls onto her robes. It's clear. Granted, it could be white wine, imported from the North. Or it could be water, and the flush on her cheeks is mere rouge.

At sixteen, Cicada is two years my junior. An infant, to this court. She must pick and choose her battles wisely. By putting on this grief-stricken act, she lures her adversaries into complacency. Feign Madness but Keep Your Balance, we strategists call it.

She won't be feigning once I'm through with her.

I step forward. "As I'm sure your scouts have told you, *Queen* Cicada, an empire fleet of two hundred junks is sailing down the waterway as we speak."

Cicada takes a swig from her jug. "So?"

"We're not asking for your fealty."

"Good, because I'm not giving it."

An outcry from her advisors.

"*Silence.*" Cicada slams down her jug. "Why should I submit while Xin Ren runs free? Answer my question, Zephyr the Traitor." Her black eyes burn at me. "Don't think I forgot who you served before Miasma."

"Ren doesn't have much going for her," I say. "All she has is her surname and honor."

"Xin. A name and dynasty soon to be history." Advisors keen

in distress. "As for honor . . ." Cicada shakes her head, her long hair rippling. "What does honor mean to a lordess without a fief? Fleeing from the empire with a horde of commoners? Facing the imperial cavalry with farmers and serfs?"

"Honor is defending what you can't bear to lose," I say, meeting Cicada's gaze. "It's fighting for a family that can't help you."

You were that family to me, Ku. She's still consumed by her stick of sugar, when I glance to her. I turn my back on her and Cicada both, proceed down the walk alone. "Ren's honor isn't for everyone. It definitely wasn't for me. The empire forgave my past transgressions and spared my life. Bow to Xin Bao now, and it will spare yours too."

Every Southern advisor adopts my mantle, voicing reasons why the South should cede sovereignty.

"The Northerners are ruthless!"

"They'll wage total war on the South if it comes to it."

"Think of all the farmland that will be destroyed!"

"Farmland?" cries an advisor in blue. He shakes his head and steps out from the ranks, bowing deeply at Cicada. "More than farmland is at stake, child. The North treats its soldiers as vanguard fodder, but the South is different. We are a land of culture. We may have the wealth and numbers to fund a war, but just because we can doesn't mean we should. The lives of our people are more valuable than theirs."

Cicada says nothing. I make it to the end of the walk, and turn to see her rising from her seat. She descends the dais steps, nimble as a doe.

The advisor in blue trails after her. "Listen to reason, child."

She ignores him, striding to one of the Southern guards flanking the walk. Before anyone can move, she unsheathes the sword hanging at his side and cuts down.

For a second, I'm back in the mountain clearing, watching Miasma swing her sword, looking away as the head thuds onto the undergrowth but catching a flash of bone, white in the center. I shake my head. The court comes back into focus. No one is keeled over; the sword isn't bloody. The lump on the ground isn't anyone's head. Just the corner of a gilt table, sheared off.

Cicada returns the sword to the stunned guard. "Next time, it'll be your head," she says to the advisor before addressing the rest of us. "It will be all your heads if I hear another word about submitting to the empire."

No one protests.

She turns on Crow and me. "Get out of my court." She says it calmly, her tone belying her next words: a declaration of war. "Tell that god of yours the South is ready."

With that, she walks past the dais, to the lacquered screen. Ku scampers down from her perch. Cicada takes her hand, and mine fist as they disappear behind the façade of silk and wood.

Cicada played right into my provocations. Her every word and action furthered my goals. But I can't savor what I've accomplished. I've won, as a strategist.

I have lost, as someone else.

‡ ‡ ‡

"That went well," says Crow when we're back on our junk.

Under normal circumstances, we'd be staying in the Nightingale

Pavilion. But having war declared to our faces has necessitated a change of accommodations. As I pace up and down the deck, Crow's eyes track me. Does he know I was goading Cicada on? Has he figured out my master plan of arranging a Ren-Cicada alliance against Miasma?

It doesn't matter either way; Crow has no evidence other than what I said, and what I said is consistent with everything I've *been* saying since I bowed to Miasma in the mountain clearing. He can't report on me yet. In spite of my theatrics, I've been playing a cautious game.

I can't anymore. Provocation got Cicada to insurrect against the empire, but it won't get her to join hands with Ren. I have to plant the idea, persuade. I can't accomplish either from this junk.

I need to see Cicada again.

But all I can see is Ku. Healthy, *happy* Ku, taking Cicada's hand.

The Ku I knew never wanted to hold hands with me.

I clutch the junk side for support, squeeze my eyes shut as Crow approaches.

"Hey." His voice sounds far away. A hand settles onto my shoulder. "Is everything okay?"

As if he cares. *Go on*, I want to say. *Ask me why I froze, back in Cicada's court.* He must be dying of curiosity. I'd be, in his shoes.

But he doesn't ask. Just repeats his first question. I can't tell if the concern in his voice is genuine. I can't tell a lot of things with Crow.

I rest my forehead against the lacquer. It's pleasantly cool. "Just let me be."

"You're always welcome to see my physician."

"And end up like you?" My chest tenses, my lungs tight. Excellent. A breathing attack now of all times. "No, thank you."

"It's my own fault I'm the way I am."

"How so?" Not that I care about Crow or how he got his consumption. My legs shake. I feel myself slide toward the deck.

Crow wraps an arm around me, stopping my descent. "The physician caught my cough in the early stages." He guides me to one of the tea tables on the promenade; I don't have the strength to fight him as he sits me down on a stool. "With sufficient rest, I could have prevented it from turning chronic."

"Then why didn't you?"

Crow gestures for a servant and sends them away with an order I don't catch. I can barely hear him when he says, "Hard to rest, given the state of the empire."

"How devoted." Sarcasm lacks its *oomph* when you're gasping for breath. "Is everything you do for your lordess?"

"Yes. Everything I do is for my lordess."

"Because you think she's the strongest?"

"Because I care."

About your own head. With so much talent waiting in the wings, Miasma can afford to kill off anyone the second they disappoint her.

My head feels huge, an overripe melon about to split. A groan slips past my lips.

"Talk to me, Zephyr."

Why should I? "Do you have a sister?" May the personal question silence him.

"No," replies Crow. He sounds farther away. "But I had a

childhood friend who was like a younger sister to me. We did just about everything together. Compose pretentious poetry. Debate the meaning of life. Chase after the same ladies and gentlemen."

"That's nice." I wish my sister were like Crow's not-sister. "That's very nice . . ."

The servant returns with a bronze teapot. Crow pours. "Here," he says, sliding a steaming cup over to me. "Have some tea."

The cup clinks as I plant my hands on the table, straining to my feet. "I have to go."

"Where?"

"To Cicada." I'm aware of my mind driving my body, my lips moving with words I don't consciously think. "War will be costly no matter who wages it. It's better for the empire if I can convince the South to cede without coming to blows."

"I sensed that we were overstaying our visit."

"Then stay here and wait for my return."

Crow catches my elbow. The force turns me around and sends me pitching into him. I grab on to his arms, then glare upward.

He doesn't react. Just gazes down at me, hair poured black over his shoulders, lips parted as he catches his breath. He still looks sickly—a bowl of marrow stock would do him good—but also ethereal, from this angle. Beautiful, I think, before realizing that I might be the sick one, considering that I'm seeing three of everything.

"You should really have some tea," he says, and I release him.

"I don't want tea."

But I don't get very far before I need to rest.

I'm shivering. I shouldn't be shivering in this summer heat.

Crow catches up to me. "Maybe not now, but you'll wish you had it in an hour."

In an hour. My arm, when I lift it, feels like a log. Something is wrong with me, and it's not just because I'm reacting poorly to seeing Ku. My thoughts are sluggish as Crow sits me down again. He pours a fresh cup of tea and wraps my hands around the warm porcelain.

Drink, his eyes say.

Drink, or else.

The fatigue. The nausea. The shaking. The insistence that I drink. "You poisoned me."

It's obvious once I accuse him of it. Of course he poisoned me. Had the drug not reached my head, I'd have figured it out sooner.

"You would have done the same," Crow says, matter-of-fact.

It's clever, I'll admit. By poisoning me, he keeps me on his leash. No matter where I go, I have to return for the antidote.

I lift the cup, hands trembling against my will. But my gaze is steady, and it fixes on Crow's over the porcelain rim as I drink, down to the dregs.

My legs are already steadier when I rise. Crow doesn't stop me, and I'm nearly at the rungs before he speaks.

"Send Cicada my regards."

"Not coming?" I try to sound indifferent. I mustn't let him think that his company is unwanted.

"You'll be running back to me soon enough."

Don't remind me. "You wish it were because of your charms," I drawl, and Crow pulls a sad face. "No one would willingly chase you without you poisoning them."

"Now you're just being—" He breaks off into a coughing fit.

Disgusting. I descend the rungs, ignoring him.

The coughing stops.

His shadow spills over the side of the junk; his voice drifts down. "For what it's worth, I'm sorry."

Regret doesn't suit him. But his apology also hands me the last word. For that, I can't complain.

"Don't be." I clear the final rung and thump into the boat waiting in the water. "Like you said, I would have done the same."

六

A CICADA'S SHELL

I would have done the same.

A laugh escapes me as I stroll down the city boulevard.

No, Crow. If I were you, I would have convinced Miasma to execute me on the spot. I would have used every stratagem in the books to make it happen, had I any doubt of your allegiance.

Instead, I'm alive. Poisoned, yes, and at Crow's mercy. But as long as I breathe, I will scheme.

The Southlands are known for their gourmet food and fine art, and it shows as I enter the marketplace. Brightly draped vendor stalls boast everything from roasted squids to tapestries woven from seed pearls. One stall hangs with silver suits of armor.

"They're handcrafted," says the vendor, noticing that I've looked twice. "No two are the same, and I sell them with a lifetime guarantee."

No one could live a lifetime in one of these. Even I can tell that there are too many gaps in the laminar. When I say as much to the vendor, she stares at me like I've grown hair between my brows.

"It's ceremonial grade, of course. Far too fine to be worn on the battlefield."

"How much?"

She names her price, and my eye twitches. One of these suits could feed Ren's army for weeks.

I reassess the marketplace as I walk away. None of the vendors appear to be living from sale-to-meal. Even the refugees—the only sign of our fractured empire—are clothed and fed. Two scholars debate politics at a tavern bar. A teacher conducts class on the porch of an apothecary, leading his students in recitation of Sage Master Shencius's couplets.

A kingdom of knowledge, I hear Cicada has taken to calling it. More like a kingdom of plenty. Compared to the North, a famine-plagued battleground between Miasma and every dissident warlord of the last decade, this land is a paradise. How Ku wound up here, in Cicada's court, is beyond me. I should be grateful she did, but—

"Lu'er! Piao'er!" A call, from a second-story window. Two girls dart in from the street. One trips and falls behind the other, screaming as she skins her knee.

Turn back around. It's not until the other girl does and helps her sister up that I realize Ku would have kept on running if I'd fallen.

Something wet splatters my nose. I glance up; the rain comes down. When was the last time a storm caught me unprepared? Too long ago, before I learned to read the heavens.

Remember who you are, and who you aren't. You're here for Ren. You're here for yourself.

I dodge the parasol vendors beelining for me, and continue in the direction of Nightingale Pavilion. The rain stops as quickly as it started. I reach the front gates and duck under one of the adorning willow trees, out of the guards' sights.

As I survey my prospects, a party of caravans pulls up, bearing a group dressed in furs that should be illegal in this climate. Some hold staves that widen at the top like a python's head, pierced through with bronze rings that jangle as the group hops down from the caravans.

Monks, mystics, fortune-tellers. Peddlers of drivel. An old court registrar comes out to the gate, and I wait for him to shoo the lot away.

Instead, he invites them forward.

Associating with the occult is normally beneath me. Today, it's my ticket in. I slip down the line while the guards inspect the caravans and find a monk standing behind the final vehicle. She's piled in pelts and leaning on her staff. I whisper, "I'll pay you for that outfit," and she straightens.

"Won't be cheap." Her mouth is a garden of mixed metal teeth, gold and bronze sprouting from her gums.

I unstring my money pouch—courtesy of Miasma—and offer it. Better spent on this than ceremonial laminar.

The monk shakes the pouch, then squints at me. "You have a strange aura to you, child."

"That's all my money. I have no more to give."

The monk circles me.

"Your furs, please," I prompt, my patience drying as she mutters some incantation. When she finishes, I'm just as soggy as before and probably still half-poisoned. She hands her furs over and I don them. I take her staff, assume her place.

The guards clear us for entrance.

We follow the registrar through gardens and into a large courtyard bordered on three sides by honeysuckle.

"The lordess will be with you shortly," says the registrar. "In the meantime . . ."

The bushes prick my shoulder blades as I step back. When the registrar turns, I do too. The fragrant blooms enclose me. I tunnel through them, out of the courtyard and into another, shucking off the furs as I go. The downpour has darkened my beige robes to dung, and my ponytail is a wet plaster against my neck. I'm hardly worthy of an audience with Cicada.

And she's not worthy of my sister.

Using my knowledge of geomancy, I navigate myself from corridor to corridor until I arrive at an ink room, large and airy. Gills of light bleed through the shuttered windows. Calligraphy hangs from the walls, the smell of freshly ground ink astringent like tea.

It's unlikely that Cicada herself will visit. But a scribe is almost certain to, and scribes will at least listen to me make my case, unlike a hot-blooded warrior or a guard. They might even take me to Cicada, if I'm convincing enough. Settling in for the wait, I sit behind a table. It's laden with more reading material than I've seen in months. I lift a scroll.

"Those aren't yours."

A voice as smooth as stone.

Slowly, I set down the scroll. I look up—*be Zephyr, not*

Qilin—as Ku crosses over to me and says, "You're not allowed to touch what isn't yours."

I rise before I can help it. Walk, closing the distance between us. I grab her by the upper arms—and stumble when she pushes me off.

"Ku—"

"That's not my name."

"Don't be silly."

"It's not my name." She dodges me as I grab for her again, but I'm faster. My hand closes around an elbow, and her eyes flame. "My name is November."

November.

The name pierces my mind. November. This sobriquet—

"Take your hands off my strategist."

Cicada sweeps into the room. Ku wriggles free and runs to the Southlands lordess.

Everything about the image is wrong. Cicada is shorter than me. Just a year older than Ku's fifteen. It looks like one child hiding behind another. Still, the lordess growls like a tiger protecting her cub. "I thought I made myself clear that you're no longer welcome in my court."

Maybe not as Zephyr the strategist. But if I were her right now, I'd say something. Do something. I wouldn't be standing so still and silent, back to being the orphan on the side of the street, staring at where the dust had cleared. Rubble on the ground, and blood. But no sister.

My sister.

Is November. The new Southlands strategist who aided in

fighting off the Fen pirates. She works for Cicada just like I work for Ren. But before she was Cicada's, she was mine.

Mine. The scream stings the back of my throat. *You're shielding what's mine.* But my training wins over, and when I do finally speak, my tone is level. "I'm here to talk."

Without replying, Cicada nods at the door. Ku cuts in front of me to exit the room. I swallow.

Cicada takes the same path as Ku, but slower. She intersects my shadow. Her cheeks are still flushed, but she doesn't smell of alcohol. Both her feet are shoed.

I was right about the façade. Her old advisors might see a girl bereft of her sister, but I see a noble, entitled. It's in the lift of her chin. Even her silence is a weapon. I wonder if she knows how much it hurts me to repeat myself. "I'm here to talk."

She stops just short of the door, figure aglow in the daylight. "I'm not interested in talking to strategists who betray their lordesses."

Her hair, long and black, reaches past her waist. She hasn't cut it once in all her sixteen years. I know that as a fact. I've read up on Cicada—and her sister, mother, grandmother—but as she places a hand on Ku's shoulder, I realize I was reading about a character. The real person makes me feel and say things I can't control.

"I never betrayed my lordess."

The truth was to be my final weapon, not a shield for my shredded pride. But I can't stand for being called a traitor in front of Ku, and my fists ball as Cicada says, "I'm listening."

She doesn't face me. Doesn't turn. If there was any doubt as to which one of us held the power, it's gone now.

"I'm still working for Ren." My fingers move to my fan. The bamboo handle is cool in my hand. "I said I came down on Miasma's behalf, but in reality I'm here on Ren's."

"Does Ren know this?"

"No."

"Then how can you be here on her behalf?"

"Because we're in agreement on the importance of an alliance with you."

"Me," says Cicada.

"Yes."

Miasma would throw her head back and laugh. Cicada simply floats back into the room, going to the document cubbies built into the walls. "And what makes you think I'd want an alliance with her?" she asks, skimming her long, pale fingers over stacks of scrolls. "Just what does Xin Ren have to offer?"

"She treats her allies like blood. Whatever she has, you'll have. Troops. Generals. Strategists." Strategist, technically, but I'm worth ten.

"And the empire's bounty over her head? Will I share that too?" Cicada eases out a volume and tosses it onto the table. It unfurls, and I recognize the sonnet by the first line. It's about an empress who chose to kill her daughter rather than send her as tribute to a rebel warlord.

This is Cicada's refusal. Poetic and indirect, but clear as day to any scholar.

I walk myself to the door where Ku is standing. She ignores me, staring instead at a dragonfly zooming around the courtyard.

Be Zephyr. Be a strategist.

Cicada had a sister too. Cricket. Three years older, a prodigy of the literary and military arts, pride of the Southlands. When the Fen pirates killed her, it's rumored that the whole of the South mourned for three months straight, abstaining from wine, meat, and music. They might mourn no more, but that doesn't mean Cricket is gone. Her legacy remains, a shadow that will hang over Cicada no matter how high she climbs.

I wait in the doorway, wait for Cicada to pad over to me when I've stood too long, wait to say, "Your sister would have listened to reason."

Her footsteps stop.

So quiet is the courtyard that I can hear the dragonfly's buzz.

She turns to Ku. "Should we show her?"

Ku looks away from the insect. "Let's."

"Come," Cicada says, brushing past me. "There's something you should see."

The humidity has returned, replacing the temporary cool brought on by the storm. Sweat coats my skin as Cicada takes us through a never-ending series of courtyards connected by moon gates. The mystics and monks have left the large courtyard, but I hear chanting in the distance. It grows louder as Cicada leads us down a gallery that ends at a padlocked door.

Cicada unlocks it.

"Watch your step," she says, inviting me to go first.

I don't know what I expected to be hidden behind the door, but it wasn't a lake, a hundred or so steps below. As I descend, shadows from the wall rippling over my head, a strange sensation overcomes me. In the lake, the monks and mystics dance. Their staves jangle as they chant to an audience of one: a boy in the middle of the waist-deep water, chained to a stone slab.

Goose bumps rise on my arms, and questions in my mind. Who is he? What are the monks doing?

Cicada joins me on the second-to-last step. The water laps just beyond our toes. Narrow stone paths divide the lake like spokes to a wheel. "Stay here," Cicada tells Ku, then starts down one of the paths. Warily, I follow.

We near the boy in the center of the lake. Lumps of greenery float around him like miniature islands. I peer closer at one such lump and reel back, almost losing my footing.

They're not islands, but bodies, overgrown with moss and ferns, the flesh taken up as food, the organs filled with roots.

Cicada stops in front of the boy. Angry red marks bracelet his wrists. Once, he must have fought against his chains. Now he barely cracks his eyes open as Cicada sloshes water into his face. It's shameful, his helplessness, and I start to look away when he lifts his head, revealing the cattails tattooed down the right side of his neck.

A Fen pirate.

He's dazed at first, gaze flitting between me and Cicada, before it stills on the Southlands lordess. His lips pull back, his veins tensing with the anger of a grown man.

Holding his stare, Cicada orders the monks to chant louder. The cries rise to keens. I wince, but the boy—he screams as if his very skull is being split.

"Curious, isn't it?" Cicada speaks over him. "The pirates

claim to be sensitive to qì. They say it gives them magic. They say it's what makes them strong. But it also makes them weak."

"Let them be," the pirate begs Cicada, his words garbled by the marsh dialect. There's no hate or anger to him now. He's just a single pirate chained to a slab of stone while the rest of his crew rots somewhere else. "Let them be."

Them.

I look back down at the flora-fied bodies in the water. Not rotting somewhere else. Rotting *here.* What were they like a month ago, before their flesh flowered? I imagine the stink, the mosquitoes. I imagine watching them decay by the day, losing dignity and form, their spirits—if I believed in such things—tortured by monks. My head spins like I'm poisoned all over again, and my gaze skates to Cicada. Miasma is the one reputed to be cruel, a reputation I've seen her live up to. But Cicada? She's been surprising me at every turn. I admire her inscrutability.

I also despise it.

"You say my sister listened to reason," Cicada says as the boy begs. "And you're right. She very much did." She faces me. "Her reason was her conscience. She was a genius when it came to waging war, but she had codes she abided by. She refused to launch a sneak attack on the pirates, and she paid the ultimate price for it.

"After they killed her, they cut her to little pieces and fed her to the marsh sharks. They left us with nothing to bury." Cicada's black eyes flicker to the mossy man-islands in the water—her version of justice, I realize. "Now the people have moved on. Only I mourn."

Mourning. Is this that? Is it even revenge? The pirates are

already dead. Their ships are mud in the marsh. When Miasma sticks the impaled heads of warlords atop the empire walls, her actions are a deterrence. This pirate—hidden, the last of his kind—deters nothing. Cicada's actions are irrational.

Emotional.

I should thank her, for giving me so much weakness to work with.

"Miasma was behind the death of your sister," I say to Cicada. "If the North cared, they would have sent troops. Instead, they let the pirates be your problem. They wanted you to buckle."

"You think I don't know?"

"You and Ren share a common enemy," I press on. "Forging an alliance only makes sense."

"It makes more sense to keep the empire focused on Xin Ren," pipes a voice behind us. It's Ku's, to my consternation. She's disobeyed Cicada and made her way down the stone path, her robes trailing into the water.

In the past, I would have rushed for her, held her arm even as she fought me, knowing that if I let go, she'd inevitably trip and topple in. But now I'm not her sister or guardian. Cicada is, and Cicada simply replies to me, "Yes, Ren and I have a common enemy. But Ren has one enemy. I have hundreds. You saw my court. It's full of old men who doubt my abilities. Every day, I have to pretend to be someone I'm not, just to pacify them. Do one thing they deem as unwise, and they'll be looking for my replacement. And you know what is unwise? Allying myself with Ren."

"That's not—"

"The South isn't powerful because of the wealth of one, but

the wealth of many. I need every noble on my side. Ren can afford to up and run from danger. I have a kingdom to protect."

When Cicada finishes, her cheeks are redder than before, a real flush bleeding through the rouge. She rips her gaze from mine. "You wouldn't understand. You have no need to hide. You present yourself as you are and speak as you like."

"You can too," I deadpan. "You did just now."

Her lips part, then close. She shakes her head, laughs once, and gathers up her robes, striding past me, and finally, I see her. A cicada sloughing off its shell. She's vindictive, stubborn, brittle. A child. I know her type.

I can control her.

"Ren won't be a burden!" I call after her. "Give me a chance to prove it to you."

"What can you do? Wave your fan and conjure a hundred thousand arrows?"

"If I fail, you can have my head."

Cicada laughs, looser this time. "What do you say, November? Should we let her try?"

And just like that, my fate is chained to Ku's again. She can't possibly know how much I need this alliance.

Say yes. Say yes. Say—

"Three days." My sister turns to follow Cicada. "A hundred thousand arrows in three days."

BORROWING ARROWS

A *hundred thousand arrows in three days.*
  Sorry to disappoint, Ku, but it'll take more than that to kill me. I may have failed as a sister, but I won't fail as a strategist. When I return to the junk that night, I lie awake in my cabin, mind on fire as I consider my options.

I could employ every arrow maker in the Southern capital to scrounge up that number. But that's an insult to my skills. I can do better. I'll demonstrate to Cicada that nothing is out of my reach, not even the unthinkable.

I won't make the arrows.

I'll borrow them from the enemy.

‡ ‡ ‡

Day one, I thatch twenty Southern junks with straw. I order Cicada's craftsmen to make dummies—blue burlap stuffed with more straw—and have them set up on the decks. Then I climb to the highest watchtower and take a seat, watching the stars migrate through the sky and laughing when they foretell the perfect conditions for my artifice.

"Should I be concerned?" asks Crow when I return to our shared junk for dinner. He doesn't know the details of my challenge, or what's at stake for Ren, just that I'll win Cicada's submission to the empire if I succeed and lose my head if I fail.

"Why should you?" I swirl my tea. "You're the one killing me."

"And saving your life daily."

"Enough of this." Servants set the table with our entrées. "Just tell me where you've put the poison."

"Everywhere." Crow doesn't sound the least bit contrite. "Does my thoroughness impress you?"

"No."

"My zither playing?"

"No."

"My good looks?"

"You're not afraid I'll overdose?"

Crow sighs as I bring us back to the topic. We've been talking more, now that I know what's the worst that can happen. Besides, I have to get closer to Crow. The poison—tasteless, odorless—could be in anything, but I've been watching the kitchens closely, and the antidote isn't brewed into the tea. Crow must add it to my cups himself. It has to be on his person.

Up his sleeve? Between his broadbelt and waist? I watch him carefully as he scoops rice into my bowl.

"You certainly stare a lot for someone who says I'm ugly."

"I never said you were *ugly*."

Crow grins as if I just complimented him. "You won't overdose, not as long as you take your antidote every day," he says, arranging pea shoots atop my mound of rice.

I snatch my bowl from him. I like him better when he's not pretending to be anyone other than my rival.

Crow begins to fill his own bowl. "I'm more worried about your transaction with Cicada."

You should be. The empire will soon have twice the number of enemies. "Save your concern." I poke around the sizzling stone pot of pork belly, looking for the leanest piece. My palate isn't used to so much meat. "It's my head on the chopping block, not yours."

A chunk of lean pork lands on my rice. My gaze rises to Crow's chopsticks, hovering just before my nose, then to his self-satisfied smile.

He withdraws his chopsticks. "I'm the one who has to explain your death to Miasma."

Turns out Crow got to the only lean piece in the pot. Rather than touch his offering, I select another and saw at the white fat with my chopsticks. "Just say you let me die, then. I exposed myself as a traitor."

"There's no harm in admitting defeat," says Crow, watching me work.

"Maybe not for you." I excise fat from muscle. "But I have a reputation at stake, seeing as I'm undefeated."

‡ ‡ ‡

If Crow's skeptical, Cicada is even more so. "I don't understand you," she says when I join her for tea the next day. She paces the length of the room. "You ruin the junks I lend you—"

"Renovate." They're more suited to my purposes than before.

"Befit them with some of the ugliest scarecrows I've seen—"

"Dummies, not scarecrows."

"You exchange pleasantries with the craftsmen and talk about market prices and the economy. You go to the watchtower and sit there for hours at a time. Then you come back here and do what? Debate with me? Drink tea?"

The tea *is* quite good, a definite improvement to the brown stuff Ren's camp serves. "I thought you enjoyed my company."

I, for one, find Cicada's entertaining enough. A Southern noble to her core, she's well versed in philosophy, archaeology, and all topics utterly useless in a war.

"Hmph." Cicada rejoins me at the low table inset with imported ivory. "I did, before I realized you're mocking me."

"I wouldn't dare."

"It's day two, and you don't have a single arrow to show."

"In due time."

"There's no time."

"I still have a day, like you said."

Cicada sweeps back her sleeves and ladles hot water over a fresh batch of leaves, releasing the scent of jasmine. "Word of our deal has spread through the kingdom. I'll have no choice but to execute you if you fail."

"I won't. Do you have the forty ship hands I requested?"

"What for?"

"Manning the junks."

Cicada raises a brow. "You're saying that all those scarecrows you made can't man the junks?"

I laugh, and Cicada lets out a rare smile. It softens her face, makes her look closer to her actual age.

"I do have the ship hands you asked for," she says as she refills my cup. "Just what are you planning?"

"A surprise."

"Strategists," huffs Cicada, raising her cup with me. "You and November both."

My cup stops halfway to my mouth.

I set it down as Cicada inhales the steam from hers. "How exactly did you come into . . . November's acquaintance?"

A breeze blows in through the half-opened door panels, sweeping bamboo leaves across the floor. One lands in Cicada's lap. Her tiny mouth tightens. She places her tea, untouched, on the table, and settles back on her heels. Her expression has cooled, just like this room. It's like she's reprimanding me for asking such a question when we were getting along so well.

"I'm aware you knew her in the past."

That's one way of putting it. *Yes, Cicada, I did happen to know my sister in the past.*

"Whoever she was to you before," Cicada goes on, "she's not that person anymore."

"Because she's yours?"

"She belongs to no one." End of discussion. But after a moment, Cicada breathes out, something giving. "She arrived several springs ago and asked to see me. Said she could help."

I picture Ku walking herself to the pavilion gates. Requesting an audience with the Southern lordess. Sitting at a table like I am now and laying out her plans for defeating the pirates. A pained laugh bubbles up in my chest. I wash it down with a hard mouthful of tea.

"Go on," Cicada says. "Laugh. My advisors certainly did. It only made me more determined to take her into my service."

"Like a pet or playmate." Adopted in an adolescent act of rebellion.

"Is that how you would describe yourself? As a pet or playmate of Ren's?" I choke on my tea, and Cicada smiles. "I don't lack vassals up in their years, with fossilized ideas of rites and dynasties. *I* think youth is brilliance. The mind at its most supple. I thought you'd agree."

Don't compare us. In the courtyard, the sky is purpling. The air smells of a yawn, the heavens unhinging before a downpour. And it will pour. I know from reading the cosmos, a skill I first learned from the ex–imperial cosmologist, then honed by spending months out in open fields, scribbling down observations, charting my predictions, marking off which came true and under what conditions. I'm as classically trained a strategist as they come. My mentors were all living embodiments of their arts. Did Ku have mentors? I can't imagine it. I can't see Ku as anything but a girl who resisted my care at the orphanage.

"What bound you to this path so young?" Cicada asks, interrupting my thoughts.

"What else was I going to be? A farmer?"

Cicada arches a brow.

"I was born in Shangu Commandery," I say, and Cicada's expression changes, comprehension settling. Shangu of the Yi province. North. It was a land of fighting warlords, famine, and plague before Miasma swept in. Then only famine and plague remained. "I could have lived an ordinary life at the mercy of the heavens. Or I could seek to understand the universe."

"Risk death by your own terms."

"Yes." Annoying, that she finished my sentence.

"You could have been a warrior," Cicada says.

"Look at me," I say lightly. In front of a fellow literati, I'm not ashamed of my build or constitution. We both know that there are more ways to be dangerous than one.

A courtier intrudes then and whispers something into Cicada's ear. She listens impassively and dismisses him.

"Just in time," she says to me. "Your lordess has arrived—"

For a fleeting moment, I think *Ren*.

"—and clogged up my waterway with her fleet of junks." Cicada lifts her now-cold tea and drinks. "Maybe I'll gift her your head when you fail."

"Maybe," I say, and drink my cold tea as well. Outside, it begins to rain. "Or I could be the one gifting you hers."

‡ ‡ ‡

The rain lets up as evening rolls around. I return to the junk to find people whispering about Miasma's arrival. Eyes glance to me, probably wondering if I have Cicada's oath of fealty to show to the prime ministress. Without engaging, I take up a seat by the stern and fan myself as the sun sets behind the Diyu Mountains.

The stars come out. I stay on deck while everyone heads below. The first of the post-rain mist creeps in on the waterway.

The mist is cotton thick by dawn. After putting on the whitest pair of robes I can find, I go to Crow's cabin and shake him awake. He comes to slowly, asks after the time.

I throw his black robes at him, then set his mustard-yellow girdle and wrist-guards at the foot of his bed. "Our lordess is here. It's time we pay our respects."

But really, it's time to borrow a hundred thousand arrows.

‡ ‡ ‡

My hand fades into the mist as I grip the boat for balance. Crow clambers in behind me, his coughs sounding wetter than usual. I look over my shoulder and see him wiping his mouth with the edge of his sleeve.

"I told you my illness worsens with my outlook," he says, and a morbid thought occurs to me—that even if he were to start coughing blood, his all-black attire would make it impossible to tell.

And why would I care to tell? "What's your outlook?" I ask as the rower at the head of the boat plunges her oars into the water.

"Let's just say I don't have a good feeling about this."

I take a seat. I'd sooner worry about my arrow-borrowing enterprise than Crow's well-being. "Our lordess has finally joined us. It's only natural that we should report to her."

"By junk," qualifies Crow. "With the rest of the crew." He leans against the hull, washed out in the weak light. His hair is completely down—he didn't even bother with tying it in its half-up style—and he seems . . . vulnerable as he sighs and closes his eyes. "This all feels very illicit." His head tips to one side; his bangs fall over his brow. My fingers fidget, and I readjust my already-perfect high ponytail. "Like we're sneaking away." One of his eyes flickers open and peers at me through his bangs. "Don't tell me we're really sneaking away together."

My heart fidgets now. Yes, we're on a boat, rowing on the famed Gypsum River, with mountains to our right and left and gossamer mist all around, but in less than ten minutes, this idyllic scene is going to hell.

As if sensing my thoughts, Crow sits up. "Say something."

If only I could tell him the truth, that everything about to happen is by my brilliant design. But even I know when to be modest. I mustn't be seen as a tool so sharp that I'm better off discarded.

"Stop jumping to conclusions," I order, which promptly invites Crow to jump to conclusions.

"You failed whatever it is that you promised Cicada," Crow concludes as our little boat glides out of the mist. "So you decided to make your escape and implicate me while you're at it."

"Hush." I motion for him to quiet, then squint at the waterway ahead. Still and silent as the river is, it feels sentient. It shivers at every kiss of our oars, every stroke delivering us closer to the escarpment where Miasma is anchored.

A heartbeat later, the menacing face of granite reveals itself. It stabs out of the water like a curved jaw, tongued by choppy waves and crowned with canine-like peaks. Miasma's junks emerge from the mist too, neat rows of them, crimson sails erect like fins.

A distant horn sounds—from behind. Crow's head jerks up, his gaze shooting to the southern banks from which we came. I look too, just to be convincing. I already know what to expect: What will first appear as a darkness in the fog will become a fleet of junks arrayed in a line. Their numbers will be seemingly impossible to count—unless you were the one to outfit each ship with straw, dummies, and two ship hands. One to steer, one to sound the drums.

"Will you look at that," murmurs Crow. "A whole navy in pursuit, just for us."

He turns to our rower, presumably to give orders, but whatever he says is drowned out by Southlands war drums. The baritone rattles my bones. Miasma is hearing this too. She'll be whipping out her spyglass to inspect the size of the force, but no amount of resolution will bring into focus the straw thatching or the dummies on deck. The fog will limit her information to just this: roughly two dozen Southern ships are headed her way in a straight-line formation.

It's a classic battle scenario, one that Miasma will handle by ordering the archers on her vanguard ships to ready their bows and fire on her command. A navy without sailors is no navy at all. Kill enough of the people aboard, and the attack is averted.

Now we wait. Miasma will want the ships a bit closer to ensure that not a single arrow is wasted. My pulse quickens. I'm so invested in seeing my ruse unfold that I don't notice Crow until he's shoving a spare oar into my hand.

"You row too."

"Me?" Does it look like I'm made to do manual labor?

"Do you want to live or—"

Something whizzes over our heads.

It's the first of many arrows to come.

They scream through the sky. Hundreds of arrows. *Thousands* of arrows, passing overhead in waves as empire archers release and reload, release and reload. Behind us, the drums have stopped. Cicada's ship hands have gone belowdecks, where they'll be safe from the arrows striking the junks, ensnarled in the thatching and dummies like needles in pincushions.

The arrows cease. Miasma has called them off. But as I instructed, the ship hands maneuver each junk around to expose the other thatched side. The drumming starts up again, and empire arrows fly once more.

Our rower has gone sheet white with fear. It's not every day that you find yourself in the middle of a war. But the middle is the best place to be. I'm explaining as much to her—how we're nestled right under the vertex of each arrow's parabolic journey—when Crow pushes me down.

"Hey!" I yelp as my shoulder smacks into the bottom of the boat. "What—"

"You too," Crow orders the rower. Then, to my horror, he throws himself on top of me.

"Get *off*." I push at him as he wraps an arm around my shoulders. "Just what do you think you're doing?"

"Saving your life, as has become tradition."

"We're safe."

"By what law? Of projectile objects in motion? Stay still," Crow says as I squirm. "You've forgotten the law of the human body." His breath brushes my right cheek, warm as the planks are cool against my left. "People tire over time, archers included."

As if on cue, a stray arrow slices into the water beside the boat. Anger sparks in me. What sort of half-hearted shot was that? But then another arrow strikes the boat itself, and in dismay, I realize that Crow is right. I didn't account for the archers who wouldn't pull their weight. Now they might be the death of us. Or of Crow, who's taken it upon himself to be my human shield.

"Get off me," I snap, elbowing him. I'd much rather die than live indebted to Miasma's minion.

"Zephyr, please—" Crow shoves my head back down and my temple hits the planks.

My vision dulls, like night is falling, then brightens with pinks and whites. Zither music fills my ears. The sky blooms above me. I'm lying in a white wicker gazebo.

It's that dream.

Of heaven.

The zither music is still ringing in my head when I come to— under Crow. On the boat. The river has gone quiet. The sky is clear. The mist is dissipating, and the thatched junks are turning back, arrows collected. Our rower is slowly sitting up. Crow ... isn't.

"Crow?" Something seeps into my shoulder. It reeks of iron. It's dripping down my neck too. I palm it.

My hand comes away red with blood.

八

LINK BY LINK

*B*lood.

It coats the arrow shaft. A hand's width of red, all buried in Crow before the physician extracted it.

Now Miasma holds it. She snaps it. The pieces hit the ground. "Explain this!"

Retainers fall to their knees, leaving only me standing to brave Miasma's wrath.

"The South refuses to bow," I say. My voice is brittle, like my composure. I want to scrub off the blood that's still on my robes. I want to see Crow. I don't want to be here, in this empire camp erected atop the escarpment, answering to Miasma. "We barely managed to escape with our lives."

"The rest?" Miasma demands, referring to the retinue that accompanied me and Crow down south.

I fold my hands behind my back. "They were detained."

"Lies."

"I dare not assume anything else."

"*Assume.* If they defected, then say so!"

"Milordess," Plum starts.

"Silence."

Plum snaps her mouth shut, but stares at me with open hostility. The tension in the tent is as thick as lard. Even the physician senses it when he enters. He wets his lips. Miasma barks at him to hurry up.

"Speak," she orders after he bows. "What's his condition?"

If I didn't know any better, I'd think she actually cared about Crow as a person.

"Master Crow will recover with enough bed rest and tonic."

"Good. His life is your life. If he dies, you die."

The physician bows again, as if this is routine. After he retreats, Miasma does too, to her chair at the front. A servant delivers tea. She curls a hand around the cup. I brace myself, waiting for her to hurl that too.

In the end, she simply knocks back the tea and slams the cup down.

Everyone around me rises by some unspoken cue. Advisors bow, then file out. I'm a second late in following them.

My sobriquet rings across the tent.

"Zephyr."

Miasma gestures for me. When I'm standing before her, she twirls her hand. I spin for her and come back around to her careful scrutiny. She eyes the bandage around my temple. The injury bled.

Crow bled more.

"Are you wounded anywhere else?"

I can't read her face, or her voice. She might be concerned, or she might be suspicious.

Honesty feels like the safest play. "It's mostly Crow's blood." My throat closes. "He saved me."

He really shouldn't have bothered. The odds that I'll die anyway—at the hands of his lordess, no less—increase as Miasma frowns. She rises from the seat. The bell at her ear tinkles as she lifts onto her toes. She's as short as Ku, but it doesn't feel that way as she touches an ice-cold hand to my jaw.

"Of course he did." I should be focusing on the nuances of her voice, but it's impossible to when her finger is crawling up my jawline. It stops just beneath my ear, like a fly at rest. "He's like me," Miasma says. "He knows talent when he sees it."

If Miasma really is like Crow, then she should also know that talent doesn't equal loyalty. She'll look at me in the same way Crow does, watching for the moment I become more threat than asset.

But there's no caution in Miasma's gaze when she lifts her hand from my face and comes down to her heels. Her pupils are dilated, hungry. "I have a gift for you."

I follow her out of the tent and onto the scarp. The winds are brutal at this altitude, and I blanch when I see the sheer cliff drop, the rapids below breaking white like bones. We could have met in a perfectly good junk, but I guess it's true that Northerners fear water more than anything, heights included.

As I hug the waxy granite for dear life, Miasma climbs the stairs cut into the rock face with ease. She reaches the top long before me, her form a mere speck against the sky. *One push*, I think, eyes trained on her. *I'll do it when I reach her.* But though she may be petite, Miasma is no weakling. Chances are I'd have to throw myself at her, which would end with both of us plunging to our deaths. Another warlord would rise up, declare themselves regent of Xin Bao, and inherit the empire's might—including this massive navy beneath us.

It's not yet time to die.

"Behold," says Miasma as I join her side, straining for breath. "The empire's fleet of warships."

It's even more impressive from a bird's-eye view. Four hundred junks—maybe five—dotted with soldiers and weaponry. For years now, the South has always had the largest navy in the empire. Miasma has come to contest that title.

"Prime Ministress." A huff from behind us. I turn to see Plum's head bobbing up the steps. "You have—"

"Plum. Just in time." Miasma sweeps a hand at the fleet. "Do you think my navy is big enough to crush the South's?"

Plum pats at her forehead with a square of silk. "I reckon it is."

"You 'reckon'?" Miasma tips her head at me. "Zephyr, what do you say?"

"It absolutely is."

"Excellent, because it's yours."

"Prime Ministress?"

"I want you to destroy the South with it," Miasma says, ignoring Plum's aghast expression. "Can you do that?"

With a whole fleet to call mine? I've done more damage with less. My heart scrunches as I look back down at the ships. It might be years before Ren has a navy of her own. The frustration I played to Crow on the zither surges within me. How can I be the master of my fate, of all our fates, when we have so little and the enemy has so much?

Simple. Take it away.

"I can't accept it," I say, facing Miasma. "My skills are in advising. The fleet is best left in the hands of your naval officers. But . . . if I may . . ."

"Speak."

"I would like to suggest an improvement."

Plum sniffs, but Miasma motions for me to go on.

"Your soldiers are strong and well trained," I start, "but I'll hazard a guess that seasickness plagues many. The Southlanders, in contrast, have lived all their lives on the water. They're in better fighting condition, and will have the advantage in any naval battle."

Miasma rubs a thumbnail over her bottom lip. "And you have a solution for this?"

"Yes. Link the boats."

Before Miasma can reply, Plum flies into a fit. "Preposterous!" She whirls on her lordess. "Prime Ministress, you mustn't listen to the fox! Linking the boats would render them immobile! If some calamity were to strike, everything would be ruined!"

"Calamity? Like a meteorite falling out of the sky and landing right atop my fleet?" Miasma clucks her tongue. "Plum, oh, Plum. You know I don't like it when you overreact."

"I—"

"Zephyr is right. My people have not been themselves on this journey south. Linking the boats will help them recover."

"What if they attack with fire?"

"In this wind?" Miasma whips off the broadbelt at her waist.

She holds it out, an offering to the gale; it flies right back into her. "They'd roast themselves. Have no fear, Plum. It wouldn't be permanent. The boats can be unlinked quickly enough."

"But—"

"Save your breath." Plum stands there, fuming, as Miasma takes to the steps. I hurry after her, shivering in my robes as she looks toasty in her sleeveless vest. "The naval officers will do as Zephyr commands," she shouts over the wind. "Link the boats, and ready for war. Treat the ones who haven't returned as defectors. The South is our enemy, and anyone who sides with them will be annhilihated."

"I have to go back."

"What?"

I raise my voice. "I have to go back." I'm improvising, saying whatever I can to justify returning to Cicada even after she supposedly chased out me and Crow. "For the defectors."

Miasma hops down the last step and turns on me, eyes flashing. "Did you not just hear my orders? The defectors are to be—"

"Not *ours*. Theirs." I rattle off the names of several Southern naval officers, and Miasma's gaze narrows with recognition. They're the talent of a generation, worth twice the gold of any empire officer. I throw in some lesser-known names for good measure and finish by saying, "They want to serve you. If not for their tip-off, Crow and I wouldn't have been able to escape alive."

"Then why aren't they here with you now?" asks Miasma, ever suspicious.

Not too long ago, she was also suspicious of me. But she lusts after talent, all the better when it's mutinous.

"They're scared," I say, appealing to Miasma's sense of power.

"Oh?"

"Many of them have served the South for decades, and directly aided Cricket in military campaigns and developing naval technology." I watch as understanding blunts the edge to Miasma's features. Plenty of her current forces once coated their weapons in empire blood. You only need to look to the diversity within her army.

"They're not sure if the empire will forgive them," I continue, "and without guaranteed amnesty, they're unwilling to risk the safety of their families. But give the word, and I will personally deliver the pardons."

Miasma waves her hand even before I've finished. "How many pardons do you think I've issued, Rising Zephyr? I'll tell you now: more than the years this dynasty has lasted. Of course I can issue pardons; I would pardon everyone in this land if they swore loyalty to me. But I can't send you as the messenger."

If Miasma's no stranger to issuing pardons, then I'm no stranger to detecting pity. "You think I'm weak."

"Only in body," says Miasma, not unkindly. "Not in mind."

My chin juts out. "I didn't die on the run from you."

That gets a chuckle out of her. "That you did not, though Plum certainly wished it."

Glad to know I've been a thorn in the senior registrar's side since day one. I wait, breath held, for Miasma's permission to see Cicada.

"Not today," she finally says. "Tomorrow."

No, not today. Tomorrow, I will gloat to Cicada and Ku and

everyone else who doubted my ability to procure a hundred thousand arrows. I will explain to them exactly how the empire plans on destroying us and how, together as allies, we will destroy them first.

But today, I owe someone a visit.

✦ ✦ ✦

The junk cabin smells of mint salve and medicinal mushrooms.

It also smells of death.

On my way in, a servant exits, bearing a tray of used handkerchiefs. I let her by, then close the doors behind me, entrapping myself not just in the room, but in my memories of the orphanage. The thin millet gruel, the flea bites and mosquitoes. We'd spend summer looking forward to winter, when the vermin would freeze and die. But when winter came, we also froze and died. And so every summer we waited on winter and every winter we waited on summer, dreaming of better days that never came.

Granted, this cabin isn't the orphanage. It's missing a touch of something. Probably fecal matter and vomit. But no amount of incense can cover up that all-too-familiar reek of illness. Vertigo roils through me as I pad deeper into the cabin, keeping my eyes pinned on the canopy bed along the far wall—my objective.

My legs weaken short of it.

I clutch a chair for support, startling when my palm meets a material that's definitely not wood. It's Crow's cloak, draped over the back of the chair, crunchy with dried blood. I yank my hand away, but not before I catch a glint in one of the pockets.

A ceramic jar.

I dart a glance toward the shadowy bed, then back at the pocket. Carefully, my hand dips in. My breathing slows as I withdraw the jar.

I pop the beaded stopper and shake out the contents: clear, little pearls. They melt as I roll them between my fingers. The residue is odorless. Tasteless, when I lick the pad of my thumb.

My vertigo recedes. My legs regain their strength. It wasn't just the smell of death affecting me, or my bruised head. It was the poison.

This is the antidote.

I roll the stopper back in. Hesitate. I can't take it. Not yet. Crow's bound to notice its absence. But I might never have this opportunity again. This could be my only chance.

A sound comes from the bed and my hand decides for me, opening. The pill jar falls back into the pocket. My other hand releases the chair; I turn, bracing myself before I reach the bedside. I'm not sure what I fear more—that Crow will ask why I was poking around in his pockets, or that he won't have the strength to.

The latter fear swells at first glance. He looks like a badly done ink painting, hair too dark, skin too pale, with no gradient between black and white, life and death. My dizziness returns; my eyes squeeze shut.

I open them to his intent stare.

Before I can speak or move, he heaves onto his side. He props himself onto an elbow and palms his cheek, hips angled in a manner that would be suggestive if his expression weren't tight with pain.

"Come to finish me off?"

Anger flushes up my neck. How can he still joke? "Doesn't look like you need my help."

"Ouch." His wince is too convincing. "I'm just trying to grace you with my good side."

"You don't have a good side," I snap, pushing him back down. He grimaces, and I blanch at the sight of his shoulder bandage, blood already seeping through.

"Are you going to cry?" gasps Crow as he settles onto his back.

"No." If anything, I'm going to faint.

"A shame." His lids clam shut, the area under his eyes smudged purple. "I have a pocketful of handkerchiefs reserved for my personal use, but for you, I'd have made an exception."

I sit gingerly at the bed's edge. "Is that what I am? An exception?"

"Do you think I'd have lived to the ripe old age of nineteen if I took an arrow for anyone?"

The room is suddenly too warm. I reach for my fan, but there's blood on that too. The crane feathers are ruined. The kingfisher feather has broken at the tip. My heart barely registers the loss. It hurts in places I didn't know it could hurt. There's a price when you rely on miracles. This, I suppose, is the price of relying on Crow.

He saved my life.

I was not in control.

"*Why?*" I demand.

Crow stares at the canopy of the bed, focused, like he sees something I can't. My need to know overwhelms me after a minute, and I lean in, crane my neck to peer at the canopy, bending close enough that his exhale grazes my neck.

"Because I like you."

My gaze sinks. To his face, his lips, his half-lidded eyes. He stares and I stare back, the canopy dark above us. It all feels surreal. Dreamlike.

But by the law of dreams, we'd wake up right about now. There wouldn't be a chance for Crow to ruin the moment by musing, "It's a bad habit of mine, liking ruinous things."

"I didn't ask you to stick yourself with an arrow."

"No, but you almost broke my rib, flopping under me like that."

My face ignites. "You—you smashed my head!"

I expect Crow to fire back a witticism.

I don't expect him to grow solemn. "Does it hurt?"

He reaches up; I bat away his hand. "*Yes.*" I hate that I've admitted it to him. I hate that the pain in my chest is worse. *I like you.* He's just saying that to throw me off guard. Or he expects something in return. "I don't like you, for the record."

"Not even a little?"

"No."

"Worry not," says Crow. "I have plenty of time to woo you. I could even take another arrow if I need to."

I shake my head. "You've lost your mind."

"Maybe I have. I wouldn't be the first of our kind."

I won't lose mine. But then I recall Master Yao's decline. It started innocuously enough. A lapse of memory. Slower judgment. He never spoke of his dreams, but now I'm thinking about my strange ones of heaven, beginning eight years ago. Maybe they're the first symptom—*no, don't spiral down the unknowns—*

Unknown: How much blood Crow lost. How much more he *had* to lose.

I don't know.

I'm back in the bottom of the boat, my heart oblivious to the arrow on course for it.

I didn't know.

Where to look for Ku, and even earlier—I didn't know what changed, during the famine, that cost me her love.

I still don't know.

I feel myself rise from the bed.

"Zephyr?"

Zephyr is the name of someone who is always in command. Right now, I don't feel like her. I'm Qilin, the orphan who lost everyone who mattered.

Live or die, I'll leave no mark on this era.

"Are you leaving?" Crow rasps when I stand there without speaking.

Someday, I will have to. I will return to my true lordess's side, and Crow and I will become enemies once more.

Someday, I won't be able to say, "I'll be back."

As I climb the stairs, the sway of the junk stills. On deck, ship hands lay down a walk between this junk and the adjacent one. A metal spike is driven through to link the two. Other junks receive similar treatments. Soon, we will have a floating, interconnected fortress of boats. It's only the start to the finale I have in mind.

A finale of my design.

I'm still Zephyr. I don't think about what my stratagem means for the servants who bring me a zither at my request, or what it means for Crow, who watches me from the bed as I sit, cross-legged, with the instrument on my lap.

"There's no need to serenade me," he says as I lay my hands on the strings. "You're free to reciprocate my feelings in plain words."

"Quiet. Just listen."

I play one of the first songs I learned. It's based on the love story of an immortal snake deity and a young scholar who over-came immense odds to be together.

It didn't end well for them; it rarely does for a deity and human in these legends. Their child was a demon who con-sumed his mortal father before wreaking havoc in both heaven and earth. But I play the courtship part of the song, which has a playful and quick melody. It'd be uplifting, if my mind wasn't straying to Crow, working for a different lordess than me. Ku, too. One day, Ren might battle the South. What then? *I don't know.* Death is closer than I think.

Crow reminded me of that today.

The air feels ten times heavier when I lift my hands from the strings.

"If I die," says Crow at last, "you can play my funeral dirge."

"Rich of you to assume that I'd attend." Then, before Crow can say anything else, I play again. This time, I remember the day I stopped searching for Ku. It was the end of a long winter. The snow was melting, puddles forming in the streets. A retinue of warriors rode past, their stallions splashing bystanders, their bodies flashing with weapons, shields, armor—all except for one. That person rode at the front. She wore white flowing robes and carried a strange instrument, a fan, and nothing else. *Strategist*, the people whispered.

It was the first and last time I saw her.

The next day, I was wandering, lost and hungry, when the sound of music wafted from a tavern. I peeked in and there, by a table, sat a wiry man with a permanent frown carved into his face. But the music he played! His *instrument*. It had a name. *Zither.* The man did too.

Yao Mengqi.

Cicada asked me why I chose this path. I offered a suitable explanation. I spared her the story of the pitiful twelve-year-old orphan who stood outside the tavern as the man played the very instrument of the strategist leading all those warriors. The man glanced up, saw me staring. His frown deepened. To him, I was just another dirty urchin.

I almost turned away.

But then a gentle breeze blew in from behind, and despite all the things I didn't know, I did know one:

Spring was in the air.

Better times were coming.

I just had to believe in myself.

九

A SOUTHEAST ZEPHYR

*B*elieve in yourself.
     99,810.
  99,820.
  99,830.

The clicking of the abacus is music to my ears. So is the creaking of the wagons carrying in bales of arrow-quilled hay from the dock and the high-pitched voice of the courtier announcing the total count by increments of ten.

"Ninety-nine thousand nine hundred!"

"Nice and loud." I settle into my divan by the counting station and cool myself with my replacement fan. It's uglier than my crane one, fashioned from pigeon feathers, but I don't care, not when I have a hundred thousand of Miasma's arrows. "I want everyone to hear."

"Yes, my . . ."

"Rising Zephyr will do." A servant floats by to refill my tea. As I treat my lungs to the fragrant steam, sunlight saws through the rain clouds over the river and casts everything—the junks waiting to be dethatched, the wagons crisscrossing the dock, the workers pulling out the arrows—in gold. It's as if the heavens know how rare this moment is for me. "Victory" usually means buying Ren an extra day, an extra hour, an extra minute to escape Miasma by the skin of our teeth. I can't remember the last time I got to kick back under the shade of a silk parasol and bask in the fruits of my labor.

"Ninety-nine thousand nine hundred thirty!" calls out the courtier, loud as instructed.

With a grin, I settle deeper into my divan.

"You don't seem worried."

The smell of honeysuckle incense precedes Cicada. Four servants carry in her ivory divan and set it down next to mine.

"Why should I be?" I ask, taking in Cicada's outfit. She's traded her white robes for sea-foam green accented with gold brocade. Matching gold glints from her coronet. Only her hair, a sleek sheet to her waist, belongs to the shoeless girl I first met in court.

"Anxiety sharpens the mind," says Cicada, sounding like a forty-year-old philosopher.

I fan a gnat off my nose. "Anxiety is counterproductive."

"Someone else I know always said that."

"They must be a strategist." And I must be a masochist. Why else would I keep on bringing up strategists when there's only one Cicada would think of?

"You're right," says Cicada. "They are."

I follow her gaze as it moves, expecting to see Ku, but she's just looking at the river, a glittering serpent that separates us from Miasma.

My fingers drum against my knee. It's the poison, I tell myself—I'll need to return for my daily dose of antidote soon—and not because I'm remembering the zither song I played for Crow.

"Ninety-nine thousand nine hundred fifty!" shouts the courtier, a welcome diversion. "Ninety-nine thousand nine hundred sixty! Ninety-nine thousand nine hundred seventy!"

The last wagon arrives at the abacus station. The count edges closer to one hundred thousand. Cicada rises from the divan, accepting a golden sword carried forth by a servant. I rise too. Our eyes lock as she rests the blade against the slope of my shoulder. She'll see blood if she presses any harder.

"Ninety-nine thousand nine hundred eighty! Ninety-nine thousand nine hundred ninety!"

The last of the arrows are pulled out of the hay, marked on the shaft with tar and sorted into baskets. The last of the counting beads slide into place. The last tallies go into the book of armaments, and everyone waits as the courtier double-checks the numbers before clearing his throat and hollering the final count.

It can't be.

"Again," orders Cicada. "Nice and loud, for the people in the back."

"Ninety-nine thousand nine hundred ninety-nine!"

The number twangs like a broken zither string.

What were the chances? One in one hundred thousand, surely, to be one arrow short, not two, not three.

"Is the prospect of losing your head amusing to you?" asks Cicada as I smile mirthlessly.

"I find coincidences amusing."

"Are you suggesting this wasn't a coincidence, but the result of some interference?"

"No." I step in, the blade sliding along my shoulder. "One arrow short is one arrow short."

Cicada checks my advance with a sword point to the chest. "You don't have to be one arrow short."

"Your meaning?"

"You have five seconds to produce the one hundred thousandth arrow on the spot." She lifts the sword. "Five." Closes her eyes. "Four."

So this is how it is.

"Three."

I *could* have brought a quiver of arrows, just in case.

"Two."

But that would be second-guessing myself, and I haven't done that since the day I stood outside the tavern.

"One."

I have nothing for Cicada when she opens her eyes. No arrows or words. I spread my empty hands, and Cicada smiles.

"That's what I like about you. You're proud to a fault." She raises the sword and points it at my neck. "One day, you'll die for it."

It's all for show. She won't kill me. She can't kill me. Not for one arrow—

The blade falls.

Onlookers gasp. I don't have the breath to. They're ogling at the sword stabbed into the ground, the golden blade split apart to reveal an equally golden arrow standing upright in the center. *Peasants*, I think weakly. Of course it was never going to be stabbed into *me*.

Cicada plucks the arrow out. "Today, your life has been spared by me."

She offers me the arrow. I want it about as much as my ego wants her charity. But I need to live to see my stratagem to the finish, so I accept it. It's ridiculously heavy. Cicada nods at the courtier.

"One hundred thousand!"

The Southern lordess faces the people gathered. "For too long, the North has taken our resources as they please. Now they sail their fleet down to intimidate us into submission. But we will not bow. Together with Xin Ren, we will defeat Miasma!"

Those were supposed to be my words, I think as the dockworkers cheer.

"Ren will be a great ally," Cicada goes on. "With her support, the Southlands will return to the height of its glory. We will regain all the territory that rightfully belongs to us, starting with the Marshlands."

Wait. I never promised Cicada *that*. But the dockworkers cheer—louder when Cicada decrees a two-day feast to commemorate the alliance. She turns to me.

"Why the long face? Isn't this what you wanted?"

Allies come at a price. I knew this. I just thought I'd have more time before Cicada brought up the Marshlands, the buffer zone between the West and South that's historically belonged to the South—until the Fen pirates stole it. By the time Cicada destroyed the Fen, Miasma had scooped up the territory and gifted it to Xin Gong. With how unhelpful he's been, I have little reason to believe that Ren's uncle will give up the lands for our benefit.

But now's not the time to downplay Ren, so I nod at the golden arrow in my grip. "You call this thing an arrow?"

"What would you call it, if not an arrow?"

"Your strongest archer couldn't make this fly."

"I thought you'd appreciate it. I was told you enjoy pomp and excess."

"By whom?" For once, Ku doesn't come to mind. She never saw me at my white-robed, crane-fanned best. We lived in squalor and filth. The most "excess" we had was a tea egg every New Year, a cotton tunic if the orphanage had alms to spare.

Cicada doesn't answer. "There's someone here to see you," she says instead, departing the dock before I can press.

I catch up to her. She dismisses her attendants, and we enter a manicured bamboo thicket. The deeper we go, the dimmer the light, tinged green as if we're underwater. We step off the path and cross a mossy bridge that wends into the forest, where bamboo spears out of the ground at random, fully grown culms thicker than my arms.

A government official would meet me in Nightingale Pavilion. A general or naval officer would meet me in a battle room or on a junk. My confusion escalates as the forest ends abruptly, the bamboo clear-cut into tea fields. "Where are we going?"

"A place you know well."

I frown. There's nothing out here but a citrus grove to the

west, an infantry training camp to the east, and . . . my favorite watchtower in between it all.

It looms out of the green-scape like a too-skinny scarecrow with four long legs, a basket for a head, and a straw roof for a hat. The other five watchtowers overlook critical mountain passes and rivers, but this one is surrounded by tea fields as far as the eye can see. As a result, it's not armored or manned. It was the ideal place for reading the cosmos to concoct my arrow-borrowing strategy, but I can't imagine what distinguished person would await me here.

Cicada stops at the watchtower's base. "Serve me, Zephyr."

"Pardon?"

"You heard me." The dying sunlight sparks on her coronet as she lifts her chin. "Leave Ren and join the Southlands as my strategist."

"No."

I don't hesitate with my answer, and Cicada's lips crimp. "What about me doesn't measure up to Ren?"

"I'd rather not insult you to your face."

"I order you to."

"You're not my lordess."

"Really?" Her eyes glint. "By the alliance, I believe what belongs to Ren now also belongs to me."

Well, then. If she insists.

"You have no ambition." Cicada's face darkens; she asked for it. "You care for your kingdom, which in your mind includes the Marshlands. But your aspirations have never reached the level of empire. You can't see the value beyond this home you know." I wait for my words to sink in. "Am I wrong?"

"And if you were? Would I ever be able to convince you of it?" Cicada sniffs. "So you won't serve me. But why Ren? She doesn't aspire after the empire either."

"She wants to help Xin Bao."

"Xin Bao is a lost cause. And don't even start on Ren's honor. I'll die if I have to hear about it one more time." Cicada's gaze narrows. "*You've* almost died for it." I beg to differ. "The populace might support her, but most of her followers are uneducated farmers and unskilled laborers. You don't respect them. Miasma might be the one claiming to be a god, but the same rumors surround Ren. Well, Zephyr? Is that why you follow her? Because she's your god?" Cicada strides in, her face in mine. "You could do better than Ren, yet you continue to risk your life for her at every turn. *Why?*"

I don't know. The words spark in my mind—a lie. I *do* know. *She has the proper surname. The righteous claim.* If the populace respects that, what does it matter what *I* respect? I stake my hopes on Ren because I see the best chance of success.

But then another voice sounds: *Why do you breathe? Why does the sun rise in the east?*

Must you follow Ren for a reason?

Without question. Ren isn't family. I'm not obligated to her in the same way I was to Ku.

"Why do you think?" I ask Cicada, who clearly has her own opinion.

"I think you follow her because she's an underdog, and you just can't resist a good challenge. Serving her is no different from collecting one hundred thousand arrows in three days. Am I right?"

"Would I be able to convince you otherwise?" I ask, tossing her words back at her. "Are we done yet?"

The fervor to her expression dims. "It seems so." She turns from the watchtower's base. "Have a safe climb."

"I will," I call after the Southern lordess, shaking my head. *A child.* At least she finally recognized my abilities as a strategist.

I roll up my sleeves and grab the ladder. Seconds into the climb, I'm already trembling. My arms give out on the final rungs, and I collapse onto the platform. Lotus and Cloud would laugh if they could see me.

"Need a hand?"

My gaze startles up—onto the last face I was expecting.

Ren helps me to my feet. "It's good to see you, Qilin."

No words come. My heart last beat this fast for Crow. But Crow scatters me. Around him I am mist, taking whichever form I please.

Ren has the opposite effect. I pull myself together for her, thoughts condensing as the strategist in me resumes control.

Cicada cornered me under the watchtower on purpose.

She was hoping I'd betray Ren to her face.

I bow as low as my aching back will allow me.

"At ease, Qilin."

I stay bowed. "How much did you hear?"

"Enough to commend Cicada," says Ren good-naturedly. "I have to give it to her; she raises valid points."

I'm less charmed. "You shouldn't be here." The lands between us teem with warlords, bandits, and empire lackeys. The few waterways not in Miasma's fist cut through treacherous ravines prone to flash floods. Besides, for Ren to be here, she would have had to set out almost immediately after my defection. What kind of impression did that make on the peasants? What kind of impression did *I* make on Ren, when I poisoned our horses?

"What do you know?" I ask, recalling my instructions to Tourmaline.

If Ren probes, say nothing.

Ren paces to the watchtower's edge. She's tanner than before. Skinnier. Marsh mosquito bites pebble her neck, already several days old. "From the moment you asked for twenty strong, I trusted you had a plan. When Cloud said you'd defected to Miasma, I trusted there was more to it. When the horses died, I trusted it was for a bigger cause, and when Miasma turned her troops away from Hewan, my trust became a hunch.

"Then our scouts reported that Miasma was sending a delegation south. I figured it was time I speak to the last person you were seen with." Ren grips the wooden rail and glances to me. "You chose your confidante well. Tourmaline refused to talk. So I told her I already knew your plan. You were going to hitch a junk ride south from Miasma. I just needed to see her expression to confirm it." Ren smiles as I join her by the edge. "Bet you didn't think I had the craftiness in me."

I mumble a no. I'm still not pleased that Ren risked herself to come. ("There can't be a Ren-Cicada alliance without a Ren, can there?" is her retort.) But Ren also doesn't seem quite like the

lordess I left in Hewan. Her eyes aren't on the stars just beginning to show themselves, but on the fields right before us, fields
that might someday belong to Xin Bao once more.

"I've burdened you enough," Ren declares to the dusk as
it falls to night. "From here on out, leave it to me. I've already
informed Cicada that we can contribute ten thousand strong."

"Ten thousand strong?" Wherever from?

"The Xin clan is big. They can spare some troops."

"They're helping us?"

"Yes."

"But why?" Her uncle has ignored our existence thus far.

"It's nothing to Governor Xin Gong," says Ren with a lift of
the shoulders. "I wrote to him, told him to think of it as a loan."

I wrote to him too. What changed? Something lurks behind
this development. Just as Cicada expects the Marshlands, Xin
Gong will be expecting repayment.

"Aiya, you're making me nervous," says Ren when I remain
silent. "The troops will be helpful, no?"

I clear my head. If and when Xin Gong becomes a problem,
I'll deal with him. I'm the Rising Zephyr, after all. "How quickly
can you get his troops situated around Pumice and Shale Pass?"

"Consider it done in three days."

Three days. Suddenly, plans that would have taken weeks to
develop unfurl before my eyes.

"We'll strike by night." I slash my fan through the air. "Wipe
them out with two blows—one from the water, one from land.
Cicada will destroy their fleet while we block both passes from

the scarp and prevent their retreat." I lower my fan, fingers tight around the handle. "Miasma won't get away this time."

At first, Ren's silent. Maybe I shouldn't have alluded to Cloud's folly, or spoken so forcefully. But then her eyes meet mine. "It'll be good to be on the offensive for once."

"Indeed." This is everything I've been building toward since joining Ren's camp. When we emerge victorious, Ren will finally represent a real threat to the empire. *As will I*, I remind myself as Ren's smile dissolves.

"You've suffered, Qilin."

My hand follows her gaze, to my own temple. "It's nothing." I touch the injury. "Already scabbed."

A cricket chirps, somewhere in the night.

"Ah, I almost forgot." Ren reaches into the cross-fold of her robes and brings out a stick wrapped in parchment. "Look what I found in the marketplace."

Through the parchment, I see the squiggly mass of spun sugar.

Slowly, I take the stick.

I dislike sweets. They hurt my teeth. I'll discard this one later, just like all the others. But in front of Ren, I hold it, and smile. From the day she bought me the first—"This one caught your eye, didn't it?"—I decided that I wouldn't do to her what Ku did to me. If she buys me candy because she saw me lingering at the stall, lost in my memories of Ku and her hard-to-win love, I'll accept it. I'll accept anything Ren gives me. Even if we're not related. Even if she has other sisters.

Other sisters. As I stare at the candy, I realize I've forgotten someone very important to Ren. "Lotus—"

"Already escaped with her foot soldiers. She endangered their lives when she rode out to meet Miasma without your orders, and I've had her punished for it."

I can only imagine how that was received. But no matter. What's important is that Ren is reunited with her swornsister. "And the people . . ." I trail off. *What do they think of me?* Why am I even asking? Since when do I care about how I'm regarded by the masses?

"What they think doesn't matter," says Ren, as if reading my mind. "You'll be given a hero's welcome when this is over."

"She's not a hero."

Both Ren and I turn, but only I flinch.

Ku pulls herself up the final rung and hops like a shrew onto the platform.

"This is . . ." *My sister.* ". . . November. Cicada's strategist," I finish, the words sour in my mouth.

Ren takes in Ku. I do too, worried that I'll find some telltale resemblance. But all I see is a fifteen-year-old with tea stains on her robes and badly cut hair.

Ren appears a lot less shabby in comparison. "I look forward to working with your lordess," she says, dipping her head at Ku.

The formality is wasted on my sister. She stares at me, and I clear my throat. "I should fill November in on our plans."

"Of course. I'll leave you to it."

Ku doesn't acknowledge Ren as she takes to the ladder. I wait for my lordess to descend. Wait some more.

Finally, I face my sister. "What do you want?"

Ku pulls something long and slender out from behind her back.

An arrow.

Not just any arrow, but one that was extracted from the felted dummies on my straw junks. Wisps of blue yarn are still caught in the red-and-black fletching, and when Ku holds it out, I see that the shaft is missing the band of tar that every tallied arrow got marked with.

My gut was right. Someone *did* sabotage me.

My own sister.

"It's for you," she says. "Take it."

My hand shakes as I do. It shouldn't. I got my hundred thousand arrows. I kept my head. But then the rest of me shakes, because it's not about the arrow. I *know* Ku hates me, enough to want me dead. Giving me the arrow is her way of telling me that. What I don't know is this: "Why?"

"Why what?"

"Why do you hate me?" *Ever since the famine. As long as I can remember. Why?*

It consumes me, this mystery of Ku.

It boils me down to nothing.

"You're not my sister," Ku says, and those words . . . I've heard them before. When I first woke up from my hunger-induced coma. "You're not my sister. You're not—"

"What are you talking about?"

"You're not Qilin!" Ku screams, and I take a step back.

"I don't understand."

"You're not my sister," Ku repeats, calm again. "That's all you need to understand."

You're wrong. Understanding everything—from who I was to who I could be—is the only reason I was able to regain control over my life after losing her. "Ku—"

"November. That's my name now."

She walks away from me. She talks about the positioning of Miasma's fleet. She speaks of the retreat routes the prime ministress will take if attacked from the front. She spins out a strategy of land and water, ending with:

". . . fire." A word plucked from my skull. "The South will strike with fire," says Ku, her weapon of choice the same as mine, and I stare—at this girl, my sister, the one reason I could have been convinced to switch sides. Cicada could have led with it.

But instead it's as if our past never existed. The cosmos shift; the wind changes. A breeze blows Ku's hair forward and mine back.

A southeast zephyr.

In three days' time, it'll fan the fire over Miasma's navy, linked and all the easier to devour. But tonight, there's only one fire. It's right here, in my heart. It burns me from the inside out as I accept that Ku will never tell me the truth about what happened. So be it, then. She can have her station, her sobriquet. She'll be November the strategist, and I'll be the stranger.

+

A SHORT SONG

I'*ll be the stranger.*

In three days' time, the Southern "defectors" will arrive on the escarpment banks. They'll travel by barge, under the cover of a grain shipment helmed by me. The news delights Miasma.

"It'll be the longest three days of my life," she declares over her goblet of wine. I agree.

Three more days until her navy burns.

Three more days until I return to Ren with our greatest victory yet.

At night, I dream of the camp—of strolling with Ren, talking to Tourmaline, even drinking with Cloud and Lotus, which is how I know I'm dreaming. During the day, while trapped on this enemy junk, I imagine them preparing for the big battle. I've given orders to both our people and Cicada's, but I itch to do more. In my cabin, I bundle up my few belongings in a large kerchief and stash them under my bunk. I remove the jar I made with help from Cicada's artisans and examine it one last time.

Both the jar and pills inside appear identical to Crow's. He won't be able to tell the difference after the swap. He'll have the look-alike, and I'll have the antidote, because once I leave to collect said defectors, I won't be coming back for my nightly dose.

The issue, it turns out, is getting my hands on his pockets.

"What do you mean, 'No visitors'?"

"It means what it means," says the servant stationed outside Crow's cabin. "No visitors. Take this, and go."

She hands me a tray with a teacup on it.

I accept it but don't drink. "He said that himself?"

"He did."

"I don't believe it." I try to move around the servant; she moves with me. "How do I know he's even in speaking condition?"

"Oh, trust me, he is," comes a voice from behind.

It's the physician, approaching with his medicine chest.

"Did he take his tonic?" he asks the servant.

"He said it's too bitter."

"Children these days," sighs the physician.

The servant opens the cabin doors for him. I raise my brows, and she primly says, "The physician is here for Master Crow's own good."

"So am I."

She gives me a disparaging look.

I cross my arms. "What are you afraid I'll do? Seduce the living daylights out of him? Charm away his soul? Well, what is it?"

"He took a turn for the worse after your last visit."

"That's . . ." *Impossible.* All I did was play him some music. He even had the energy to flirt.

But he wouldn't be like this at all if it weren't for me. He saved my life, and here I've come to repay him by trying to steal the bottle in his cloak.

Leave, says a voice in my head. *The maid is right. You're the last thing he needs.*

But I don't leave. Mission calls, and I want answers.

"How is he?" I ask the physician when he emerges. He shakes his head. My gaze falls to his medicine chest; bloodied linens peek out from under the lid. My heart goes cold.

"I can help." My fan is in my hand, like I can strategize health back into Crow. "I can convince him to take his medicine." *More like force-feed it to him.*

"You?" The physician scoffs. "Just who are you to him?" Then he leaves a set of tinctures and instructions with the servant and hustles himself up-deck, his throwaway question haunting the air like the smell of herbs.

Who am I to Crow? No one. A rival at best, enemy at worst. What can I do for him? Nothing but drink my tea and leave as well.

Night sets. Dawn breaks. Two days left. I stew in my cabin, almost jumping when the door opens, but it's just a servant bringing another cup of antidote tea. I down it, then go to Crow's cabin and pace outside it.

Took a turn for the worse. Took a turn for the worse.

He could be comatose. He could be dying. Or, I think as I watch clean bowls and cups exit his room, he's not at death's door at all. He's eating. He's drinking.

He's avoiding me.

He knows I'm leaving. He doesn't want me to get my hands on the antidote. But then why not withhold it and let the poison take its toll? He must have his reasons. Nothing is accidental with Crow. I remind myself of that as I walk away from his cabin, the look-alike jar clenched tight in my hand. But there's a tighter knot in my throat.

He knows you need to see him for the antidote.

But he doesn't know you want *to see him, antidote or not.*

Or maybe he does. *He saved you. He said he likes you.* No—half of what Crow says is probably an act. Taking the arrow for me? A risky act, but not without reward. He could be trying to gain my trust just to stab me in the back. Injure Yourself to Wound the Enemy. It's Stratagem Thirty-Four. I *know* this.

And yet I spend the next day, too, outside of his damned cabin doors.

When I finally return to my own cabin that evening, a group of servants awaits me. The prime ministress is throwing a feast on her junk tonight, they say. My presence is required. They bring in the robe Miasma had specially tailored, and for a split second, I wonder if Crow told her of my preference for white.

But the robe inside the chest is black. It slips over my skin, weightless like water. Three servants fuss with the sash while another reaches for my head. I jerk away. "What are you doing?"

"Styling your hair."

"My hair is fine the way it is." Wearing black for Miasma is where I draw the line.

But none of this is for Miasma. Everything has been for the Ren-Cicada alliance.

Endure one more day.

I reach up and take out my clasp. My ponytail tumbles loose. My head feels off-balance.

The servant braids some of my hair around my crown and leaves the rest hanging down my back. When she's done, I look at myself in the mirror and see the kind of girl who might be tempted by Miasma's riches, and certain dark-haired strategists. But I'm too much of a strategist myself to fall for any of it. I'm acting, just like Crow is. Every bone in my body remembers this as I step onto Miasma's junk, into the feast. Flame-blowers, knife-jugglers, and face-changers mingle with the company on deck. Dancers shimmy in diaphanous dresses. An orchestra of lutes and mouth organs plays, and tables stretch from port to starboard. Above, pennants that used to whip hang limp and still. The winds have stopped.

By tomorrow, they will have reversed direction and blow in a true southeast current.

"Rising Zephyr!" Miasma gestures me over to her table and flicks her hand when I reach her. I spin for her, just like I did atop the escarpment.

"Stunning!" She turns to the rest of the table, seated with countless generals, advisors, and strategists, but no Crow. "A real gem, isn't she?"

I force a coy smile onto my lips.

"Come." Miasma pats the spot to her right. "Don't be shy. Have a seat!" She grabs a bronze vessel and fills my cup. "A shame that Crow isn't feeling well enough to join us."

"Yes," I venture. "I was hoping I could see him today."

"Miss him, don't you? I know you must miss Ren," Miasma

says without giving me a chance to recover. Her breath already smells of the wine she just poured me. "I don't blame you. She has this effect on people"—she gestures with the vessel—"drawing them to her. But in reality, all she does is take. Your trust, your values—she takes and reshapes you without reshaping herself. She is a thief of everything you think yours. But there will come a day when I take everything she thinks hers." She leans in, the bony tip of her nose nearly touching mine. "It begins with you."

Then, before I can process where any of that came from, Miasma sits back. "Servant!"

A servant appears and Miasma orders her to serve me the best cuts of a mountain goat.

"Lordess—"

"Now what did I say, Zephyr?" scolds Miasma as the servant piles meat onto my plate.

I wet my lips. "Mi-Mi. I don't—"

"Eat up," says Miasma, pushing the plate in front of me. "I want your body to grow as strong as your mind."

I don't eat meat. At least not the glistening, gamey stuff mounded before me. But under Miasma's eye, I chew and swallow a piece of goat. And another. Cold sweat beads down my spine. I vow never to eat meat again.

I finish the plate and sit back, my stomach frothing with acid.

Miasma suddenly rises. "A toast!"

Goblets and dishes rattle as she leaps onto our table.

"To our empress, Xin Bao," she declares, pacing over plates of food. "May her star stay bright and her reign long!"

She reaches the end of the table and throws back her wine. Everyone drinks. I toss the contents of my cup over my shoulder.

A servant clambers onto a stool to refill Miasma's goblet. Wine in hand, she resumes pacing. "And to Xin Ren and Cicada! What entertainment they've provided! But we've played with our prey long enough. I say it's time we closed in for the kill!"

Shouts of consensus. Another round goes down, and everyone drums their goblets as Miasma grins, her skull-like features exaggerated in the torchlight. She accepts a second refill and raises it to the sky.

"The heavens may have blessed me with the power to reunite the empire, but I couldn't have done it without you! Yes, you! And you!" Wine bleeds from the goblet as she points it around. "All of you! You, my most dear and loyal retainers! For you, and for our imminent victory, I will perform a short song. Or poem." Miasma knocks back the wine and tosses the goblet before snatching up the pitcher. "As many of you know, I can't sing. But a poem, I can make!"

She takes a long gulp from the pitcher spout and swipes her knuckles over her mouth. "Man's life," she shouts, marching down the table, "is but the morning dew. Past days many—"

Her boot crunches into a bowl.

"—future ones few. The melancholy my heart begets/comes from cares I cannot forget.

"What can unravel these woes of mine?" She teeters, and generals rise, reaching out to steady her. "I know but one drink—Du Kang wine!"

A riot of laughter.

"Disciples dressed in blue—"

A guard sweeps to the tableside and kneels. "Report!"

The prime ministress takes one more swig, then tosses the pitcher. As servants scamper to retrieve it, Miasma bends down to listen to the guard's message. "Right here will do," she replies.

She straightens, facing the rest of us. "It seems we have an interruption. My poem will have to wait for another day."

Cries go up in protest.

"Have no fear!" Miasma declares. "You will be just as entertained. Guards!"

A hush descends over everyone but the dancers, who squeal and scurry out of the way as the guards drag a person to the bow of the ship. They're thrown down, and I half rise out of my seat.

Crow?

No. Same black cloak and long black hair, but a stranger. My mind empties with relief—relief that I have no business feeling. I focus.

With the exception of Crow, most of Miasma's retinue is older. This girl is young. She's either an outsider, or a—

"—servant," drawls Miasma, "was caught sending doves to Cicada's court. What does that make her?"

"A traitor!" everyone says in practiced unison.

"And what happens to traitors in this camp?"

"They die!"

Miasma jumps down from the table and crouches before the

girl, grabbing her chin. The spot under my ear tingles, remembering the bite of her nail.

"I like your eyes." The girl whimpers through her gag, and Miasma releases her. "I wish you'd thought twice before giving me reason to gouge them out."

She forms a claw with her hand, poising it above the girl's temple, as if she might do the deed right here, right now. Advisors cover their faces with their brocade sleeves. The generals and warriors look on because they have an appetite for blood. I look on because I have no more appetite to speak of.

But then Miasma's hand closes into a fist. "Plum."

"At the prime ministress's service."

"How many coffers of gold do I have to spare?"

"Two hundred and fifty-three, my lordess."

Miasma rises. She turns to us, eyes gleaming. "I know what my enemies say about me. That I'm cruel. Mercurial. Irrational.

"But no one has ever picked a bone over my generosity. I give people what they earn. Now is your chance." The bell at her ear tinkles as she opens her bare arms to the crowd. "Answer me. Anyone. What is the most painful way a traitor can die?"

Suggestions flood the air, each more gruesome than the last. Voices claw at each other, until all I can hear is my own silence, and a whisper from behind me.

"Steaming."

The whisperer is a servant with a tattooed face. A convict-laborer. I stare at him and he stares back, dazed, as if he can't quite believe what he just said.

But it's too late. Like a snake sensing motion in the grass, Miasma whips her head toward us. "What did you say?"

The convict-laborer glances helplessly at me, as if *I* can claim his words.

"The prime ministress asked you a question," barks Plum. "Speak up."

"S-steaming." The convict-laborer keeps his eyes on his feet. Maybe he worked with the girl. Maybe they were friends. It wouldn't matter. A person with nothing has everything to betray. "D-death by steaming."

"Steaming . . ." Miasma rubs the side of her face, contemplative. "Steaming it is, then. But pluck her first. I like my swine hairless."

The servant wails through her gag.

Miasma waves at the guards. As they drag the girl down-deck, the prime ministress gestures at the convict-laborer. "Plum, see that he receives his coffer."

"That's—"

"Too wasteful?" Miasma shakes her head. "Plum, Plum, what did I say about your stingy ways? Well?" She faces her audience. "What do you all say? Am I wasteful or generous?"

"Your lordship is most generous!" everyone shouts, but the atmosphere has changed. Wine sits in cups. Food goes untouched. A servant runs to report that the cook has started the largest of the steamers, and an advisor across from me excuses himself and dashes to the side of the junk.

"Excellent," says Miasma. I pray that this marks the end of the feast, but she leaps back onto the table. "Now, where was I?"

A general clears his throat. "'Disciples dressed in—'"

"Mi-Mi." Gazes swing to me.

I should keep silent. That girl could have been me, but for one difference: I'm too smart to get caught.

I rise and address Miasma. "Allow me to play you a song."

"Oh? Do you not like my poem?"

"A poem is a song without a melody. Yours deserves one. Allow me to arrange it."

Miasma's face is still as porcelain. Then a grin cracks it. "Well said! Bring the Rising Zephyr a zither."

"And an accompanist," I add, hoping that she'll think to summon Crow. But a member of the orchestra is called forward. His eyes are wary as he takes a seat across from me, behind his zither.

I watch his wariness fade to revulsion as the smell of steaming flesh wafts above deck.

"What is it that you have for us?" asks Miasma as people blanch right and left.

I lift my hands. "The screams of Ren's soldiers under your cavalry's hooves."

"Excellent!" roars Miasma.

I mouth "Battle hymn" at the other zitherist, then nod. His cue to start playing. As his notes hum, I pinch the strings hard and drag my hands up and down along them. My fingertips burn from the friction, and I grit my teeth as the sound is birthed into existence.

These will be the screams of Miasma's soldiers as they burn alive, the shriek of her junks as they fall apart at the seams. I slam a hand into the wood of the zither—a single, strained heartbeat—then throw my fingers out, cutting the screams short.

One ship sinks. Another catches fire. One lordess falls. Another rises.

I add melody to the screams, send them trembling with vibrato, render the hate, the anger, the sorrow of the last ones standing. I hope Miasma is among them. I hope she lives just long enough to see all her efforts fall to ash.

I hope she regrets ever thinking less of Ren.

The emotion behind the thought startles me. Then I embrace it. I've never played the zither for Ren; a strategist is no common entertainer. Now I play for Miasma because I'm *not* her strategist. I'm here for a lordess who wouldn't steam a person alive, even if they betrayed her. *I* betrayed Ren.

She believed in me anyway, beyond reason.

When I finish, the whole deck is silent. Even the flames crackling in the braziers are quieter, feeble sparks compared to the firestorm to come.

Miasma breaks the spell. "A masterpiece! What do you call this song?"

I bow my head. "I was hoping you'd honor it with a name."

Miasma thinks for a moment. "A short song for a short battle should go by the name of 'Short-Lived.'"

Everyone praises the name. Eating and drinking resumes. I guess it's true that you can grow desensitized to anything, the smell of cooking flesh included.

I rise from the zither.

"Wait." My accompanist rises too, his eyes glittering with awe. Normally I'd soak it up, but today it does nothing for me.

"Rising Zephyr. You also go by the Tactician of Thistlegate, don't you?"

Thistlegate. For a second, memories of that hermit town swamp me. The zitherist approaches.

"It's not my preferred sobriquet," I finally say.

"I'm Lu Pai. What's your birth name?"

Bold of him to ask. "You, Lu Pai, need only refer to me as—"

"Zephyr," says an all-too-familiar voice, stealing the sobriquet right out of my mouth. "There you are."

There you are yourself, I want to say but can't, my tongue too flustered.

The zitherist quickly bows. "Master Crow."

"Run along now," says Crow, before grabbing my elbow and escorting me away. I glance to see if Miasma has seen us, but she's deep in conversation with her generals.

"What are you doing?" I ask as we leave the junk and cross onto another by the linked planks. Servants and ship hands bow as we pass. I try to free myself, but Crow's grip is iron. "Let go."

"Only if you promise to follow," Crow says as we cross onto another linked junk.

"What if I want to stay?"

"For what? Lu Pai?"

"Really, Crow?" I dig my heels in and rip my elbow free. "You've avoided me for days, and now you show up with no explanation."

"We're strategists. We don't need to explain things to each other."

His voice is as slippery as the night he challenged my defection, and I shiver.

But he doesn't reach for my elbow again. "Don't fall behind," he says, before walking on.

Who is he to give me orders?

And who am I, obeying them?

"Where are we going?" I ask one more time as we hop off the last junk and onto the rocky shore.

He doesn't answer, and I sulk.

We walk for a long, long time, made longer by the fact that I'm still feeling unwell from stuffing myself on goat. *But you're not the one who was struck by an arrow.* I eye Crow's back as he pulls ahead. If he's in pain, he's silent. If he's flagging, he hides it. Everything about him is an enigma.

I don't know if I've ever been able to resist one.

The wind picks up, severing my thoughts and cutting through my too-thin robes. My ridiculously styled hair flies into my face and I swipe at the strands as we clamber over a series of jutting rocks, only to face more rocks, sloping on either side, creating the perfect wind tunnel to blow my hair right back into a disarray.

Abruptly, Crow stops.

"What are we looking at?" I ask to his back. We're in the bottom of what appears to be a dried-up riverbed. "Rocks?"

"We're looking at your one means of escape."

I stare at him as he reaches under his cloak and draws out the culprit of his bulkiness: a bedroll, stuffed with supplies. He hands it to me. "It's a long way from here to the nearest town, and I don't presume you know how to hunt and trap. You'll need this."

"I don't understand."

"I'm setting you free."

"I'm perfectly happy where I am."

"Zephyr." He closes in and I, on a whim, remove his hat. This is how we met: moonlight slanting between us, his face much too close. "I've served my lordess for many years. I'll serve to my death. But that's my choice. You don't know Miasma. What you saw tonight, that's just the surface. She unlocks the best and worst of a person. She has hundreds of us in her wings, and we're all her puppets, outdoing each other just to please her."

He draws back and glances up at the sky. It's clear tonight, a sickle moon shedding light over the rocks. "It's why I am the way I am. I meant it, when I said my cough is my weapon. It's a weapon, and a shield. I may be Miasma's strategist, but I'm not worth anyone's time or notice. My illness will take care of me eventually, and someone will be ready to replace me."

Of all the things Crow has said to me, this may be the truest. The admission is raw, disarming. I don't know how to reply. "If a person like you can survive in the North, so can I."

"I'm pleased you think this is surviving. But I don't." Crow glances down, and before I know it, he's taken my hands into his. I thought mine were cold, but his are ice. "You deserve to live."

Then he's releasing me and pushing me forward. "Go."

I'll go. Tomorrow, I'll go. I *must* go. But not now. I need to hold out one more day. Miasma can't suspect a thing.

"*Go!*" orders Crow when I don't move.

"I don't want to go." The bedroll falls out of my hands and

onto the rocks. "I'm staying," I say, squaring my shoulders at Crow.

"I don't care if Miasma is evil," I shout against the wind, for the entire riverbed to hear. I step in. "I choose her. I'm staying with her." I bring myself chest to chest with Crow. "I'm staying with *you*."

He smiles, rueful and skeptical. "Zephyr—"

Silence him. So I do—in the most efficient way I know how.

I grab his face and smash my lips to his.

He pulls away, as I thought he might. "The consumption—"

I throw my arms around his neck and silence him once more. I'm a piece put into play, a strategy already in motion. I'll do whatever it takes, forfeit whatever I must. Besides, consumption isn't a guaranteed death sentence. I'll live long enough to see Ren restore Xin Bao. I just have to stay in Miasma's camp tonight.

I just have to convince Crow.

I don't have field experience or books to guide me. This kiss— it's my first. But I'm a quick learner. I raise myself to capture his upper lip, and he stiffens. His hands close around my shoulders, but he doesn't pry me off. He holds me as tightly as I imagine he's holding himself, his mind at war and his muscles locked. He's shaking. Resisting. Fighting.

He forgets I always win.

I forget too, because when he pulls me in, I bite down. Salt runs over our tongues. His fingers slip through my loose hair and my head tilts back, my throat exposed. I'm no longer leaning into him but clutching him for balance. He's the only thing holding me up off the ground, and for a heartbeat, I let him. I envision staying and working beside him. But it wouldn't last. One day, I'd wake up and hate myself for betraying my goal.

I break us apart. With each gasp of air, I taste.

I taste blood.

Crow regards me silently, his lip split down the middle. "Is this what you decide?" he finally asks, voice breathy.

"It is."

He raises his sleeve to my mouth and wipes it. "I'm sorry."

Says the one who's bleeding. "It was me. I—"

He wraps his arms around me.

—*bit you.*

As I hug him back, I stare at the sky and the moon and the stars over his shoulder. They are the only ones watching as I slip my hand into the pocket of Crow's cloak.

Out comes the real jar.

In goes the fake one.

—†—

BEFORE IT ALL BURNS

Dear Crow,

By the time I write this, I'll have left to collect the Southern defectors.

I won't be back.

You don't know this, of course. Neither does Miasma. Together you'll watch the river from atop the escarpment. A southeast gale will clear the mist from the water as night falls, and as the moon glows, smaller moons will appear on the horizon, the lights of lanterns swinging at the helms of the grain barges.

Miasma will delight to see them. You, I suspect, will be more circumspect. At what point will you notice that the barges aren't sitting low enough in the water? At what point will you realize they're moving too fast?

Let me tell you a secret: the barges aren't weighted down by tons of grain at all. Only pots of sulfur and black powder, and the brave soldiers who've volunteered to man the hellfire straight into your navy. You'll alert Miasma the moment it hits you, and she'll yell at the ship hands to unlink the boats.

But the fire will have already started.

Before it all burns, I wanted to write to you. I wanted to tell you, for what it's worth, that I don't expect you to forgive me. Blame me, or blame the heavens for placing us on different sides of this war.

May we meet in another life.

Qilin

十二

BATTLE OF THE SCARP

May we meet in another life.

The moment it happens is quiet. I'm too far away to hear the shatter of sulfur pots on deck, the roar, the crackle of the inferno. There's just a glow in the distance, the birth of a new day in the night. Sunrise courtesy of the Rising Zephyr.

From my perch on a rock uphill, I can see rows and rows of Ren's troops standing at attention. Tourmaline rides Pearl at their front. Her voice rings out like a gong.

"Unsheathe!"

Blades and pikes stab the air.

In the past, we ran.

"In the past, we ran."

In the past, we retreated.

"In the past, we retreated."

Not anymore.

"Not anymore!" Tourmaline wheels her mare around, and I say the next words with her. "It's our fight now, and we don't stop fighting until we're in the capital streets, leading our lordess to where she belongs . . ."

Tourmaline pauses there, then shouts, ". . . by Empress Xin Bao's side!" like I instructed her to. "Vultures and buzzards circle our young monarch. She needs a protector. She needs Ren!"

The troops raise a cry. No matter how Miasma tries to frame us, our mantle isn't sedition. It's to restore the empress, protect the throne.

"Hey, Peacock." Lotus clambers onto the rock beside me and sits with her legs sprawled out. "What's the strategy today?"

"Watch Fires Across a Burning River," I murmur, my attention on our troops.

"Really?" Lotus looks over her shoulder. "Can't see the river from here."

Fool of me, to forget how literally Lotus takes everything. "No. It means we wait." The winds are strong. The fire will spread. Miasma will order a retreat. Cloud and the Xin clan's forces will then attack her from behind, funneling her and her demoralized soldiers toward the ambushes I have laid. "We wait for Miasma to run right into my snares."

"What if Skull-face doesn't show up?"

"Oh, she will." There are only three ways to the empire capital from here: go through the westward passes, Shale and Pumice, or go direct north. Direct north is the most obvious route—for both a retreat and an ambush. Miasma knows this. She'll take the longer, harder westward passes, even if it means putting her troops through hell, just to avoid a humiliating defeat by the books.

Out in the field below, Tourmaline explains as much to our soldiers. I move my pigeon fan as she gestures, pointing west when she does, north when she does.

"Shouldn't you be down there?" asks Lotus. I look up at her, and she nods her ax head at the troops.

Slowly, I lower my fan. "I'm fine where I am." Above and away from Ren's camp, filled with narrow-minded soldiers who might not appreciate receiving orders from a defector—

Lotus tugs me to my feet.

"What are you doing?" I splutter as she drags me after her.

"Putting a peacock where it belongs."

I'm hauled down the hill, almost colliding into her as the ground flattens. Heads turn to Lotus; eyes narrow when they spy me in tow. I grit my teeth, drop my gaze. This must be Lotus's revenge. Word is that Ren awarded her with twenty lashes for disobeying my orders and riding out to meet Miasma.

Definitely revenge, I think, once we're standing in front of everyone, the silence taut as a bowstring.

Then Lotus wraps my hand around her ax handle and thrusts both high above her head.

"Who's ready to crush some skulls?"

The response is an earsplitting roar. Lotus roars right back. Her cheeks are ruddy, her eyes alight. When they meet mine, I expect to see bitterness, but all I find is fire. It's in everyone's eyes, when I finally dare to look again.

"Down with the empire!" shouts Lotus, and I whip a glare at her; this is most certainly sedition. But then the cry spreads, catching like kindling.

"Down with the empire!"

"Down with the empire!"

"Down with the empire!"

"Down with the empire," I whisper, tasting the words. Cicada's mistaken. Not every follower of Ren's is a Xin loyalist. To these soldiers, Empress Xin Bao is *Miasma's* property. They fight for Ren and Ren only. Their fury becomes my fury, and our fury is for one enemy alone.

"Down with the empire!"

The wind rises; the cries die. Lotus releases me to round up her troops. According to my plan, she will take half of our forces to one of the two passes Miasma might use. Tourmaline will take the other half. As for me, my job is done. My orders have been issued. I make my retreat—

"Peacock!"

Spine stiffening, I turn back around to see Lotus waving at me from atop her stallion. "With me, Peacock!"

I shake my head, but Lotus is already riding over. She dismounts; I back up from her.

"You're mistaken, Lotus. I'm—"

—lifted off my feet, dropped atop her stallion. The ground is suddenly frighteningly far away.

"Lotus, let me down. *Now.*" I clutch the saddle horn and look desperately to Tourmaline across the field. *Save me.* But her back is to me. *Turn around, Tourmaline!*

"Don't you want to see Skull-face's head roll?" asks Lotus, taking the reins.

"*No.*" Lotus's bushy brows hike in confusion, and I wonder

if I really have to explain that it's enough for me to simply *win* without witnessing the bloodshed firsthand.

But before I can, Lotus's confusion melts. "Don't be afraid." She strokes her stallion's huge nose. "Rice Cake is gentle."

And I'm humble. "This isn't funny," I hiss as Lotus swings up behind me, into the saddle. "Ren will whip you for—"

Rice Cake breaks into a gallop.

Teeth clicking like summer cicadas, I cling to Lotus's leather-guarded arm. The ride goes on and on, a lifetime and then some, before we arrive at Pumice Pass. I push away from Lotus after she helps me down and totter to the mouth of the pass, searching for a hiding place from which to watch the battle. Over the horizon, smoke hangs like an executioner's blade.

It had to be done. The servants who tended to my daily needs, the ship hands who linked the boats by my order—they all would have died in an empire conflict eventually. Still, I see their faces. I see *his*, pale but flushed, blood dripping from his lip. I remember the feel of his body against mine, our music entwined.

He'll be safe. Strategists don't enter the fray (one more reason for warriors to scorn us). But he'll encounter Cloud's forces just like all of Miasma's people. There will be arrows, and there will be swords. There will be Cloud too. I doubt she'll be merciful.

A wave of nausea hits me, almost as bad as the times I was poisoned. But I took the antidote from Crow. I should be fine. I lean against a hunk of pumice, breathing hard, thoughts foggy. "What are you looking at?" Lotus asks, and I jump to find her next to me.

"Nothing." I left nothing of me behind—not even the letter to Crow. Any strategist worth their salt would have done as I did, I think, touching the folded-up paper in my sleeve. It's what makes me strong.

I'm not afraid to lose everything or anyone.

Unsteady, I sink to the ground, back against the rock. Lotus sits beside me. I ignore her; she's the reason I'm in this wretched place and state.

"You were right. About Skull-face. She gives you gifts if you're strong, and those gifts kept my soldiers strong." Lotus bumps me with the handle of her ax, and I flinch. "Lotus owes Peacock."

She certainly does. If she were really grateful, she wouldn't have dragged me out here.

But I can't take credit for what I didn't do. "You wrestled Miasma's soldiers and won. You got away with everyone."

"Not everyone." Lotus pushes up her sleeve and holds out her arm. The four scabbed lashes on her skin ripple as she makes a fist and flexes. "For Moss."

Moss, I assume, was the underling who lost his head to Miasma. He'd still be alive if Lotus had listened to me from the start. But I don't say the obvious, and for a while Lotus doesn't say anything either. We sit in a rare, almost perfect silence.

A scream shatters it.

We jump to our feet. Well, Lotus does. I stumble, my legs full of pins and needles, and hobble after her. Midway down the pass, we reach a group of soldiers. They part for Lotus, and I suck in a sharp breath when I see the soldier at their center.

The worst of it isn't that he's lying on the ground with an arrow shot clean through his neck. It's that he's still twitching, like a fish on the mallet board.

Lotus crouches beside him. "Wei? Wei!"

The twitching stops.

Lotus rises. Her gaze lifts to the pumice formations on either side of us. As she scans our surroundings, my attention goes to the arrow. The fletching is half-crimson, half-black. I'd know the markings anywhere; I collected one hundred thousand of them.

Empire.

But an ambush from Miasma? Here? Impossible. She couldn't have predicted the beats of this battle. Even if she had, she's not the kind to sacrifice her entire navy just to capture me. It's Ren she should be going after. And Ren is fighting at the vanguard alongside Cicada. Not here.

Something isn't right. I know it on a visceral level.

"Shields up!" yells Lotus, but too late. A *zing*, and another soldier falls. Arrow to the chest. I stare at the body until my gaze is ripped away by Lotus. She shoves me behind her and whirls, ax out. "Tortoise formation!"

Our soldiers rearrange their shields just as arrows shower down. Most thump off the bronze. Some penetrate. An arrowhead stops hairs short of a soldier's nose; another pins the hem of my robes to the ground. Our formation holds. The hail stops.

The clicking starts.

Rocks. Small ones, dislodged as feet find purchase on the pumice overhead. The soldiers around me tense in their positions, and my grip on my fan tightens as the enemy rappels into view.

They drop to the ground like spiders, clad in the black of mercenaries, with scarves bound around their heads and lower faces. But the swords and bows on their back are of empire gold.

Something isn't right. My mind stalls, sluggish. I'm missing a detail, a sign, a shift in the cosmos I failed to foresee—

I crumple to my knees as zither music rakes through my head.

Far, far away, Lotus is shouting, but I can't make out the words. *What's wrong with me?* I'm awake, not knocked out or dreaming. And yet—this music. It's deafening.

Before my eyes, close-range fighting breaks out. Swords cross. Pikes redden. A man loses a hand; a chord rips out of his mouth instead of a scream. I see red, like my mind is bleeding, then pink. Pink sky, white limestone, a white wicker gazebo.

The flutter of a figure behind a curtain, playing the zither.

My feet move, bringing me to the gazebo. I reach to draw the curtain back.

A spearhead shreds through the gauze.

The battlefield floods back in. A flash of her ax, and Lotus severs the spearhead from its pole, saving my life. She severs people too. Then she's throwing me over her shoulder and sprinting down the pass, to the bend where we tethered the horses. She's setting me atop Rice Cake. She's handing me the reins and screaming something into my face, over and over again until I hear it through the music.

"Get out of here!"

She's turning and lumbering away, disappearing into the thick of the conflict.

Get out of here.

I look down, at the reins in my hand. I look up, at the fighting down the pass.

My fingers close over the reins.

Run. I know a lost battle when I see one. *These troops are expendable. You're not. You're the only strategist Ren has.*

Run, and don't look back.

But I look back. I spy Lotus in the tangle of bodies. Three empire minions fly at her from a chunk of pumice overhead. She guts them midair. Another comes at her from behind. She snaps their neck with one hand.

She'll be fine. Lotus can return as the hero, and I'll return as the coward everyone hates. As long as I can strategize by Ren's side, our mission lives on.

She'll be fine. I press my heels into Rice Cake's side. He doesn't move.

"Come on," I mutter. I tug at the reins. "Come *on*. Lotus will be fine." I look back again to prove my point. "See? Lotus—"

—blocks a spear before it can skewer one of our soldiers. As she finishes off the attacker, motion ripples from one of the pumice forms overhead. A glint, and my blood freezes over.

The arrowhead finds Lotus before I find my voice. It hits her square between the shoulder blades.

She goes down.

She'll get back up. She'll survive against the odds. She has to. And if she doesn't—there's nothing *I* can do. I can't pick up a sword and save her. I can't do anything but set the board, play my pieces, and minimize my losses when I'm outplayed.

And tonight, in this pass, I've been outplayed.

Run, the strategist in me says. I squeeze the reins, damp with sweat. *You're not a warrior.*

Out there, you'd be a burden.

But Lotus is Ren's swornsister, and I can't fail Ren.

I can't be the girl I was again.

I tumble off Rice Cake and slap him on the rear. "Go! Gallop away!"

Rice Cake whinnies but stays put. *Millet-brained horse.* I snatch an arrow from the ground and stab his rump. *"Run, you fool!"* I scream as he screams, rearing. His front hooves slam down—and keep on slamming as he pounds out of the pass.

I gasp for breath, already winded, then turn to face the bloodshed.

No one cuts me down immediately. Everyone's locked in a fight to the death with their opponent. I trip over bodies—some ours, some empire—step into puddles of blood—all the same— the chaos, so much chaos—as I search the ground for Lotus. My panic builds when I can't find her.

I can't find her.

I can't find her—because she's up and fighting, the arrow sticking out her back. Another strikes her in the breast. She yanks it out, throws her head back, and roars. The stones around us shake. Birds take to the night sky, and for a split second, enemy soldiers stand in a daze. Lotus fells them like timber.

But more pour down the cliffsides like ants into a cellar, and I'm three strides away from Lotus when one drives a spear behind her knee. Lotus buckles. Another follows up with a spiked club to the head.

Lotus falls.

She hits the ground, and I collapse with her, the strength threshed from my legs. Something cracks into my skull; someone stomps on my spine. The butt of a polearm punches into my cheek, and I choke on my own blood. *I'm going to die.* Right here, in this pass, before I ever see Ren march into the capital. I had a chance to live and make my mark, a chance that younger, grubbier me seized by stepping into that tavern. Now I've thrown it away.

For what? I can't feel half my face as I crawl to Lotus.

"Pea . . . cock. What . . . strategy . . . this . . . time . . ."

"Injure Yourself to—Wound—the Enemy."

Lotus gurgles. "Lotus . . . knows . . . that . . . one . . ."

She'd better. It's one of the few stratagems that sounds like what it means. Inflict a wound upon yourself, induce the enemy to lower their guard, and attack when they least expect it.

Except I have no attacks left in me. If only I could do more than reach for Lotus's hand with the last of my strength. My trembling fingers meet her still ones.

Is it worth it? the strategist in me screams. *To hold her hand? To be by her side as she dies?*

Is it worth your life?

No. It's not. I had plans. I betrayed Crow for them. I gave up Ku. I made hard decisions and sacrificed the people's love.

But Ren—she would stay with Lotus. My eyes close weakly. The zither music is back again, ringing through my mind. I listen to it, to the fight, still raging on as we lie on the ground, bodies thudding to join us.

A boot crunches by my head.

Whine of a bow, *whoosh* of release. My back blazes. Everything fades. No sensation. Just blackness, like the inside of a thatch hut shuttered tightly against the noonday sun.

Then someone opens the door. Light spills in. A woman in her early twenties strides across the tiny space. The two warriors at her side scowl as she kneels and bows low. She touches her head to the mat before my feet, then raises it. Her gray eyes are plain but warm, like rocks soaking up the very sunlight I was trying to avoid.

My name is Xin Ren, she says. *And I've come to beseech you for your help.*

The mat is damp beneath my feet as I rise. The snow is melting, dripping through the roof. Spring is my favorite season. It represents new beginnings.

This, unfortunately, is an ending.

‡ ‡ ‡

On the doorstep of death, I have something to confess.

I told the truth, about why I am a strategist.

There just so happens to be another truth, about a girl who lost herself again after her fourth and final mentor died. No matter how many warriors she might go on to command, there would still be meteors. Floods. Disease. Death. Despondent, the girl withdrew to a valley called Thistlegate, a paradise for hermit sages. She closed the door to the world.

Ren opened it.

She, and no one else, needed me to be a strategist.

In these final moments, I'm inside this memory. With Ren.

This is her third visit. Flanked by Lotus and Cloud, she strides before my bed, kneels, bows.

She made me give myself a second chance.

I'm sorry, Ren, I now whisper. Somewhere in the distance, I think I hear a zither. *You thought you might fail me.*

But it is I who will fail you.

The music dies.

STANZA TWO

To the north, a miasma
retreated, defeated but alive, the pass
ambushed before they arrived.

To the south, a cicada
stepped out of its sister's shadow
and set sights on the west.

To the west, a lordess
had won a battle
but lost her strategist.

And in the skies above,
a star blinked out of existence.

WHAT IS WRITTEN

When I open my eyes, everything is pink. Birds sing up high. Closer by, someone plucks the zither. I raise myself from the cloudlike bed, enclosed by a gauze curtain, and the notes stop. Footsteps sound, gentle against stone. A shadow appears beyond the gauze. A slender hand parts it.

We stare at each other through the opening, the zither player and I.

Her hair is pulled back, held in place by a living snake. Another one drapes from her arms like a decorative sash, while the skin of a third snake binds her bosom. Below her exposed midriff hangs a long emerald skirt, falling short of her bare feet.

But my attention is consumed by her eyes.

The whites are black. The irises are red. They're like suns in eclipse, ringed with golden coronas.

Demon. Monster.

"Zephyr?"

The monster knows my name.

"Zephyr," whispers the snake-woman again, no longer as a question. "Dewdrop! She's back!" She sits on the bed, cups my face.

I scuttle backward. "I'm not dead?"

"Dead?" The snake-woman laughs. "Of course not, silly."

Not dead . . .

Before I can process that, a small child clambers onto the bed, wearing nothing but a pair of yellow pantaloons and sporting a clean-shaven head—save for a clump of bangs. She crawls into my lap and I flinch as a cloud of multicolored bees materialize around her. But the bees become the least of my concerns when she hugs me tight around the middle and nuzzles my stomach. Suddenly a voice is in my head, sounding nothing like a child's and everything like a hungry beast's.

Mmm. A little skinnier, but still nice and soft.

"Welcome home, Zephyr," says the snake-woman.

About time, says the demon-child without opening her mouth.

Home.

All my life, I've been a home for knowledge, but no place has been a home for me. Not the orphanage, or the residences of my many mentors, or my hut at Thistlegate. I may not know what home *is*, but I know what it isn't.

This isn't home.

I shove away the child called Dewdrop and push off from the bed. Shock splashes onto the snake-woman's face. The moment she doesn't reach for me is the moment I make my escape.

"Zephyr!"

I dash out of the gazebo, across the white terraces. The skies above me bloom pink. *This place—I know it.* It's heaven. But just like before, I'm not dead. In the real, waking world, I'm lying passed out somewhere, drooling and bruised but still breathing and *needed.* I am missing the most important battle of my life.

I have to get back.

"Zephyr! Wait!"

I run faster. If they capture me, I'll never be free. As they gain ground, I look for something—anything—that I can use to slow them. I'm surrounded by a lake of pink clouds; the carved terrace edge is the only thing standing between the sky and me.

They want me alive. That much I can glean. And they speak my language. So long as we have a common tongue, I can negotiate.

I just need leverage.

I hoist myself onto the terrace edge. "Don't come any closer! Or I'll jump!"

The snake-woman glides to a stop.

The child stops behind her, but the bees continue zooming forward. One reaches me and lands on my nose. I reel back—and fall through air—for a single heartbeat.

It ends before I can even scream. My senses plunge into pitch blackness.

Shapes appear, hazy at first. My eyes adjust to lines of a small room and the irregular contours of a person sitting in the center, a person none other than Ren.

Ren. I almost laugh, as if I've come out of a terrible nightmare. I enter the room. It's lit by candles. Ren doesn't turn, and I don't call for her. The silence feels sacred, and Ren looks lost in thought, hunched over some object.

It's a zither, I realize when I'm close enough to peer over her shoulder. *My* zither, the inscription on its side faded, the mica inlay on the fingerboard worn clean. Ren cradles it as she runs a cloth over the strings—seven in all, I count. Sweet notes of apricot oil rise from the repaired instrument.

"There's no need," I murmur. "The shine won't stay."

Ren doesn't respond.

I walk closer, then stop. Three sticks of incense burn in front of Ren. The smoke drifts over a bowl of peaches, then rises up, passing over a name plaque usually reserved for the deceased.

Pan Qilin
Rising Zephyr
Age 18
Her brilliance rivaled that of the stars.

But I'm not dead. The snake-woman said I'm not dead.

I *can't* be dead.

"Lordess." I reach for her, shake her shoulder. "Lordess—" I break off, try her name. "*Ren.*"

My breath snags as she looks up. Her face is so close. Her eyes gradually focus. "What is it?" she rasps.

"Thank heavens—"

"Xin Gong requests your presence at tea."

Slowly, I turn.

Tourmaline stands hunched at the tiny threshold. A newly

scabbed cut runs across her left cheekbone, joining the scar on the bridge of her nose. Was it from the Battle of the Scarp? Did we win? My heart drops at the thought of the alternative.

"Tea," repeats Ren, voice dull. She returns to polishing my zither. "Another day."

"You said that yesterday," Tourmaline says.

The polishing cloth stills over the strings.

"We won, my lordess." I breathe out, but Tourmaline goes on, "At a terrible cost. But the people need—"

"Don't you have troops to train, Tourmaline?"

Despite Ren's rebuff, Tourmaline doesn't leave. She remains in the doorway while Ren dips the cloth into the pot beside her and starts on the fingerboard.

I snap out of my daze and throw myself at the warrior. "Tourmaline!" I grasp her armored forearms. "It's me! Zephyr! Tourmaline, say something! *Tourmaline!*"

She turns away.

I back into the candlelit room—into this *shrine*—tripping over the threshold as I do. I can still react to this world, but it won't react to me. What am I, then? A ghost? Have I become the very superstitions I never believed?

Someone grabs me. The snake-woman. "Zephyr, come back to the sky palace," she pleads as I fight her. "I'll explain everything."

"You can start right here. Why are you following me? Who are you?"

"I'm your sister."

"No." Wrong question to ask. "No, *what* are you? What am

I? Are we—" I glance back at Ren, at the incense. The orphan-age was always burning incense to appease the souls of recently departed children. "Are we ghosts?"

"No, Zephyr." There's something about the way snake-woman says my name . . . something about those demon eyes of hers that seems almost human. "We're gods."

‡ ‡ ‡

Her name is Nadir.

The little one's name is Dewdrop.

They call themselves gods.

Now where have I heard that one?

We're real, Dewdrop insists, offended at my mention of Miasma. I suppose it's a little more convincing (and concern-ing) that she communicates through thought. *The new star that appeared? It was yours.*

I don't deign to reply. Why should I to a child claiming to be thousands of years old?

You were shot with an arrow to the spine. No human could survive that. Dewdrop shimmies off a giant pouf and waddles toward me, bees and all.

"Stay back," I bark, and Dewdrop stops. I glance to Nadir, expecting a reprimand—I did just yell at her toddler sister—but Nadir is silent. She stands by one of the arched gazebo entrances, staring at the sky and its stationary sun.

You know this place. Dewdrop redirects course, going to the zither. She takes a seat at the instrument. *You know this music.*

She plays. Notes emerge, the same notes I've heard in my

dreams, growing up, and more recently, when I was flung from that rearing horse, when Crow knocked me unconscious on the boat, when we were ambushed in the pass. Each time but the last, I escaped death.

Or, if I can't die, each time was this . . . *place* calling me back.

Dewdrop stops playing and smiles, as if she can see me connecting the dots. *You control the weather. It bends to your will.*

"I *read* the wea—"

You wished for a rainstorm on the mountain, so there was a rainstorm. You wished for fog on the river, so there was fog. You wished for a southeast wind, so there was a southeast wind. You are a sky deity like us. You specialize in controlling the atmosphere. Granted, your powers were sealed in your human form, but like calls to like. No seal could have severed the alignment your qì has with the cosmos.

Nonsense, all of it. *I* read *the weather!* I could scream. *I don't wish for things like some monk or medium.*

But one word of Dewdrop's catches me off guard. *Qì.* The essence of universes, the elusive thing that makes a zither *sing.* Master Yao gave me so much grief for not being able to connect with it. Surely—

Still not convinced? Dewdrop spreads ten chubby fingers. *Look at your hands—your* real *hands. See? Lineless. Only humans are ruled by the lines of fate. But even in your mortal form, you were slightly different from them. You heal faster. You didn't contract infectious diseases in the orphanage. You had intercourse with that other strategist, and you didn't contract his consump—*

"Intercourse?"

Dewdrop frowns. *Intercourse, the exchange of fluids high in qì.*

I shake my head. I'm a fool for listening to any of this. "If I'm a god, then what the hell was I doing in the human world for eighteen years?" Wait—eighteen years. "The star—it appeared only eight years ago."

I sit back, smug. There. *Take that, demon-child.*

Dewdrop glances over me. *You really don't remember, do you?*

"No, she doesn't." Nadir drifts toward us. The ground beneath her feet turns to mud wherever she steps, then hardens back to stone.

"A part of her is still trapped in the human shell," she says to Dewdrop. "Unless we destroy it, the Zephyr we know won't return."

We'll have to find the body if we're to destroy it.

"Or we can destroy a representation." Nadir reaches down and scoops up a chunk of mud. In her hands it becomes a doll. She holds it up, and the snake at her elbows lifts its head and opens its mouth. Flame jets out; the mud hardens, whitens, turns glossy.

Nadir contemplates the finished figurine in her palm.

The bees around Dewdrop hum. *It'll be painful.*

"It's the only way."

"What—"

Nadir hurls the figurine and it shatters. *I* shatter. My bones fracture, and I scream until there's nothing left of me to scream with, no lungs, throat, mouth. I don't exist—until I do. The pieces come back together.

I remember.

‡ ‡ ‡

I remember the days. The years—forty thousand, from the moment of my genesis to the moment I was cast out of the sky.

That's right. The Masked Mother, empress of all deities, sealed my memories of being a god and banished me to the human world because I did something foolish. I did a lot of foolish things, now that I recall, but this particular incident involved a drunken bet with some other deity over who could stir up the strongest winds by . . . well, by flatulating over the edge of the sky.

Like I said, foolish. Thoughtless. Worse, Zephyr-as-a-real-god cared even less about the mortal peasants down below. It didn't occur to her that her winds would cause a blight, and the blight a famine, one of many that had plagued Xin Bao's reign.

When the Masked Mother's guards came for me, Nadir pleaded that it was an accident. But humility was—is—not a strength of mine. I couldn't be known as Zephyr the Accidental Murderer. So I confessed and awaited my punishment. No-good gods were allegedly chained to the Obelisk of Souls and struck repeatedly by lightning.

Instead, the Masked Mother took me farther down, past the storm clouds of the lower heavens.

Into the mortal realm.

We materialized in a tiny, dark room that smelled absolutely vile. I stayed back as the Masked Mother went forward. Two girls lay on a bedroll. Both were young, but one was slightly younger. Both were starved, but one was more dead than the other.

"Come back," whispered the younger, less-dead girl. It was Ku.

"Come back. Come back." She stared at me all the while, as if she could *see* me. That was disconcerting. The qì of a god was supposed to be too pure for mortal eyes to detect.

Then I spotted the spirit between us. A mortal soul in the likeness of the girl who'd already departed. In human terms, a ghost. I could see her, and it seemed like the younger girl could too. Somehow. I wanted to ask the Masked Mother how. Maybe I'd have known, if I'd taken the time to educate myself on humans, like Nadir. Nadir loved humans, had once breathed life into her clay figurines and used them to populate the mortal world, back when it was young and still possible for gods to mold.

But obviously, I wasn't anything like Nadir, and I never got the chance to ask.

"Behold a soul that you extinguished," the Masked Mother said, looking down at the body of the dead girl and paying no mind to her lingering spirit. "Thousands more like her exist." Yes, I got the message. The smell of the place was killing me. Was it too late to request the struck-by-lightning punishment? "Now you are to take her place."

"Wait—*what?*"

The next thing I knew I was coming to, my powers as a god sealed away, forgotten with my identity. I had the girl's— Qilin's—identity instead, this fuzzy concept of parents long dead, the sharper concept of starvation in my stomach, and Ku. A sister who, to some extent, realized I wasn't hers.

Now my sentence has expired with my last human breath. It's over.

It's all over.

When I wake up, I'm flat on the bed. Dewdrop is braiding my hair and Nadir is hovering over me with worried eyes. My sister's eyes. Not a demon's.

"Hey," I whisper, and Nadir closes them, tears spilling down her cheeks. I don't know how to comfort her. I'm back, but I've been gone eight years. A blink to a god. A lifetime to me.

Eventually it won't be. "Me" will be Zephyr the deity, a master of the cosmos all along. The years spent in the human world? That will be the blink.

I reach for Dewdrop and tug on her tuft-like bangs. She hates it when I do that.

Back to normal, I see, thinks Dewdrop.

"Yes," I whisper. This is my home. My family. They will never die on me, never leave me like they left Qilin. I don't know why, then, it hurts so much to say, "Back to normal."

‡ ‡ ‡

After monitoring me for a day, Nadir deems me ready to face the Masked Mother. She'll be the judge of whether or not I'm fit to regain my powers. I put on the robes my sister sets out, and pause when I notice her staring.

"What's wrong?"

"You're wearing what I asked you to."

"I trust you know best."

The snake around Nadir's arms tightens and I find myself reading her body language. *She's nervous.* "You usually prize your own opinions."

Translation: I was even more arrogant as a god.

"What else . . . seems different to you?" I ask as we leave Aurora Nest—the name of our home—and head down the terraces.

"Well . . . your diet, noticeably."

She's right. Dewdrop strolls between us, her head bobbing below our hips. *You've been sober for a record number of hours.*

"I didn't mean that," Nadir says quickly.

We both know it's true. And you eat like a monk.

"You've taken up a vegetation-heavy diet," Nadir amends.

Same difference.

We reach the end of the terraces and the beginning of the endless lake.

Since my powers are still sealed, Dewdrop summons a cloud to take us to the Masked Mother's Zenith Palace. As we step onto it, I consider Nadir's and Dewdrop's words. It's true, I did consume a lot more meat and wine as a god. I don't know why I lost a taste for both in the mortal world. Perhaps because Qilin was deprived at the orphanage, or the rich food and drink reminded me unconsciously of the person I no longer was.

The tall gazebos of Zenith Palace pierce the distant clouds as we near the Masked Mother's domain. We step onto the backs of Qiao and Xiao, the twin serpents in bondage to her. Their bodies arch into an iridescent bridge that leads to the main hall.

A Masked Guard stops us at the apex of the bridge. "Only one may accompany," he says through his mask, a solid sheet of gold.

Nadir's snakes hiss. I vaguely recall her fear of the guards. More vividly, I recall the way she barged past them in spite of her fears, to plead on my behalf before the Masked Mother. When Dewdrop offers to go with me now, Nadir's gaze firms with resolve.

"I'll take Zephyr."

See you two soon, then, says Dewdrop. She's a yellow blip beside the massive guard when I look back at her, across the bridge.

I face forward. Sights seem new for all of two seconds before the memories return. There's Lantern Gate, which I once set on fire, and there's the statue of a qilin beast, where I etched my name on its rump—again, under the influence of drink and dare.

Maybe Nadir's recalling my past indiscretions too, because she stops just before the threshold to the hall. The two pillars on either side of us tower like giants' legs into the light of the sun.

"Remember," Nadir murmurs. "It's the Masked Mother."

"Right. And she hates me." I wouldn't blame her. Both Nadir and Dewdrop are much older than me—at one hundred thousand years and seventy thousand, respectively—yet I'm the only one who bored of being a good little god.

"She possesses no concept of hate or love," Nadir corrects. "She knows no emotion but that of others. Whatever you hide, she will see. Whatever you feel, she will use to test you."

I'd much rather she just hated me. "I'll be fine," I say for Nadir's sake. "I'm the Rising—"

—*Zephyr.*

The snake around Nadir's arms constricts. "Remember who you really are, Zephyr."

Then the Masked Mother's bond servants are announcing

us and Nadir is saying, "Head down." She dips her chin. "You mustn't look the Mother in the eye uninvited."

We cross the threshold.

Entering the hall feels like entering Miasma's war camp. I reach for my fan—which doesn't exist. Nadir is too busy bowing to notice my slip. I quickly follow in observing the obeisance, and a voice, neither masculine nor feminine, sounds from the dais deeper in.

"At ease."

Nadir straightens, lifting everything but her head. I mimic her, plastering my gaze on the turquoise-, peach-, and white-agate floor as the Masked Mother descends the dais. Her shadow cascades over the steps and overlaps with mine.

"Well, hello again, Zephyr."

My gaze flies up.

It's Crow, standing before me, smiling. No—it's Ku. I blink, and it's Cicada, circling me.

"Did you enjoy your time in the human world?"

My mouth opens. No words come out. Two sets of eyes sear into my skin—Nadir's, in growing concern, and Cicada's, ink black.

No—*the Masked Mother's.* Creator of the universe, empress of all deities. To regain my powers, I need to prove that I'm fit for godhood. If I fail to do so, I don't know what will happen. No one does. Gods can't die, but the gods she sends away are never heard from again.

My fingernails dig into my palms. I focus on the pain, let it be my compass. "I did enjoy my time."

Nadir stiffens. Too late, I realize it's not the right answer.

"Oh?" The Masked Mother stops behind me. "How much . . ." Her voice changes, from the adolescent pitch of Cicada's to a perfect tenor, ghosting over my earlobe.

". . . did you enjoy it?" asks Crow, before pressing his lips to the side of my neck.

My heart plunges. My stomach burns. My body is confused, but my mind isn't.

I jerk away from Crow.

"I've learned my lesson." My voice shakes. My fists do too, closed at my side. "I won't do it again."

"Won't do what again?"

Do no harm. That's the first rule of being a god—the rule I broke eight years ago. "Hurt humans."

"Is that so?"

I nod.

"Good. Good," says Crow—the Masked Mother. She steps in front of me and turns into Miasma. "Excellent," murmurs the prime ministress, bell tinkling at her ear, scalp half-shaved. "But what about help? What if . . ."

Miasma falls, and *melts*. A stew of skin, organs, and bones bubbles on the ground, the grotesque scaffold underlying every human displayed right before my eyes. Structure re-forms, and a person, naked like a newborn, rises from the stew, vertebrae audibly clicking into place as they straighten their spine.

"What if I need help, Qilin?" gasps Ren.

It's an illusion, I tell myself as she collapses again and immediately begins to liquefy. *An illusion.*

But then Ren-not-Ren, half pooled on the ground, looks at me with what remains of her face. Her mouth opens, and my name, a wretched sound, comes out.

"*Qi . . . lin. Help . . .*"

It doesn't feel like I've moved at all, but I must have, because something yanks me back.

Nadir's snake hisses around my arm, ending my dash to my lordess, who is completely unrecognizable now, looking the same as any human would when you boil them down.

I'm not them. We might all be composed of qì, but there's still a world of difference in the purity of our physical matter, of our energy. *Like calls to like.* I'm a god. I'm unlike humans.

I'm not supposed to care about them.

Do no harm. The first rule of being a god.

It has a counterpart.

Do no good, I think, as the puddle on the ground assumes the shape of someone else. I have to show the Masked Mother that I don't care. That I won't interfere. The Library of Destinies has already penned every mortal's fate.

What is written cannot change.

The new person rises and approaches, features morphing into a familiar face.

My breath stops.

"I knew you weren't my sister," says Ku. "I always knew. My sister left me that day. I saw her float away. You were an impostor. That's why I hated you."

"I'm sorry. I'm sorry. I'm sorry." The words are out before I can stop them.

"I forgive you." Ku nears me. "I miss you." Nadir's snake releases me. "Please come back. Come back, sister."

Shaking, I breathe in. I reach for the well of qì buried deep inside me, always there, never gone, but now—the seal cracks. Behind Ku's face, I sense another presence. The Masked Mother's. She's watching, waiting to see what I'll do with this sliver of power she's released for me.

Show her, then.

Show her that you don't care.

I draw up the energy. I turn my palm out, facing Ku.

I reduce her to mist.

For a second, nothing happens. Then the wind rushes through me. I *am* the wind. I am the clouds outside this room, the beat of distant wings, the vibration of a zither being played, thousands of lǐ away. But as my power over the atmosphere settles into my bones, their voices return.

They are all I can hear.

十四

A WORLD APART

Come back, sister.

Dewdrop lies belly-down, skimming her fingers through the clouds below as we journey home. I sit beside her, silent.

That wasn't Ren I watched die. That wasn't Ku I destroyed. Just illusions, inspired by my deepest fears.

Whatever you hide, she will see. Whatever you feel, she will use to test you.

Nadir stands at the edge of the cloud, her eyes pinned ahead. She's the first to step off when we reach the terraces. Dewdrop and I follow. We're barely past the threshold of the atrium when Nadir stomps her foot. The mud beneath her feet expands, hardens, cracks. Shards of earth rise and fly to me.

"Uh . . ." The broken pieces cocoon around me, glowing red-hot when I get too close. I look to Nadir through the cracks. "What's this for?"

"You can stay here and reflect on what you did today."

The words open a chest of memories—of Nadir feeding me hangover tonics, laying cool cloths on my forehead, dressing me in clean clothes. She's always been closer to a mother than a sister. But the sternness of her tone is a first.

"I passed whatever that . . . *test* was," I protest. "I got my powers back. I did as you asked."

"Did you?" Nadir's voice shakes. "I told you to remember *yourself*. Instead you remembered . . . those mortals."

"What you saw back there was . . ." *An accident. A mistake.* I swallow, unable to say the words. "It won't happen again."

"Promise me." Nadir extends a hand, and a green bottle materializes in her palm.

It takes me a second to remember what it is.

I stumble back, as if the Elixir of Forgetting can take effect on sight alone. "No."

The bottle vanishes. Nadir closes her hand. "You're not how you were before."

"I don't want to return to before," I blurt, to Nadir's horror. But it's true. I'm remembering more. Other gods were either obsessed with making love or obsessed with making war (the heavens never lacked for either), or they were like Nadir, devoted to self-cultivation. Me? Beneath my juvenile debauchery, I remember the crushing apathy, knowing that nothing I did mattered in this unending existence. "I was *terrible* before."

"But you were *you*. *Our* sister." The snake at Nadir's arms writhes. "Not theirs."

"Nadir . . ."

"I've never begrudged you anything, Zephyr. Never. I let you do all the reckless things your heart desired. But I can't lose you again. As long as you refuse to forget the human world, I'm not letting you go."

She walks away.

"Nadir, wait." I reach out without thinking and hiss, fingertips singed. "Nadir!"

But she's gone. There's no one left in this atrium but Dewdrop and me.

"I don't get it." I shake my head. "Nadir—she *likes* humans."

She doesn't interfere with them. None of us do. You know the rules.

I do. *Do no harm. Do no good.* But they weren't always so. As someone who could barely be bothered with mortals, I never asked why the paradigm shift happened, why the gods of old could interfere and why it's now forbidden. It's so arbitrary. So unfair. I growl, and Dewdrop's bees hum as if to comfort me.

She'll come around. Just give her some time.

"How much?"

Maybe a month. Maybe a year.

"A *year*?" I can't afford to be in this clay prison for a year. Dynasties can rise and fall in a year.

It's short compared to eight. If you love us, then do as Nadir asks. Forget your mortal life. Forget the people from it.

"I can't. They need me."

So do we.

"But you don't. Not really." Not in the same way the peasants needed me. I can't believe I'm thinking of them, but they're all I can see. "You've never been alongside them, wading through muck just to live another day. You've never—" *met Ren* "—served someone who would rather die than leave her people behind.

You've never—" *been saved by someone working on the opposite side*. I break off, swallow. "I don't want to forget them." Either of them.

For a long time, Dewdrop doesn't speak.

There's something you need to see.

The next thing I know, I'm standing on a floating, moss-covered boulder. A chain of them stagger up the cloud-filled sky, into the higher heavens.

Come. Dewdrop leaps from boulder to boulder. *Our destination is at the top.*

At the top is the biggest boulder, the base to a red lacquered pagoda, in which shelves also float, made of the same mossy rock. Dewdrop waves a hand, and the shelves rearrange themselves. One shoots forward, stilling right before us.

"Where are we?" I should know, but my memories are still dusty.

The Library of Destinies. Dewdrop rummages through the summoned shelf, dislodging scrolls. Her bees catch them. At last, she finds what she's looking for. She hands the scroll to me, held shut.

There was a reason why you served Ren, out of all the warlords, thinks Dewdrop as I unroll it. *And that reason is written right here.*

I read the words once, twice, three times, unbelieving. This can't be true. This . . .

You were meant to live and die as a mortal, thinks Dewdrop. *So, like any mortal, your fate was written by the Masked Mother's Scribes. You were ordained to serve the weakest lordess in the realm.*

You were never in control. The bees lift the scroll out of my hands and return it to the shelf. *You had no say in the lordess you served. This was a loyalty already decided for you. It was part of your punishment.*

The Library vanishes, and I'm back to being surrounded by clay shards.

Consider it, Zephyr. Dewdrop turns away from my prison and, like Nadir, steps out of the atrium, taking her bees with her. *You didn't choose Ren. You never had a choice at all.*

‡ ‡ ‡

Times passes. Night does not fall. The sky stays a maddening pink as I pace in my prison. I might as well be standing still.

So I do.

I stop in my tracks, chest heaving.

You didn't choose Ren.

You had no say in the lordess you served.

The weakest lordess in the realm.

My hands clench. I *did* choose Ren. I chose the lordess with the people's support. Weakest? Only in the eyes of the ignorant, like Cicada. Miasma. They all felt threatened. I trust my judgment.

Some prewritten destiny couldn't have imprisoned me.

Nothing can. I turn on my heel and blast the clay shards with qì. I try again and again, before doing what any human would do: I grab the shards with my bare hands. The clay heats. The stink of singed flesh is worse than the pain itself. But I hold on, until the cracks start to widen. It's working. It's—

The cracks reseal.

I let go, gasping. The gory mess of my hands heals before my eyes. I wipe the spit off my chin and grab the clay again.

This time, I suppress my own healing. The qì controlling the shards weakens. It's designed to hold me in, not harm me, and as I blister and bubble, the clay pieces move and part.

I burst out and run, my hands only half-healed when I hoist myself up onto the terraces. The fresh pain robs me of my breath. But I'm free. The pink sky above is the home of the gods.

Mine is beneath.

As I teeter on the narrow ledge of stone—the boundary between worlds—Dewdrop's words come back to me.

A loyalty already decided for you.

To hell with them. If I have to leave Ren, it'll be on my own terms.

The clouds shift, lapping at the terraces like waves at a bank.

They close over me when I jump.

‡ ‡ ‡

I'm not supposed to be here.

It's the first thought that comes to mind when I end up in an unmistakably empire room. Red lacquered walls press in. Candlelight flickers off bronze partitions, urns, and a decorative gong, round and polished.

I'm not reflected in it.

Neither are the ghosts. I can see them now, these supernatural things I never once believed in, never *could* see because of my sealed qì. Here, they take the forms of servants. Generals.

Officials. They stare at me from the red-tinged shadows, and I stare back, chin up. We might both be made of qì, but ghosts are abominations. Incense is burned to dispel them. They linger in a world that's no longer theirs.

I'm a god, not a ghost. We're different.

I turn away from them, to the room.

Two people face each other across a chessboard. One is Miasma. She sits with a knee bent under her elbow, rubbing a black stone piece over her bottom lip. "You let me win on purpose."

The other is Crow. "It's commendable that you noticed," he says, and my neck tingles where the Masked Mother kissed it.

For once, I'm more interested in a person's face than his play. My eyes pin on Crow's, then slide down the bridge of his nose. His complexion is paler than I remember. Did Miasma blame him for the empire's defeat at the Battle of the Scarp? Or for failing to predict my betrayal? My stomach contorts, and a *clunk* makes me jump.

But it's just Miasma, dropping the chess piece. "Oh? Why's that?"

The black stone bounces off the ground, lands by the hems of my robes.

"Because it's dangerous to think you've won when you've actually lost," says Crow as I bend down, driven by instinct. My fingers pinch the stone. It won't budge. I can *feel* it—solid and humming with qì—but I can't exert force on the inanimate object.

"You know what I like better?" Miasma leans forward. "Thinking that I've won when I've actually won."

Silently, Crow clears the board, depositing white and black stones into their respective pots single-handedly. He doesn't use his right hand, not even to hold back the billowing sleeve of his left.

Clunk. A piece falls at the same time as my stomach.

"Do you resent me?" asks Miasma, and my stomach falls even more. She couldn't have.

"No." Crow continues to drop pieces into the pots, one by one. *Clunk. Clunk. Clunk.* His left elbow rests over his right hand, blocking it from my view. "I miscalculated. Our troops paid the price. So should I."

Behind me, the ghosts murmur.

No. I reach for him, grab his arm. I feel him—his energy, his warmth, familiar and pliant—but beneath the qì of his body is that of his soul, unyielding as armor. It resists me like the chess piece, for the opposite reason. The soul's qì is too alive, a repelling storm. I can't push or tug his elbow away from his hand.

"We've been through a lot, haven't we?" muses Miasma.

"We have," agrees Crow. "Since the Battle of the Central Plains."

"You were still working for Xuan Cao." Miasma shakes her head. "A boar, just like the leaders of the Red Phoenixes. So many boars, followed by fools. We've put them all down. Now . . ." She touches her middle and index fingers to two white stones still on the board. "A nobody and a bug remain."

Crow stares at the board, quiet. "You shouldn't underestimate Ren."

"Then shall I overestimate her like the rest of the world?" Miasma licks her lips. "Did you know, Crow? Our empress once offered Xin Ren a royal title. I was here. I saw it. She did not take it. Xin Gong's lands are now at her disposal. She does not grab them. Back when that star was still in the sky, she could have spread rumors of being a god herself. Did she? *No!*"

"Others spread the rumors for her," Crow points out, and Miasma's eyes glitter. He shouldn't have said that. "I'm sorry about the star," he adds, and my heart pounds at Miasma's silence. I worry that she'll misinterpret his words as pity.

But then she throws her head back and laughs. "Crow, oh, Crow. Twenty-five years now, I've lived without the blessing of a surname like Xin Ren's. I'll live without the blessing of the skies. I will seize what I like, whether they think me deserving or not. Isn't that what it means to be a god?" She picks up one of the two white stones and gazes at it, smiling. "I may have lost a star in the sky, but Ren lost more. Without her little strategist, she's nothing. I'll end her myself."

I don't remember moving, but my hands are in Miasma's hair and I'm *yanking*. She winces and palms her head.

"Should I summon the physician?" asks Crow without missing a beat.

"Don't bother. The old mule is as useless to me as he is to you."

"I haven't worsened under his care."

"I'd have his head if you did." Miasma rises. I wish I could do more than give her a migraine. I wish I could burn this whole place down.

But then I'd also be burning Crow. *As you should*, argues another part of me. *He's the enemy*. But had he not been a friend, then I wouldn't have been able to swap out the antidote. The empire killed me anyway, but I didn't die by his hand.

Enemy. Friend. Rival. My confusion grows when Miasma says, "Get some rest, Crow," with a nauseating tenderness. How can she still care for his well-being after harming him?

How can *I*?

"Forget about that," Miasma orders as Crow continues to clear the board. "Have a servant do it."

He rises and a servant kneels in his place. He starts for the draped doorway, and pauses by it. "Mi-Mi."

"Yes?"

"Did you ever trust her? Zephyr?"

My heart stills at the sound of my name.

Say no, I think to Miasma. It has to be no. Why else would she have arranged an ambush for me in Pumice Pass?

Miasma traces a finger down the shell of her ear, stopping at the bell. "What about you, Crow?" she asks, as if she's already answered.

But she hasn't, and instead it's Crow who says, "No."

The silence goes watery. I shake my head, trying to clear my ears of it.

"Then why didn't you say something?" asks Miasma.

"I wanted to respect your wishes."

Miasma's face wrinkles. "Well, don't in the future."

"I'm afraid I have to," says Crow, mild. "You might kill me otherwise."

Have you no fear? Why remind her?

But Miasma simply laughs again. "You're right. You, Crow, are right and wise. I was the fool this time. I thought someone so smart would know better than to follow Ren."

I don't hear Crow's reply.

Miasma trusted me.

But Crow never did.

Or so he says. I don't accept his answer like Miasma does. Respecting her wishes isn't worth losing a whole navy. Respecting her wishes isn't enough to explain why he didn't withhold the antidote from the start. He saved my life, on the boat. He had to have trusted me, at least a little.

"Why lie?" I demand.

Crow doesn't answer. I'm left trailing after him down a narrow corridor and, before I know it, into his room. He closes the door, his arm brushing mine. It feels so real. I'm living. He's living.

We're both living, a world apart.

He peels off his cloak and hangs it from a peg on the wall. Without it, he's slim, almost diminished. He begins unwrapping his outer robes as well, and I'm about to look away when he stops, in a state of half-undress that might as well be complete, judging by the temperature of my cheeks.

He wears the untied robe like a shawl as he sits at his desk. I sit beside him. He lifts his right arm, the sleeve slipping back as he reaches for a brush, and finally, I see the bandage. It's wound around his hand and bound over a gap between his third and index fingers.

A finger, gone.

I don't know whether to feel relief or horror. Miasma could have easily taken his whole hand. He could have lost his life, like the ghosts in that room, perhaps also once in Miasma's service.

He's already lost too much.

The brush handle, meant to be stabilized between the third and middle fingers, wobbles in Crow's grip. After watching him struggle for several minutes, I can't take it—I wrap my hand around his. I pretend I'm helping even though I'm not. I'm hurting him, if anything, because Crow's face pales. The bandage reddens.

I jerk away, breathing hard. "Go to bed."

He doesn't listen. Can't hear. Wouldn't listen, I imagine, even if he could hear.

The night deepens; the room chills. At last, Crow sets down the brush. He leans back in the chair, closes his eyes.

His breath evens and slows.

I came for Ren, not Crow. Crow, who only suffers because of me. I deceived him. He fell for it. I've seen the cost.

I should go.

But for just another heartbeat, I stay. I sit beside him at the desk. I relearn his face even though I never forgot it. When his head lolls and the collar of his robe slips, I try to tug the fabric back into place even though I know it's useless. My knuckles brush his skin.

His eyes fly open.

My pulse ricochets. He sees me. I'm certain of it.

Then his eyelids shut. He sighs, the sound so frayed that I hold still until he drifts off again.

It's clear I have some sort of effect on Crow, just like I had on Miasma. Could I exist like this, a god in the mortal realm, and somehow still serve Ren?

Not as a god.

My gaze jerks over Crow's shoulder to find Dewdrop standing by the wall, her head barely reaching the bottom of his cloak.

As a god, you can't do anything to revise the lines of mortal fate, she thinks as she enters the room, accompanied by her cloud of bees. She draws near.

And hops onto Crow's lap.

"Get off him." I grab for Dewdrop, but her bees form a blockade. "You're going to—"

Dewdrop jumps up and down. Crow sleeps on.

—wake him.

Dewdrop pokes at his face. Stretches his cheeks. *What's there to like about him?*

"Why are you asking me?"

Because you're the only one here who knows the answer.

"I don't like him."

Your qi says otherwise. Dewdrop does a handstand off Crow's knees.

"Enough. Stop that." I lift her. A bee tries to fly up Crow's nose. "*No,* Dewdrop."

Why not?

"Because I say so."

He won't feel it. I've had practice, unlike you.

"No is no." I lift up Dewdrop, almost dropping her when Crow's lips suddenly move. Two tremors. Syllables, like a name.

It doesn't look like mine.

Something flares in me. I squash it. I won't be so pitiful. I carry Dewdrop out of Crow's room without looking back.

She hugs my neck. *Nadir is right. You've changed.*

"Is that why you're here? To spy on me for Nadir?"

No. I wanted to see her. Your human sister.

I stop in my step.

Mine. Not mine.

Not my sister.

Still, there's a part of me that wants to shield her, to protect her like a secret.

"Okay," I finally say.

The landscape changes. We're in another room, very different from Crow's. The walls are more air than timber. Rush mats hang unrolled from the beams, their shadows alternating with stripes of moonlight on the bamboo floor.

Ku sleeps half-cast in both. She's kicked off her blanket, her legs poking out from under her tunic like the whites of scallions. She mutters, over and over again, the same two words:

"Come back. Come back. Come back."

She's not asking for me, I know, but Qilin's ghost.

Here is someone else I hurt.

I crouch beside Ku, a lump in my throat. Dewdrop places a hand on my bent knee. *Her name is Pan Ku, isn't it?*

"Yes," I whisper, and shiver. The South is never cold, but the night is damp and Ku always sickened easily, catching everything there was to catch in the orphanage. A draft blows through the open walls, and my teeth clench. Where is Cicada?

Dewdrop's bees lift the blanket by its corners and resettle it over Ku.

"I thought you couldn't do that."

She wasn't fated to be cold tonight.

"And Crow was?"

Dewdrop smiles innocently.

"None of this makes sense," I huff.

We can bend the rules in small ways. Respect your elders, and I'll teach you how. Then Dewdrop stops smiling. She looks to Ku. *Your qì is full of fear.*

"It's part of being mortal." To fear losing them. Hurting them. Failing them.

"There's someone else important to me," I say, taking Dewdrop's hand. "Let me show you."

I think her name, and the moon-silver room dulls. The walls solidify to stone. We're someplace underground; torches on the dirt walls throw light over the table in the center. At its head paces a boy on the cusp of adulthood. He's dressed in purple, hair swept into a topknot, two side bangs left long.

"Where is Bracken?" he asks, making a half turn. Torchlight catches on his golden mask. *Not a Masked Guard*, I think to calm myself. We're in the mortal world, and this boy's mask only covers the left half of his face. Besides, whereas the Masked

Guards are huge, he's scrawnier than even my human form. Yet people reply to his query with deference. "On their way, Young Master."

The "young master" continues to pace. A second later, three raps—two long, one short—sound from the door. People spring to answer it. The newcomer is ushered in and shuffled before the masked boy.

"Were you followed, Bracken?"

"No, Young Master."

The boy nods. "Then let this meeting begin. Have you reached out to Xin Ren yet?"

"She refuses to see anyone," says Bracken. They're wearing a mask too, like all the others seated at the table. "Not even your father for tea."

"Then have you contacted her swornsister?"

Sister. My heart plunges at the singular.

"No."

"Are you eating rice for nothing?" snaps the boy, and Bracken flinches. "Try harder."

"Yes, Young Master."

You don't know him, do you? Dewdrop scans the earthen room. She tugs on my sleeve. *Let's go.*

I don't move. They might not be Ren, but they're talking about Ren. If that weren't enough to transfix me, then the boy's next words are.

"I've been waiting for a leader like Xin Ren for a long time. Get through to her, or I'll have you all stripped of your titles."

"But, Young Master," someone says from the other end of the table. "Even if your father doesn't deserve these lands, don't you?"

"Me?" The boy laughs without humor. "I'm—"

The underground room disappears before I can hear the rest. "Hey!"

Dewdrop pats my hand. *There'll be plenty of time for you to snoop later.*

Will there be, though? How many chances will I get to slip away? And how am I to find this place again?

Speaking of which: "Where are we?"

On a cloud.

Yes, I'm aware. But the land we're hovering over is indistinct, until the cloud descends. A patchwork of prefectures, bordered to the east by marshes, cupped by cliffs in every other direction. The region is a basin, and there's only one in the realm.

The Westlands.

The cloud lowers us into a town square at least twenty times the size of Hewan. Lacebark elms line the roads. The roads themselves connect like latticework. Alleyways collapse to sunken pavilions; bridges swell over canals. As Dewdrop and I cross a bridge, dawn cracks slow and blue over the mountains to the north. The sky—one star short—lightens.

I make a series of deductions.

We won the Battle of the Scarp. We forced Miasma to retreat, even if we didn't successfully capture her. Ren went west with our troops to return Xin Gong's, and Xin Gong beseeched her to stay. An about-face, but that's what happens when an army successfully defeats Miasma's.

Ally with the South. Establish a stronghold in the West. The first two points of the Rising Zephyr Objective, before the final step: *March on the North.*

We're closer than ever to bringing the war to the empire.

I won't be there to see it happen.

My hand tightens around Dewdrop's, and she squeezes back. *You owe them nothing.*

"I know." Except I don't. Even if everything I gave Ren was preordained, everything she gave me—the shoes she wove when my pair fell apart, the books she'd snag as we fled from town to town—was of her own will. She never seemed surprised when I delivered results. She believed in me, and that *meant* something.

As if sensing my thoughts, Dewdrop tugs on my index finger. *Would you come back to us?*

"I didn't say I was going to leave."

We start walking. When our legs prove inefficient, I flick a hand and a gust of wind carries us instead. The Westlands are huge, but I seem to know exactly where we're going. The perks of being a god.

If you left, how long would it be? Dewdrop asks as red-walled wards and emerald rice paddies blur by.

"Not long."

You're certain?

"We're less than two steps from realizing our objective."

If you say so.

"What, don't believe me?"

I believe you. It's the humans I don't believe.

"They're not so bad."

Are you really sober?

The gust slows as we enter a path formed by a canopy of banyan trees. The path winds to a stone-pillared gate, beyond which lie stables, barracks, and training fields. The wind vanishes, setting us outside a barrack raised on stilts.

Ren is in that barrack. I just know. Before stepping in, I glance to Dewdrop. Her expression is unreadable.

"I just want to see her," I say, mostly for myself. "That's all."

Inside, I'm assaulted by the smell of herbs. Ephedra, licorice, wolfberry—they hang from the ceiling in baskets, a testament to the Westlands' fertility. But my gaze homes in on Ren. She's sitting by a bed. I edge closer—and freeze when I see the person under the sheets.

The last time I saw Lotus was on the battlefield. Both of us were in bad shape. But I never believed I'd witness Lotus—slayer of tigers, reigning champion of drinking contests—so motionless and quiet. A bandage covers her eye. The skin around it flames violet. There's no energy rising from her skin when I hover a hand above her. No qì of her spirit. Just a whisper of a breath. A stutter of a heartbeat.

I spin to Dewdrop. "Where is she?"

Here.

"Where is her *spirit*?"

Dewdrop sits on the edge of the bed, yellow-pantaloon legs dangling. *Gone.*

"What do you mean, 'Gone'?" My breath catches. "Like a ghost?" No. Lotus is alive—she's still breathing—

Not a ghost. Just gone. Scattered. Dewdrop swings her legs. *On the minuscule level, human and gods are not so different. We both have spirits made of qì. But the mortal spirit is more unstable. You and I can travel in whichever form we like, without bodies. Mortals can't. If the spirit leaves—*

"It comes back. I know it can." Mine did, after accidents of the equine variety.

Perhaps, if the spirit had stayed close to the body. But hers has been gone for too long, Zephyr. Even if parts of her are still trapped in this world, they're scattered. You could spend your endless existence searching for them in the ether, and you still wouldn't find all of her.

"So she's never going to wake up?"

Dewdrop shakes her head.

I shake my own. "No, Lotus will come back."

As a reincarnation, after her body expires and her spirit is recalled to the Obelisk of Souls.

"That's not what I mean!" If Lotus goes, so will Ren. She's already leaving. Her eyes are vacant. Her cheeks are hollow, thinner than when I last saw her in my shrine. They swore to live and die together, Lotus and Ren, when they swore sisterhood. Lotus *has* to wake up.

Listen. Dewdrop closes her eyes. *Her heart is already weakening.*

I don't want to listen. I want to shout. I want to yell.

"Ren." I grab her by the shoulders; she hunches them in. "*Ren.* You can't—"

"—do this to yourself."

A shadow falls over us, and I look up to the clean-cut angles of Tourmaline's face. The scab to her wound has peeled away. "Please. The troops need to see you."

"I don't want to see them."

"Then what do you want? What can we do to help?"

"I want to be left alone, Tourmaline. I want you to go." Ren says all of this without lifting her eyes from Lotus. "Can you do that for me?"

"No."

Ren takes Lotus's hands. "Then you're free to stand where you are."

I'm so close to Ren, yet unable to help. She's lost, as am I. I want to escape and hide.

But Tourmaline doesn't budge, and so with her I remain, the two of us facing our lordess, Ren kneeling by the side of the bed, Lotus on it.

Then Cloud storms in. *Clang.* Suddenly, I'm no longer under Tourmaline's shadow, because Tourmaline has been shoved aside. Ren is standing, her sword crossed with Cloud's glaive. "What are you doing?"

Cloud presses in. "Checking to see if you still remember your vow."

"We made a vow to die as one."

"A vow to ourselves. But we vowed to the people of this realm to defeat Miasma. Are you willing to break that vow for ours?"

Ren doesn't answer.

"I'm not." With a spin of the wrist, Cloud whirls away her glaive and slams the butt into the ground. "I'm going to flay whoever did this to Lotus. Until then, do your job. Live and lead."

Slowly, Ren looks at the sword in her hand. The instinct to live is still there, buried deep. Cloud's attack unsheathed it.

"Go where you're needed," urges Cloud when Ren doesn't speak. "I'll keep watch."

Do as Cloud says, I think for the first time in my life, breath held.

At last, Ren nods. Her sword sighs back into its scabbard, and I sigh too. She's back. Not completely, but in time, she will return.

After Ren steps out, Cloud turns to Tourmaline. "Go with her."

Tourmaline doesn't argue. Once she's gone, Cloud clasps Lotus's hands just like Ren did. But whereas Ren's hold was loose, Cloud's is tight. Her tendons strain against her skin.

"She can't feel you," I whisper as Cloud stares at Lotus, her dark eyes focused. Qì thrums off her rounded shoulders in waves, as if to compensate for Lotus's missing energy. I place a hand on Cloud's, trying to relax her grip. "Don't do this."

As I pry at her knuckles, my pinkie brushes Lotus's skin.

I'm suddenly falling. It feels just like jumping off the terraces in the sky. But unlike then, I know exactly where I'm going to land—in this empty vessel before me.

In Lotus.

I yank back. The momentum of my qì, left with nowhere to go, catapults up my spine. Gasping from the rush of it, I look up to find Dewdrop's gaze resigned. The questions she asked on the way here—those hypotheticals . . .

Are suddenly not so hypothetical. Without further elaboration, I know:

I could stay this way. The body before me has no spirit. My qì is compatible with it. I might even be able to affect fate, if the mortal body masks my godly essence. I could come back, help Ren.

Give her the second chance she gave me, when she visited my hut in Thistlegate.

"Will you stop me?" I ask Dewdrop.

No one has ever been able to stop you, Zephyr.

"Then will you tell Nadir for me?"

What do you want me to say?

"That I love her. That I'm sorry. I'll be back before you know it."

Dewdrop is silent. *Be careful,* she says at last. *The Masked Mother doesn't mind gods visiting the mortal realm, but if she knows that you're here to meddle . . .*

She doesn't need to say more. Neither of us really know what kinds of transgressions cause a god to be sent away instead of merely punished, but I have to assume that deliberately meddling in mortal fates would be one.

"Come here," I say, breaking the silence. When Dewdrop comes, I hug her close, release her, and tug on her tuft hair. "I'll be careful."

Dewdrop gives me a skeptical look.

"I will!"

You'd better. The bees condense around her. A blur of color, and she's gone.

Just me, Cloud, and Lotus now.

In the distance, a gong sounds. The shadows on the ground move with the sun.

Slowly, I place my hand on Lotus's bandaged forehead.

Forgive me, I think as I release my existence. It's like uncorking a jug and pouring out my spirit like wine. *I hope you understand.*

I imagine somewhere, scattered as she may be, Lotus might hear.

I imagine that she would say, *Do what you need to, Peacock,* before raising her jug in a toast. *For Ren.*

十五

IN HER NAME

For Ren.

Everything is pain when I wake this time. My knee, my back, my head. A fire rages in my left eye. But there's a quieter pain on the skin of my face.

Tears fall onto me like rain.

I rest my hand over Cloud's bowed crown, and she looks up. A tear rolls off the tip of her nose. It must land on my cheek, because it seeps through the bandage. Stings.

"Cloud." My voice is too deep. Too rough. "Cloud," I say again, testing the vibration of Lotus's vocal cords.

Slowly, Cloud wipes her nose, her eyes. "Lotus." Her lip trembles. "Lotus," she says again, now smiling, so brightly. Too brightly. It hurts to see. Hurts more than all my pains combined, especially as the sting on my cheek fades and the other aches dull. Dewdrop was right; I do heal fast. I just never had the chance to notice, as a strategist, or maybe Lotus has a tougher hide. The muscles in her legs twitch, itching to be exercised.

"Hold on," Cloud is saying, new tears catching at the corners of her upturned lips. "Let me get Ren. Ren will want to be here . . ." She looks around in a daze. "What's the hour?"

The gong sounds then—once, long. An hour past noon. Has Cloud been here this whole time?

The answer is an obvious *yes*. Cloud is Lotus's swornsister. *My* swornsister. I have to convince myself of it first, if I'm to convince others. But for a moment, I waver. I don't want to do to Cloud what I did to Ku. If I could just tell her the truth, that I'm here in Lotus's form for Ren—

"Of course." Cloud slaps her forehead. "She's at the shrine."

"Shrine."

A nod, restrained. It doesn't match the dark fire in Cloud's eyes. "The traitor had to go and get herself killed."

Traitor.

Me.

Zephyr.

My shrine, which Cloud looks like she would torch if she could.

The truth dissolves on my tongue. Cloud would never let me see Ren if she knew who I really was. I doubt she'd let me make it out of this bed alive.

I push off the covers.

Cloud helps me sit up, then stand. "Easy there, Bobcat."

"I can walk."

My first few steps are shaky, my depth perception skewed through my unbandaged eye. Cloud steadies me; I shrug her off, igniting the wound to my back. A curse—much too foul—rips past my lips.

"Where's the shrine?" I ask, gripping the doorframe.

I'm scared Cloud won't tell or—worse—insist on accompanying me.

My fears are misplaced. "Down the banyan path," says Cloud, without asking if I need to be shown the way. There's worry in her eyes, but also confidence, and she only has one caveat: "Ren doesn't like anyone to disturb her."

I look out. Fog blankets as far as the eye can see, like that morning on the river. I had a plan then. A strategy. Arrows flew for me.

Now I have nothing but a quiver full of lies. "Lotus isn't *anyone.*"

‡ ‡ ‡

The banyan path is squishy and sweet, perfumed by the figs released from the branches overhead. But the scent is overtaken by that of incense when I reach the shrine.

My shrine.

I don't like a single thing about it. Not the choice of incense— the perfect stimulant for a breathing attack—or the windowless, ink-black space. I especially don't like seeing the darkness cling to Ren, who kneels before the altar inscribed with my name. The offering of peaches in the bowl seems freshly replaced, and she's bent over something. My zither, I worry. Maybe Ren can't get over the fact that she never fixed it before my death. I wish I could tell her that I could care less.

I *can* tell her.

"It's important to move on."

I sound nothing like Lotus, I realize after the words are out. I stand, rooted in place, as Ren turns. The frown knotting her brow comes undone. "Lotus?"

My name is a question in her mouth. In Cloud's, it was a fact. Ren lurches to her feet, face slack. "Is that you?"

Cloud never truly accepted the idea of Lotus never waking up. Ren had. She'd believed her swornsister gone.

She was prepared to follow.

I'm here to give my lordess strength, not take it away.

I nod.

Ren spreads her hands. "Come here." I walk toward her. She holds my arms, scanning me from head to toe.

"You're standing." She blinks rapidly, as if checking her vision. "Your . . . your wounds." Her hands shake as she releases me, and I recall that Ren had Lotus whipped for insubordination. "I—" Ren chokes off. I hear the guilt in her sob.

I can assuage it, in this new form.

"Lotus is fine." I thump my chest with a fist. *Ow.* "Strong."

"Good," says Ren. "I'm glad. I'm glad . . ."

I steady Ren as she sways. She's like straw in my arms. Was she always this fragile, or is it Lotus who's strong? I frown, and Ren pats my shoulder. "We'll be back to sparring in no time."

She pauses, and I struggle to think of Lotus's reply.

But then Ren is speaking again. "You were there. When the ambush happened, you were with Qilin, weren't you?"

Qilin.

I nod.

"The empire denies having a hand in her death. But it was empire soldiers, wasn't it?"

Another nod.

Ren crouches before the altar, reaching for the thing she was bent over. Not my zither, but a box, lined with white silk. It's filled with possessions—mine. Seeing them is like seeing my own dead body. I look away, but not before Ren pulls out the arrow.

Like the one that was buried in Crow, half of the shaft is darker than the rest. Stained. Ren's fingers curl over it. Her knuckles bleed to white.

"People say a lot of things, Lotus." Her voice is quiet, inward. "They say I don't fight for the empress, but for myself. They say I battle Miasma because I hate her. In the eyes of some, our conflict is personal.

"But I never felt it to be so. Will one of us end under the other's blade? I suppose it's inevitable. But our disagreement over how to run the world wasn't personal.

"Until now." The arrow trembles in Ren's grip. "She could have taken my life, or dueled you or Cloud, warrior to warrior, and I would have respected the outcome. But I can't respect this. She murdered my strategist. She made it personal."

Silence. Ren's breathing is loud.

She shouldn't be this hurt. I was her strategist, not her sworn-sister.

"It's war," I finally say, trying to sound like Lotus. "People die."

Instead I just sound callous. One of these days, Ren will surely catch on.

Just not today. "I feel Qilin's pain, right here," says Ren, pressing the arrowhead to her chest. "I'll make Miasma bleed for it."

Every gain we've secured will be for naught if we march on the North prematurely.

"Revenge later," I urge, trying not to screech. "Base-building first."

Unhearing, Ren sets the arrow down among the other items in the box. She rises, and lays a hand on my back. "Let us feast tonight, in celebration of your recovery."

A feast sounds like the last thing either of us wants or needs. But Ren's pretending to be whole, and I'm pretending to be Lotus, so we pretend on this too.

‡ ‡ ‡

When I return to the infirmary, Cloud has already set out Lotus's pieces. I ask for a moment alone, not caring if it's uncharacteristic, and pick up Lotus's tiger-pelt skirt. So rough, so crude. Flesh was once cleaved to this fur.

Stomach turning, I force my fingers around the handle of Lotus's ax next. To this body, it's as light as my fan. I touch the blade—and jerk away when I remember the bones and organs severed by it. I see the soldiers Lotus gutted in her last moments. All enemies. I've killed enemies too.

It's not the same.

I put on Lotus's outer robes and skirt and leave the weapon behind as I exit the infirmary. Who takes an ax to a feast?

I stop in my tracks.

Lotus, that's who.

I go back.

‡ ‡ ‡

The night is warm like an embrace. We're safe—safe as followers of a landless lordess can be, enjoying the hospitality of the West-lands governor Xin Gong in Xin City.

But arms that hold can also strangle. And tonight at the feast, I keep a hand on Lotus's ax, my every sense attuned to the press of danger.

My deductions have been confirmed: We won the Battle of the Scarp but suffered defeat at Pumice Pass. Miasma retreated safely through it and made it back to the capital. Her command of the empire still stands. And Ren—she's more unstable than I've ever seen her.

I thought Lotus's return would fix her.

"To the recovery of a warrior who inspires fear across the realm," says Xin Gong.

Goblets drumroll down the long tables.

Xin Gong faces Ren. "And to the reunion of the greatest fam-ily under heaven."

Says the uncle without the backbone to back Ren, or Xin Bao for that matter, against Miasma. Xin Gong takes no stand, cham-pions no cause—a travesty in an era when even robbers declare themselves king. I look to Ren and see a shadow in her eyes. The crowd doesn't notice. To them, she's ever the smiling, benevolent lordess. A servant pours her a goblet of wine, and she raises it to all the Westlands vassals assembled.

"Governor Xin and I will be working toward the same goal: to strengthen our troops and save our crops, so that the people may weather the war to come."

At the mention of "war," Xin Gong's smile stiffens. He *should* be nervous. He'd have been torn apart by Miasma long ago if not for the mountains enclosing the Westlands, a natural deterrence against invaders. He has no biological children of his own. His army may be one of the few that have triumphed over the empire, but for that he has Ren to thank. Ren could declare herself governor right now and the populace would support her. Honor holds her back. She refuses to betray blood.

But she must; it's step two in the Rising Zephyr Objective. *Establish a stronghold in the West* is but a euphemism for "wrest control from Xin Gong." There cannot be two leaders in a land, and we need the land. A base to train and feed our troops. A place to retreat to. Relying on Xin Gong in our weakest hour would be more fatal than losing a battle. Ren *must* betray him, family or not. I knew this from the start. I just never imagined having to convince her from my current spot. Physically, I'm no farther from Ren than I was as Zephyr: Cloud and I sit to her immediate left. But all I can see is the empty seat to Ren's right.

A seat that I called mine.

The space to Xin Gong's right, meanwhile, is filled by two young men, one a burly warrior, and the other—

My gaze freezes upon him.

—the boy with the golden mask, the boy from that underground meeting who spoke of waiting for a leader like Ren.

"Cloud," I murmur without taking my eye off him. "*Cloud.*"

"Yeah?"

"That person." I nod at the boy, who's saying something to Xin Gong. "What's his name?"

"Him?" Cloud sets down her drumstick and squints at his backlit, half-masked face. "That's Sikou Hai."

My mind lights up at the name. He's Xin Gong's adopted son, his closest advisor.

"What's so interesting?" asks Cloud at my obvious fixation. "Don't tell me you fancy him."

"N-no." I should say more; sisters would say more. "Do you?"

Cloud blinks, then flicks me on the nose. "Looks like that head injury of yours was no small bruise."

She tears into her drumstick before I can ask what she means, and I'm left with a platter of goat in front of me—Lotus's favorite, apparently—and friends to either side. I force down a piece of goat, quiet and waiting. A new platter comes out. Everyone digs in, and only then do I risk another glance at Sikou Hai.

He's gone. My teeth grit.

But then—a flash of gold.

I jump up; a wine jug tips over. No one bats an eye, to my surprise, except for one soldier who thanks me for the "drunken goat."

"Outhouse," I still feel obligated to blurt, then hurry away in what I hope is the right direction. Out of the town square, into the thicket. Critters flee the undergrowth as I crash through it, almost running into a tree when I misjudge Lotus's longer strides.

In no time, I've caught up to Sikou Hai.

"Wait!" I call, and he stills, turning around slowly.

"Are you speaking to me?"

I come to an awkward stop, short of words instead of breath for once. But Sikou Hai isn't Ren or Cloud. He doesn't know the real Lotus.

Around him, I can be myself.

"It would appear so," I say as I approach, "considering there's no one else here."

"You must be mistaken." Sikou Hai's eyes narrow, flitting from my bandaged face to my armored chest. "I don't deal with warriors."

"I'm—" *not a warrior.* "I'm here to talk about Ren."

I know an opening when I see one, be it on a chessboard or in a person's face. At my lordess's name, Sikou Hai's guard falls. His eyes practically gleam, and I grow wary. As Xin Gong's adopted son, his devotion to Ren is certainly a mystery. But even if I don't trust him, I need to learn the mission behind his underground meetings. "I understand that you—"

Want to rise against your father? Oust him for Ren? He'll ask me how I know. As I vacillate, Sikou Hai's expression closes.

"You'd be better off speaking to my brother," he says, voice cold, his gaze fixing on something over my shoulder.

"You've got that right."

I turn to find the burly warrior from dinner lumbering toward us. "Sikou Dun, at your service." His hands are suddenly upon my arms. "Whatever you need, I'm your person."

Sikou Hai. Sikou Dun. Brothers, though I can hardly tell. Sikou Dun is twice the size of Sikou Hai, with a mallet for a chin and stubs for teeth. Spit webs between them as he grins.

"Get your paws off me." I twist out of his grasp and turn, but Sikou Hai has already slipped away.

"Feisty," says Sikou Dun. "You're lucky I like my girls with—"

My knuckles crunch into his nose.

He stumbles back, and I stare at my fist. Punching anything always seemed like it'd hurt me more than my target. But Lotus was made for this. My knuckles crack as I unclench them, and my nerve hardens as I stare down Sikou Dun.

"Lotus, right?" With a grunt, Sikou Dun wrenches his nose back in place. "I've heard a lot about you."

"I haven't heard anything about you." And I don't care to. "Bring your brother back to me," I order, the strategist in me coming out in the face of this warrior.

"My brother?" Sikou Dun repeats, incredulous.

"What's his relationship like with Governor Xin?"

"Like advisor."

Unhelpful. "And yours?"

Sikou Dun thumps his chest. "Like son!"

Predictable, that Xin Gong has picked an heir as incompetent as himself. "Your surname isn't Xin."

"I've earned it, unlike your lordess."

"Ren is as deserving as they come."

"Because of her honor?" Sikou Dun sneers. "Attacking the prime ministress from behind doesn't sound very honorable to me."

"She's a sage ruler who listens to the advice of her strategists."

"You know what else is good at listening? A bitch."

"Take that back."

"I'd make you my second-in-command or maybe my wife. But how does Ren treat you? By whipping you." Sikou Dun leans in, oiling my face with his gaze. "A rabid bitch."

My hands are somehow at his collar. "Take. That. Back."

He grins. "Beg for it."

I'll kill him. I'll pull out his intestines and feed them to him.

But this—this isn't me.

I stumble back.

First the curses, now this. It has to be coming from Lotus. Bodies, like everything in this world, are also made of qì, and qì is fluid. Lotus's spirit might be gone, but her physical energy is mingling with mine.

"What, scared now?" I back up as Sikou Dun advances. "I thought you'd like it rough."

Disengage. Don't respond—

"I challenge you, in Ren's name."

Sikou Dun stops, then smirks, triumphant. "Weapon of choice?"

"Fists."

"When?"

"Whenever you dare."

He bows—too deep, the gesture a mockery. "Looks like we'll be tumbling after all."

If I break him in the right places, he'll never tumble again.

But after he leaves, I realize what I just agreed to. Not a game of chess or a duel of zithers.

A fistfight.

Skies, oh skies, what have I done?

十六

TWO LORDESSES IN A ROOM

What have I done?

"There you are," says Cloud when I finally find my way back to the barracks in the dark. "Thought you'd fallen into the outhouse for a second there."

If only. Then a bath and change of clothes would do.

"You left this." Cloud hefts something into her grip, and I could groan. It's Lotus's ax. I forgot it at the table. Good for Sikou Dun. Not so good for me. I take the weapon. Do I sleep with it? I might cut myself. But I've never seen Lotus without it, so I set the ax—blade facing away—by the bedroll already spread beside Cloud's. Now, to undress in front of everyone.

I thought I'd left these days behind me at the orphanage.

As I strip down to Lotus's under-robes, activity flutters around us. Soldiers bet on who will win tomorrow's one-on-one training duels. An arm-wrestling match starts in the back of the room. An argument next to us sends someone falling onto my bedroll. "Oooph, Lotus, sorry," she says, shoving her opponent back. I will myself to leave my bedding as is, rumpled.

"So what did Sikou Dun want with you?" Cloud asks as I sit. Her glaive blinks on the horizon of my vision as she polishes it.

"You heard?"

"Word's all over camp."

Always knew warriors were gossips. "He insulted Ren."

"Gather 'round," someone shouts, and suddenly I'm at the center of a crowd. Faces—young, old, but few older than Ren herself—peer at me, eager and expectant.

I have no idea whom Lotus considered a friend other than Cloud. Who owed her a life on the battlefield. Whom she owed in return. All I know is that I've never held an audience of warriors so rapt. My mouth thins.

"And you?" they ask. "What did you do?"

"I punched him."

From the hoots, you'd think I cracked his skull. An orange is chucked at me. I catch it—with my hands and not my face, like I would have before. Then Tourmaline strides in, and my audience disperses, murmuring "General" to the silver-armored warrior even though Tourmaline is no higher in rank than Lotus or Cloud.

"Good to see you back, Lotus," Tourmaline says when she nears. "How do you feel?"

Better question is how do I answer? Were Lotus and Tourmaline close? I look to Cloud, who's very focused on polishing her glaive. Taking that to be a no, I go for the safer reply.

"Ready to beat Sikou Dun up." I crack my knuckles for punctuation, and Tourmaline's gaze grows solemn.

"Have care tomorrow."

It's such a Tourmaline response, I almost smile.

Cloud saves me from exposing myself. "Have a little faith," she grunts to Tourmaline.

"It's not just Lotus I'm worried about."

"Who, then?" scoffs Cloud. "Sikou Dun?"

"Our lordess."

Silence drops like a hatchet, lodged between the two warriors. Both avoid looking at me, which makes it obvious that they're thinking about me. Lotus nearly took Ren's fighting spirit. Maybe she would have taken Ren's life, if she'd died. No matter what happens tomorrow, I can't die to Sikou Dun, or anyone. This is the responsibility I carry, as Ren's swornsister.

A responsibility I didn't realize I also carried as Zephyr.

"Ren's fine," Cloud finally says. "She's only *not* fine because of that shrine, which you could do us all a favor by torching."

"It wouldn't solve anything," Tourmaline replies, voice dry as sand. "She'd build another."

"No one's gonna build a shrine for Dun," I intrude, misinterpreting the subtext on purpose. Lotus would.

Cloud, being Cloud, undoes my work. "Just admit you liked the traitor," she says to Tourmaline, and my mind slows.

Liked. Not *tolerated*, as I'd assumed. As Tourmaline followed my orders. Gave me advice.

Lent me her horse.

"Zephyr wasn't a traitor," Tourmaline says, voice so low it's almost a growl. No one argues with her, but Cloud makes no secret of her disagreement. Her face, reflected in the crescent blade of her glaive, is high in color. When Tourmaline finally strides across the room, Cloud chucks down the polishing cloth. I wait for her to curse Tourmaline out. Instead she sighs. "Hells, I messed up."

"How?" I ask, but Cloud is already shaking her head. Her leather under-armor crackles as she unstraps it. She lays it under her pillow, then slides into her bedroll.

"I wish she weren't so goddamn..." Her lips puff with pent-up words and air; she blows out both. "I don't even know."

"You mean Tourmaline?"

Without denying it, Cloud bends an arm over her eyes. "I'm never going to be worthy of her."

"You. And Tourmaline."

"What about it?"

Aside from the fact that Cloud seemed to hate Tourmaline's guts just now? "Nothing."

"Hmph." The blankets rustle as Cloud turns her back to me. "You're a horrible liar."

Coins jingle as bets are collected. The last candle dies under a breath.

Cloud's snores join everyone else's.

I slip into my bedroll—Lotus's, that is—and choke as the material exhales a throat-clogging odor. The smell of Lotus, concentrated. When was the last time she washed this? I don't even want to know.

Alone in my wakefulness, I stare at the beamed ceiling. I pretend it's the universe, the knots in the wood representing galaxies near and far.

But here, at the bottom of the Westlands basin, not even moonlight can cut through the fog. Everything is dark to me, ceiling included.

I flop onto my side, bumping a bruise. Lotus would have known what to say to Cloud. Yet Sikou Hai would have stopped for Zephyr. Ren needs her swornsisters, but to build a kingdom, Ren needs Zephyr. Is it possible to be both? Is it possible to be even *one*?

Sleep sucks me under before I can find the answers.

‡ ‡ ‡

The next morning, I wake to a ruckus of snapping buckles and clanging pikes. Helmets glimmer as Ren's soldiers don them. In a flash of silver armor, Tourmaline is out the barrack doors before I can rub my eye.

"Cloud?" My mouth is fuzzy, my senses more so. Everyone's dressing for war, but not to the blare of the horn or beat of the drum. "Cloud, what's going on?"

"Huh?" Cloud ties off her braid with a blue ribbon before turning to me with a confused expression. "What are you doing up so early?"

Early? I've already lost the dawn. But Lotus, I'm finding, isn't a morning person. My head and limbs are weighted with lead, and my stomach croaks like a frog. "Everyone else"—I'm interrupted by my own yawn—"is up."

"Yeah, because people from the Southlands are here." Cloud says it like *breakfast is here*. She goes back to getting ready, throwing on her blue cloak, as I blink.

The Southlanders are here.

Our allies that I secured.

I rise—too fast. Pain explodes through my left eye. Cloud grabs for me before I topple. "Whoa, whoa. You really don't have to be up."

On the contrary, I really do. "They're in a meeting? Ren and the Southlanders?"

"I would assume."

"I want to be there."

"Then you will," says Cloud, to my relief.

This is all I need, I tell myself, slipping into Lotus's ochre outer-robes and tying on her tiger-pelt skirt. *To be there. To listen.* I'll figure out how to advise later, but as long as—

"Report!"

A soldier bursts in and gets down on one knee, presenting us a square of paper on his upturned palms. "General Cloud. General Lotus. A message."

Cloud takes it. "From the South?"

"From the general of the governor's guard, Sikou Dun."

"Him?" Cloud wrinkles her nose as she unfolds the square. "What does he want?"

My stomach drops even before the soldier says, "It's addressed to General Lotus."

Silence.

Cloud looks up from the message. "He says he'll be awaiting you in training field number two, between the chén and sì—"

The gong sounds for eight short notes.

"—hours." Cloud's brow drops low. "Right now."

She sends the soldier away, then crumples the note. "Is this the time you agreed upon?"

For a frightening moment, I can't remember. My brain is foggy despite the sleep, the most I've ever gotten as a mortal. My stomach growls again, and I suppress another yawn.

Then last night returns. Sikou Dun, asking me when I'd like to duel. Blood aflame, I told him whenever he dared.

I, Rising Zephyr, the Dragon's Shadow, am caught in my own snare.

I curse the Masked Mother's mother, and Cloud slaps me on the back. It's how warriors show sympathy, I guess, and it really hurts.

"You know how these things go." I don't know the first thing about fights. "Pointless pleasantries, sentences looping in circles," Cloud goes on to say, and I realize she's talking about the meeting with the Southlands. The art of diplomacy, the kind of wrestling I am—was—built for. "I promise you won't be missing anything."

No, just the first meeting since our joint victory as allies.

"I'm jealous of you. I could do with some exercise."

You're free to take my place. I bite back the words. Lotus would never think them. She'd march out there and make quick work of Sikou Dun. I . . . just have to do the same. I *can*. How hard can it be?

"Save me a spot," I say to Cloud, then stride to the doorway. "Lotus won't be long."

‡ ‡ ‡

I can do this. I can do this. I can—

My mind blanks at the sight of Sikou Dun.

Sunlight gleams over his shoulders. They're bare like the rest of him. He's nearly naked, save for his trousers, which he's tied up to his calves.

"Good morning!" he calls to me across the training field. Soldiers of both Ren and Xin Gong have already gathered around. Xin Gong's snicker as Sikou Dun says, "You look lovely as usual."

"Oh, you think so?" I can fix that.

War cries erupt as I undo the bandage around my ruined eye. A puddle of rainwater on the ground reflects something angry, mangled, red. I don't look too closely, just wind the bandage around my right hand. Sikou Dun slides his feet apart and grips the ground with his toes. I mirror him. The only sound is my heartbeat for a long, long moment before a lark calls.

Dun charges.

There's no time to craft a plan of attack. My hands shoot out and meet him by some stroke of luck. I grab him, lift him, hurl him across the yard.

Well, that was interesting.

The crowd cheers as he lands—hard. Yet not hard enough to knock him out. Foot by foot, he staggers upright, nostrils flaring. His eyes show whites as he turns his gaze on me.

I've dined with Miasma. Conversed with enemy generals. Been poisoned by Crow. But never have I been confronted with someone who wants to eat me alive.

Lotus faced worse than men, I remind myself, wiping my mouth with the back of my hand. *She faced tigers.*

She would peel Sikou Dun's hide and wear it as a skirt.

Sikou Dun rolls back his shoulders and cracks his neck. We circle each other. I angle myself accordingly. His body is all lines and points, hills and valleys, weak spots and strongholds. I analyze it as I would a map. But right as he lunges, an unaccounted for piece of information enters the picture.

A silk palanquin, coming down the dirt path ahead.

Bam. The world flips, trees upturned as Sikou Dun slams me, back first, into the ground. He sits astride my stomach as the palanquin is set outside one of the smaller barracks, and an upside-down Cicada steps out, followed by an upside-down Ku. An upside-down Ren greets them with a bow before seeing them both inside.

I should be there.

I should be by my lordess's side. I should be facing Ku as a fellow strategist, not here, pinned beneath Sikou Dun.

Bam. My good eye flashes black. His blows are spaced out just enough for me to scream, to feel things bruise, bleed, break. Blood runs into my eye, bloating the outline of Sikou Dun's face as he leans in. "How do you like that?" Sweat slicks off his neck and onto me. A bee buzzes around his head. "Say the word 'please,' and I'll stop."

Can't. The weight of him on my chest is so heavy, I can barely breathe. But air isn't needed for what I do next.

Dun reels as my bloody spittle flies into his face. He paws at it, dumbstruck. Then the veins in his temples flex. His fist rears back like a python. I see the trajectory of the strike. I know what will happen. My skull will fracture, broken beyond healing. I've done this before.

Died before.

But the world doesn't turn black, like last time. It turns blue like Cloud's cloak, flying overhead before she descends onto Sikou Dun.

She tears him off me, and I lie there, an oozing lump, as she beats him into the ground an arm's length away.

"A three-way tumble! I love—"

Smack.

"Go tumble with a horse," says Cloud. Then there's no more talking. Just punching. I warrant Cloud gets two more in before the shock wears off for the spectators, and Sikou Dun's lackeys try to save him. Another scuffle probably breaks out, ending with another victory for Cloud. Then she'll wipe the blood off her knuckles and turn to me—or where I used to be.

‡ ‡ ‡

By the time I hear my name, I'm already halfway to the barracks.

"Lotus! Wait!"

I push on, fueled by raw adrenaline. The ground bubbles like it's boiling as I stumble down the dirt path, past the stables and the Southlands palanquin.

"Lotus." Cloud catches up to me, her voice urgent. "You can't go in there. Not like—"

"It's where I belong!"

The roar is Lotus's, but the pain of it is mine. My gaze dares Cloud to stop me. For a second, she's too stunned to.

Then she grabs me. I throw her off. When she tries again, I use the last of my strength to shove her. Caught off guard, off-balance, Cloud falls. "Lotus . . ."

I lurch past her, any guilt overpowered by my desperation. I need to know what Cicada wants.

I need to be Zephyr.

But I'm stuck as Lotus, and when I slump against the barrack doors in an attempt to eavesdrop on the conversation inside, the frame buckles under my person, more muscular than Zephyr's ever was. The door falls. I fall.

We clap the ground like thunder.

Get up, I think as voices rise and feet approach. *Stand*. But I can't. I'm out of adrenaline. I moan and drool, half-delirious, as three sets of shoes approach. Black peasant sandals for Ren. Foam-green silk slippers for Cicada. And Ku's. Her robes, just out of reach, trail white like the tail of a meteorite before dissolving into nothingness.

十七

SWORN

Ku. Cicada. Ren.

In my nightmares, I'm sprawled on the floor as Cicada eyes me in disgust. Ku sits on my back like I'm a water buffalo while Ren bends down to ask, *What were you thinking?* And I, for the life of me, don't know what to say. I wasn't thinking. I was scared.

Scared to have become a good-for-nothing.

I come to on an infirmary pallet, the beds around me unoccupied like before. We're in a lull between battles, and no one else but me seems to be going around picking recreational ones. I ease myself up with a groan.

At a glance, the room seems empty. Then I see Ren. She stands at the windows, hands clasped behind her back. I wait for her to notice me. When she doesn't, I can't stop myself. I have to know.

"Is Cicada still here?"

"Just left," murmurs Ren, her willingness to answer surprising me. Maybe she and Lotus *did* discuss state affairs and all is not as hopeless as I think. "She's on the road south."

So is my luck. "What did she want?"

"The return of the Marshlands. I told them to speak to Xin Gong," Ren continues. "The land isn't mine to give."

It will be, soon enough.

"But they said their alliance is with me, not Xin Gong." Ren pauses. "What do they take me for? A betrayer of my own clan?"

"That's not true."

"First, Miasma spreads rumors that I'm after Xin Bao's throne. Now it's Xin Gong's lands. Is honor dead in this kingdom?"

"No, but good rulers are. Xin Gong's only lasted this long because of the mountains. The second Miasma draws him out into an engagement, he'll fall quicker than a stalk of sorghum. His troops will pick sides, and the people will be left defenseless. Before this happens, you must establish . . ."

"Lotus?" Ren turns. Light from the window silhouettes her, shrouding her gaze from me as she takes a seat at the edge of my pallet. "You're awake."

I am, but Ren? She doesn't seem quite present as she takes my hands into hers. When she says, "I don't need you to defend my name," it's as if our conversation before didn't happen. Or, as if she was speaking to another person.

Such as Zephyr.

What am I to Ren if she can't consult me like she did before?

"Ren . . ." I moisten my lips. "Would you have still liked Zephyr if she couldn't strategize for you?"

A breath of silence. "Why do you ask?"

"Lotus misses the peacock."

For a heartbeat, Ren is tight-lipped. "Do you know what I liked best about Qilin?"

I shake my head.

"It wasn't her strategy, though skies know we needed it." Ren rises from the pallet. Her eyes rove the room, settling on an incense urn. She plucks out three sticks. "It was her fan and how she'd point it—" Ren waves the sticks around and I cringe. "It was how seriously she took herself, and the people around her." Smiling, Ren shakes her head. "Did you know, Lotus? I once saw her throwing out the candy I got her. I know!" Ren cries at my horrified expression. "I was almost tempted to retrieve it from the muck!"

"Then why—" I catch myself and pivot. "Ungrateful Peacock."

"Aiya, that's what you don't get about Qilin! She was just too polite. But I must confess: I thought she'd eventually tire of saving me face and tell me outright. I thought I was offering her the chance with every candy I gave. When I realized she was committed . . ." Ren lowers her voice and I lean closer. "I'd give her candy just to see her eye twitch."

Ren, a prankster. Maybe Lotus has seen this side of her, but I haven't. As I let it sink in, the light leaves Ren's eyes. She looks at the incense in her hands, now burned down. Ashes rain from the stubs. "She was just a kid. She died too young."

Neither of those things are true. I'm older than all the dynasties combined. But around Ren, I really do feel young. I may no longer be compelled by fate, but I feel the same calling to follow her as I did in my Thistlegate hut. I couldn't stand by.

I still can't.

"Ren." I wait until she's looking at me, really looking at me. "You have to take over the Westlands. It's the penultimate step in the Rising Zephyr Objective. It's the only way we'll be strong enough to attack the North."

Ren smiles midway through my directive. "Focus on recovering," she says when I've finished, patting my shoulder. "I've got the rest."

"But—"

A cough comes from the doorway. Sikou Hai stands in it. "Lordess Xin."

"Young Master Sikou. What brings you here?"

Not me, clearly. Sikou Hai looks at me like I'm a meal he finds unpalatable before bowing at Ren, his sleeves a waterfall of violet. "May I have a word with you . . . alone?"

"Consider Lotus a part of me."

His brow spasms. I silently gloat.

"Please," insists Ren, and finally, he enters.

It's my first time seeing Sikou Hai in daytime lighting, and I can't say it's very flattering. His face is narrow like a poorly crafted blade, his forehead lined even though he's close to Lotus's age. The skin left uncovered by his golden mask is pocked. As an orphan, I know sickness like I know strategy.

But if we were still in that dark underground room, I'd only be able to see the elegance with which he now presents the scroll. "For you."

Ren unrolls it. Her expression flickers. "I have no use for this."

"I don't think you understand my intentions."

"I think I do." Ren hands the scroll back. "And I can't accept them."

The scroll hangs from Sikou Hai's slack grasp. I glimpse a detailed map, dense with line work of the Westlands capital. It's the sort of map that belongs in war rooms, a map that should never fall into enemy hands. The meaning of the gift is clear.

As is Ren's rejection of it.

When Sikou Hai scrunches the map shut, I can't help but empathize. We're in the same predicament. Trying to convince Ren of reality, and failing miserably.

Sikou Hai takes a breath. "They say you love the people. You never abandon the young and old. You give the weak shelter and protect them with your troops."

"People are free to say what they want about me," says Ren, but Sikou Hai won't hear it.

"They say it because it's true! Miasma? She once rode down the line and gutted her wounded soldiers when they slowed her retreat from Xuan Cao. You're different. If there's a deity in this world, it's you!" I gawk, and Sikou Hai backtracks. "You can't possibly sit by and be content with Xin Gong's rule," he mutters, eyes dropping.

"The people here don't seem discontent."

"We are not the people. We can't look to our full bowls today and stop planting. We can't look at the roof over our heads and stop building." The blotches on Sikou Hai's face redden. "The North almost fell to the Red Phoenix Rebellion and the Ten Eunuch Cabal," he says, and I find myself both rooting for him and wishing I were the one speaking to Ren. "The South almost fell to the Fen pirates. The peace in the West is ephemeral. In this era of rogues, we need a protector. And Xin Gong, father to me as he may be, is not the one."

Ren doesn't immediately reply. At least she isn't dismissing his words like she did mine. The objective matters more than my pride, I tell myself, ignoring the pang in my chest. If Sikou Hai can convince her—

"You say my popular appeal is built on my honor." Ren touches the pendant at her neck, the Xin nearly effaced. "If that's the case, then where is my appeal if I usurp my own relative?"

"Relative." Sikou Hai spits the word. "I know a thing or two about relatives. I reckon you do too." I grow nervous at his tone. "Xin Gong may have offered you a place to rest and train your troops, but where was he before you sealed an alliance with the South? Even before that, after your mother died—"

"I think we're done for today," says Ren quietly as I pass off my groan as one of pain.

"Lordess—"

"You've given me a lot to consider. I need time."

What was I thinking? If *I* can't convince Ren, then how can Sikou Hai?

Definitely not by thumping down to his knees. "If you won't accept the map, then accept my loyalty. I know I will never live up to the talent of Rising Zephyr—"

At least he acknowledges it.

"—but you need a strategist." He knocks his head thrice upon the wood. "I swear my life to your cause."

"That won't be necessary, Young Master Sikou." Ren's voice is kind but firm. "I have all the support I need."

She helps him up, sees him out. After he leaves, she paces to the windows and clasps her hands behind her back, pose identical to before. But everything else has changed, and I know better than to speak when Ren whispers, "What would you do, Qilin?"

She's not asking me.

‡ ‡ ‡

When Lotus's friends visit the infirmary that afternoon, they curse Sikou Dun and blame him for taking the fight too far.

They could just as easily blame me for botching it.

Cloud stays behind after the others. She was the only witness to my outburst. Now she may be the only person to realize Lotus never would have lost to the likes of Sikou Dun.

"Anything you need?" she asks innocuously, but my mind detects danger and decides to employ Stratagem Seven: Stomp the Grass to Scare the Snake. Cloud's suspicion is the snake; any poor imitation of Lotus will arouse it.

So I stomp the grass by saying the completely unexpected. "Sikou Hai."

"Sikou Hai?" Cloud's eyes narrow. "Really? You and I both know he's not your type."

For a flash of a second, I see black feathers, the snick of a grin, *his* fingers flying over the zither strings. I grumble something incoherent. Let Cloud think me embarrassed. I am interested in Sikou Hai for strategic reasons. I need him and his ready-made network of supporters; he needs me to convince Ren. It's the perfect partnership. I can't say the same for whatever game of lies I had going with Crow.

"So what do you want me to do?" asks Cloud. "Lead him here?"

Like a horse by the reins? I'm not that desperate. "Tell him to come here."

That night, Cloud returns alone. "He says he's busy."

In other words, I'm not worth his time. I could write my intentions to him, but when I try to, with a candle in the corner of the barracks among a sea of snoring warriors, the brushstrokes emerge shaky and thick. I crumple the paper, breathing hard, then unclench my hands. Ink is smeared all over, blackening the fate lines carved deep into Lotus's palms. At the base of every finger is a callus. The ax isn't just light because Lotus is strong, I realize. She practiced wielding the weapon, just like I practiced my calligraphy. We both have skin that we thickened, day by day. Our calluses are just in different places.

But Lotus's skills are useless to me, and after another failed writing attempt, I throw down the brush. Someone grunts in their sleep.

Giving up, I join them.

‡ ‡ ‡

I don't care that Lotus's face still looks like a bruised squash come morning.

I seek Sikou Hai out in person.

He senses me coming for him and avoids me like the plague. At dinner, he'd rather excuse himself than catch my eye. Invited to tour Xin Gong's favorite courtyards, he'd rather plead unwell than spend a moment in my vicinity. Even at the outhouse, he'd rather hold his piss than walk past me.

He can't evade me forever.

The next night, I knock on his study's doors. They open— and start to close.

I jam in an arm.

After a few fraught seconds, Lotus's bones of steel triumph. Sikou Hai lets go of the door. "I've said this before." He stalks back into his study. "You're better off dealing with my brother."

"Your brother"—I turn him around by the shoulder and point to my face—"was a *great* help."

Sikou Hai flinches. His hand goes to his mask, adjusting it even though it never slipped. "Isn't that how the lot of you communicate?" He retreats behind his desk. "Your fists—"

My palms crack down onto the surface.

"—are your words." He eyes me haughtily. *See?*

So I just proved his point. What of it? He should know that I can do much more damage with my words. I could threaten to expose his treasonous underground meetings and force my way into them.

But I can't force my way into his respect. I release the desk. *Know your terrain*, my third mentor, the chess master, would say. My gaze trails over Sikou Hai's study—fastidiously organized— before landing on a scroll. It hangs between two tall windows, a bolt of plum-and-gold brocade backing a sheet of rice paper. On the paper—

Are my words.

Written under the tutelage of the poet.

Left behind after his death.

I reexamine Sikou Hai. His speech and his conduct resemble mine. He knows of Zephyr. He *admires* Zephyr. He wants to *be* Zephyr.

How, then, would I have earned my own respect?

Skies.

I wouldn't have.

"Can you go now?" Sikou asks when I continue staring at my poem. My words. My calligraphy, back when my strokes were dragonfly-leg delicate. My hands clench. Unclench.

Control yourself—

I leave the study, as requested, right after swiping everything off Sikou Hai's desk.

‡ ‡ ‡

"So ... you and Sikou Hai," says one of Lotus's friends at target practice.

My arrow hits a tree.

"Again, Lotus," says Tourmaline, stern but patient. It helps that I'm still injured. That, and I don't think Lotus was known for her archery, seeing as everyone avoided taking the targets nearest to me.

Cloud, meanwhile, is firing arrows like none other. She hits two bull's-eyes in a row. Tourmaline nods in approval and Cloud, too deliberately, ignores her. I can't believe I didn't notice her feelings before. "Any progress?" she asks me after Tourmaline passes.

"No," I grumble, stringing another arrow.

"I wouldn't think so, from the way you've been stalking him."

"I'm *not* stalking him."

A soldier titters to my right. "I heard he shit his pants the other day because you cornered him at the outhouse."

"He did not."

"But you admit to cornering him," says Cloud.

So much for being on my side.

"At least I'm making moves," I say loudly when Tourmaline laps around again.

Cloud goes lychee red. The others cackle.

"Focus," orders Tourmaline, and we hush. As we wait for Tourmaline to pass, Cloud mimes pointing her arrow at me. I do the same thing, and everyone around me shrieks and scatters.

My eye is too bruised to be rolling as much as it is. "I'm not *that* bad," I yell at the others, then swing my bow to the target, intending to demonstrate. A bee lands on my knuckles. I blink, and suddenly my arrow is across the field, caught in Tourmaline's fist.

Everyone stares at me, then Tourmaline.

Cheers erupt for the silver-armored warrior.

"Focus!" Tourmaline orders again, as if getting shot at by Lotus is a daily occurrence.

When target practice ends, Cloud won't even look at me. "I hate you," she mutters as we walk our equipment to the armory.

I hate myself too, Cloud. What warrior doesn't master archery? As I put away the damned bow, the bee buzzes by me again. I swat at it.

Be gentler with your elders.

That *voice.*

"What—" I cough to mask my slip. *What in the heavens are you doing here?*

I never left, thinks Dewdrop the Bee.

How?

Like I said, respect your elders, and I'll teach you.

But you're not allowed to interfere with mortal fate.

You aren't exactly a mortal, are you?

You—

"Stalking Sikou Hai or not, you'd better stop spending so much time by the outhouse," says Cloud, hanging up her quiver. "You're attracting flies."

Flies! Dewdrop cries. *Do mortals not have eyes?*

"Come on." Cloud slings an arm around my shoulders. All is forgiven, it seems, even though I did nothing to earn it. Uneasy, I let her guide me out of the armory. "I have something that you'll like more than archery."

Mmm . . . surprises, thinks Dewdrop as we go to the stables. *I don't think you'll like this one though.*

Stop distracting me.

But Dewdrop is right. The surprise is Rice Cake, mane braided, a garland of flowers around his ears. Two of Lotus's underlings stand at the stallion's side, grinning. I try to grin back. When an underling hands me the reins, Rice Cake nickers in protest. Others might think I'm Lotus, but her horse isn't so easily fooled, shying away from me when I reach for his nose. I get it. I wouldn't want to be touched by someone who stabbed me in the rear either.

Everyone is grinning now, waiting for me. With a gulp, I swing into the saddle and somehow actually land on Rice Cake's back. He startles, but I'm already urging him on, out of this cramped space where someone is bound to notice something amiss. Ignoring Cloud's "Slow down, Bobcat," I dig in my heels.

Rice Cake tears out of the stables like he's running for dear life. I hang on for mine as we fly past the camp gates, through the villages of the next prefecture, past a field of wheat. The road tapers, turns to dirt, rises. We're galloping up the basin side before I can redirect us. Pebbles spray off the narrow ledge. Something fuzzy lands on the nape of my neck, and I yelp, the reins slipping in my grip.

Stop trying to get me killed!

Dewdrop crawls under my collar. *My wings got tired.*

Gods. I'd shake my head if it weren't bouncing so violently, every impact quaking through my jaw. If Rice Cake thinks he can outrun me, he's wrong.

"We're stuck with each other now," I shout above the wailing wind. I jerk on the reins, and we slow from gallop to canter to trot. I clutch fistfuls of Rice Cake's mane to keep from tumbling off. As I wheeze, hooves clip from behind.

Cloud joins us. Her hair is tousled, her eyes bright. "Remember when we used to race?"

No, considering I can't seem to access any of Lotus's memories. "And I'd win," I hedge.

"*Rice Cake* would win." Cloud faces the land below us, and I wonder if she's thinking about how far we've come. All I can think of is how far we have yet to go.

"Remember when we swore ourselves?" I ask as we ride. This is hardly a memory private to Lotus. Everyone knows of how she, Ren, and Cloud met each other while enlisting to put down the Red Phoenix Rebellion. They swore sisterhood not long after.

"As if I could forget," says Cloud. "You got drunk on that peach liqueur and tried to kiss the tree."

I laugh as if it's funny. How mortifying.

"And then you went ahead and flogged that imperial inspector who slandered Ren." I take it back; I'd rather kiss ten trees. "I'll never forget the look on Ren's face when she found him stripped and tied to the horse post," says Cloud, laughing now too. "I bet she regretted swearing sisterhood with you then. But oaths cannot be broken." She throws her arms out at the open sky. "She's stuck with us forever."

"Forever," I echo. A word too big for this world, but one that I knew well, as a god. Making light of things was how I coped with my endless existence. In a way, I suppose I wasn't too different from Lotus. We both lived as if every day were our last. A delusion for me. A warrior's reality.

We ride down the basin, pass by the wheat field again, then under the town gate, into the prefecture's marketplace. I jerk on Rice Cake's reins to stop him from trampling an auntie. A wagon is overturned beside her, figs spilled onto the street.

I find myself dismounting before I know what to do. Cloud

goes to the woman, and I mimic her. By the time we right and fill her wagon, a small crowd has formed around us.

"Are you Ren's swornsisters?" ventures a carpenter.

"Yes," says Cloud—the last word either of us get to utter for a while.

"Heavens bless you and Ren!"

"She's a gift from the gods. Empress Xin Bao is so lucky to have her!"

"You'll let me know when she's looking to settle down, won't you?"

"Shut up, Lǎo Liao. Xin Ren would never marry you!"

"Will she bless our newborn? Will you?"

The crowd swells, a deluge. Floundering, I hear Cicada's voice. *The populace might support her, but most of her followers are uneducated farmers and unskilled laborers. You don't respect them.*

In stark contrast to me, Cloud is perfectly at home with the people, like a true sister of Ren's. She accepts their gifts— handmade charms, antiques that are about as useful to us as ox dung. She lifts a child up into her saddle and soon more children flock over for a chance to ride the beast. Some begin to sing.

> *"When Miasma does bad deeds,*
> *her enemies wee.*
> *Cicada drinks tea.*
> *Xin Gong says, 'No, please,'*
> *which makes Ren the lordess for me."*

Cloud laughs in delight. I tug on her arm. "Let's go. If this reaches Xin Gong—"

Shouts, up ahead. Another mob has formed. The children run to it.

"Let's see what's going on," says Cloud.

Let's not. But Cloud's already joined the herd, leaving me with no choice but to follow.

The same people who crowded around us just moments ago are now crowded around their new fascination. The ranks are too dense for me to see what it is, but their whispers reach me when I reach them.

He's from the North.

Says he's Miasma's strategist.

Nonsense. I don't believe it. I push my way through to the front. Then there's no denying it. It's him.

It's really him.

十八

OF A FEATHER

It's him.

Pale-faced, darked-haired Crow. I want to go to him. Touch him.

See if I only feel this haunted by his appearance because he's a ghost.

Your pulse is racing, Dewdrop observes as he's seized by Ren's people and shoved before Cloud. His knees hit the ground, but his gaze does not. He fixes Cloud with it, and I recall the night those same eyes arrested me, his suspicion slicing deep. *Why don't we start with the real reason why you're here?*

Now our places have switched, and it's he who answers to the enemy. "I'm here to pay my respects."

"Respects?" Cloud spits the word back at him. "Since when has the North respected us? Tie him up!"

Ropes go around Crow's arms and wrists. His hand is still bandaged, and my heart twists as he's yanked to his feet. "This isn't very in line with Master Shencius's codes."

Cloud stiffens, surprised. I'm hardly. Crow *would* know of

Cloud's favorite philosopher and use it against her. He's a strategist, through and through.

He *must* be here for a strategic reason.

"Neither was your ambush," hisses Cloud, recovering. "Blindfold him!"

Crow chuckles as a kerchief is pulled over his eyes. "Your strategist had one planned too."

What an interesting specimen of human.

Silence, I think furiously at both Dewdrop and Crow. Doesn't Crow realize he's in hostile ground? Thousands of lǐ from safety, with no backup in sight. He can be as vague as he wants about his true motives, but he has to give Cloud one good reason not to beat him up. But Crow doesn't offer one, and Cloud turns without a word and jerks him along.

We arrive at camp just in time for the noonday meal. Ren still hasn't returned from her meeting with Xin Gong. I pray that she's on her way. As much as Ren hates Miasma, it's not in her blood to beat the opposing strategist to a pulp. I can't say the same for the others, who abandon their food when they hear about our Northern catch. They amass around Crow, degrading everything from his intellect to his size. Crow is silent through it all. He's led before the stables; Cloud hands off his rope to two soldiers. "Don't be too gentle."

"Wait." I snatch the rope. "Lotus wants him."

Lotus *should* want to have a hand in Crow's brutalization, and no one stops me when I shove him into the stables. He tumbles into the hay, the doors shut, and for a moment, I might as well also be blindfolded, my heartbeat sounding like a gong in the too-intimate dark. Crow struggles back to his feet, and I swallow. We used to be close to the same height. Now I'm taller. Even when he stands, he looks small. Frail.

His tone, though, is as arch as ever. "Spare my legs, please. I still need to get back."

I shove him, and he falls again. "Who said anything about you getting back?"

He pushes upright. I wish he would stay down—it's easier to think when his face is at a distance. "Killing me really isn't prudent. Your lordess will agree with me when she returns."

"Then you'd better hope she returns quick." *Hurry, Ren.* The longer we're in here, the less of an excuse I'll have for leaving Crow unmarked. Outside, the others must be listening for his screams, or betting on how many bones I'll break.

Five, thinks Dewdrop unhelpfully. My palms moisten. I close them.

Compose yourself. I *died* because of the North. I recall the fire in my spine when the arrow hit, and the ice in my heart when I later learned that Crow never trusted me. I marry the sensations like notes in a chord, let the song of vengeance sweep down my arms and harden my fists—

"Can you hurry up?" interrupts Crow, shattering my focus. "I'm dying of—"

He breaks off, hacking into his left hand. The sound raises the hair on my arms, and my eye widens as he uncovers his mouth.

For a heartbeat, I can't feel. Can't think. All I see is red—glistening like a gem in his palm. "It's worsened."

"Pardon?"

"N-nothing." A warrior like Lotus wouldn't know the health status of a Northern strategist. She wouldn't even know his name.

Crow wipes his mouth clean. He rises. Approaches. I back up, foot crunching in the hay, giving away my location. He closes in as if he can see through the blindfold, cornering me against the wall. He reaches out and I stop him, grabbing him by the wrist like he once grabbed me.

I'm the one who could crush his bones if I so wished. But he's the one who pins me with four words.

"You said it's worsened." His voice is quiet, like we're sharing a secret. "What did you mean by that?"

"Nothing."

"Try again, General. Do you even know my name?"

He's got you, thinks Dewdrop.

He wishes. "It's Crow," I blurt. "Zephyr told me about you."

Crow winces. I really *am* crushing his wrist.

Before I can let go, the stable doors fly open. Light floods in, blinding me to everything but the shape of Ren.

"Release him, Lotus."

I stumble away, and Ren goes to Crow. "Are you hurt?"

"No, Lordess Xin."

"Your hand—" The blood, Ren means.

"Of my own doing," Crow assures her, tucking it into his sleeve.

Ren remains skeptical. She casts me a scolding glance; I duck my head, sheepish *and* indignant. At least I didn't whip him. "What brings you to the Westlands?" she asks Crow, and I bristle with the same need to know.

Crow bows. He takes his time doing it, and my anticipation grows as he remains half-bent. Even if his answer is a lie, it'll help me figure out what in the heavens Miasma has up her sleeve, sending her strategist all the way out here like a sacrificial boar—

"Your strategist." My lips part as Crow says again, to the ground, "I'm here to pay my respects to your strategist."

‡ ‡ ‡

Liar. Trickster. The gall of him, to use *me* as his excuse. Seething, I watch from behind a banyan tree as Crow steps into my shrine. Outside, Tourmaline stands guard by Ren's orders; evidently, our lordess didn't expect me to show the same restraint twice.

Minutes later, Crow steps out. I follow in secret when Tourmaline leads him out of camp and all the way to the eastern outskirts. There, a chute-like path, barely wide enough for a mule cart, cuts through cliffs that would otherwise be too steep to cross.

"Walk straight from here," Tourmaline orders, undoing Crow's blindfold. "Turn around, and we won't be so hospitable."

"I understand. Please pass my gratitude on to your lordess."

"Express it someday when it matters." Tourmaline extends her arm, inviting Crow onward. Her hawklike eyes track him over the first cliff. Once he's beyond that, she turns. I duck behind a chunk of sedimentary rock as she passes, wait for her footfalls to fade. Then I squeeze up the path myself.

It doesn't take long for me to reach Crow. I stop behind him as he walks on. My mouth opens—then shuts. My mind is scattered, my wrath lost like dandelion seeds to a gust.

Well, say something, thinks Dewdrop.

Like what?

Confess your feelings.

I have none to speak of.

Stubborn. At the very least tell him to stop.

I shouldn't.

Then why are you here?

To confront him. To make *him* confess. *Stop pretending*, I'd say. *How could you possibly be here for me?* Except it doesn't make sense to say any of this. Not as long as I'm Lotus.

Look, he's almost out of sight, thinks Dewdrop. *Speak, Zephyr. This is your last—*

"Stop!"

I don't know if that was intended for Dewdrop or Crow. I *do* know that I'm playing with fire, when Crow actually stops. With his back still toward me, he says, "I was just taking my leave."

I know. If I were really Lotus, I'd tell him to get out of my sight or else I'd peel his hide. I wouldn't ask, in a cracked whisper, "Why are you here?"

Crow doesn't answer.

"Turn around." I give the order, a direct contradiction to Tourmaline's. I want him to see me.

And he does turn around, but it's not me whom he sees.

He takes me in, the warrior I am, and I take him in. His cloak seems more overgrown than ever, his frame gaunter, his eyes darker. I didn't imagine it; he really does look more unwell. Like something died inside of him.

Or someone.

"I asked you a question." I wish I could ask more. "Why are you—why are you *really* here?"

I wish, for a wild, wild second, that he would say *because of you*.

But no matter what form I'm in, I'm still a strategist, as is Crow.

"I already explained to your lordess." His voice is flat. It's not the voice of someone who entered enemy territory just to burn some incense for a rival, and right before he turns back around, I catch a flash of something more in his gaze.

He goes, and I let him. I have to. He heads over a rise and past the scrub bushes, until the fog on the cliffs thickens and I can't see him anymore. But then all I *can* see is him. His lips, his nose, his eyes. The look of remorse he failed to hide.

I go back down the path, through the banyans. Crow journeyed across the realm for me. *For me. No*, I think. *He lied to you.* He told the truth to Miasma: *I never trusted her.* But he could have respected me enough to mourn me. No—there has to be a real reason he came. I step into the shrine, neither Zephyr nor Lotus, but a girl too curious for her own good.

There's nothing that Crow could possibly have gleaned from this place.

Then what did he do while in here?

The answer rests on the cushion in front of the altar. A fan that wasn't there before glows, iridescent, in the candlelight. I lift it by its bamboo handle, stroke the silky peacock feathers. I press it to my chest. The shrine bears down on me, as if it's collapsing. Dewdrop's silence rings loud. I can almost hear her voice in my head. Or maybe it's the voice of my regret.

You should have confessed your feelings to him.

A sound comes from behind me. Slowly, as if emerging from a dream, I turn to find Cloud.

She steps over the threshold. "Do you know who that was?" The question sounds rhetorical.

I answer anyway. "Miasma's strategist?"

"More."

"More?"

Cloud gestures for me. I rise, fan still in hand, while she reaches beneath her breastplate and draws out a piece of paper. It crackles as she unfolds it.

Oh dear, thinks Dewdrop, before I've even seen the words. Then I do. The shrine rushes into silence.

It's . . .

My.

Letter.

To.

Crow.

The heavens must hate me. A boxful of items recovered from Qilin's body, and Cloud just had to go ahead and confiscate *this* one. I reach for it, and Cloud's face darkens. Too late, I realize that Lotus may not have known how to read. Most of the population can't. There's no way to confirm the suspicion; I take the paper and squint at the characters. "The peacock sure scribbles," I force out, handing it back.

"Want to know what it says?"

"Yes."

Cloud clears her throat.

I wrote this letter by starlight, while the junk swayed on the river and everyone else slept. I bled my emotions into every stroke. The words, as innocent as they are, aren't meant to be spoken.

Now Cloud reads it out loud, and it's humiliating. When Cloud reads "I wanted to write to you" with dramatic emphasis, I want to burn to the ground. Then my face gets hot for another reason. I'm angry. At myself. I should have given Crow the letter. He traveled over two thousand li to deliver a parting gift.

I left him with nothing but ash.

Lotus isn't used to suppressing her emotions. The muscles in my face bunch as Cloud reads "I don't expect you to forgive me," and when she finishes with "May we meet in another life," my hands are balled tight.

Cloud crumples the letter. "Can you believe it? She had feelings for the enemy."

She knows. She has to. That's why she read this letter to me. To see me crack. To have me admit to taking over her swornsister's body. When she grips me by the arms, it's to shake my spirit out of it.

"Did you hear me, Lotus? Zephyr wasn't the friend you thought she was. She had a way of using words, of using *people*. She convinced the *enemy* to like her."

Lotus thought I was a friend?

Lotus. I'm still Lotus.

"She saved me, though," I croak.

"She handed all of you over!" Cloud roars. "And now she's warped your mind."

"She didn't," I say, even as I find support for Cloud's argument. I didn't pulverize Crow. I've been pursuing Sikou Hai, who is supposedly not my type. I'm *here*, in Zephyr's shrine. Even small details, like reaching for a letter I apparently can't read, can be construed as evidence.

I sweat in Cloud's fuming silence.

Finally, she releases me. "You're fine the way you are," she says, so sincerely that my throat aches. Even around my kindest mentors, I had something to prove. I deserved to exist in this world because I was more than an orphan. I was different. Skilled. A strategist. I was *needed*. This kind of unconditional acceptance is . . . a first.

But it's not meant for me, and I don't want it. "I know," I say, swallowing the pain in my throat. "Lotus doesn't need to be Zephyr."

"That's more like it," says Cloud, bumping me with her shoulder. "Heavens knows she kept too many secrets for her own good."

Her gaze drops to the fan in my hand. I'm still holding it to my chest like it's my most precious possession.

I snap it in two and toss the pieces.

‡ ‡ ‡

That night, I dream of him.

I dream of us.

We're on Miasma's junk—a setting I know. He wears his black robes. That's the way it is with dreams, I remember the poet telling me. Even the most fantastical are composed from things you've seen, heard, felt. The ensemble might be new, but the notes come from life. A repertoire of sensations, transposed.

And at first, the dream isn't so different from what I've lived. Crow and I sit across from each other, our zithers before us. We play, the song familiar though I can't name it. "Faster," I say, and Crow grins before complying. We race each other, our music galloping like stallions across a never-ending plain.

All of a sudden, the music stops.

Crow cradles his hand to his chest, wincing. I rise from my zither and go to him, crouching at his side. My heart seizes at the sight of the bandage around his fist. It's the first time I'm noticing it in this dream, but it's as if it's been there all along.

I draw his hand into mine and meet his gaze. He nods.

Unwinding his bandages, layer by layer, feels like baring myself. My heart pounds fast, faster when Crow places his other hand over my eyes. "Think twice before you look. It's unsightly."

"So it matches the rest of you."

"You wound me."

I remove his hand and meet him in the eye. "No worse than I already have."

I let the bandages fall.

It could be worse, I tell myself as my throat closes.

It could be worse.

Because this is a dream, the scar tissue isn't scar tissue at all, but new skin, baby pink. Smooth, when I brush a thumb over the gap between his fingers.

Cool on my lips, when I kiss it.

Everything seems to fall away. When I finally lift my gaze, it's just Crow, only Crow, his eyes as dark as the sky outside. I look into them and find myself reflected.

I'm Zephyr.

I look down at my hands. *My* hands. Skinny and pale, matching Crow's as he takes one into his. With his other hand, he brushes the hair from my face. I wasn't aware that it was down until now, flowing loose like it did on the night I took the antidote from his pocket.

"You never trusted me," I whisper, breath catching. "You never liked me."

I wait for Crow to pull back, but he remains, his eyes like bronze mirrors. "Must they be mutually exclusive?" he asks, a smirk on his lips. Then the smirk falls. "Who are you?"

"What?"

"Who are you?" demands Crow again, pulling away, but not before I see the face reflected in his eyes.

It's Lotus's.

十九

NO ONE'S SKY

Who are you?

I don't know. Not in these barracks, trapped in the breath of my dreams. I have to get away, from myself and the sleeping bodies of friends who aren't my friends, escape this place that feels less welcoming than Miasma's junk. There, at least, I knew who I was and what I wanted. I may have been a traitor in the eyes of the world, but I was true to my heart.

I run.

Rice Cake whinnies in dismay when I barge into the stables. I saddle him regardless. The doors swing shut behind us; I walk us out. At the gate, I mount and urge him into a gallop.

We soar through the night, whipping by the wheat field, up the basin side, past the place I rode with Cloud. The sky breaks out in stars as we rise, out of the fog. The land streams by like water.

"*Yuu.*" I slow Rice Cake down as we ride into a scrubplain. Trees, straggly at first, poke out of striped chunks of sedimentary rock. Ahead looms the Tianbian mountain range, a gate of limestone between North and West. But here, I'm neither North nor West. I'm in an in-between land. Neutral territory, according to empire cartographers, though I doubt bandit kings respect maps. I ought to stay on my guard, even as Lotus.

Reckless as always, thinks Dewdrop.

Perhaps. But I've come a long way from farting over the edge of the sky.

The undergrowth thickens. Conifers stretch tall. When the forestry grows too dense, I dismount and wrap Rice Cake's reins around a mulberry tree before proceeding on foot. The spicy scent of pine clears my mind. Wind rustles in the leaves. Water—a trickle from hidden streams—and the susurrus of music.

Zither.

I stop in my step.

The last real zither I heard was in the heavens. I turn, thinking I'll see the Masked Mother and her guard. *The sky*, Dewdrop suggests, and I glance to it. Every star is where it should be.

I haven't been detected yet.

Exhaling, I look down from the sky—and stiffen.

At first, it seems like a trick of light, a mirage of a huge lake, silver beyond the trees. I shoulder past the foliage. The lake remains, real. Stone formations rise out of the water like islands. I could almost mistake it for an inlet, except I know there are no oceans nearby. But it doesn't matter what I know, what I want, who I am. The sight is so otherworldly that it makes me forget my three identities. The music, though imperfectly played, finds its way into my heart, and something drips off my chin. Tears. I'm crying, for no good reason. This must be Lotus's doing.

The music stops just as I sniff, the sound going off like a fire-cracker in the silence.

"Need a handkerchief?"

I'm dreaming.

But his voice couldn't be any fresher in my head, and a part of me is not surprised when motion ripples from the banks—a distant Crow, his bulky, cloaked silhouette rising from a sitting position. Behind him is the zither.

Pebbles cluck as he nears. "No need to hide." He stops a dozen stride-lengths away. "I don't bite."

I have the opposite fear from my dream.

I fear that he'll recognize me as Zephyr by the moonlight.

But it's hard to look past appearances in reality. Even a strategist like Crow can't see me for who I truly am.

"How do you know I haven't been sent to kill you?" I ask, stepping forward from the trees, but still staying in a cone of shadow.

"That loud?"

"Hey!"

"If you really were an assassin," Crow goes on, "you would have killed me already." I step into the light, and his eyes narrow. "It's you."

I wait for him to say something else.

"It's a far way from camp."

I scowl. He speaks to me as if I'm a child.

"Here." Crow pulls out a handkerchief from his pockets and dangles it like a turnip. "It's clean." I snatch it. "Alone?" he asks as I wipe my eye, then my nose.

"Yes. Something wrong with that?"

"Just observing."

"You're alone too." I toss the handkerchief onto the ground, and Crow makes a sound. As if I was going to hand it back snot-drenched or—worse—tuck it into my breastplate like a keepsake. "Does your lordess know you're here?"

"Of course. Why do you ask?"

"Someone like you could have done with some guards."

"I'm stronger than I seem." I snort, and Crow smiles. "But I do have a group of guards waiting for me just fifty li over."

It's a small comfort, to know that Miasma didn't send Crow on a cross-country trek alone. "Why are you here, then?" I ask, gesturing at the lake.

"A person needs to sleep, right?"

"Sleep is for the weak."

I'm not prepared for Crow's laugh. It's crisp as frost, but also soft as a breath. "I suppose neither of us will know old age." He turns from me to face the lake. "I had a day to spare. Wanted to enjoy my first foray into the Westlands."

"Aren't you scared?" With his attitude, he'd sooner die from carelessness than consumption.

"No," says Crow.

"I could still kill you."

"I don't think you will."

"Oh really?" I crack my knuckles.

"You haven't already tried." He moves back to his zither and sits. "People are more predictable than they care to admit."

Unless you're a strategist. Then you're the least predictable of them all. No matter what Crow claims to be doing—paying Zephyr his respects or sightseeing—he has an ulterior motive. But even so, I don't feel like interrogating him, not when the tears on my face have barely dried.

"Besides," adds Crow, flicking a pebble into the lake, "your lordess is Xin Ren."

"Watch yourself."

"A compliment." He flicks another pebble; this one skips. "It would take a special kind of lordess to let someone go, then secretly kill them."

"Like yours," I say, and Crow chuckles. "Do you ever regret working for her?"

"No. Do you regret working for yours?"

"Why would I?"

"People change."

"You just said they were predictable."

I wish I'd made Crow laugh as Zephyr. "Fair enough, Lotus," he says, and I shouldn't be surprised he remembered my name. My heart shouldn't stumble when he pats the pebbles next to him. "Care to join?"

Yes. No. I don't know. His demeanor is so different from before, when he faced me on the path out of the Westlands.

"Ah. Right," says Crow when I don't reply. "We have to define our relationship tonight." My flush deepens, but then he says, "Does this lake belong to you?"

"No?"

"This sky?"

"No."

"They don't belong to me either. I believe that makes us pass-ersby."

Passersby. Not enemies. Not strategist and warrior.

Slowly, I sit beside him.

"My turn to ask a question." Ever the strategist, Crow. He could ask me why I followed him, earlier. He could ask why Zephyr told me about his consumption. He could ask me what I was doing, riding in the night, and I'd have to lie. *Because I dreamed of you.*

I wait, braced, as Crow gazes into my eye.

"Was it my music that moved you to tears, or something else?"

Or he could ask me to stroke his ego. "The music." I resist the urge to add, *I cried from how bad it was.*

I wait for Crow to puff up. Instead he's quiet. Perhaps he finds it strange that someone like Lotus can be touched by zither music. Does he share Sikou Hai's contempt for warriors, and would it be hypocritical of me to judge, if he does?

"Do you want to try?"

I blink. "What?"

"I sense a curiosity about you," says Crow. He nods at his zither. "I'll indulge it."

"N-no!"

"Is that fear I hear?"

"Why would I be scared of a piece of wood?"

"A piece of—" Crow coughs—and keeps on coughing. He turns away from me, a sleeve raised over his mouth. Concern has me leaning in, and he holds his other hand up in warning.

He doesn't know I'm a god, protected from his illness.

That doesn't mean you should engage in more intercourse, thinks Dewdrop.

Will you stop *using that term?*

What would you like me to use, if not the accurate term?

The accurate term is kissing. Nadir would know it. I glance to the sky, suddenly morose. I thought it'd be Nadir and not Dewdrop who would understand my need to return. *People are predictable. People change.* Both can be true, I muse, as Crow finally stops coughing. He goes to the lake bank, washes his hands, and my stomach turns, queasy with worry. Just how much worse has he gotten?

"My apologies," he says upon sitting beside me again. "As I was saying, before we were so rudely interrupted . . ." Crow gazes down at his zither, lashes lowered. "Do you believe in gods, Lotus?" He glances sidelong at me and interprets my startled expression as a no. "Legend has it that all the ancient zithers are blessed by them. They can make the qì of the player visible to the naked eye. But even if you don't believe, a zither is so much more than a piece of wood. It's a way for the like-minded to communicate." His voice lowers a notch, and I shiver at the reverence in it. "A way to hear another's truth."

I want to play. I want to play with every fiber of my being. But I also don't want to embarrass myself or the instrument. "Prove it, then," I say to Crow. "You play."

Crow presses a hand to his chest, as if wounded. "I'm no common musician. I don't play on demand." Oxshit. He did on the junk. "But I'll play if you play."

I shake my head. "There's only one zither."

"I think we'll both fit."

"I'm a warrior."

"Plucking a string can't be harder than picking up a sword."

"I don't know how."

I'd rather lie than be reminded of all that I've lost.

"Here." Before I can get another word out, the zither is placed in front of me. Behind me, Crow sits. His bandaged hand is on mine—*someone has butterflies—shut up!*—and with his left hand, he presses on the third string. We pluck, and to my astonishment, the air around the instrument *ripples*. It's qì. The zither's. Crow's. And mine. It rises like a stream of vapor, mingling with the other streams to form colors, lines, shapes in the air. Images mist above the strings: Crow, riding across the Central Plains with Miasma. Entering the court with Plum. And *us*.

Him and me, playing in that empire pavilion.

How strange, Crow had said, and I remember my frustration. Now I see what I couldn't for years. My playing was technically perfect, but my qì, sealed away with my godhood, couldn't interact with the zither. I couldn't pour my soul into the music the way Master Yao wanted.

My shock wearing off, I glance to Crow. His face is a mask, but the hand he has around mine is frozen. As the note fades, so does the image of us in the pavilion. He must think it came from him. But it could have just as well come from me.

I jerk my hand out of his before I unwittingly divulge more. "Told you I don't know how to play."

"You say." His voice is silken. "There's more to you than meets the eye, Lotus."

It's absurd, that I'm feeling jealous of *me*. "I didn't do anything. I played one note."

"One note . . ." Crow gestures at the air above the zither strings, still and dark once more. "Some strategists can't unlock the zither to converse with their playing partner at all."

He's referring to me. To Zephyr. I itch to defend myself. It's not *my* fault I had a divine seal on me.

Well, actually, it is—

"Zephyr was my friend," I blurt, cutting off Dewdrop and catching Crow off guard for a turn. A beat passes.

"She didn't strike me as the kind with friends," he finally says.

He'd be right, thinks Dewdrop.

Quiet! "What did she strike you as?"

"Ruthless and secretive."

That makes two of us. "But you still came to pay your respects."

The lake laps at the banks, sucking at the pebbles.

The silence grates on me. Grates on Lotus. Blood rushes to my head and I hear myself say, "She liked you," before I can stop myself. *What am I doing?* Strategy. It's for strategy. Somehow. "Say something. It's not as if she'll hear you. She's gone."

My heart pounds as Crow breathes in, slow. "Is she?"

"Well, she's certainly not *here*."

Crow smiles wearily. "Some people never leave."

The words sit between us.

A weight lifts off my chest.

Crow, for all his flaws, treats Lotus with respect. But he will never like me in this form—or any form for that matter—because Zephyr still lingers. My lungs feel bigger with my next breath.

At least you were a sincere flirt, I think as Crow picks up another pebble. He skips it over the lake. I lie back, face to the sky. Like the stars when I close my eye, I remain in this world. In some minds.

I'm out of sight, but not unseen.

"Thank you," Crow says, minutes or hours later. "For not breaking my legs."

You're welcome, I try to say, but Lotus's body betrays me yet again. It's dawn, when I blink awake.

I sit up. Something slips off my shoulders. Crow's cloak.

A gentleman, thinks Dewdrop as I lift it. I remember the blood crusting the feathers, the last time I touched it. I remember more: his amorphous figure atop that horse the night we met. How I barely recognized him cloakless in the gallery, his body so close. My cheeks warm.

I don't know when our paths will cross next. If I'll be able to give the cloak back to him. I hold on to it for a moment longer, then throw it onto the rocks. Ratty thing. I'd much prefer if he'd left his zither.

He took it with him, of course. An indentation in the pebbles is all that remains. The hollowness echoes through me. Maybe it's better this way. From plucking that one note, I could already tell that my music won't sound the same.

But in this era of war, we're bound to lose things. Crow didn't let his changed hands hold him back. I don't have to either. I can play as Lotus and Zephyr. Under no one's sky, I am both and neither.

If only Sikou Hai could see me in such a light.

Wait.

I could *make* him see.

I plunge into the trees—return and grab Crow's cloak—plunge again and untether Rice Cake. We race back to camp, the land flying by. It's only later that I realize I'm riding with more ease than I ever have in my life.

‡ ‡ ‡

I wait until night, bumbling through combat training, enduring dinner with Ren, Xin Gong, and Cloud in Xin City. Usually, mealtime conversation with the Westlands governor revolves around his own nonaccomplishments, but tonight, Xin Gong is quiet. He picks up and sets down his chopsticks three times. He's heard the children's songs in the streets, I'm thinking, when he says, "My guards tell me a Northern spy was caught yesterday."

Strategist, I'd correct, but Ren isn't as contrary. "He came to visit my late strategist's shrine," she says.

"And you let him?"

"We took all the necessary precautions. General Tourmaline herself saw him out. I assure you that he acquired nothing that would be of use to his lordess."

"But you set him free."

Beside me, Cloud's lips part—and shut as Ren tugs on her earlobe. Smart of our lordess. Across from us sits Sikou Dun, and behind Xin Gong stands his personal guard. At the end of the day, we are only guests, here on Xin Gong's terms. Until I can convince Ren to take over the governor's seat, all we can do is listen to Xin Gong as he says, "It's a risk to host you and your troops, Ren. Should the empire sweep down, my neck is on the same chopping block as yours."

He finally emerges, the man who didn't have the courage to support us before our victory against Miasma.

"I understand," says Ren, her voice betraying no emotion. "If we ever become too much of a burden, then just say the word and we'll be out of your hair."

"No," says Xin Gong immediately. "That's ridiculous. Where would you go?"

"Anywhere." Ren's smile is graceful. "We're not picky. How can we be? For the last few years, we've lived off the backs of our horses."

Cloud *hmph*s in approval, but the rest of the table tenses—and jumps when Sikou Dun's goblet slams down.

"Be grateful, or be homeless." His face is still bruised. Rumor is he told Xin Gong that he fell into a ditch. Couldn't let his ego take a beating too.

"Sikou Dun," admonishes Xin Gong, as if rehearsed.

Sikou Hai is quiet through the performance. He leaves as soon as dinner is over, and I follow, knowing that Cloud won't. Once I'm out of her sight, I detour to my shrine and fetch my zither, bundling the instrument and strapping it around my back. I make for Sikou Hai's.

He's at his desk when I barrel in. Unlike Crow's, his state of half-dress doesn't affect me. I'm on a mission and nothing can stop me, not even Sikou Hai's white under-robes.

"Put on a cloak," I order as he bolts back in his chair, still masked.

"Falling empires. Have you any propriety?"

"You've one minute. Put on some extra layers, or come the way you are. And bring your zither."

"I don't take orders from you," Sikou Hai snaps.

"Fine by me." I stride over and lift him by the armpits. I could get used to this.

"Wait!" He wiggles out of my grasp. "What is this about?"

I unwrap my zither in reply.

Sikou Hai's eyes widen as he reads the inscription running down the fingerboard's side.

When the lotus leaves are no longer standing
And the chrysanthemum stalks are two frosts from bending
Be sure to remember this year's best time and scene
When the oranges turned yellow and the tangerines glowed green

The poet wrote these lines. The zither is Master Yao's. If Sikou Hai is as devout an admirer of me as I think he is, he must know that I was the disciple of both.

Sure enough, his eyes rise to me. "Is this . . . the Rising Zephyr's?"

"It is."

He reaches for the instrument. I let him touch a single string before wrapping the zither back up. "Bring yours," I repeat. "I'll allow you to play if you follow me."

Shaking his head, as if he can't quite believe what he's doing, Sikou Hai goes to the back of the room and opens a bureau. He returns with his zither, wrapped in silk. "Where exactly are we going?"

"I'll show you."

Moments later, I'm plopping Sikou Hai onto Rice Cake.

"Th-this is improper!" he shouts as I swing myself into the saddle behind him.

I'm not thrilled with the seating arrangement either. "You're going to want to hold on."

By the time we reach Crow's lake, my arm is numb.

"We're here," I say, prying Sikou Hai off.

He doesn't respond. Doesn't even object when I lift him and set him to his feet. The silence makes me wary, and instinct has me stepping back just as he doubles over and retches.

"You—you—" His words are garbled and I feel a burst of sympathy—of *empathy*—before he spits out the rest of his words with a dribble of vomit. "You *animal.*"

Animal or not, I keep my promises. I unwrap my zither and set it on the pebbles. Nothing cures a strategist quite like their favorite obsession, and since Zephyr is Sikou Hai's, he pulls himself together and takes a seat behind it. I sit down myself behind his zither, and his gaze flashes up.

"What are you doing?" he demands, as if I'm stripping naked.

"Accompanying you. Don't think I know how?"

His brow spasms. "You'll break it."

"I won't." I hope. While my spirit is more aligned with the music now, playing is also a mechanical endeavor. I may have retained my knowledge of technique, but will it transfer through these fingers? Or will the music be butchered, like my calligraphy?

There's only one way to find out. "Go on," I say to Sikou Hai before I can overthink it. "Start."

He sucks on his teeth, reluctant. "Subject?"

I regard him under the moonlight. He might be masked, but I intend to change that. "You."

Sniffing, Sikou Hai spreads his hands. I can already guess his selection before he strums the first string. A song without a melody, designed to highlight a player's technical prowess.

But music speaks what the heart cannot. The tighter Sikou Hai's refinement, the more I hear his lack of control. He plays no melody because he has none. His song is not a statement, but a contradiction. His soul is shadowed—by a person.

You're better off dealing with my brother.

Your fists are your words.

An animosity simmers beneath his notes, spiking when I play a sloppy chord. Sikou Hai sharpens his technique. Correcting. Overcorrecting. I play another chord, and Sikou Hai silences his strings. "What—"

My right hand plucks out his tune. My left maintains the chords. One chases the other apart, like two identities existing categorically. Strong or weak. Them or me. Orphan or *somebody*. I wouldn't have a place in the world if not for my role as a strategist, so I embraced it, conformed to the identity rather than bend any part of it.

I didn't want to break how I was perceived.

Twang. I resurface from the music. Beneath my hands, the intact strings vibrate, emitting the final ghosts of notes. The broken string curls like a frond of fern.

I brace myself for Sikou Hai's rage.

Instead I'm met with silence.

Then, like the string, he snaps. "Who taught you?"

No images formed in the air when I was playing, because Sikou Hai wasn't playing with me. *Two are needed*, I note to myself. But even though Sikou Hai couldn't see my qì, he clearly heard my skill. He didn't think I had it in me, as a warrior.

He can puzzle out my backstory on his own. Tonight, I'm here for his.

"Play," I order, then find the complementary notes on my remaining strings. I weave my song through his, playing the harmony to his melody. The air between our zithers ripples. The music reacts to our qì. The tapestry of sound becomes a misty image that I can see: two boys. One smaller, one bigger, raised during a famine. By candlelight, a thin man and woman come to a difficult decision. The bigger boy grows stronger with every extra scrap placed into his bowl. The smaller boy grows weaker without. Four winters later, he falls to fever first. But the pox doesn't discriminate, and the bigger boy ails next. Again, by candlelight, the man and woman whisper—choose—they've always had to—one or the other—one scrap—one cure—two children—one chance—which is better spent—

The music cuts off. Staggering to his feet, Sikou Hai backs away from the instrument. His face is blotchy, his breath ragged. For a heartbeat, I see myself. I chose to be a strategist, but truthfully, could I have been anything else? I got to pick Qilin's body no more than Sikou Hai got to pick his.

I want to say *I understand.*

But I'm here for Ren. And as much as I have changed, I'm still me. I have bent, but I have not broken. Sikou Hai is just a piece in my plans.

"We may be different," I say to him, also rising. "But we share a goal. I want to give Ren the kingdom she deserves." I pause meaningfully. "You do too."

I'm at least a head taller. To meet my eye, Sikou Hai has to look up. In stature, I must remind him of his brother.

But tonight, I'm not just a warrior. I'm the zitherist accomplished enough to unlock his soul.

"Tomorrow," he says at last. "Meet me by the banyan at the dusking hour."

二十

CORPSE AND SOUL

Meet me by the banyan at the dusking hour.

For the first time since becoming Lotus, I wear white. The color no longer suits me, but it's still mine.

Short of the fig trees where Sikou Hai and I are to meet, I'm stopped by the sight of Ren.

She stands in a field just off the path, her gray robes blending in with the surrounding rocks, which aren't rocks at all, I realize when I approach, but graves. The field is a cemetery. The headstones all belong to members of the Xin clan. Ren is staring at someone by the name of Xin Dan.

I join her side. "Who is that?"

"I don't know," murmurs Ren. "A stranger. But this stone . . . it should be my mother's."

My mother's. I know of Ren's mother: a physician who came of age on the eve of Empress Chan's assassination. Her peers went on to serve the warlords of their hometowns as the unrest crested under Xin Bao's reign, but Ren's mother left the Westlands and wandered from North to South, treating hundreds across the realm before getting caught in the typhoid epidemic in year 401 of Xin.

I know that Ren doesn't like speaking of her.

But then Ren asks, "What do you think, Lotus?" and I remember that what I know as Zephyr may no longer be true. "Would she be proud or disappointed in the calling I've chosen?"

"Proud." The word feels right for a swornsister. "You're a leader."

"A warlordess."

"You're waging a righteous war on behalf of our empress."

Ren's mouth twitches at the word *righteous*. Her fingers rise and close around her pendant. If I could feel her qì, I imagine it'd be tumultuous. The Ren I knew shared her doubts in careful quantities, diluted with self-deprecation. Clearly, she's more vulnerable around Lotus. I sense the sadness I've always felt to be there, but also an anger.

If only I could use it. "Do you blame Xin Gong?"

It's a far shot. Xin Gong may have been the brother to Ren's mother, but even he can't be blamed for a typhoid epidemic.

"Yes," Ren says, to my shock. "How could I not? He drove her out."

The pieces on the board change.

Driven out. This is news. Her mother didn't leave by her own volition. She died far away from her childhood home, a place that she had every right to return to. And Ren blames Xin Gong. It's the motive I've been searching for. A way to convince her to take over.

But before I can, Ren continues, "It's because I blame him

that I'll show him he was wrong. On his deathbed, he will realize he banished my mother for a sham of a prophecy." Ren turns to me, eyes flashing. "I will never, ever betray a clansman."

The board changes again. Another new piece. A prophecy that involves betraying a clansman.

Ren never told me. To be fair, I wouldn't have cared to know, as a strategist. Superstition doesn't impact my stratagems.

But it impacts Ren.

She can't fight fate, Dewdrop later says, when I at last have to leave Ren for my meeting with Sikou Hai. *She's bound to it like any mortal. Do you see why she's the weakest now? Do you regret your choice?*

At first, I don't answer. I glance back and see Ren standing among the graves. She may be mortal, but I'm not. What sort of god am I, if I can't punish the people who mistreat her? Lotus did exactly that. She wasn't afraid of breaking the rules or suffering the retribution incurred by doing so. She was reckless.

She was brave.

‡ ‡ ‡

"You're late," snaps Sikou Hai. "Put this on." He shoves a cloak at me, then draws out a ceramic mask glazed black, red, and white. "And this later, before we see the others."

I take the mask and feign ignorance. "What others?"

"There are more who support Ren."

We walk. The aroma of caramelized boar smokes the air, wafting from the distant mess halls. Everyone is distracted by dinner. Sikou Hai picked a good time for sneaking around.

Still, my nerves hum. As he leads us out of the town and to the basin side, where we duck under a shelf of rock and into a cave, I think about the audience I'm about to meet and the first impression I'll have to make. It would be so much easier if I could introduce myself as Zephyr.

Too soon, the stairs are bottoming out. Before a set of doors, I put on my mask. We enter, and the people at the table rise. Most are disguised like me. Some show their faces. All sit when Sikou Hai sits—with the exception of one.

"Who's this?" they ask, voice suspicious.

"Our newest member," says Sikou Hai. In this earth-packed room, his authority is absolute. "Sit, Bracken," he orders, and eventually Bracken does. I take my place between two cloaked figures masked as grasshoppers. "Who else has something to say?"

Silence.

"Then we may begin." Sikou Hai spreads his hands upon the table like it's his personal zither. "I've made contact with Xin Ren."

The silence takes on an anticipatory edge.

"And it hasn't been successful."

"So what now, then?" The speaker's voice is strong and proud, matching their tiger mask.

"We persist," says Bracken.

I say, "We go on without her."

Bracken turns to me. "And act in her name?"

"Yes."

"Why?" This time, it's Sikou Hai who speaks.

I meet his gaze across the table. "Because she'll never agree."

"Don't you have a means of persuading her?"

He's thinking of how I persuaded him. But the situations are incomparable. Sikou Hai is a strategist at his core. I drilled past his prejudice, but I didn't *change* him. Ren's honor runs too deep. It's all she had to hold on to when the world doubted her, when a prophecy maligned her.

I won't take it away from her. Ren can stay in the right; I'll commit the wrong for her, just like Lotus did when she whipped that inspector. "We can't afford to wait," I say.

"Why?" asks Bracken. "We have no shortage of time."

These people have never felt the empire breathing down their necks, living in a natural fortress as they have.

"The Westlands do not exist in a bubble. Outside events will still have calamitous effects." I stand, fingers twitching for my fan. The closest thing to it is a brush on the table. I grab it by the handle and point the bristles north. "How long has it been since the Battle of the Scarp? Six weeks?"

It's actually been seven. I wait for someone to correct me, and am pleased when Tiger-Mask does. Attention to detail is an underrated skill.

"Miasma will have regrouped," I continue. "Her retaliation campaign will launch any day now. And seven weeks since the battle also marks seven weeks since we arrived. Unless Xin Gong is living under a rock, he'll have seen the people's affection for Ren. He's on the verge of making a move."

"He wouldn't," says Sikou Hai, confident. "In the face of previous adversities, he never did anything to strengthen his position."

"A fire next door is more pressing than an earthquake ten lĭ away. To your father, Ren poses a greater threat than the empire and Fen pirates combined. He will betray us, mark my words."

I speak with assurance. I hide my unease. For seventeen years now, Xin Gong has barred Ren from the Westlands, all in apparent fear that she'll betray him per some prophecy. But the situation has changed. Ren has Cicada. She challenged Miasma. From Xin Gong's perspective, Ren may still betray him—when she is too powerful to touch. So he lent us troops, lured us into his lair. He must intend to neutralize us soon. What eludes me is *how*? Kill Ren or hand her to Miasma, and he'll lose the popular support.

What exactly does Xin Gong have planned?

Hesitate too long, and I'll lose my audience. I point the brush back north. "If we delay in raising Ren, our operation risks overlapping with Miasma's march." Downward goes the brush, to the southwest. "The sooner we complete the transition of power, the sooner the people will stand behind their new governor and unify against enemy forces. We must act now."

The room is quiet when I lower the brush.

Maybe I overstepped. I was invited to attend Sikou Hai's meeting, not commandeer it.

But then Sikou Hai turns to Tiger-Mask. "How prepared are the soldiers?"

"Trained and ready."

"And the decree to the people?"

"All set to go," says the grasshopper to my left.

Sikou Hai faces me. "How soon is 'now'?"

"As soon as an occasion arises. Do you have one in mind?"

280 : JOAN HE

Sikou Hai's gaze lowers in thought. "Xin Gong's fortieth birthday banquet." He looks up, eyes ablaze. "Soldiers will be present for the sake of ceremony. Ours will have no trouble blending in. And given the venue, most will be inebriated. Figuratively and literally, Xin Gong's guard will be down."

Brilliant—and brutal, when I remind myself that Sikou Hai is Xin Gong's adopted son. "What fate do you have in mind for your lord?" *And why are you so determined to help Ren?*

Sikou Hai rises from his seat. "Things will be chaotic," he murmurs, circling the table. Torchlight illuminates the masked half of his face, casting the rest in shadow. "In the melee, lords are not so different from guards." He stops at the opposite end from me. "Anyone can be struck down."

His voice has risen to address us all, but his gaze targets me. It dares me to pass judgment. I'm a warrior; I'm supposed to prefer stabbing people from the front.

He doesn't see the strategist who proudly wore the crown of a defector, who left Crow to burn.

If Sikou Hai is set on supporting Ren, he must be prepared to end his adoptive father. Likewise, the people in this room must be prepared to betray their lord. There can't be two leaders in a land, just as there can't be two suns in the sky. We all recognize that.

But this coup jeopardizes Ren's honor. She deserves legitimacy in legacy. A trustworthy name.

She can't be tainted, not when there's a prophecy at play.

"A new era begins with us!" I interrupt the discussion of logistics, tearing off my mask.

The cries of recognition are immediate. "General Lotus!"

Sikou Hai looks too peeved to speak.

"Warriors make history." I rip my broadbelt free. "Literati write it." I spread the white fabric out on the table. "But tonight, we can be both."

I bite my forefinger until blood rolls, then write our mission at the top of the broadbelt in red. Below, I draw out the strokes of Lotus's name. My calligraphy comes out better than expected without a brush to negotiate. "Who dares to bleed with me?"

"I dare." Tiger-Mask is the next to unmask. Another name goes down in blood.

"This is too risky," the grasshopper to my right protests.

"Only if you think we'll fail," says the grasshopper to my left. They take off their mask, and I stare.

Tourmaline. She puts down her name as well. Others line up after her, until Sikou Hai is the only one left. I pass him the brush; he knocks it aside and adds his name in blood like the rest of us. He seems confused when he finishes, as if he can't quite believe he did something so bold and fearless. I can. I see someone smart, with the potential to become dangerous. I nominate him to safekeep the belt of names, and his confusion mounts. I conceived the idea; I should be hungering for the credit.

Little does he know I'm not being generous.

As the others leave, staggering their departures, I pull him aside. "Best to steer clear of Ren in the coming days."

Sikou Hai tugs his sleeve free. "I have common sense." His disdain doesn't reach his eyes. He looks at me as if seeing me as an equal—and perhaps a threat.

He's two steps slower than Crow, who was wary from the

very start. Like knives, we honed each other whenever our minds crossed.

I miss it.

But I'll have to learn to live without it, just like I'm learning to live without my reputation and sobriquet.

I made it through my first meeting as Lotus, I think as Sikou Hai and I leave last. And it wasn't a disaster. My words combined with Lotus's heart made us impossible to ignore. People heard us.

"Wait here," says Sikou Hai as we come to a footpath sheltered under an overhang. Below the cliffs, the nearest town is a glowing square that I could cover with my hand. "Allow five minutes."

His head disappears beneath the sloping rocks, and I start to count. After three minutes, I tilt my face upward. The sky is black, fog veiling the stars. No extra ones have appeared, but I can't shake the sense that time is running out.

Lowering my head, I sigh—right into another's hand.

The hand claps tight, muffling my scream. My arms are pinned, my legs barred behind a hooked leg. With a twist, I'm spun around, brought face-to-face with my attacker.

Twice in one night, Tourmaline has stunned me.

Her hand drops from my mouth.

The Tourmaline I know doesn't go around ambushing people. Nor does she struggle for words.

"Zephyr?" she finally chokes out.

She couldn't—how could she—how could she *know*?

She doesn't. Zephyr doesn't have to be a name. It could refer to this breeze that is picking up. Clouds move. Fog thins.

Starlight hits the plane of Tourmaline's forehead, her eyes left in shadow under her browbone.

"The brush." She approaches. "You held it just like you held your fan. The words. You spoke—"

—like Zephyr. I thought I was addressing a room of strangers. I wasn't careful.

I fall back as Tourmaline closes in, lurch as a soft bit of stone crumbles out from under my foot. "What are you talking about? How could I be Zephyr?"

"I don't know," says Tourmaline. "I don't know how. I don't know why I can't believe what I see. I don't know what to ask."

Then don't ask anything.

"Are you who I think you are?"

I am a resurrected corpse.

"Tell me."

I am a transplanted soul.

"Are you Zephyr?"

I am—I am—

"I am."

It escapes me as half a gasp. Two words, to which I have no idea how Tourmaline will react. This is more than reincarnation. I've essentially told her that the person before her eyes is dead and the dead person is alive.

"The leaves," Tourmaline finally breathes. "What kind of leaves did you tell me to feed to the horses?"

I have a basin at my back, a steep drop at my feet. By all means, I should feel trapped.

Instead, I am free. "Yew."

When Tourmaline's arms first go around me, I hasten to do the same. It's the only way to pass as Lotus, who receives at least a dozen tackle hugs and shoulder bumps a day.

But then I hug Tourmaline back because I want to. There is no hidden agenda, like when I embraced Crow. And this isn't goodbye.

This is hello.

‡ ‡ ‡

Where to even begin?

"Start from after the ambush," says Tourmaline. We're sitting on a hill of shale overlooking the eastern Marshlands; below us, the Mica River carves past like a moat. The seclusion is a breath of fresh air. Earlier, at lunch, Xin Gong invited Ren to his quarterly hunt, and Sikou Dun went on and on about all the deer he was going to kill. Being here with Tourmaline feels healing.

I tell the silver-armored warrior about my home in the heavens, my sisters. The sentence I served as a mortal, how it ended, and how I want to help Ren before I'm detected. She listens with a deathly straight face. I scrunch mine when I'm finished.

"Do you believe any of that?"

"I have to," says Tourmaline solemnly. "You're right here."

"Even the god bit?"

"I always thought you were a god."

"Because I was insufferable?"

"Because I had no idea how you survived every accident." Then Tourmaline smiles—a first. Her smile dims when I ask her how she ended up in Sikou Hai's meetings. "After you . . ."

"Died," I supply. Because I did die. Somewhere out there, there's a mortal body rotting in the dirt.

A blade of sun reflects up from the marsh below, and Tourmaline squints. "You left behind all your unfinished plans. The visions you had for Ren. It opened up this . . ." She gestures with her hands. "Hole in the camp. When Ren refused to find a new strategist . . ."

"You tried to fill it."

Tourmaline recognized Sikou Hai as a key player of the Westlands. She worked her way into his circle of trust just as I would have done. I'm humbled and impressed.

But Tourmaline's eyes flicker down. "I shouldn't have tried to replace you."

"You were right to." She meets my gaze and I hold it. We've always had things in common. It's just taken this long for me to realize it, to see ourselves as more than our roles in Ren's camp. "I couldn't have asked for a better replacement."

† † †

"You've been friendly with Tourmaline lately," says Cloud as we wind down for bed.

With a wince, I pry off my laminar. "Trying to make moves for you."

I wait for a rebuke or a scowl, but Cloud turns over in her bedroll without a word. She's asleep in minutes.

An hour later, I'm the only wakeful person in the room.

Everyone around me is still as a log. I'm a kayak stranded in their midst. I've trained with these people. Laughed and dined as friends. But while I've grown to know them, they only see Lotus. They don't know me. Not like Tourmaline.

They'll reject me if I show them who I really am.

I plunge outside, into the stables. Rice Cake makes no sound as I saddle him. I stop us by my shrine to pick up my zither.

We ride.

Out of the town, over the basin, into the trees, until we reach Crow's lake. I pull out my zither. I play.

The next day, I do it all over again. Combat training at noon. Coup meeting at dusk. Zither playing at midnight. Even without a partner, it's enough, just to play. The music allows me to be whoever I want to be under the stars, so that under the sun, I am a better Lotus.

‡ ‡ ‡

My mind is sharp when I go into my third meeting, three days from Xin Gong's birthday ceremony.

The logistics of coup have been hammered out. But Sikou Hai is pondering something; I know from the way he cradles his mask.

Finally, he rises from his seat. "We should enlist aid from the South. Let me explain," he says as people mutter. Seems like Cicada isn't popular out West. "With our existing numbers, we can guarantee a smooth transition of power for Ren in Xin City. But we shouldn't overextend. It would benefit us to utilize Southern troops in prefectures out east and by the Marshlands, where the predominant dialects and customs are Southern. Besides, Ren and Cicada already have an alliance. It ought to be strengthened."

Sikou Hai sits back down, and the room erupts in debate. I keep silent, rising only after everyone has voiced their opinion.

"We can't rely on the South, not before we've paid them back for their help at the Battle of the Scarp."

"But—"

"Lordesses are like wolves," I cut over Bracken. "You can invite them to wars, but not to feasts. The last thing we want is for Cicada to gain an appetite for the Westlands."

I'm already worried about the appetite she's gained for the Marshlands, a buffer zone we can't afford to lose.

"So no help from the South," says Tiger-Mask.

"Absolutely not," I say, well aware of the nods going around. Sikou Hai is too. Our dynamic has shifted. Concerning to him, but not to me. As we leave the meeting, all I can think is this:

I could have stayed silent.

Let everyone agree on enlisting Cicada's help.

It would have brought Ku closer to me.

She's not even your real sister, thinks Dewdrop.

I know, but as Lotus, I dream of her more than ever. Yesterday, I dreamed of meeting Ku and Crow on a boat. Ku caught dragonflies and showed them to me in her cupped palms as Crow rowed.

Tonight, it's just Crow. "This was the moment that I knew." His oars dip into the water. "As you made the heavens rain arrows, I realized that the two of us could not coexist in this world."

Fog rises around us like steam. There's too much of it to tell if we're on a river or a lake.

Too much silence.

I break it. "You'll never be rid of me."

Crow smiles. "Who's to say you won't rid yourself of me?"

The oars slip free and sink under.

Crow clutches his chest, and I—I'm stone. Cold and inhuman. *I was right*, I think as his hand falls. His black robes don't show blood. The arrowhead does. It's crimson, just like the trickle at the corner of his mouth. He slumps against the boat, and the force chaining me breaks. I'm at his side; I'm holding him by the shoulders; my voice is ugly, weak, panicked:

"Stay with me, Crow. *Stay with me.*"

I try to stop the bleeding but I can't touch him. It's like I'm a spirit again, and when Crow stares up at me, only the clouds and sky swim in his eyes.

His final words are still in my head when I wake, soaked in sweat.

Play that song, at my funeral.

I clench my face in my hands.

He's not dead.

Not dead.

Not dead, Dewdrop confirms, and I shake—first with relief, then with rage. I storm out of the barracks and ride to the lake. I play the damned song, over and over again, as if he might hear and regret requesting it. But eventually, my rage cools, and I shiver. Even if I'm not mortal, everyone around me is. So fragile. *I'm* fragile, if I'm this rattled by a dream. I play louder. Faster, as if every note could be my last—

Crack.

HUNT

C*rack.*

My gaze snaps over my shoulder and lands on the branch, before rising to the person who broke it.

Blue cloak, dark braid, broad shoulders.

Cloud.

I scramble up from my zither, but there's nowhere to go, and the damage is done. It's written all over Cloud's expression. She knows. How much, I'm not sure. But at the very least:

"You're . . . not Lotus." Her voice oscillates, dropping in pitch before swinging up. "Who the hell are you?"

"Cloud, I can explain—"

"Don't come any closer."

My feet still. The world quiets, as if it's listening to our exchange.

Then the sounds bleed in: water, wind, the wheeze of Cloud's breathing.

"I didn't want to believe it." The cords in her neck tense.

"I didn't know *what* to believe." Her fists ball, but she doesn't attack. My panic wanes. Can this be salvaged?

Depends. Is this the first time she's followed me, or one of many? I try to discern by her next words, but her voice is too jagged.

"You didn't say the right things. You acted strange. That fight—you shouldn't have lost it."

I know, I want to say. I almost do when Cloud's eyes well with tears.

"Then at night, you were heading out without telling me. Lotus never keeps secrets. I should have realized it then. But I didn't. I didn't suspect a thing."

"Yet you followed me."

"Because I wanted to know where you were going." Cloud scrubs at her eyes, the whites red. "Do you know how far out this place is? How many li you have to ride to come out here and back? But I didn't think anything of it as I rode. I didn't think you'd come this far because you had something to hide. I thought..." She chokes up. "I thought..."

It doesn't matter what she thought. The moment she heard the music, she'd have known. Lotus would never play the zither.

My hope of mitigating the damage crumples with Cloud's face. She advances. I retreat. "Give her back," she growls, and my heel hits the water. "*Give her back.*"

The lake closes over my ankles, its grip icy cold. "I can't."

To anyone who doesn't believe in the supernatural, Cloud sounds deranged. I could capitalize on that. But when Cloud doesn't move, I say louder, clearer, "I can't. Lotus isn't here any-more."

I don't know why I just admitted that.

"Then where is she?"

"She's dead, Cloud." Or this.

Cloud shakes her head. "You—her body—"

"Is just a body. Her soul is gone. It's not coming back."

"Who are you to say any of this?" Cloud looks from me to my zither. Her fury rekindles.

"Who are you?" Waves lap at my calves as Cloud strides into the water, fracturing the mirrored stars. "*Who are you?*"

I hold my ground—my silence too. It's one thing to hear someone else say my sobriquet, another to say it myself. But when Cloud is close enough to throttle me, my choice evapo-rates. Lotus was her swornsister.

I owe her the truth.

"I'm the other person who died that day," I say, and Cloud freezes in the water. The lake becomes a mirror once more, reflecting both our faces. "I'm Zephyr."

The stars glitter on the obsidian surface. Not one celestial body less, not one more. The Masked Mother doesn't know I'm here, but the Masked Mother was never my only foe. Cloud won't forgive me for using her swornsister's body. She'll kill me. I should defend myself.

And I can. I wait. Wait for her rage. Rage is emotion, and emotion can be manipulated.

I'm still waiting when Cloud turns.

She sloshes back to the bank.

She unties Rice Cake.

She leads him away.

‡ ‡ ‡

It takes me all night and all day to get back to camp on foot. By the time I stumble past the gates, I'm parched and dizzy from lack of sleep.

"Lotus!" Someone ducks under my arm to support me, and in a second of wish fulfillment, I think it's Cloud. Last night didn't happen. I hallucinated it.

But my helper is one of Lotus's underlings. "What's wrong?" she asks.

Everything. "Water," I croak.

We hobble to a well; Ren's soldiers flock around. The air thickens, odorous.

"Give her space," orders the underling. A bucket is drawn up and put into my hands. I drink until my stomach threatens to rebel, toss the rest onto my face. I need to be alert.

I need to think.

From the concern I'm receiving, I infer that Cloud hasn't said anything—yet. It's just a matter of time before she does. Even if people don't believe her, the seed of doubt will be sowed. I'll fall under closer scrutiny. My act will unravel.

I have to speak with Cloud before it comes to that.

"Where's Cloud?" I ask as someone hands me a sesame flatbread.

"At training ground number three."

I cram the flatbread into my mouth, wash it down with more water, then rise against the underling's objections.

Dust clouds hang above training ground three. Soldiers lean over the palisaded half wall, spectating the two figures facing off against each other. Tourmaline and Cloud. Cheers rise as Cloud dances behind Tourmaline, tapping the butt of her pole to the warrior's back. She wins the round, but her gaze is flat. When Tourmaline comes at her again, Cloud blocks, parries, whirls, and sees me. Her attention falters.

The win goes to Tourmaline.

Reactionless to the loss, Cloud watches me like a hunter as I swing myself over the palisades. Spectators hoot, and Tourmaline looks up, frowning at my presence.

What are you doing? her eyes ask.

I grab a pole from the rack. "I'll take the next match."

It's not the answer Tourmaline was expecting, and her frown deepens when Cloud kicks her pole into her hand. "You're on."

Trust me, I think to Tourmaline as she joins the other spectators.

I face Cloud.

Bets fly back and forth. The excitement is tangible, the air abuzz. It's a battle between swornsisters. A fight to remember—or, in my case, a fight to fix the mess I made last night.

The rise and fall of Cloud's chest syncs with my own breath, as if our qìs are aligned, and my body knows exactly how to respond when she comes at me. My pole meets hers overhead. Lotus must've blocked this move a hundred times.

I block the next too, but Cloud bears down. Her face eclipses the sun.

"*Why?*"

The word sears my cheek. I recall her bowed form over Lotus's bedside. Her joy when I opened my eye.

I push her off. "I'm here"—she jabs at my side; I block—"for Ren."

She slams my pole down into the ground. "Oxshit."

I wrest myself free. "She needs—"

Cloud leaps backward, forward. I dodge, meet her again in the middle.

"—a strategist. She was already gone, Cloud," I rush on to say. "Her body was a shell. When my spirit came back—"

Cloud breaks away.

"It was too late. I'm—"

I thrust my pole overhead as Cloud repeats the opening move. We connect with a smash.

—*sorry.*

Cloud's pole breaks. One half falls to the ground. The other, Cloud tosses away.

I lower mine. "Cloud—"

Her hands close around my neck.

There are shouts, and there is movement—of people from the periphery, running toward us. But I lose sight of the fringe. My hearing fuzzes, until all I can pick up on is the sound of my pulse and Cloud's, drumming together in that tender place where her fingers dig into my jaw.

Panic rushes through me; the mortal body doesn't take well

to a strangling. Then panic is overcome by relief. I was waiting for this moment. Now that it's finally arrived, I don't fight it. I have a good grasp on how it'll end.

It plays out as I predicted. Just as the first people reach us, Cloud's angry expression cracks. She lurches away, face stricken. The images have been branded into her mind: her hands on my neck. My lips turning blue. Her swornsister on the verge of death.

She'll see it every time she closes her eyes.

She won't do or say anything else to harm me. My secret is safe. But as Cloud turns and flees, some part of me—or Lotus— wants to run after her and apologize.

I know Cloud better than I did before.

I know just how much this fight hurt her.

‡ ‡ ‡

Cloud may be absent from dinner that night, but she's present in everyone's minds. It's only out of respect that people don't ask what happened. It's our business. And, as our swornsister, it's Ren's. In fact, if Ren were here instead of at Xin Gong's, she'd demand answers. I thank the stars that she's not.

At dawn, Cloud still hasn't returned. Ren is in the camp armory when I pay my morning respects. Her lips compress as I approach, and I nervously adjust my scarf, which hides the bruises on my neck.

But the source of Ren's displeasure is a piece of paper in her hand. She reads me the message—*Northern battle preparations complete*—written by our scout two weeks ago. He posted it from

Dasan, a merchant hub one thousand five hundred lǐ south of the empire capital. Miasma is due to launch her offensive any day now.

"About time," says Ren, tone light. But I still hear the vow she made in the shrine, the vow to make Miasma bleed.

Vengeance isn't Ren. I won't let her be led astray by it. I start to caution her, but she's already striding to the weapons rack. She unhooks her double swords. "Ready for the hunt?"

Hunt? What hunt? Then it comes back to me. Xin Gong's hunt. The one he invited us to during lunch four days ago.

The empire is in fragments, Miasma is on the march, and Xin Gong chooses to shoot at deer. My expression sours, and Ren chuckles. "A hunt, I said! Not a negotiation." Right. I'm Lotus. *Still Lotus.* My throat tightens, like Cloud's squeezing it. *Be Lotus.*

"Aiya, how long has it been since we last hunted for fun?" Ren muses, rubbing her neck. The marsh mosquito bites have faded since I last stood next to her as Zephyr, in the Southern watchtower. "Who do you think will shoot the first deer, me or Cloud?"

"Lotus will."

Ren smiles conspiratorially at that. "Then you will. And I'll help. I'll steal Cloud's arrows for you. Knock out the competition."

I should be laughing at Ren's arguably dishonorable tricks, but instead I'm fixated on the words *knock out*. End Cloud; keep my secret for good. The scarf around my neck feels like rope. I'm here as Lotus to help Ren succeed *without* losing any one of her swornsisters.

"Hey." Ren cups my elbow. "You're not cold, are you?"

Lotus's stomach comes to my rescue with a growl. "Just hungry." I don't care if it's irrelevant. So long as it works.

And it does. Ren relaxes. This is the Lotus she knows. "I think I smell something cooking. Go on." She walks with me out of the armory. "Meet in Xin City at noon."

Nodding, I start for the mess halls.

"Wait, Lotus."

I turn.

With her swords, topknot, and simple clothes, Ren looks like one of us, equal parts soldier and sister. "Speaking of Cloud— have you seen her today?" she asks, a would-be casual question, marked—at that exact moment—by Cloud's entrance. Ren's back is toward the camp gates, but mine isn't. My gaze meets Cloud's, and even from this distance, I see her freeze.

"No," I manage. "I think she went out for a walk." Then I escape before Ren can say anything else.

Of course, once we set out from Xin City, Cloud and I are expected to ride together. If things seem strange between us, Ren doesn't notice. Normally attentive, she appears preoccupied with the news of Miasma's preparations.

We rise out of the basin and into the highland forests. Cloud pulls ahead, and Tourmaline takes her place. "What happened yesterday?" she mutters under her breath.

"She found out." The crackle and pop of undergrowth helps to mask my words, though I doubt anyone but Tourmaline would understand their significance. When I reassure her that I have the situation under control, she looks skeptical. I suppose it's only fair, given Cloud's attack in the training ground yesterday.

But Tourmaline should remember that I'm a god. Almost dying is a minor setback.

It's fascinating, thinks Dewdrop.

What is?

How much you're willing to sacrifice.

Can't be called sacrifice if I don't sustain permanent damage, I think back, defiant. The bruises, the scrapes—all of that will heal. But lost time cannot be recaptured, and as the hunt drags on, my annoyance builds. This was Xin Gong's idea, and he isn't even making kills. Only Cloud and Sikou Dun are. When Sikou Dun shoots a rabbit, Cloud outdoes him by shooting a partridge. I bet she wishes she could shoot me.

"You have many impressive warriors in your ranks," says Xin Gong to Ren. His mood is good—too good—and my focus pivots from Cloud to the Westlands governor.

Could this be it? Will he make his move against Ren at this hunt? In terms of venue, it's fitting. Everyone important from the Westlands court is present, excluding Sikou Hai, who had the right idea in skipping the odious affair. At least fifty servants trail us, bearing chests and poles to carry any felled game, and two lines of soldiers border us, bearing Xin Gong's insignia. It's a miracle that there's any prey left in the undergrowth.

Unless we are the prey.

It doesn't add up. Xin Gong is too calm. This isn't the behavior of a man on the hunt.

It's the behavior of one who has already won.

But how? He didn't fight in the Battle of the Scarp, or negotiate for an alliance with the South. He can't reassert power over his lands without his own victories to boast of. I miss an easy shot, and Sikou Dun gloats. *Try again*, Ren mouths. Before I can, Xin Gong is speaking.

"Ren, why don't you try your luck?" He offers her his gilded bow.

It's not Ren's preferred weapon, but no one would be able to tell from the ease with which she accepts and notches an arrow. The woods quiver, quiet, as she scans the trees.

She spots the deer at the same time as Sikou Dun. Their arrows fly in unison, streaking into the brush.

At Xin Gong's signal, our entire party moves in. Behind the brush, we find the deer on its side, Ren's arrow sprouting from its neck.

Ren dismounts and strides over. She yanks out the arrow. A servant passes her a linen cloth, and she wipes the shaft clean before presenting it to her uncle.

"A token of our gratitude, for the hospitality you've shown us so far, and for lending us strength when we needed it most."

Xin Gong waves a hand. "Don't speak of it. We are family, are we not?"

"We are."

"Then you should know that by investing in you, I am also investing in all of Xin."

As Xin Gong speaks, Sikou Dun dismounts. The burly warrior comes to stand before Ren, looming like a bull.

I remind myself that Ren is older. To her, Sikou Dun is just a boy. But the age difference doesn't deter Xin Gong from what he says next. "Son, do you accept this deer as a dowry?"

"I do."

"Then on behalf of the Xin clan, I'm pleased to announce this betrothal. Wine!"

Thunk. Servants set down the chests and bring out ceramic pots of wine. One pot is passed to me; it breaks in my grip as Xin Gong says, "I thought I might find no one worthy of my son before I turned forty." His raises his wine, and Sikou Dun takes Ren's arrow. "But you, Ren, have proved me wrong. Tomorrow, it would be my gift and honor to preside over your wedding."

FIRST BLOOD

Wedding. Tomorrow.

I should have predicted this. I *would* have, had I been myself and not busy masquerading as Lotus and dreaming of Crow. Instead, I'm just as blindsided as everyone else. Shackling Ren to his son and anointing himself as father-in-law is the perfect plan, and so painfully obvious in hindsight.

We ride in silence all the way back to camp.

‡ ‡ ‡

In Ren's room, Cloud whirls on her. "You're not accepting this betrothal."

Ren unbuckles her armor and hangs it in her bureau. "That's for me to decide."

"There's *nothing* to decide."

"And there's nothing to debate." The calmer Ren's voice, the redder Cloud's face. "When I asked Xin Gong for his help at the Battle of the Scarp, I agreed to a future condition of his choice."

"How could you?" Cloud grips the pole of her glaive.

Ren moves toward the window, her gaze hard. "We needed a proper army," she says. "Qilin was the reason we lasted so long without one."

"She's the reason Lotus—"

Cloud breaks off, her expression torn.

"The peacock did what she had to do," I quickly offer, covering Cloud's tracks.

"You're right, Lotus," says Ren. To Cloud: "Qilin risked her life and reputation to trick Miasma. She secured an alliance with the Southlands even when we had nothing to offer. The least I could do was show Cicada that we could bear our own weight."

"But—"

"*Enough.*" Cloud falls silent. I've never heard Ren snap like so. "We're in a better position to crush Miasma than we were ever before. Our names are known in the realm. Our forces are trained. My nuptials are a small price to pay for these gains."

"We won't keep these gains," growls Cloud. "Not if we're under Xin Gong's thumb."

"He won't betray a daughter-in-law."

"*He betrayed your—*"

I smash my foot over Cloud's. I know what she was going to say. *He betrayed your mother. His sister.* If she wants to change Ren's mind with persuasion alone, she can be my guest.

I have my own tactics.

Your plans, Dewdrop thinks when we leave Ren's place. *I assume this marriage throws a wrench in them?*

Does it? The wedding is set for Xin Gong's birthday feast. That hasn't changed. As for how the coup might be perceived,

I've already severed Ren's connection to it by having every participant write down their names and entrusting the tangible record with Sikou Hai. The insurrection, if discovered, would be linked to him, not Ren.

But this was before the betrothal. Now I revise the scene: Ren, dressed in wedding red. Our soldiers leaping in, killing Xin Gong and Sikou Dun. Their red bleeding into Ren's, their fates forever intertwined. *She seized control of the Westlands to break off the betrothal*, historians will write. They won't portray the acquisition as a strategic move, necessary for marching north and restoring Xin Bao. They'll paint Ren's actions as reactions to a man's. Heavens forbid, they might even say that she fulfilled the prophecy.

The sun starts to set, burnishing the banyan trees around me to bronze. I pluck a crimson fig and roll it in my palm.

Blood *will* spill. It's unavoidable. But as for who draws whose . . . the narrative would turn in our favor if Xin Gong attacked first. Then we wouldn't be the aggressors. Whatever violence ensued would be out of self-defense. Problem is, Xin Gong has no reason to lash out. Unless I create one. Or . . .

I bite into the fig, let the honey sweetness wash over my tongue. My chess master mentor always ate plums. *When cornered, amateurs feel limited by what's on the board*, she'd say, one hand holding a piece, another holding the fruit. *Masters see potential in existing conditions.*

What do I need? Or rather, who? Someone who wouldn't stand for an insult. Someone with Lotus's vices, and none of her selflessness.

Someone like that on Xin Gong's side already exists, I think. But how to provoke him?

"What are you doing here?"

I turn to my answer.

Sikou Hai, stopped six strides away from me in the banyan path. He's only just heard of Ren's betrothal, judging by the look of murder on his face. But he doesn't act on it. His eyes, hard as flint, don't spark. Call it defeat, or self-control borne out of necessity. There's not much you can do against a brother like Sikou Dun. Confront him, and he could break your ribs, knock out your front teeth.

Spill first blood.

"I asked you a question." Sikou Hai scowls, striding forward. "What are you—"

"Waiting for you." I drop my fig, my fingers already stained by the juice.

Sikou Hai whips past. I follow, examining the idea. It could work. It's ruthless, yes, but Killing with a Borrowed Knife almost always is.

We arrive at the underground room, and everyone rises. "Young Master—"

Sikou Hai stalks past. He reaches the head of the table but does not sit. "We act as planned, commencing with Xin Gong's feast. Bracken and Tourmaline, have you notified the soldiers you trust of our plans?"

"Yes."

"Aster, have your forces been instructed to quell disorder in the surrounding prefectures?"

"Yes, Young Master."

Sikou Hai nods. "Good. Then everything is settled—"

"What about your brother?" I interrupt.

"What *about* my brother?"

"It's in his interests to side with Xin Gong. How should we treat him?"

"The same way we treat the rest of my father's supporters," Sikou Hai snaps. In his voice, I hear the anger and the pain he conveyed in his zither song, the grudge he bears, growing with him like the pox scars he probably hides under his mask.

But I also hear a lack of consideration for Ren. His worship of her objectifies her. He thinks she's immune to the public's narrative. She isn't, and I lose my reservations about using the stratagem as the meeting concludes. The coup won't go down in history as a conflict between Xin Gong and Xin Ren, not once I've had my way with it. It will irrevocably be remembered as a conflict between Sikou Dun and Sikou Hai.

Moments later, I get the sense I'm being followed.

You'd be right, thinks Dewdrop.

Who is it?

I think you already know.

Why, thank you, helpful sister.

You're welcome.

Annoying as it is, I do have an inkling of who my tail might be, and when they continue following me from a cautious distance, I stop in my tracks. "Well? Was what you heard to your liking?"

Cloud emerges from behind a boulder on the cliff face. "So this is where you've been going at supper."

"A worthwhile pastime, I would say." A vein of quartz flows between us, glittering like a galaxy. When Cloud doesn't speak, I continue, "If you want to break the betrothal for Ren, this is how."

"By overthrowing Xin Gong. Stealing his lands."

"War isn't easy, Cloud. Our means cannot be as honorable as our cause."

"You know who else would say that? Miasma. So why don't you go serve her, huh?" Cloud shakes her head. "No. This isn't how Ren would want it."

"So she wants this marriage?"

"No. She—"

"—is in a bind because she's a leader, considering one too many factors." The people she fears disappointing. The prophecy she fears fulfilling. "You think I don't understand?" I cross the vein of quartz and stand before Cloud. "It's precisely because I do that I choose to stay by her side, even if it's in a body that isn't mine. For the pain this decision has caused you, I'm sorry. But I'm not sorry for doing what Ren herself can't and won't do. She needs a land to call hers. She needs me, and she needs you."

A fine drizzle mists over the basin, muffling the night.

"What about Ren's reputation?" Cloud finally asks.

"I have that covered."

"And what if you're wrong to trust Sikou Hai? I heard everything in that meeting. He's willing to betray his own father and brother for Ren, but we have no idea why."

Cloud is more astute than I gave her credit for. I've wondered why myself. What are the chances Sikou Hai is like me, a god in disguise, fated to serve Ren? Next to none, I think, at the same time Dewdrop thinks, *He's not. The question is, do you want to know why he serves Ren?*

I waver for all of a heartbeat before thinking, *No.* Stratagem Twenty-Eight: Remove the Ladder After the Ascent. Once a decision has been made, extraneous information will only complicate.

"If things go according to plan," I say to Cloud, "Sikou Hai's motivations won't matter. So, are you with us or not?"

I'm certain I've convinced her. My argument came from the heart. Even the staunchest believer in Master Shencius's codes of virtuous conduct would be swayed.

But Crow was onto something about the predictability of people: just like she did by the lake, Cloud leaves without a word.

The drizzle opens to a downpour. In seconds, I'm drenched to the bone. Sighing, I start down the basin. Cloud's always been ox headed. I'm the last person she'd break her ideals for. In retrospect, I don't know what I was expecting.

Luckily, I don't need Cloud's cooperation. "Dewdrop," I say when we reach Xin City.

Talking to yourself is supposed to be off-limits.

Asking for favors most likely is too. "Can you fly?"

Who do you want me to spy on?

"Don't be so quick to jump to conclusions."

Is it Sikou Hai?

She's right, and she knows it; I can tell from her smugness. "That's a very human emotion, you should know."

Why can't immortals be smug?

"Because you have an eternity to be proved wrong."

I've never been proved wrong.

"Now I see where I get my arrogance from."

You could have turned out humble like Nadir.

Lightning flashes at the invocation of our sister, bleaching the night to silver. My heart trembles with the thunder that follows. The faster I can give Ren the Westlands, the sooner we'll march north. The sooner I'll leave the mortal realm and return for the heavens. An inexplicable sadness fills me at the thought.

Sikou Hai, Dewdrop prompts as we walk to the inner city, where Xin Gong, Sikou Dun, and Sikou Hai live.

"Can you figure out where he's keeping that belt of names?"

I don't need to fly for that. He hung it behind your poem.

"Perfect." I turn left when I come to the outer reaches of Xin Gong's massive complex.

This isn't in the direction of Sikou Hai's study, thinks Dewdrop.

"Of course not." Why dirty my hands when can I use someone else's?

But as I travel down an outdoor corridor, my stomach gurgles. I may know the origin of Sikou Hai and Sikou Dun's animosity, but I don't know its end. They might have gone down in infamy—like so many brothers through the dynasties who killed over thrones, land, and wives—without my helping hand. They might not have. One thing is certain: If their relationship wasn't past the point of no return before, it will be after tonight.

I draw short of Sikou Dun's courtyards. "Do you know what's funny, Dewdrop?"

What?

"When I was a mortal, I thought myself a god."

I thought I knew everything. I was like a frog at the bottom of the well, thinking that the circle of sky above me was the cosmos. Now I see just how limited I was. I know so much more about both myself and this world, and I feel weaker as a result. Mortal emotions such as guilt and loss sit heavy in my stomach. The heavens themselves bear down on me as I pass under the moon gate.

I spot Sikou Dun immediately; even with all the steam rising from the hot spring, he'd be hard to miss with his girls, as numerous as the rose petals floating in the milky water. Bamboo trays glide, carrying ewers of wine and plates of oiled nuts. The drunken chatter continues as I stride down the pebbled path. It's not until I'm by the spring that one of the girls sees me—and the ax in my hand. She shrieks and clambers out, fleeing with an arm pressed over her breasts.

The mature human form seems quite impractical, thinks Dewdrop, while the rest of the other girls, like birds in a flock alerted by a warning call, also take flight. They abandon Sikou Dun in the spring. His look of utter bewilderment is priceless, however short-lived. His leer returns when he sees me.

"Decided you wanted my company after all?" he drawls as I close the remaining distance. "Too late. I'm keeping myself pure for your swornsister."

This time, I'm prepared for the rush of Lotus's temper. My grip melds to the ax handle, but my voice is level when I say, "Keep spouting lies while you still can."

Then, slowly and deliberately, I touch the edge of Lotus's ax to his neck.

I've never taken a life. Never driven steel into flesh. Orchestrating deaths is more my expertise, and it's a challenge to steady my hand when Sikou Dun laughs. The cords of his neck bounce against the sharpened edge. "You wouldn't."

"Try me." I apply a bit more pressure and blood scrawls down his chest.

"But you know what'll be more satisfying?" I keep the ax in place a second longer to show that I mean my word. Then I withdraw the blade. "Watching you die at your brother's hands."

"My brother, you say?"

"Yes."

Sikou Dun smiles. "Remind me not to bash your head next time."

I could reply with something witty, but why waste intellect on the likes of Sikou Dun? I simply walk away, knowing that being ignored will anger him more than any retort.

Sure enough, I'm two steps from the spring when water sloshes behind me. Three steps, and his arm locks over my neck. "Just what are you suggesting?"

"Find out for yourself."

"I'm asking nicely."

"Don't. Beat me. Kill me. Do anything you want. Tomorrow, you're still going down."

Sikou Dun is quiet. Tomorrow is Xin Gong's feast and the wedding, taking place in an epic ceremony with a thousand opportunities for disaster. Even he must understand this.

"I'll ask you one more time." His arm shoves into my windpipe. "What are you talking about? What's happening at the ceremony?"

"Ask—brother." I'd answer him faster if he'd just let me breathe. "He's—planning—your—demise—within—walls—of—study."

With the little air I have left, I emphasize *walls* and *study*, and when Sikou Dun doesn't release me, I go on. "*He—is—not—alone. He—has—support—*"

Sikou Dun pushes me away. I fall to my knees. He strides into the house behind the spring—presumably to get dressed—and I lurch to my feet.

What now? thinks Dewdrop as I race out of the hot springs.

"Now we save Sikou Hai."

‡ ‡ ‡

Anyone else might sleep on my words before taking action. Not Sikou Dun. The moment he's armed, he'll storm his brother's study. First blood might spill right then and there.

I have to get to Sikou Hai first.

"Zither playing," I say without preamble when I arrive at his study. I lift him from his seat just like last time. Unlike last time, he doesn't put up a fight. He might still believe me a brute, but I'm a brute who won't hurt him.

"Can I at least get a cloak?" he asks, but there's no time. I plop him onto Rice Cake, and we tear out of the town, up the basin, into the forest. A lǐ or so from Crow's lake, I slow. This should be enough distance to occupy Sikou Hai for a while.

I dump him unceremoniously on the ground and kick Rice Cake into a gallop.

"Wait! Come back!"

I ride on. *It's the only way*, I think over his shouts, before the wind swallows them. Loyalty means putting one person above all. Too bad for Sikou Hai, that one person is Ren for me.

And now? thinks Dewdrop as we break out of the trees and gallop over the scrubplain.

Now we wait. It'll be up to Sikou Hai to get himself back to town. If he keeps a steady pace, he'll arrive just in time for the feast—and realize he was better off staying in the forest.

二十三

GUESTS OF HONOR

Now we wait.

I've never attended a wedding. The few processions I've seen in passing only reminded me of the chaos that swept Ku away, a storm that left nothing but detritus in its wake.

Today, I make the storm. As Xin Gong's servants deck the courtyards with red silk bouquets, I see the red of blood. When artisans arrive with hangings inked with the character for *union*, I think of the only union that will actually be happening: that of a lordess and her land.

In the barracks, we don our ceremonial laminar and strap on our weapons. Those who can keep a secret know what is to come. Those who can't will know soon enough. I tie on my tiger-pelt skirt, lift my ax, then head to Xin City. The wedding procession is set to start and end there. Ren went over at dawn.

She's in one of Xin Gong's spare courtyard complexes when I arrive, sitting at a vanity, surrounded by Xin Gong's servants. The tarnished topknot pin she usually wears rests on the vanity top, as does her Xin pendant. I cross the threshold, and Ren, catching sight of me in the mirror, orders the servants out. She rises, her dress dyed a blinding red. The color lingers in my vision even after I've lifted my gaze to Ren's.

I meant what I said to Cloud. I'd rather stand by Ren as Lotus than not at all. I'd rather give her false happiness than be the cause of the pain in her eyes when she says, "I take it that Cloud still hasn't come around."

"She will." Or, if all goes according to plan, she won't have to.

"And you, Lotus? What do you think?"

"I think you deserve to be empress."

I don't quite realize what I've said until I've said it. With Lotus's tongue. Mouth. Heart. Or maybe mine.

"Aiya, sedition, Lotus!" Ren says it jokingly, lovingly. She doesn't take me seriously because all she sees is her warrior of a sister with a heart of gold.

"Let me tell you something, Lotus." Ren picks up her pendant and slips it into the cross-folds of her red dress. "An empress has others fight her wars. I can wage my own."

Hearing Ren speak lesser of Xin Bao, direct or implied, is surprising. More surprising is my feeling of frustration. *How will you march on the North, knowing that your retreat routes and grain depots are in Xin Gong's control?* Ren starts to unstrap her double swords, and I wish I could tell her to keep them on. Then my mind clears. She'll be well protected at the scene. I've made sure of it.

Why is your stomach in knots, then? asks Dewdrop as I walk Ren to the palanquin outside. A servant drapes the red bridal silk over her head. Right before it falls, Ren catches my eye. "You're my family, Lotus. This marriage doesn't change that."

The silk settles over her face.

In another life, Sikou Dun would unveil his bride in his bed-chambers after the ceremony. Not this one. Before night falls, no one will dare to undermine Ren ever again.

‡ ‡ ‡

Horns and firecrackers blast into my ears as I march into the Xin City pavilion with the rest of Ren and Xin Gong's warriors. A shared tension hovers between all of us, but while the others have been told to draw their weapons when Sikou Dun and Ren make their three bows to the ancestral deities, I know that the bloodbath will begin much, much earlier.

We take our places along the perimeter. Xin Gong's personal guard position themselves at the base of the erected stage—a massive thing of gilt and stone, divided lengthwise by a table before which Ren kneels. Sikou Dun, who should be at her side, stands behind it so that Ren is also kneeling before him. Xin Gong sits at the center, flanked by towering plates of glazed figs.

No amount of fruit, however, can hide the empty space to the governor's right. He turns to whisper to Sikou Dun, and I don't need to read his lips to know what he must be asking:

Where's your brother?

By now? Due to arrive any moment.

Sikou Dun doesn't know that, of course, and his face darkens at Xin Gong's query. By the time I returned last night, I heard the servants muttering about how he'd overturned every inch of Sikou Hai's study. He would have overturned Sikou Hai him-self had he been present. When I checked the study later, the sash of names was gone, and this morning, Sikou Dun purportedly ordered a servant to taste everything being prepared in the kitchens.

But the poison was never going to be in the food or drink. Foul play in such a vein would be too easily pinned on Ren. No, the poison is—has always been—in Sikou Dun's mind. All I've done is activate it by showing him the warriors who follow a brother he considers inferior, the many supposed allies who've switched sides. A warrior like him won't tolerate the slight.

Eventually, Xin Gong stops waiting for Sikou Hai and faces his assembled vassals.

"Welcome! Welcome! Another year, a few more white hairs . . ."

I grip Lotus's ax and scan the pavilion. Still no Sikou Hai. I sent Tourmaline out to check on him at dawn. By her report, he was close.

Come on. A droplet of rain lands on my nose. *If I can outrun Miasma, you can make it to this feast on time.*

" . . . But the gifts of life improve with age, and I can think of no better gift than the union of a young couple. This toast is for them. To family, and to our guests of honor—"

Movement ripples near the back of the pavilion. Voices rise. Xin Gong stops his speech, and goblets lower as everyone turns to behold the last guest, late to the feast.

Finally.

Sikou Hai staggers down the pavilion. Mud cakes his shoes. Rotted leaves cling to the hem of his robes. He trips when he's nearly at the stage, and the servants rescue him from taking a premature spill. As they hold him upright, his gaze spins wildly from face to face.

Inevitably, it lands on me.

His eyes ignite. He starts in my direction, but never reaches me.

"Move aside," he barks as Sikou Dun blocks his way, a hand shoved into his slighter brother's chest. "I have business to discuss."

The hand curls into fist, pulling fabric with it. "Haven't you discussed enough business already?"

The sky is so dark now that it could be night.

"What are you talking about?" asks Sikou Hai, all impatience.

"Don't take me for a fool," growls Sikou Dun.

Sikou Hai yanks off his brother's hand. "Then act less like one."

This is it. As much as I willed it, I want to look away. I don't take perverse pleasure from seeing anyone disemboweled, let alone Sikou Hai, whose nerve I've grown to respect.

But before Sikou Dun can move, Xin Gong speaks.

"Sons, you're disgracing yourselves. You especially, Sikou Hai, showing up in such a state—"

"*He betrayed you, Father!*" Sikou Dun's voice is noticeably slurred. Blood, apparently, isn't the only liquid reddening his face. "He plans on killing you. They all do!"

In the silence, a dried fig leaf scurrying across the sanded stones sounds like a slithering snake. The breeze hisses.

Sikou Dun's sword shrieks out of its sheath.

"Come on!" he goads, pressing the blade to Sikou Hai's neck.

He spins his brother around with him, shouting at the entire assembly. "Show your true colors!"

Westlands vassals immediately rise, remonstrating with Sikou Dun, pleading with him to have sense. But none of the secret meeting members move or speak. I know what they're thinking: How does Sikou Dun know? And how much? One wrong move, and the bloodshed might begin.

Then Tiger-Mask—Aster—steps forward. "Release him, General Sikou."

Sikou Dun spins. When he sees it's her, a warrior under his command whose name was on that sash, his lips pull back. "And if I don't? Will you die for him?"

Aster doesn't reply. "Release him," she repeats, while making a fist with her right hand behind her back.

A signal. The soldiers around me tense. Another raindrop lands, this time on my brow, as Sikou Dun slowly lowers the curved blade from his brother's neck. He backs away.

Thrusts.

A beam of sunlight startles through the clouds. It catches on the scimitar tip that curves out from Sikou Hai's back like a claw. Scarlet spills down his front. I've seen blood before, but somehow, this seems like more. More than war and honor and pride.

Like murder.

You've committed plenty already, thinks Dewdrop, in a presumed attempt at comfort. And it's true. Hundreds died when Miasma's navy went up in flames. But I pulled my strings from afar. I didn't hear the screams, or see flesh blacken on the bone.

This close, I can hear the pained rasp of Sikou Hai's breath, the *squelch* of Sikou Dun's scim as it exits. The scim morphs into a spearhead, and I'm suddenly back in that street, fleeing from the warpath of the raging warriors.

Then reality bleeds in. *I* am the warrior now. The realization shudders through me, and I almost step back as Sikou Hai wobbles in my direction. He's still on course for me when he crumples, his robes puddling around him, a fallen flag on the battlefield. Sunlight burns through the rest of the clouds.

Hell descends with the rain.

Tables overturn. Platters break. Figs roll across the ground, splashing through rainwater and blood as soldiers clash with soldiers—ours, Sikou Hai's, Sikou Dun's. I'm immediately ensnared in a fight with members of Xin Gong's personal guard. Better that they're preoccupied with me than the stage, which our people should be securing. A special force, headed by Tourmaline, will whisk Ren to safety while another, headed by Bracken, deals with Xin Gong.

But someone cries my name and I look up to see Tourmaline defeating her opponents, before shouting another name.

Ren.

My gaze cuts to the stage. It's a tangle of twisting bodies and flashing steel, red hangings fallen onto the table and over the dead. I see Xin Gong and his guard. I see Bracken and their men, taking down Sikou Dun.

I don't see Ren.

Lightning tears the already-sunny sky asunder. Rain pounds on my shoulders as I frantically search for Ren, my heart a pestle grinding against my chest.

Another clap of thunder. Another flash of lightning. Another soldier I down, before I see her.

She's dragging a body out from the thick of battle.

It looks like Sikou Hai's.

Leave him! He's dead! But this is Ren, who insisted on evacuating the peasants when we could barely evacuate ourselves. Ren, who repays her debts, no matter what the personal cost. Honor is her asset. Her curse.

It'll kill her.

I start slashing indiscriminately, cutting through every obstacle in my way. Bones. Tendons. Arteries. Blood sprays into my face. I barely blink. I have to get to Ren. Have to protect—

Zephyr, Dewdrop interrupts.

"What?"

Behind you.

I whirl around, ax held out. Everyone is engaged in battle.

"Dewdrop, what . . ."

I trail off.

A beast, no bigger than the size of a wild dog. It picks its way over the carnage. Turquoise scales armor its body. Hooves of a goat cap its feet. Horns of a bull twist from either side of its head, lifting to sniff the air with a dragon's snout.

The creature is like none I've ever seen in the flesh—as a human or a god. But something about it is familiar, and slowly, I recall the likeness of it painted on vases, woven into tapestries, carved into statues. I've etched my name on the rump of one. It's the homophone for Qilin's name, a chimerical creature that heralds the death or birth of a ruler.

A qilin.

No, thinks Dewdrop, sounding almost fearful. *It's—*

The qilin's head swivels to us. It regards us with its large liquid eyes. Its face changes—to Sikou Hai's.

My vision blurs. I glance to the sky before I remember it's daylight. Not a star to be seen. Not that it makes a shred of difference. The beast vanishes into thin air, and dread spills through my blood like ink.

The Masked Mother was here.

She knows *I'm* here.

The zing of a sword forces Lotus's body to react. But my grip is slack, the ax handle is slippery, and my attacker is too fast. As his blade comes down, it hits me that I won't reach Ren. This mortal body will expire. My soul will be taken to some prison of the Masked Mother's making, or wherever it is that gods are vanished. I roar—in fury and in pain. But the pain doesn't end. It goes on and on, reverberating in my skull—

My skull. I still have a skull. My eye focuses on two perpendicular lines dividing my vision. One is bright: the sword that was meant for me. The other, smacked against my crown, the only thing between the blade and myself, is the pole of Cloud's glaive.

With a grunt, Cloud heaves off my attacker—Sikou Dun. I stumble back, stare as the crescent blade catches under his arm. Limb and sword thud to the ground. He screams. So does Cloud.

"*Go!*" She takes down another warrior lunging our way, creating an opening. "*To Ren!*"

I dash the rest of the way, relieved to find Ren battling our mortal enemies instead of something godly. She slices one of Xin Gong's soldiers with a sword she's picked up. I chop the other in the back. He takes Lotus's ax with him as he falls. *Ugh.* I brace a foot against the corpse and yank free, spurting blood onto myself. I've had enough of being a warrior.

But without the strength and courage of Lotus, I wouldn't be able to protect Ren. I face her. "Are you hurt?"

Dazed, Ren shakes her head. She looks to Sikou Hai, a pool of blood forming beneath him faster than what the rain can wash away, then to the battle still unfolding on the pavilion. "Why, Lotus? Why is this happening?"

Before I can explain, a cry rises from the stage. Upon it stands Bracken, fists thrust toward the heavens. One holds a sword.

The other holds Xin Gong's severed head.

The fighting slows with the rain. Under the beaming sun, the atmosphere shimmers and steams. Twin rainbows appear in the sky; ally and enemy look up. Awe erases the killing-intent from their eyes; the rainbows must seem a heavens-sent sign. And they are, which is why my mouth goes dry. The two arches of color bear an uncanny resemblance to Qiao and Xiao. Like the Masked Mother's serpents, I can't escape. If I'm still here, it's for a reason of her choice. She is a force I can't reckon with, a phenomenon I can't read. My greatest fear come to immortal life.

An enemy no one else can see.

"*All hail the governor!*" cries one of Lotus's underlings. The chant spreads, until every voice sings it and every head bows to Ren.

Only she and I are silent.

THE ENEMY UNSEEN

All hail the governor.

When we gather our wounded and count our dead, Ren's not with us. Normally, she's the first and last figure on the battlefield, making sure no one has been left behind. But she needs time alone, to digest what just happened. I expected this.

What I didn't expect was for Sikou Hai to survive.

Even Sikou Dun succumbed to his wounds, but Sikou Hai—I rush to the infirmary when I hear the news, moving past occupied bed after occupied bed, until I find him, lying in the very back.

For a flash, I see Crow. It's his motionless form, his chest that was sliced open. If it were Crow and not Sikou Hai, could I have sacrificed him for the sake of my stratagem? For Ren?

It shouldn't even be a question. My heart hardens as I stand by Sikou Hai's bedside. A sheet of white linen is pulled up to his chin. That it's not pulled over his face is the only thing distinguishing him from the dead. His mask has been removed. I knew it was hiding his scars, but that doesn't make them any easier to behold. The telltale mottle of pox corpuscles speaks to months of pain.

I have no idea what compels me to touch it.

Maybe it's because I know Sikou Hai would prefer that his scars be hidden, or because a part of me already senses the emptiness, waiting to be filled. Regardless, the moment I cover the left side of his face, I'm falling again. I already have a human form, but my qì is still that of a god, and it takes to a hollow body like water to a sea sponge.

I jerk back, gasping. It's too late. I've seen. The particles of his soul still holding on, the memories attached to them. Misty memories, as if we were playing the zither. Distorted memories, as if I'm experiencing them through Sikou Hai's eyes:

A woman, bending over our head.

A Xin pendant—same as Ren's—dangling from her neck.

The woman straightens. She turns away from us and presses a pouch of herbs into the hands of our parents, shaking her head when they try to offer a pouch in return. *Life has no price.*

She leaves, but we remember. She saved us when no one else would. We vow to find her and repay her. But years later we learn that she died in the same typhoid epidemic that claimed our parents. So we shift our vow from mother to daughter. We bide our time, patiently serving our new father, collecting the letters from the Rising Zephyr that he discards, forming connections behind his back. We wait for the day Xin Ren, the lordess without a land, the daughter of our savior, will need our help.

I asked if you wanted to know, thinks Dewdrop as I stare at Sikou Hai in growing horror.

And I'm glad I said no. I gather my wits. What is done is done. As macabre as this is, Sikou Hai *did* end up helping. He helped more than he can ever know.

Can his spirit come back? I ask Dewdrop.

It's uncertain. Time will tell.

You knew for Lotus.

Because it'd been weeks. The longer the soul is away, the less likely it is to return.

Then what are the chances?

Slim.

Slim, but not impossible.

Unless I made it impossible.

I kill the thought. Fate can decide if Sikou Hai lives or dies.

Ren joins my side. She looks so much like her mother. Same eyes, nose, lips. Same pendant, in her grip as she gazes at Sikou Hai. Her expression is unreadable, even when Cloud storms in with a scout on her heels.

"Report! Miasma has marched down to Dasan!"

Right on schedule, I think grimly. We have less than a month to consolidate Ren's power over the Westlands.

Ren dismisses the scout. She turns on me and Cloud. "Explain what happened today."

Cloud scowls at the ground. I feign confusion.

"Speak," Ren commands.

"We don't know anything," mutters Cloud. A child could lie better.

"Do you remember when we swore sisterhood under the peach tree?"

"Yes—"

"Do you remember our oath to speak truth and only truth to each other?"

Cloud falls quiet.

"All of our soldiers seemed well prepared to fight," says Ren, voice toneless.

"Because you were in danger," I offer.

"And how do you explain the number of Xin Gong's men fighting on our side? How do you explain the escalation to Sikou Dun losing his life and Xin Gong losing his head?"

The quicker Ren faces the reality—that we live in an era of wars and warlords, where army is everything and land is strength—the better prepared she'll be when I'm gone. "It was to raise you to the governor's seat."

"What?"

"It was to give you a land to call your own stronghold, just as Zephyr intended."

If Ren hears the last part, she doesn't react. "So Xin Gong's death was orchestrated."

I nod.

"And Sikou Hai—was that orchestrated too?"

Another nod.

"By whom?" Ren looks between me and Cloud. Her expression hardens. "*Whom?*"

"Me."

The answer comes so naturally—and not from me.

"It was my idea," Cloud goes on as I stare. "I didn't want you to marry Sikou Dun, but you wouldn't listen. So I took matters into my own hands."

"You went behind my back." Ren's voice hushes like the heavens before a storm.

"She—"

"I did." Cloud speaks over me, loud and clear.

"Ren—"

Ren holds up a hand, and I'm silenced again.

"Gao Yun." The sound of Cloud's birth name hangs between us as Ren breathes, in and out. "You *knew* the prophecy," she finally says, and there's a world of hurt in her voice. "Everyone in my clan thinking I'd betray them—"

"You didn't betray Xin Gong," I blurt. "We—"

"I did," interrupts Cloud.

"*We are one*," Ren thunders. "Your life is mine, and mine yours. Do you know what the military punishment is for instigating rebellion? For going behind my back?"

"Death," Cloud says, unflinching.

In the silence, my heart pounds. Ren wouldn't. Not one of her swornsisters.

"And did you think of a way of controlling *that* narrative too, for when I spare you?"

I breathe out, but Ren's not done. "How do I explain playing favorites to my enemies who'd love nothing more than to declare me unfit?"

"I'll kill them," deadpans Cloud at the same time I say, "They won't."

We glance at each other.

It is possible . . . it is possible that I erred. I was so focused on reclaiming my identity as Ren's strategist that I forgot it's not just me who has a relationship with this body. To the people, I'm more than a warrior. They see me and Cloud as extensions of Ren. It's like what Ren said.

We are one.

The fury in Ren's eyes flickers in and out, a fire fighting against a bone-chilling rain.

The rain wins. There's no anger in Ren's voice when she finally says, "Get out. Both of you. Cloud, tomorrow you're to ride to the Marshlands with news of Xin Gong's death. You'll stay there to keep the peace." There is only pain. "You're not to return without my orders."

‡ ‡ ‡

"Why?"

Cloud doesn't answer, even though we're alone in the barracks. She strips off her laminar and hangs it up in the bureau before stepping out.

"*Why?*" I demand, following her. Cloud saving me in the heat of battle, I can understand. But this? Claiming responsibility for the very manipulation she loathes?

"For someone so smart, you're thicker than bean paste sometimes."

I start to fire something back, then think better of it. I travel with Cloud through camp, waiting for her to elaborate.

She stops by the armory. It's been picked clean. So are the ancestral shrines beyond the cemetery. Despite our best efforts to limit disorder, some soldiers still profited off the chaos caused by the coup.

"Look," starts Cloud. "The whole standing by Ren thing? It requires Ren to trust you."

"I've done worse as Zephyr, and she trusted me fine."

"But Ren thinks you're Lotus." Cloud's face darkens. "And in her eyes, Lotus would never do such a thing."

"You wouldn't either," I mutter. But now, I'm just being contrary.

"You don't know me, so don't assume." We move on from the field of graves, going down the banyan path. "I want to stand by Ren just as much as you," says Cloud, "but on my own terms, and by my own values. Just because I went along with you this time, don't think for a second I'll back your schemes again."

She stops. We've come to my shrine.

It's burning.

Cloud unties her cloak and starts beating out the flames licking at the bamboo steps. I jog to her side. "Let it burn."

"Can't. Ren's upset enough."

"But it's my shrine."

"Too bad. I'm the one getting exiled." Smoke puffs into Cloud's face, and she coughs. "Are you going to help or not?"

With a sigh, I tear off a banyan branch and beat out the flames with Cloud.

"At least it's uglier than before," she says when we're done.

"I didn't know that it was possible." Cloud snorts, and I almost smile. But there's still blood caked under my nails, and when a rustle comes from the trees, I jerk around, expecting to see another face-changing qilin. But it's just a crow, hopping from branch to branch.

Cloud tosses aside her burned cloak and together, we step into the shrine. It reeks of smoke now instead of incense. A small improvement. The broken pieces of Crow's peacock fan are still on the floor. I pick them up, my heart knotting. Our rematch with Miasma is imminent. I'm both looking forward to it and dreading it.

Slowly, I deposit the pieces of fan into the chest containing the rest of my belongings. Cloud watches, quiet. A moment later, as if sensing my need to be alone, she retreats outside.

I should shut the chest. But the Masked Mother's appearance has reminded me of the unpredictability of this life. For all I know, I could be looking at my possessions for the last time.

So I let my eye linger—then eventually my hands. I trace my mud-stained white robes, the pigeon-feathered fan that replaced my crane one. All that's missing is the clasp I used for my ponytail—lost, probably, in the battlefield. The chess master gave me that clasp when her own tresses started thinning. I think of all the mentors who took me in after I lost Ku, all the mentors who died. By the time I retreated into Thistlegate and adopted the life of a recluse, I truly believed that it was in my stars to lose the people close to me.

It was.

What?

For Qilin, Dewdrop clarifies. *Her fate, like the fate of all mortals, was written by the Masked Mother's Scribes. She was fated to lose everyone she loved.*

For a second, I blink, unbelieving. Then I laugh. It makes perfect sense. Why my mentors, young and old, died before me. Why I lost Ku to the senseless chaos.

One of these days, the reason why the Masked Mother hasn't recalled me yet to answer for my sins will reveal itself too. Until then, I will overcome whatever the heavens throw my way.

Or rather, *we* will.

I close my eye, let the strength of Lotus's body flow through me. When I reopen it, I realize my hand has stopped on the arrow that ended my life.

I lift it from the chest. The fletching is as I remember it, black and red. But as I roll the shaft between my fingertips, I see a mark I didn't before.

Ice crawls down my spine.

"Cloud. *Cloud!*"

Cloud comes in, and I hold the arrow up. "Was this extracted out of me?"

"Yes."

"And has the mark on the shaft always been here?"

"I think so."

"Yes or no?"

Cloud considers for a moment. "Yes. Yes, it was. What's wrong? It's an empire arrow, is it not?"

Yes, it's an empire arrow.

Specifically, it's an empire arrow that I borrowed, marked by Cicada's counters with a stripe of tar.

Bile rises in my throat. Denial. They helped us win the Battle of the Scarp. Ku works for them.

They are allies.

But no alliance is unbreakable. What is united must divide. It's the first rule every strategist learns.

"Zephyr?"

I should reprimand Cloud for using my name. But I can't speak.

I rise from the chest, not bothering to close the lid, and walk to the shrine's entrance. Outside, rainwater drips off the wide banyan leaves. The air is moist. It smells of earth.

It tastes of blood.

"The empire wasn't behind the ambush, Cloud," I finally say.

"But the survivors said they were," says Cloud, joining me. "The soldiers wore empire uniforms and carried empire weapons."

Of course they did.

As the cicadas begin to sing, I clench the arrow. "That's what the South wanted you to believe."

INTERMEZZO
Cicada

Everything stinks of horse in the North, Cicada thinks, including the people. The servants have an odor that can't be masked by the incense smoked onto their silks. This very sitting room reeks of hay. Steel. War.

"The prime ministress will be with you shortly," the servant says, pouring the tea. Cicada does not touch it, or the pastries stacked before them. She stops November from taking a lotus cake. The Southlands are expert at poisons and have every antidote under the sky, but better not to risk it.

Peeved, November pushes around her cup. Tea sloshes, the puddle on the tabletop growing with the passing minutes. "She's late."

Indeed, Miasma is. If they were going by the water clock in the middle of the room, she should have arrived ten minutes earlier. But if they went by status and power, she's not late. She's the prime ministress of the empire. She can afford to make her visitors wait.

Moments later, she emerges from behind a silk screen at

the front of the room. Her footsteps are wraith-light. Only the bloodred bell at her ear announces her arrival.

"You've traveled far to come here." She takes a seat on the cushion opposite Cicada and November, crossing her legs, her posture open. "I wouldn't want you to leave empty-handed. Please, speak frankly: What can I do for you?"

Her voice is pleasant, a hostess's to her guests. If Cicada didn't know of her before this meeting, she wouldn't be able to tell that Miasma's the same person who splits opposing warlords belly-open and lights them on fire by their own lard.

But Cicada was there ten years ago, when Miasma, a mere soldier, paid her respects in Cicada's mother's court. Since then, the planes of her face have thinned out. She has nearly everything she could possibly want under the sun, yet she still looks starved.

I am dealing with a wolf, Cicada thinks as she says, "I believe we can help each other."

"Oh?" Miasma grins. "Had a change in heart after burning my fleet?"

A trap of a question. Cicada asks one of her own rather than answer. "Do you know how the Rising Zephyr died in the Battle of the Scarp?"

The prime ministress chuckles. She lifts a pastry and takes a bite. November gives Cicada a rueful look. "A person of her constitution? It could have been the common cold."

Pretending at ignorance would be one thing, but lying so blatantly to Cicada's face? It's more than a little insulting. She *knows* that Miasma's soldiers retreated through the pass before

Ren's reinforcements could arrive. The prime ministress herself saw the corpses, the remnants of an ambush already dealt with.

She even took some heads as trophies, according to Cicada's scouts.

But if Miasma wants to play this game, then Cicada will play it with her. "It wasn't the common cold. She died because *I* willed it. I ordered an ambush made to look like an empire one. All this time, Xin Ren thought *you* were behind her strategist's death. But it was our arrows that took her out."

The prime ministress's chewing slows, her interest sparked. Cicada has finally said something worth her attention. "You expect me to believe you."

You'd be dead if I were lying to you. "Why don't you ask your strategist? I hear he made a trip to the Westlands recently."

Another spark of interest; Cicada's information network is wider than Miasma assumed. "Summon Crow," she orders.

Not long after, he makes his entrance. Cicada doesn't look at him, lest her expression give her away.

He is a Northern strategist. He is no one to you.

But when the prime ministress takes her sweet time finishing her pastry, Cicada cannot help herself; she risks a glance at her childhood friend.

So the rumors were true. The prime ministress punished her strategist for the loss of her fleet. Cicada's hands tighten in her lap and Crow, as if sensing her fury, tucks his into his sleeves. *A finger for her navy?* Cicada can almost hear him say. *I'd consider it a bargain.*

But he's given up much more in the years he's spent spying on the North for her, and her fury boils over as the prime ministress licks *her* fingers, one by one. "Finally," she says to Crow. "An opportunity to put your little trip to use. Did you look at any of the memorabilia while paying respects to the Rising Zephyr's shrine?"

Cicada doesn't miss the way Crow stills ever so slightly at the strategist's name. It was always their plan to dispose of Zephyr. She was simply too dangerous a weapon to be in any arsenal but Cicada's own. But before the Battle of the Scarp, Cicada received a handkerchief by dove. A message, coded. Still a risk to send— their spies, disguised as Miasma's servants, had been caught in the past—and suffice it to say, Cicada was surprised to see the message's contents: Crow was asking for a chance to spare Zephyr.

Being his friend, Cicada acquiesced. Zephyr sealed her own fate by refusing to join the Southlands.

"Yes," Crow now says. "I did happen to find an arrow among her things."

"Describe it," the prime ministress orders.

"It was empire-made, fletched black and red."

"But was there a mark of tar on the shaft?" Cicada asks.

Crow ponders for a second—all for a show. He already knows. "There was indeed."

"This might seem unrelated, but will you explain to your lordess how Zephyr reacted when the empire fired arrows across the river?"

Feigning a look of mild confusion, Crow obliges. As he does, Cicada thinks about all the vassals back in her court who advised her not to come north. They'd wet themselves if they knew she was breaking her alliance with Xin Ren. Then, if she told them that it was too late, that she'd already killed Ren's strategist, they'd beg her to consider how the same betrayal might come for her. And to think they were shaking in their boots at the thought of joining Ren just months ago.

I'm not like Zephyr, though, Cicada thinks. *I wouldn't ally myself with the enemy without an eye on the inside.*

Crow finishes recounting Zephyr's behavior, and now it's Cicada's turn. She explains the deal she had with Zephyr, illustrates how the South marked every "borrowed" arrow with a stripe of tar. All the while, the prime ministress rubs a thumbnail over her bottom lip. She dismisses Crow, and Cicada has to pin down November's sleeve to keep her from running after him.

Soon, she thinks, squeezing November's hand beneath the table. *Soon, we will all go home.*

"Let us envision this alliance for a second," the prime ministress says once they're alone. "What do you need from me, what would you give, and what, ultimately, would be your objective?"

An audience with the prime ministress feels no different to Cicada than an audience with her vassals. She says what she's expected to say. Answers as she's expected to answer. She keeps her real motives hidden, her true allies far away. She extinguishes threats before they grow out of hand, such as Zephyr. She reserves her energy for the real enemy: the woman sitting in front of her, the secret sponsor of the Fen pirates.

First, Cicada will crush the empress and her loyalists, for the empire is complicit, and then she will kill Miasma nice and slowly.

She will show this realm, filled with people who act like gods, that she is not to be underestimated.

TO BE CONTINUED IN
THE NEXT VOLUME

‡ ‡ ‡

AUTHOR'S NOTE

Three Kingdoms, the novel that *Strike the Zither* reimagines, is a work of historical fiction—emphasis on the fiction. For the historical record, Zhuge Liang[1] did not borrow a hundred thousand of Cao Cao's[2] arrows. We do not know if the real Zhou Yu[3] coughed blood whenever Zhuge Liang provoked him, or if Liu Bei[4] was really that honorable.

We do know that the novel draws from the Three Kingdoms era (220–280 CE) at the dusk of the Han, the Han being a long and prosperous dynasty that, like many long and prosperous dynasties, collapsed to lost Heaven's Mandates, strife, and war. This is a theme in Chinese history.

---

1 Zephyr's primary inspiration

2 Miasma's inspiration

3 Crow's primary inspiration. Zhou Yu coughing blood whenever Zhuge Liang outsmarted him was adjusted in *Strike the Zither* to be a less dramatic reflection of the often unnamed "blood coughing" illness that plagued ancient China. Now we know it to be tuberculosis; the motif is prevalent in literature and media.

4 Xin Ren's inspiration

It's also a theme in Luo Guanzhong's novel.[5]

Luo Guanzhong lived during the Ming Dynasty (1368–1644 CE), a dynasty that finally saw stories from the *Three Kingdoms*, already dramatized and told as oral texts,[6] adapted to the vernacular. Just as Luo Guanzhong's story underwent a shift in format, mine has too. *Three Kingdoms* is 800,000 words long; *Strike the Zither* is 80,000. Some details have stayed: Sun Quan's[7] youth and ascension after the death of his older brother, Zhuge Liang's own brother[8] working for Wu (the South in my book), Zhao Zilong's[9] iconic white horse, Zhuge Liang's deployment of the Thirty-Six Stratagems, and the vast majority's loyalty to the emperor, out of no reason other than tradition and Confucianism.

But many other details have changed, starting with the Confucianism—particularly, its view and treatment of women. *Three Kingdoms* features few female characters, and fewer with agency.[10] My story doesn't unpack the patriarchy as much as it imagines an alternate universe where societal roles are open to anyone, regardless of their gender assigned at birth.

---

5 Luo Guanzhong is often credited as the author of *Three Kingdoms*, but Mao Zonggang and others also made contributions.

6 The carryover of words from the end of a chapter into the beginning of the next is *Strike the Zither*'s nod toward the story's oral origins. Some vernacular editions maintain the oral tradition as well, ending every chapter with *What happened next? Read on.*

7 Cicada's inspiration

8 Ku is loosely based on Zhuge Jin.

9 Tourmaline's inspiration

10 Female agency in *Three Kingdoms* usually culminates with the women dying for their men. See Lady Gan and Lady Sun as examples.

Much differs on an event level too. Zhuge Liang never defects to Cao Cao; remaining Liu Bei's strategist, he convinces Sun Quan to side with his lord. I found the glorification of Zhuge Liang's verbal prowess here (and Sun Quan's submission to it) to be quite biased toward the story's obvious heroes. Would the South really be moved to support an underdog without more subterfuge and deception? Surely not, if *they* were the story's heroes.

For the sake of simplicity, Hanzhong and Yizhou have been turned into the Westlands, and Liu Zhang[11] into an uncle. While Sikou Hai is based on Zhang Song (and a few other characters I won't spoil now), Sikou Dun is largely my creation, and his third act conflict with Ren is my brief nod toward Liu Bei's political marriage plot—a plot that I personally have no interest in exploring further. The South's betrayal at the end is something I took liberties with too, to foreshadow a major turning point in *Three Kingdoms*—stay tuned.

Character aesthetics (such as preferred clothing, hairstyles, and weapons) have also been tweaked, forgone, or streamlined. The list of changes here is not exhaustive.

Of course, if you've read both *Strike the Zither* and *Three Kingdoms*, you'll know that there are three major narrative differences, which I've saved for last.

One: Zhuge Liang does not die—not this early. Countless other strategists do, however, most notably Pang Tong.[12] One of his sobriquets is Young Phoenix; Zephyr has his arrogance.

---

11 Xin Gong's inspiration

12 Pang Tong, who comes up with the Linked-Boat Stratagem, dies by a stray arrow.

Two: Zhuge Liang never lives a day in another's body. But if he had to, then the most humbling choice felt obvious, as you could not get a character more different from Zhuge Liang than Zhang Fei.[13]

Three: Zhuge Liang isn't explicitly deified on the page, even though feats of his, such as his fog summoning, are shrouded in mysticism. Beyond the page, however, he and Guan Yu[14] are worshipped. They certainly have been immortalized in Chinese culture; like many diaspora kids, I was told stories of them before I ever encountered the text. The stories made me feel connected to my parents, and to my identity, as a second-generation Chinese American.

But this identity was not always celebrated. As young as I can remember, I was warned by my parents that *they will see you as an Asian first, a person second.* "They," here, referred to peers, teachers, and, later, colleges and colleagues. In any industry in this country, my identity would be judged before I was. It would be quantified. Tokenized. And so I always struggled to be *more* than the identity I was born with, the identity that was most visible, the identity a stranger could glean before learning my name. In school, I built a persona based on my skills and personality; I liked being perceived as *the quiet one, the artist, the good student.* But I also felt boxed in as a result. What if I wanted to be different? Act different?

What if people could see all the sides of me, instead of knowing me for one?

---

13 Lotus's inspiration

14 Cloud's inspiration

If the Confucian ideal is to be believed, a ruler should act like a ruler; a minister, a minister; a father, a father; a son, a son. But as Luo Guanzhong explored in his novel, a novel shaped by the unique struggles of *his* life in a dynasty of authoritarian government, such ideals will be challenged by war and politics. And now, in my fictionalization of the fictionalization, I explore a story that is also colored by my experience. I bring to you Zephyr—strategist, god, warrior.

Person.

ACKNOWLEDGMENTS

I know we, as authors, are not supposed to pick favorites among our books, but I, like Zephyr, have something to confess: *Strike the Zither* might be my favorite book.

I say this having written quite a few. I've written books as a teenager, and I've written books inspired by what was being published when I was a teen. But *Strike the Zither* is, without a doubt, the book I wrote *for* teen me. The story is crammed with everything I love, and for instilling that love, I have to thank my parents. Mom and Dad, watching the old epics with you will always be one of my happiest childhood memories.

I also have to take this moment to thank Jamie Lee: You're the reason I stumbled into my first Penn EALC class. The rest, we could say, is history.

To my fiercest early readers, Heather and William. Heather, for loving Consumption Crow. And William, who reads all of my books but devoured this one in a single sitting.

One of Zephyr's sobriquets is Fate Changer, a title that should also go to my editor, Jen Besser. Jen, thank you for seeing something worthwhile in my weird brain, and for championing this story in particular. I carry your voice in my head when I write Zephyr and Crow these days.

Gratitude goes to my agent, John Cusick, for making the magical connection in the first place. To the team at Macmillan, with shout-outs to Luisa, Kelsey, Teresa, Johanna, Jackie Dever, Taylor Pitts, and Kat Kopit. To Aurora Parlagreco and to Kuri Huang for another beautiful cover. The portrait illustrations at the front are by a gem of a human, Tida Kietsungden. The map is by Anna Frohman.

I appreciate all the early eyes on this work, particularly from Jamie, Kat, Leigh, June, and Em. Hafsah, you and I seem destined to be deadline buddies, and I'd have it no other way.

Lastly, to my readers: If you followed me from *Descendant of the Crane* or *The Ones We're Meant to Find*, I applaud you. Thank you for reading this far despite knowing what kind of ending was in store. A series is a special thing, and not one I take for granted. I'll do my utmost to deliver in book two.

Tutankhamun's Egypt

Cyril Aldred

Keeper of the Department of Art and Archaeology
at the Royal Scottish Museum

British Broadcasting Corporation

Acknowledgement is due to the following for permission to reproduce illustrations (colour plates are referred to in Roman numerals): Ägyptisches Museum, Berlin, 60; Ashmolean Museum, 9, 11, 17, 72, 76, 78, 79; British Museum, 6, 7, 74; Brooklyn Museum, 38; Peter Clayton, 32, 57; Egypt Exploration Society, 14, 16, 53; Hirmer Archives, 4, 12, 21, 24, 25, 26, 37, 45, 54, 61, 75; Michael Holford, V, VI, VIII; © F. L. Kenett, 13, 15, 18, 35, 46, 55, 66; Mansell Collection, 27; Marburg, 22, 41, 42, 44, 77; Tom Scott, 2, 3, 10, 19, 57, 63; Staatliche Museum, Berlin, 47; Roger Viollet, 28; John Webb, cover and title page, 5, 8, 39, 51, 67, IV; ZFA, II, III.

The map on page 4 was drawn by Nigel Holmes and the Chronology on page 6 compiled by Paul Jordan.

The illustration on the front cover shows mourners at the burial of the Vizier Ramose (detail of plate V). The wife is supported by an attendant. Their garments are ungirt, they pour dust on their heads while tears course down their cheeks. 'The great shepherd departs,' they wail. 'He passes by us! Come, return unto us!'

Published by the British Broadcasting Corporation, 35 Marylebone High Street London, W1M 4AA.

ISBN 0 563 12214 5
First published 1972
© Cyril Aldred 1972

Printed in England by Sir Joseph Causton and Sons Ltd, Eastleigh, Hampshire.

Contents

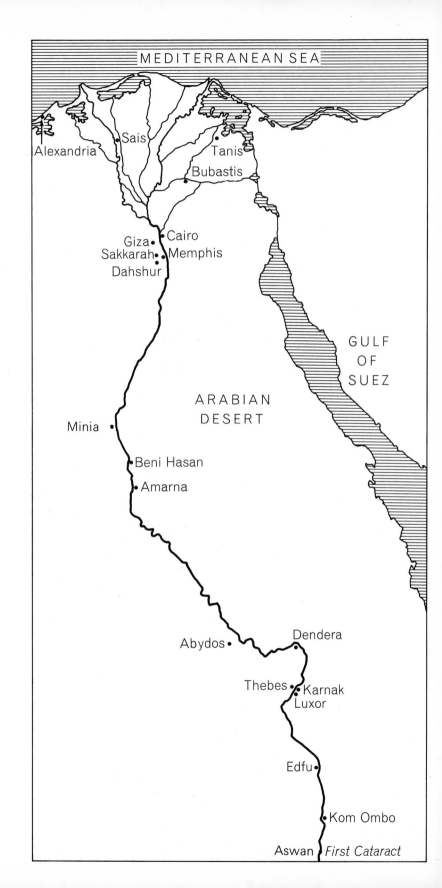

Introduction

When the boy Tut-ankh-amun came to the throne of his ancestors about the year 1362 BC, Egypt had already existed as a kingdom for over 1700 years with a characteristic culture which, however, had adapted itself to the changed conditions of the Late Bronze Age. The great stone pyramids of Giza, Sakkarah and Dahshur had by then fallen into ruins, their mortuary cults had lapsed and they were visited only by sightseers looking at the past. In a song which the young king must have heard, the poet pointed to them as examples of the vanity of human aspirations as he exhorted his listeners to eat, drink and be merry, for tomorrow death would come to them, too.

Such moralisings did not prevent the Egyptians from burying their Pharaoh with a wealth of treasure which, when it was found virtually intact in 1922, did nothing to dispel that aura of sensational mystery and exotic obscurity that has always surrounded the Ancient Egyptians from Classical times right down to the Romantic Age in which they were re-discovered. Many of the hoary old misconceptions still remain. In the following chapters, as in the television programmes on which they are based, the aim has been to show the Ancient Egyptians as a people trying to grapple with the problems of living in the world of the century in which Tut-ankh-amun reigned.

Chronology

<table>
<tr><td>PREDYNASTIC PERIOD</td><td>This is the period when the foundations of Egyptian civilisation were laid.
Egypt was not at this time a united country. It was only at the close of this period that Narmer, a king of Upper (Southern) Egypt, united the 'Two Lands'. An interesting King of Upper Egypt in late predynastic times was the 'Scorpion King'.</td></tr>
<tr><td>THE ARCHAIC PERIOD
1st Dynasty 3100–2890
2nd Dynasty 2890–2686</td><td>The First Dynasty of the newly-united country was founded, according to tradition, by Menes, whom archaeologists identify with King Narmer.</td></tr>
<tr><td>THE OLD KINGDOM
3rd Dynasty 2686–2613

4th Dynasty 2613–2494</td><td>Imhotep built the 'Step Pyramid' for King Djoser.
This was the great age of pyramid building. Cheops and Chephren are among its famous kings, Hemon and Ankhaf among its architects. The splendid statues of Prince Rahotep and his wife belong to this time.</td></tr>
<tr><td>THE OLD KINGDOM
5th Dynasty 2494–2345

6th Dynasty 2345–2181</td><td>A time when the power of the great nobles was beginning to grow at the expense of the King's. The lavishly appointed tomb of Mereruka at Sakkarah belongs to this time.
After the long rule of the last Pharaoh of this dynasty, Pepy II, internal strife led to the complete breakdown of national government.</td></tr>
<tr><td>THE 1ST INTERMEDIATE PERIOD
7th–10th Dynasties
2181–2133</td><td>During this troubled feudal period, with its ephemeral and local dynasties, pyramids and tombs were ransacked.</td></tr>
</table>

THE MIDDLE KINGDOM

11th Dynasty 2133–1991	Egypt was gradually brought back under unified rule. Mentuhotep II centred his new government on Thebes. The Governor Mesehti took to his grave two sets of wooden model soldiers.
12th Dynasty 1991–1786	A period of strong central rule, under the powerful Sesostrid pharaohs. A jar of Nile water from the tomb of Sit-Hathor Yunet belongs to this time.

2ND INTERMEDIATE PERIOD

13th–17th Dynasties 1786–1567	A confused period, dominated in its latter half by foreign (Hyksos) rule, especially in Lower (Northern) Egypt.

THE NEW KINGDOM

18th Dynasty 1567–1320	The kings of this dynasty, the first of whom expelled the foreign rulers, were among the most powerful and celebrated of all the pharaohs of Ancient Egypt. Among them, Amenophis I, II, and III; Queen Hatshepsut; Tuthmosis III; Tuthmosis IV; Akhenaten and Tut-ankh-amun. The jewellery of Queen Ah-hotep and the splendid tombs of the nobles at Thebes belonged to this period. Rekhmire was a great vizier of the time, and Amenophis-son-of-Hapu raised the Colossi of Memnon for Amenophis III.
19th and 20th Dynasties 1320–1085	During these two dynasties, Egyptian imperial power went from its zenith under Seti I and Ramesses II into decline under the later Ramessids, when the Asiatic dependencies were lost and another bout of tomb-looting began.

THE LATE DYNASTIC PERIOD

21st–30th Dynasties 1085–341	A succession of foreign rulers interleaved with native Egyptian pharaohs oversaw Ancient Egypt's final decline. The last real Egyptian pharaoh was Nectanebo II, who built extensively all over Egypt until driven out of power by the Persians.

THE PTOLEMAIC PERIOD

332–30	During this period of rule by the descendants of Alexander's general, the great temples of Philae, Edfu, Kom Ombo, Esna and Dendera were built.

I

Scene in the tomb-chamber of the craftsman Snedjem at Deir el-Medina, Western Thebes, showing the owner and his wife performing agricultural labours in the Fields of Yalu – the Egyptian equivalent of the Elysian fields. Like Egypt, this Netherworld, ruled by Osiris, has its fields, canals, ponds, and groves of date and dom palms and its flowering plants. The Egyptian farmer could readily visualise Paradise as a land where perpetual spring prevailed and the corn grew to a height of nine cubits. The good life consisted in tending the domains of Osiris eternally as he had once cultivated the fields of Egypt.

1 The People

For the most part the Ancient Egyptians, like their descendants today, were farmers laboriously tilling the soil of Egypt, draining its marshlands and extending the cultivation little by little every year. The development of their natural resources was the constant preoccupation of countless generations who boasted of the produce of their fields and were no less proud of their prize cattle fattened and garlanded for sacrifice to the gods, or for display on the day they were counted for census purposes.

The power and prestige of Ancient Egypt reposed mainly in its agriculture, and in this respect it was the wealthiest country in the ancient world, though its immense gold reserves and monopoly of tropical products made it esteemed and courted by the other great nations of antiquity. Nevertheless it was its fleshpots that were celebrated among the contiguous hungry nations, its surplus grain succouring the Hittites in their days of famine as well as the city mob a millennium later in the time of Imperial Rome.

Here is how the poet Paibes described the great city of Raamses on the building of which in the thirteenth century BC the Israelites were supposed to have toiled:

Its fields are full of all good things and it has provisions and sustenance every day. Its channels abound in fish and its lakes in birds. Its plots are green with herbage and its banks bear dates. Its granaries are overflowing with barley and wheat and they reach unto the sky. Fruits and fish are there for sustenance and wine from the vineyards of Kankeme surpassing honey. He who dwells there is happy: and there the humble man is like the great elsewhere.

For the Ancient Egyptians were a greatly privileged community inhabiting a rainless land that straggled a long narrow oasis for hundreds of miles in the African deserts but was blessed with a prodigious fertility. It was independent of the caprice of the weather for its prosperity and in favoured localities could bring forth two crops each year.

For most of its length, the Egyptian looking across the Nile could see the boundaries of his world in the rich mud that was deposited each year by the inundation of the great river. Beyond this narrow fertile belt was tawny desert, mostly sterile and inhospitable. The division between cultivation and aridity, life and death, good and evil, was therefore clear and complete and gave the Egyptian his characteristic awareness of an essential duality in his universe.

The Ancient Egyptian believed that the waters that were under the earth welled up each year from subterranean caverns and submerged the land in their flood. To this simple circumstance Egypt owed her fertility, indeed her very existence and the character of her ancient civilisation. Except at rare intervals when a succession of low Niles brought 'the years of the hyaena when men went hungry', or when too high a flood destroyed the ancient protective dams and dykes, the beneficent river spread its life-giving waters and fertilising mud over the exhausted land in an annual miracle of rebirth out of aridity. In the semi-tropical climate abundant crops could be rapidly produced each season and an ample surplus was available for next year's seed and for lean times.

The farmer's labours, though well rewarded, were burdensome and almost continuous except at the height of the inundation. They were largely concerned with irrigation, with the raising of dams to hold back flood-water in shallow basins so that silt could settle on the fields and the ground become thoroughly soaked; or the piercing of dykes to allow water to flow from one area to another as the river receded; or the building of moles to protect towns from the flood-waters. In spring and summer the higher-lying fields had to be watered by means of the *shaduf* or well-sweep, or from jars suspended from a yoke.

Besides its arable farms, Egypt had a large population of domestic animals such as oxen, sheep, goats, pigs and donkeys, and later the horse. The cattle-breeders and herdsmen led a freer and more nomadic existence in the natural habitat of such animals, the marshlands, particularly those of the Delta with their lush pasturage and thickets of rush. But the vast majority of the Egyptians were committed to the cultivation of land as much by predilection as of necessity. They were deeply attached to the soil and un-happy away from their valley.

They did not, however, function spontaneously but had to be organised and directed on a national scale so that the gifts of the Nile could be developed to the full. They were merely the governed. In our next chapters we shall look at the men who governed them.

2

To the right above, the scribe Nakht sits in an arbour watching with a benevolent eye the work in his fields. Before him are sacks of corn and a meal of dates, bread, onions and wine. A farmer guides his plough pulled by two heifers which are yoked at the horns. Other labourers fell trees or hack at scrub. Below, a farmer and his men plough and seed the fresh earth. On the higher ground the inundation has left pools and mud in which the hoers sink to their ankles. A thirsty worker takes a pull from a water-skin slung in a tree.

3 (above)
In the upper register grapes are picked from vines grown espalier-wise, and brought to the press where five men tread them out. The wine gushing forth is bottled in large amphorae closed with a rush and mud cap and stamped with an oval seal. Below, three men at a signal given by the look-out in the papyrus thicket are trapping fowl over a pool set with a clap-net. Two men are plucking, cleaning and 'jerking' the birds before preserving them in jars with salt. Offering-bearers bring pomegranates, birds, grapes and fish.

4 (left above)
Userhet in his chariot hunts gazelles, hares and other creatures of the desert. A pair of hyaenas have been flushed out; one flees with the rest, the other sinks wounded. The desert wadys in ancient times had not been reduced to complete aridity by over-grazing by goats and camels. They supported wild game, ibex, gazelles, ostriches, hares and their predators, the lion and his relations. Userhet is shown in the usual convention of dashing into the chase, either of men or animals, with the reins tied round his waist. Actually, he would be driven by a groom.

5 (left below)
A scribe, right, registers the tropical products brought from Nubia and the Sudan. In the upper row, these consist of logs of ebony, ostrich feathers, a basket of ostrich eggs, gold in the form of rings and bags of dust, a green monkey on its special stool and six jars of ochre. In the lower register, besides gold of various grades, there are cheetah skins, elephant tusks and baskets of carnelians and green-stone. The ivory and ebony were exported in finished products all over the Near East. Both names in fact reflect their ancient Egyptian origins.

6 (above)

Farmers delivering their cattle for an annual count and tax assessment. If an animal had died, its hide had to be produced instead. The scribes on the left with their document chests and writing cases are entering numbers and checking inventories. A farmer, above, kneels to greet the chief accountant, kissing his foot. The cattleman with the rolled halter calls out to his companion: 'Buck up! Don't natter to the effendi. He detests blitherers. He'll do what is right and won't listen to your tale. He records the silent man properly and is not hard on folk. He knows what's what.'

7 (right)

Offering-tables piled high with some of the produce of Egyptian farms. On the left is an ornamental bouquet made of papyrus stalks, lotus flowers and mandrake fruits. In the foreground are four wine-jars on light wicker stands draped with vine leaves and floral caps. Such jars were inscribed with the year of vintage, the names of the vineyard and vintner, and often the assessment of quality. Behind them is a rush mat heaped with loaves and cakes, honeycomb, baskets of figs, pomegranates, bunches of grapes, cuts of beef, a goose and a bunch of lotus flowers.

8 (above)

The Egyptians personified the Nile as Hapy, a fat, well-fed denizen of the marshlands, often painted blue and bearing gifts including jars of water, river plants, pond-fowl and fish. The waters of the Nile, which could turn desert into fertile land, were thought to be charged with divine power able to create life out of death. A hymn to Hapy describes him as 'The Father of the Gods, Abundance . . . the Food of Egypt. Everyone rejoices on the day you come forth from your cavern,' – a reference to the annual inundation of the Nile.

9 (right)

At each inundation all the able-bodied men were called up for service in the national corvée when the peasantry were thrown out of work by the rising waters of the Nile. They reported for duty with their earth-moving equipment – a hoe, pick and basket – with which they cleared irrigation channels and raised dykes. A similar compulsory service was thought to exist in the Osirian Hereafter, and the Egyptian provided himself with magic substitutes, *shawabti* figures, which would perform such onerous labours for him. Even kings were not exempt and this shawabti of Tut-ankh-amun is one of many that were buried with him.

10

A scene in the tomb of Ipy shows the house of the owner, left, with steps leading up to the portico. The garden is being watered by a hunch-back working at a *shaduf* or well-sweep. A leather bucket on the end of a pole is counterbalanced by a mass of limestone at the other end. The pole pivots on a support of whitewashed mud. With such a device the Egyptian watered his high-lying fields during the summer cultivation. The machine is still used in rural areas of Egypt. The garden grows papyrus, lotus, cornflowers, poppy, mandrakes, pomegranates, willow, persea and figs.

2 The Divine King

While Egypt may have been the gift of the Nile, as the Greeks affirmed, the peculiar nature of its culture was the creation of their Pharaohs. Civilisation arose in river valleys elsewhere in the Near East with economies based upon agriculture: they, too, had a unifying system of communications afforded by a great river and knew the art of writing and keeping records, without which no great civilisation can flourish. Yet they remained a collection of rival city-states, whereas Egypt displayed a national conformity under the leadership of a deity.

For the Pharaoh is a prime example of the god incarnate as king. This concept comes from that stratum in Egyptian culture that belongs to Africa, where similar rulers have existed until recently. A tangible god, whose sole authority could produce results by the exercise of the divine attributes of 'creative utterance', 'understanding' and 'justice', appealed to the Egyptian mentality and gave the nation confidence to overcome formidable obstacles. The Pharaoh from the start was a divine leader whom the entire nation united in following.

The prehistoric rain-maker or pastoral chief who was thought to keep his people, their crops and their·cattle, in health and prosperity by exercising a magic control over the weather was thus transformed into the historic Pharaoh, able to sustain and protect the nation by having command over the Nile in a rainless land. Each year he performed ceremonies which were designed to ensure that the waters of the Nile rose with unfailing regularity and were properly used. It was not only the magic throne that he sat on that made the king divine; an ancient folk-yarn relates how the first three kings of the Vth Dynasty were born of the wife of a mere priest by the sun-god, Re himself; and this fiction of a theogamous birth for the Pharaoh is preserved for as long as the kingship lasted in Egypt. The Divine Marriage is represented on several temple walls. The sun-god takes the form of the Pharaoh and fills the Chief Queen with the divine afflatus by holding the sign of life to her nostrils. As a result of this union the heir apparent will be born. Perhaps the most celebrated version of this myth is the one represented on the walls of the funerary temple of Queen Hatshepsut at Western Thebes.

Similarly the coronation of the king, though conducted on earth by chamberlains who had the royal insignia in their charge, was thought to take place in heaven and to be performed by the gods, as is represented on so many temple walls. King Tuthmosis III in the fifteenth century BC claims that it was Amun of Thebes who recognised him as his son as he was serving as a mere boy in the temple at Karnak; and he thereupon flew like a divine falcon to heaven and was crowned by the sun-god: though this is probably a fanciful way of saying that it was his earthly father Tuthmosis II who crowned him in the sanctuary of the temple as his co-regent. The harmony between the divine kingship and the natural world is seen particularly in the intimate connection between the Pharaoh and the Nile on which the prosperity of Egypt depended. Even the sun-worshipping monotheist, Akhenaten, was hailed as 'A Nile which flows daily giving life to Egypt.' The coronation of the king took place at a time which was heralded by the rising of a bright star, Sirius, at the beginning of the inundation. This moment was the auspicious point for the sympathetic rising of a new king and a new Egypt out of the old land drowned in the chaotic waters of the inundation.

Each king, therefore, at his advent was regarded as recreating the old universe anew in the primal pattern that had come down intact from the time when the gods had ruled the earth. Their son and incarnation was on the throne of his ancestors and when he died and was assimilated to Osiris, the god of the dead, his son would reign in his stead. Thus Egypt was eternally under the beneficent rule of God.

Rejoice, O land, in your entirety! A goodly time has come. A Lord has arisen for all countries .... The water stands and fails not and the Nile carries a high flood. The days are long, the nights have hours and the months come aright. The Gods are content and joyful, and life is spent in laughter and wonder.

So sang the scribe at the accession of Mineptah in 1237 BC. 'A Lord has arisen for all countries' – it was not only that the Pharaoh was Lord of Egypt, he was the master of the circuit of the sun's disk. The neighbouring nations recognised that the divine ruler of so rich, so unified and so powerful a state as Egypt was a god indeed. At his advent they journeyed to him bearing rich gifts and seeking his blessing.

The idea of this god incarnate, his birth and coronation, bequeathed a legend and a tradition to the nations of the Near East which persisted for thousands of years.

II

Ceremonial macehead of Scorpion, an early ruler, showing him celebrating the rite of 'Opening the Dykes', performed when the inundation began to fall. The king 'cuts the first sod' with a pick while an official waits to remove it in a basket. Beyond the thicket of rushes the Queen waits in her carrying-chair: women dance before her. In the background are standards from which hang plovers and bows signifying Scorpion's sovereignty over Egyptians and foreigners. He wears a tall cap, the White Crown of Upper Egypt, and a tail at his back. In a boat moored nearby he will sail into the new basin he is opening. The prehistoric rainmaker now controls the Nile.

12 (above)

Pyramidion of a fallen granite obelisk at Karnak showing Queen Hatshepsut, who usurped supreme power and is represented as a Pharaoh, kneeling before Amun to have her crown affixed by the god. The crown she wears is the Blue or War Crown, a helmet-like headpiece which makes its appearance in the XVIIth Dynasty. The crowning is performed under the sign for the vault of heaven. The coronation of the King, like his procreation, is the concern only of the gods.

13 (left)

Gilded wood statuette of Tut-ankh-amun as the god Horus of Lower Egypt. He wears the Red Crown and stands upon a papyrus skiff, harpoon in one hand and a chain in the other to capture the animal of Evil who has taken the form of a hippopotamus and hidden in the marshes. Horus, an ancient sky-god, was manifest as a falcon and incarnate in the King. This relationship is expressed in many ways. The King rules – 'while yet in the egg', and on death 'flies to the horizon'. Two of his names bore the title of Horus, and he often wears garments of a feather design.

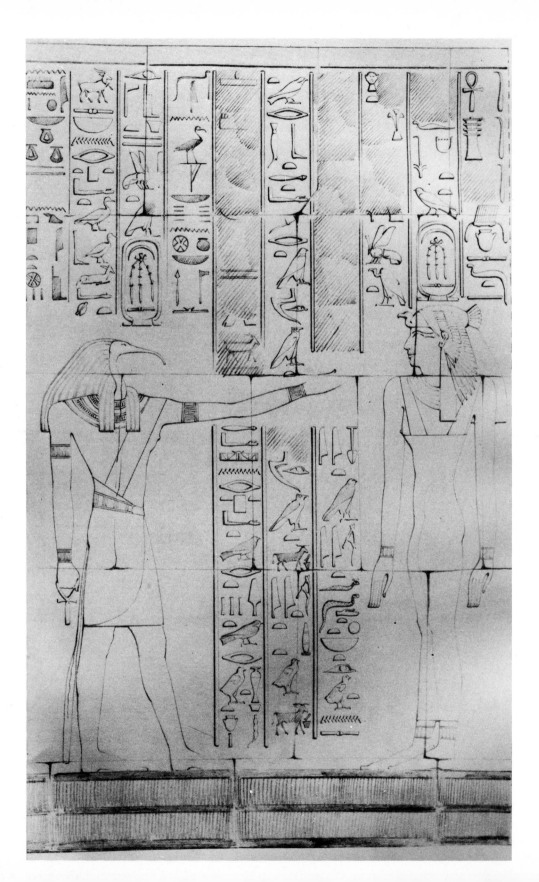

I (above)
Wall-painting from the tomb of Sobek-hotpe showing a delegation of Syrians bringing children and rich gifts to the Pharaoh at his accession. The leaders in their ornate garments fall to the ground and 'smell the earth', before the new god-king upon his throne, in order to beg his blessing. Their gifts consist of gold and silver vessels, an ivory horn full of precious oil, and an eagle-headed rhyton of Mycenaean design probably acquired by trade from the Aegean region. Such scenes also show contingents from Nubia and occasionally from the 'Isles in the Great Green [Mediterranean]'.

14 (left)
The myth of the divine birth, recognition and coronation of the Pharaoh is depicted in several temples. The sun-god takes the form of the Pharaoh and begets the heir-apparent by filling the Chief Queen with the divine afflatus. The drawing opposite shows Thoth, the ibis-headed messenger of the gods, announcing the glad tidings to Queen Ah-mose, the mother of Hatshepsut. Other stages of the myth show the Creator Khnum forming small figures of the 'king' and his soul on a potter's wheel, and the procession to the birth-chamber where the infant is born, recognised by the sun-god and suckled by the divine nurses.

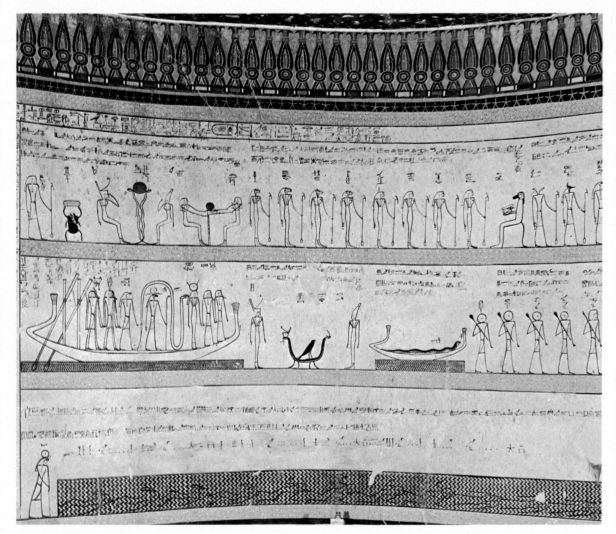

II (above)

The pith of the papyrus sedge which grew abundantly in the marshes of Ancient Egypt could be easily sliced into strips which, when laid edge to edge and crossed with similar strips at right angles, only needed a light pressing to dry into sheets of paper. Such sheets could be pasted together to form rolls. New papyrus was white and pliable but as it aged it became yellow and brittle. The walls of the burial chamber of King Tuthmosis III are decorated as though an ancient copy of 'The Book of What is in the Underworld' has been unrolled against them, and the ground is painted yellow to show its antiquity.

III (right)

At the redness of sunset, Re stepped from the day-boat into the night-boat. The sun-god, now in the form of a ram-headed being called Flesh, bears the sun-disk on his head and is protected by the coils of a huge serpent. He is accompanied by divinities in the boat as it is towed on the waters under the earth through the regions of the night hours, illuminating the Underworld, overcoming its hostile denizens and undergoing transformations which will result in his being born at the next dawn as Kheperer, the scarab, a name which means 'coming into existence'. This painted relief of the night-boat with its crew is in the tomb of Sethos I. Below, the sun-god Atum overcomes the serpent fiend Apophis.

IV

Scene on the side of a painted box, showing Tut-ankh-amun vanquishing Asiatics who fall headlong before his strong right arm. He is mounted in a chariot, shooting into a disordered mass of the enemy distinguishable by their heavy beards, long-sleeved garments and rectangular bucklers. The king is accompanied by his mounted suite and two negro fan-bearers. The scene is more fantastic than real. The ordered calm of the Pharaoh, the embodiment of right, contrasts with the confused mass of the enemy, symbols of error and evil.

V

'A goodly burial' was the ideal to which every Egyptian who was rich enough aspired. 'Remember the day of burial, the passing into bliss when the night shall be consecrated to you with oils and bandages. A procession is formed . . . your coffin is gilded, its head inlaid with lapis lazuli, a canopy above it. You are placed on the bier and oxen draw you. Then the musicians shall await your coming and the mourners dance before the door of your tomb.' Part of the funeral procession of the Vizier Ramose, showing professional mourners beating their breasts and pouring dust on their heads while servants carry objects he used in life for deposition in his 'mansion of eternity'.

VI (above)

A scene painted on a wall in the tomb of the King's land agent, Menna, showing scribes with cords knotted at standard lengths measuring the standing crops to estimate the yield. On the right a farmer and his small son conduct the scribes through the fields while another tenant and his wife bring them a corn-dolly and first-fruits. Below, scribes with their writing palettes and document cases record the yield of winnowed grain as it is measured out in standard containers. From such records, a document like the Wilbour Papyrus (plate 38) would be compiled.

VII (right)

At his advent Tut-ankh-amun claimed that Egypt was 'topsy-turvy' through the religious revolution of his predecessor Akhenaten, who had banished the old gods in favour of his sole deity, the Aten. Tut-ankh-amun had to restore the nation's morale and prosperity by returning to the former way of life and the worship of the old gods. Their neglected shrines were rebuilt, their estates re-endowed and their destroyed images remade. This statue at Karnak shows Amun, the god of Thebes who had suffered most under Akhenaten, carved in the reign of Tut-ankh-amun with his features.

VIII (above)

The cycle of the reincarnation of the god who ruled Egypt at each new reign is seen in the features of the Osiris myth where his son, Horus, took his place on the throne of the living, while the murdered god was resurrected to rule the realm of the dead. Each new Horus, who was usually the son of his predecessor, in turn was assimilated to Osiris on death (plate 78). In this wall-painting from the tomb of Tut-ankh-amun, the successor, Ay, in the dress of a living king, performs the last rites for his predecessor who is shown as the mummified Osiris, even though Ay was much older than Tut-ankh-amun and not his son.

15 (right)

Carved and painted wooden head of the infant Tut-ankh-amun emerging from a lotus flower. According to a myth popular at Hermopolis, creation began when out of the ocean of Chaos a lotus arose and opened its petals to disclose the young sun-god whose light dispelled the darkness on the face of the waters. The advent of the new Pharaoh is often represented as the appearance of a child upon a lotus, since he was the son of the sun-god and each king was believed to re-create the Egyptian universe in the old form at the beginning of his reign.

16

Relief from his temple at Abydos showing Sethos I, c. 1317 BC, wearing the *Atefu* Crown, with horns, feathers and sun-disks of his coronation. He holds the crook and 'flail' and has a false beard attached to his chin – all reminders of the prehistoric origin of the Pharaoh as a pastoral chieftain. He sits on a throne personified by the mother goddess, Isis, who thus 'makes the King', an idea common in Africa where chiefs' stools play a similar role. Sethos is supported by the goddesses of Upper and Lower Egypt, here represented as elegant queens. The gods Horus and Thoth bind the symbolic plants of Upper and Lower Egypt beneath him.

3   The Pharaoh as Hero

The horse-drawn chariot, introduced into the Eastern Mediterranean about the eighteenth century BC during the latest phases of the Bronze Age, wrought a greater revolution in the world of the time than the motor-car has effected in our own day. It was not only that a new and formidable armoured vehicle was introduced into the warfare of the period, but great changes were precipitated in the entire social system of the Ancient World. The warrior society that is mirrored in *The Iliad*, with its aristocracy of armoured chariot fighters, expert in the use of the javelin and the composite bow, and with its emphasis upon athletic contests and the management of horses, spread all over the Near East forming a professional military caste who established feudal states in Syria and Palestine among the petty rulers.

The Pharaohs of the New Kingdom, who were the Egyptian contemporaries of this last period of the Bronze Age, did not escape these novel ideas. Instead of the remote divine king of former ages, more of a god than a priest, and more of a priest than a warrior, the Pharaoh himself now took the field in person at the head of professional armies, the incarnation of a war-god like Baal, or Mont. To the traditional garb of a prehistoric divine king the Pharaohs added a new crown, the Blue Crown or war helmet, and replaced the old mace by a modern scimitar which even became a sceptre like the pastoral 'crook' and so-called 'flail'. Like the heroes of *The Iliad* they boasted of the harness that they had stripped off their vanquished foes. Above all, they delighted to show themselves as vainglorious Homeric champions mounted in a chariot and charging into the thick of the foe or herds of wild animals; while their prowess as athletes, archers or sportsmen is vaunted as truly superhuman. In particular Amenophis II, in a stela found near the Great Sphinx at Giza, is fulsomely praised for his sporting and military exploits. Such a divine hero had to have a memorial that not only sustained his mortuary cult but left some record of his great deeds to posterity.

It was at Thebes, the birth-place of their dynasty, that these champions chose to have their last resting-place dedicated to their own cults and that of the hero-god of Thebes, Amun. For this purpose they selected a remote and wild gorge on the western bank of Thebes, now known as the Valley of the Kings, where their tombs were hewn, some of them, like that of Sethos I, vast complexes of halls and corridors, decorated with extracts from the sacred books; but some, like that of Tut-ankh-amun, a few modest chambers, mostly bare. Only the tomb of Tut-ankh-amun has been found substantially intact. The last resting-places of nearly thirty of his fellow rulers had been plundered by the end of the New Kingdom and their occupants stripped of their opulent trappings. The royal tomb with its treasure and its occupants was in a secret place. The public part of the memorial was the mortuary temple built in a row of such structures in the plain that flanked the west bank of the Nile at Thebes, separated from the Valley of Kings by a ridge of hills.

Most of these temples are little more than heaps of rubble or mere ground-plans under the sand, but the ruins of one or two others are more impressive, such as the mortuary temple of Queen Hatshepsut dominating the amphitheatre at Deir el-Bahri, and the temple of Ramesses II, known today as the Ramesseum. The most complete, however, is the mortuary temple of Ramesses III at Medinet Habu. Ramesses III, the last great native Pharaoh of Egypt, in the twelfth century BC had the task of beating back from the borders of Egypt invasions of land-hungry Libyans and assaults by con-federations of migrants known as the 'Sea Peoples', whose incursions into Asia Minor, the islands of the Aegean and the North African coast destroyed the old cultures of the Late Bronze Age in the Eastern Mediterranean, a mere decade after the fall of Troy VII. These great deeds are depicted on the walls of the mortuary temple at Medinet Habu, the defeat of the two waves of Libyans being dated to years five and eleven, and the repulse of the Sea Peoples to year eight. The latter, among whom appear forerunners of the Philistines, Dardanians, Lycians, Sicilians and other peoples of the Classical World, are shown in their peculiar ships in a great naval battle off the Nile mouths, the first representation of such warfare in history.

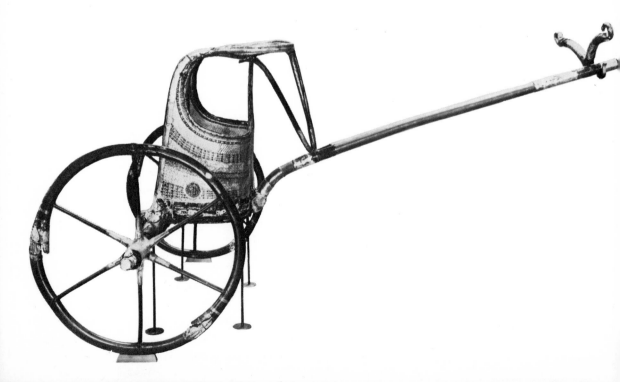

17 and 18

The horse-drawn chariots of Ancient Egypt are masterpieces of wood-working, many different species of woods being selected for the particular part they had to play in the construction. It is certain that their invention and development arose elsewhere, though there are representations of chariots being made in Egypt. They were frequently sent as gifts to the Pharaoh by the rulers of Asia. The bodies of the great state chariots were ornamented with reliefs, gilded and inlaid with coloured glass and glazes, so that when the king appeared in them it was likened to the sun-god arising in his glory. Above, is a detail of the decoration of the chariot. The bodies of these vehicles were made of wood coated with gesso, modelled in relief and covered with gold foil. The scene shows a Northern foe, an Amorite, between two Southern enemies, both negroes. All the foreigners are represented pinioned and kneeling in supplication, bound by cords in the form of the plant of Lower Egypt.

19 (above)

Part of the reliefs in the mortuary temple of Queen Hatshepsut (plate 24) showing the reception of an Egyptian trading mission by Pairohu, the Chief of Punt, a mysterious land in East Africa reached by vessels from a Red Sea port. Nehesi, the Egyptian commander, accompanied by a bodyguard, offers in exchange for myrrh, myrrh-trees, gold, ivory and other tropical products, the traditional goods of all such traders to Africa – beads and weapons. Other scenes in the same reliefs show the loading of the boats, the journey to Thebes, the unloading of the cargo and its dedication to Amun of Thebes. The scene illustrates one of the great 'deeds' that the Queen accomplished during her reign.

20 (left)

A granite stela found at Karnak showing King Amenophis II, like a Homeric champion in his chariot, shooting arrows through an ingot of bronze and a wooden target. A stela found near Memphis says of him, 'He drew 300 strong bows comparing the skill of the different bowyers . . . And afterwards he mounted a chariot like the war-god Mont in his might and shot his arrows in turn at four targets of copper each a palm thick mounted on posts .... It was a fabulous deed to shoot at such targets so that his arrows went right through them and dropped to the ground.'

21 (above)
The third King of the XVIIIth Dynasty began the tradition of having the tomb of the Pharaoh hewn in a barren wady at Western Thebes, the birthplace of his family. In this spot, now known as the Valley of the Kings, were buried thirty Pharaohs who ruled from 1510 to 1085 BC. Their tombs were robbed in antiquity and their stripped mummies hidden in two caches not discovered until the last century. Although the tomb of Tut-ankh-amun had also been violated, it is the only one to have remained substantially intact. The view in the foreground shows the entrances to the tombs of Sethos I and Ramesses I.

22 (right above)
Some of the tombs have been discovered only during the past seventy years. Others have stood open since classical times and still bear the scribbles of Greek visitors, such as the tomb of Ramesses VI (c. 1150 BC), a hall of which is illustrated above right. This chamber is elaborately decorated with scenes from the Book of Gates and the Book of Caverns. The four pillars show the King making offerings to the gods of Thebes.

23 (right below)
Ramesses II at his accession receives sceptres handed to him by Amun, seated upon a throne and supported by his consort, Mut, shown as an elegant woman wearing the vulture headdress of a queen-mother and the united crowns of Upper and Lower Egypt. The emblems of rule consist of the traditional pastoral crook and flail and also the new curved scimitar that was introduced from Asia in the eighteenth century BC with other chariot weapons such as the composite bow and the war helmet, a version of which, the Blue Crown, is here worn by Ramesses II.

24 (above)
The mortuary temple to sustain the cult of the dead King was built about a mile away from the tomb in the western plain at Thebes. One of the earliest to survive, though in a greatly ruined state, is this temple of Queen Hatshepsut at Deir el-Bahri, built on three terraces. The walls of the colonnades are decorated with scenes showing the Queen's great deeds, such as the erection of obelisks (plate 64) and the trading expedition sent to the spice-lands of Punt (plate 19). It also depicts the Queen's divine conception, birth and recognition (plate 14).

25 (right above)
The mortuary temple of Ramesses III is the most complete of such edifices. It was surrounded by a stout wall pierced by two fortified gates. Here the entire population of Western Thebes took sanctuary in the later years of the XXth Dynasty when marauding bands of Libyans were roving at large. In the foreground is a palace adjoining the First Court where the King and his suite stayed during his visits to Thebes. On the exterior North wall, reliefs show the King attacking foreign foes including the ship-borne Sea Peoples who overran Asia during his reign.

26 (right below)
The Ramesseum is the modern name for the mortuary temple of Ramesses II which stands in picturesque ruin on the edge of the cultivation at Thebes. Its Egyptian name was The House of Usimaré (i.e. Ozymandias, Ramesses II) in the Estate of Amun. Its pylons, courts and halls are considerably dilapidated but scenes of the King's exploits still remain on some of the walls (plate 49); chiefly his wars in Syria against the Hittites and their vassals. The First Court had a colossal seated statue of the King nearly 60 feet high hewn from a single block of granite and weighing over a thousand tons which now lies shattered (far right), and inspired the sonnet *Ozymandias* by Shelley.

27

The great deeds of Ramesses III are depicted on the outer walls of his temple (plate 25) where he drives evil, in the form of the enemies of Egypt and the animals of the wild, from the holy precincts. Here, with his sons acting as beaters, he rounds up wild cattle in the papyrus thickets by the banks of a stream. Above, still in a chariot, he hunts the animals of the desert.

4   Officials of the King

It was the officials of the Palace, a sort of Privy Council, who helped the king to govern and who in the tomb of Tut-ankh-amun are represented in a unique scene showing them wearing their white mourning bands, faithful to the end, hauling the catafalque of their dead lord on his last journey to the West.

This scene belongs more to private tombs and a splendid example may be seen in that of the Vizier Ramose. These are also the high officers of state at the time of Tut-ankh-amun, and the Egyptian equivalent of the military aristocracy that had spread with their chariots all over the Near East. Such intimates of the king might be related to him by marriage, but some claim to have been men of lowly origin who had distinguished themselves by valour in the field. Others had been brought up with the king, their mothers having been wet-nurses of the royal children. Such families tended to form dynasties of officials, their sons or nephews succeeding them in turn.

The chief offices were those of the two Overseers of the Treasury, concerned with the reception and allocation of raw materials and finished goods, plunder, tribute, and other commodities. Also important was the Overseer of the Granaries of Upper and Lower Egypt whose responsibility was the harvesting, recording and storage of the annual crops of wheat and barley. There were many other court posts such as the Chief Steward, the Master of the Horse, the Scribe of the Recruits, the First Herald, Secretary and Butler besides various underlings, chamberlains, pages and fanbearers – though the title of 'fanbearer on the right of the king' was claimed as an honorary position by the highest officers in the land.

Two officials during the New Kingdom were of especial importance. The first, a new post, was the Viceroy of Kush, the king's deputy in Nubia and the Sudan as far as the 4th Cataract. His seat of government was at Aniba, 140 miles south of the 1st Cataract, and from here he ruled his provinces in the names of the Pharaoh with an administration modelled on that of Egypt itself.

The other official was the First Prophet, or High Priest of Amun at Thebes, whose temple received such enormous endowments and gifts from grateful Pharaohs that the person who administered its considerable wealth could not fail to become an important power in the state.

The chief official under the king during the New Kingdom, however, was still the vizier whose office goes back to the dawn of history and persisted until the fourth century BC. Generally at this period there were two viziers serving in Upper and Lower Egypt. One of them, Rekh-mi-re, who served Tuthmosis III, has left in his tomb a detailed account of his duties. These included not only a daily report to his sovereign on the state of the nation but also the delivering of judgements in his Audience Hall, the receiving and issuing of instructions to the various branches of central government, and the making and rescinding of appointments.

He was chiefly concerned with the collection of taxes in Upper and Lower Egypt, but he also mobilised the king's personal bodyguard; saw to the cutting of timber and general irrigation; directed village headmen as to summer cultivation; made a weekly inspection of the water resources; considered deficits in temple revenues and assessments for taxation. He also confirmed the state of the fortresses on the borders; took measures against raids by robbers and nomads, and saw to the fitting out of ships. He presided over important civil cases referred to him from lower courts; he dealt with questions of land tenure and the witnessing of wills; and he considered criminal cases requiring heavy sentences, all in his capacity of Chief Justice. He also received foreign embassies, and supervised workshops and building enterprises including the work on the Royal Tomb. No wonder that the Pharaoh, in delivering the homily that it was customary to address to high officials when they took office, should say to Rekh-mi-re:

Look to the office of the vizier. Be vigilant about what is done in it, for it is the mainstay of the entire land. As to the vizierate, it is not sweet, indeed, but it is bitter as gall. For the vizier is hard copper enclosing the gold of his master's house.

The king went on to warn the new incumbent against using his rank to further his own interest. He is to show favour to no one.

These then were the king's high officials and some of the principles by which they were supposed to govern. Such officials were well recompensed because, as an early Pharaoh remarked to his son, a poorly paid official is open to corruption. Such men formed the administrative arm of government.

28

High officials of Tut-ankh-amun wearing white mourning bands around their heads and drawing the catafalque of their dead lord to his tomb. They comprise the privy council that helped the King to govern. In the penultimate row are the two viziers of Upper and Lower Egypt with their shaven heads and long gowns. The last man in the cortège must be the King's Deputy for the Army. Probably also included, though not identified, are the Viceroy of Nubia and Kush, the King's First and Second Heralds, the Overseers of the Treasury, the Chief Steward, the High Priests of Amun, the Elders of Thebes and the Overseer of Works.

29 (above)
King Amenophis II as a child on the lap of his wet-nurse, Amen-em-ipet. He is shown as a miniature Pharaoh complete with regalia, his feet resting on a footstool decorated with the bound figures of the traditional nine nations whom he leads captive with cords. Ken-amun, a son of Amen-em-ipet and therefore the King's foster-brother and companion from earliest days, was appointed his High Steward upon his accession to the throne. Such families of officials tended to follow one another in office, the son succeeding the father for several generations.

30 (right)
The audience chamber of the Vizier Rekh-mi-re, in his capacity as Chief Justice, showing its windows and the tall columns that support the roof. Lesser magistrates are drawn up in two lines to the left and right with their scribes holding writing palettes. In the central aisle, and outside the hall, ushers are introducing the litigants or debtors. Two messengers arrive at the double with dispatches and are met by janitors. The vizier is said to be 'holding a session to hear [law suits] in the hall . . . dispensing justice impartially . . . no petitioner weeping because of him.'

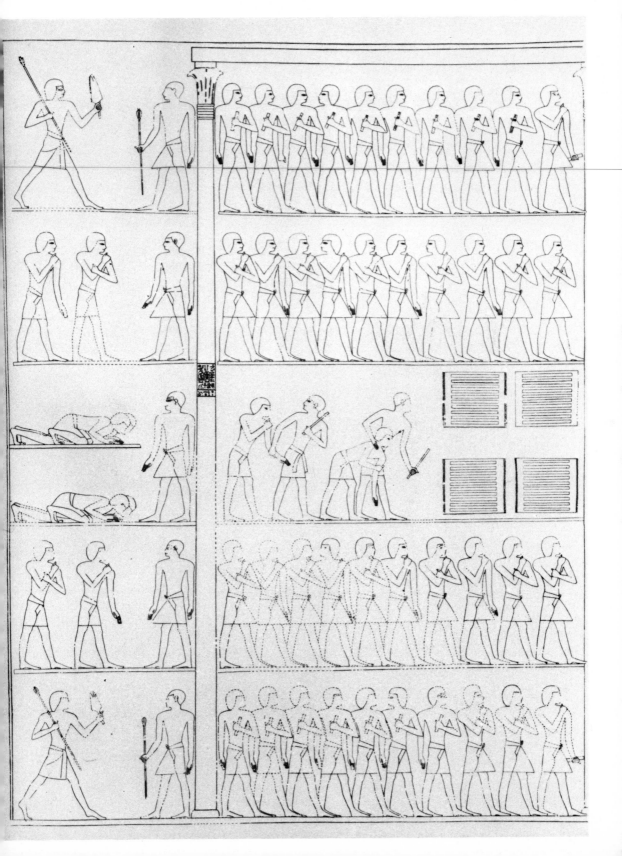

31 (above)

Huy, the Viceroy of Kush, who governed Nubia and the Lower Sudan in the name of the King during the reign of Tut-ankh-amun. He is shown on the right carrying two formal bouquets as he leaves the palace after his appointment, and is accompanied by his sons who also carry flowers. One of them succeeded him as Viceroy. On the left, in the upper register, holding his fan of office, Huy receives his commission from a Chief Treasurer who says, 'Thus decrees Pharaoh – "there is handed over to you from El Kab to Napata"' (the extent of the province he is to govern). In the lower scenes Huy receives a gold signet ring, his seal of office.

32 (far left)

A black granite statue, now in Turin, of the Second Prophet of Amun, Anen, wearing the leopard skin of his office. The princes of Thebes, who drove the Asiatic Hyksos kings off the throne of Egypt in the sixteenth century BC, gave large endowments to Amun, the god of their native city who had promoted their fortunes. This great wealth was administered by four prophets or High Priests who became very influential in state affairs. Anen, who held office for much of the reign of Amenophis III, was the brother-in-law of the king and the uncle of Tut-ankh-amun.

33 (left)

Black granite statue, in Cairo, of the Vizier Woser and his wife, showing him wearing the distinctive gown upheld by a halter. Woser was preceded in office by his father, and succeeded by his nephew, during the long reign of Tuthmosis III. All these officials left detailed accounts in their tombs of their duties and appointments. Every morning, explains one, the Vizier 'is to enter the Great Palace, and as soon as he appears at the portal the Chief Treasurer is to advance and meet him saying, "All your affairs are safe and sound, and the Royal Estate is safe and sound."'

34

The Southern Vizier was also responsible for the collection of taxes in Upper Egypt from the First Cataract almost to Amarna in Middle Egypt. Here the headmen of Elephantine bring their taxes in kind, to be recorded and checked by the officials. In the top register, chests of cloth, gold and silver beads and gold rings are received. In the central register the gold is weighed. In the bottom register a policeman escorts a tax-payer who presents cloths, bundles of sticks, cordage, baskets of fruit and ten grindstones. In addition, cattle, honey, pigeons, grain, beans, gum and grass mats were delivered.

5 Scribes

In a land so dependent upon the control of the flood waters for its prosperity, the Egyptians had been accustomed from earliest times to an organised way of life, but their highly centralised administration would not have been possible without the discovery of writing and it is probable that the development of the machinery of state and the art of writing went hand in hand.

The character that writing took in Egypt was due to the invention of a remarkable material – papyrus – one of the great contributions of the Egyptians to civilisation. As early as the fourth millennium BC, the Egyptians had learnt to make a flexible paper from the pith of the papyrus sedge which grew in profusion in the undrained verges of cultivation.

The Egyptian practice of writing in ink on this paper, and very occasionally on leather, was already in force at the very dawn of history; but all the evidence is that the art of writing was used not so much to create works of literature as to preserve records and documents of a profusion and complexity that can only be paralleled in modern times with the widespread use of a paper made from rags.

The extreme compactness and portability of Egyptian documents made it possible to develop filing systems and to keep repositories of records for hundreds of years. There are several references to the consulting of ancient archives in temple libraries and sometimes of papyri so old that gaps had been worn or eaten into the texts. No other nation of antiquity had such convenient means for retaining a memory of its past and documenting every aspect of its life and activities.

Despite the wealth of papyri that exists in the storerooms of most great collections, the mass that has survived is an infinitesimal proportion of what was written in antiquity. The paper-work by which the Egyptian machinery of state functioned was obviously very voluminous and highly organised, but it is clear that it could never have operated without the existence of an educated and busy legion of scribes, able to read, write and calculate and keep such records. This class formed a bureaucratic élite versed in the art of writing and aware of its privileges. 'The scribe,' wrote one of their number in a composition that was popular with schoolboys a century after the death of Tut-ankh-amun, 'directs the work of everyone. For him there are no taxes, he pays his dues in writing.' 'It is the scribe,' wrote another, 'who assesses and collects the taxes in Upper and Lower Egypt. He governs the entire country and every affair is under his control.'

The training of a scribe began at a very early age and was completed by the time he reached manhood at about sixteen. The pupil was sent to one of the schools attached to the great departments of state such as the Palace, the Treasury and the Army, or to the 'Houses of Life', the scriptoria attached to the larger temples where books and inscriptions were copied and compiled. The wealth of school exercises that has survived shows that most scribes had to spend part of their time instructing pupils, probably their sons or relations, since education in Egypt was largely on the master and apprentice system.

In learning the classical utterance of the Middle Kingdom which was used for some monumental and religious purposes down to Roman times, the pupil often had to contend with a language which was already dead and which he understood only imperfectly as his copies of the classics clearly reveal. But it is often only in this garbled form that Egyptian literature has come down to us. When the young scribe had graduated from school he had his foot upon the first rung of a career in the higher ranks of the Army, the Treasury or the Palace. While a career open to all the talents was hardly possible in Ancient Egypt, where the tradition was to appoint the son to the place of his father from the Pharaoh down to the merest field labourer, it did sometimes happen that a man from humble circumstances attained to high office. In the exhortation to be a scribe which the master set his pupil to copy, the rewards of successful graduation are enticingly set forth.

A man of worth is sought for, and you are found. The man that is skilled rises step by step until he has attained the position of a magistrate.

It was through his command of writing in the hieratic and hieroglyphic scripts that the scribe for so long made Ancient Egypt the most highly organised and prosperous state in the Near East. We have in this chapter been concerned only with the scribe as a civil servant; but in addition to his accounts, reports, legal texts, letters and government files, he also produced a wide literature – novels, poems, lyrics, hymns, meditations, instructions and lamentations, as well as mathematical, surgical and medical treatises. That these were not the least esteemed of their writings is clear from a eulogy on the ancient authors written by a scribe in the thirteenth century BC.

Their monuments have crumbled in pieces. Their mortuary priests have gone; their tomb-stones are covered with sand; their chambers forgotten. But their names are pronounced because of the good books that they wrote and their memory is for ever more.

---

35 (right)
Part of the writing equipment of Tut-ankh-amun comprising an ivory palette with reed pens and two ink-pans, and a pen-case in the form of a palm-column made of wood overlaid with gold and inlaid with coloured glass. The writing palettes of several members of the royal family at this period, men and women, have survived as reminders that the Ancient Egyptian Pharaohs and their children, unlike medieval European Kings, were able to read and write. Earlier, the Pyramid Texts of the Old Kingdom had spoken of the Pharaoh as acting as the scribe of the sun-god after death.

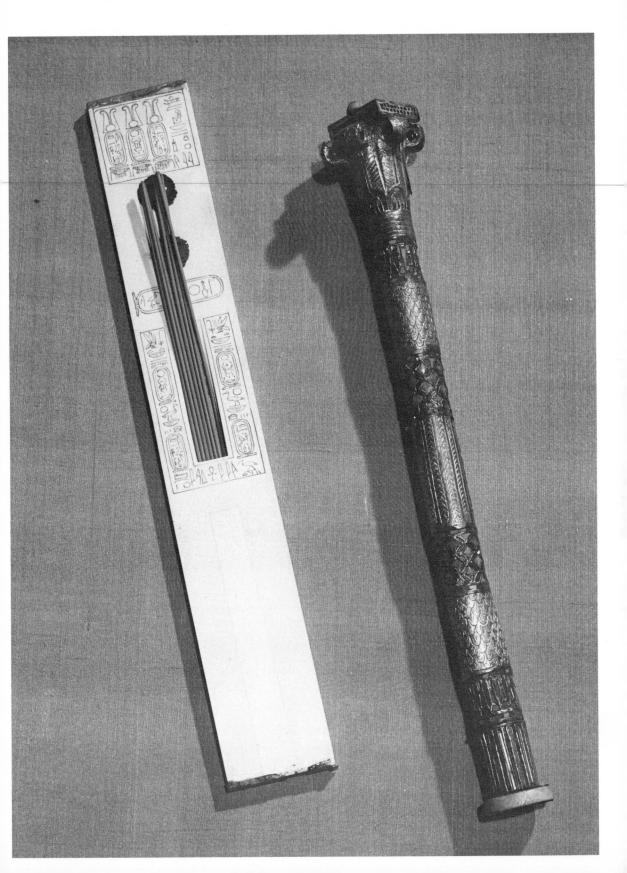

36 (above)

While Egyptian society tended to be fixed in rigid patterns, in which the son followed the calling of his father, it did sometimes happen that a man from humble circumstances attained to high office, particularly if he had been taught reading and writing. A notable case is Sennemut, the Chief Steward and general factotum of Queen Hatshepsut, whose father bore only a vague and probably posthumous title of 'worthy'. He rose by merit to high office under the Queen and was given the honorary position of tutor to her daughter Neferu-re whom he is seen nursing in this statue in Cairo.

37 (right)

Egyptian hieroglyphs are the most beautiful forms of writing ever devised, and it is probable that their aesthetic qualities as well as their hallowed tradition kept them in use for so long, especially for monumental inscriptions. At the end of their life in the Ptolemaic and Roman periods when they were employed as an esoteric mystery, they display remarkably ugly forms and a confused 'typography'. In the high periods of Egyptian culture, however, they reveal the same elegant proportions and drawing as the contemporary reliefs. In this panel two of the titles and names of King Sesostris I of the XIIth Dynasty, protected by the flying falcon Horus of Edfu, are spaced out in elegant glyphs carved in great detail.

38 (left)

The Wilbour Papyrus in the Brooklyn Museum, shown here before it was unrolled, is a fiscal survey of the various plots of cultivated land in a continuous portion of Middle Egypt, from near modern Minia to a point some eighty miles north, made in about a month during summer in the fourth regnal year of Ramesses V (c. 1156 BC). This register gives in meticulous detail particulars of the different institutions that owned the various tracts of land, the names of the farmers, the estimated yields and their assessments for taxation. Such a chance survival enables us to estimate the enormous mass of paperwork by which the Egyptian State functioned.

39 (above)

Hieroglyphs were used only for monumental and religious purposes. A more cursive and abbreviated way of writing them, called today hieratic, soon developed. In hieratic the resemblance to the original picture sign is often vestigial, and the system underwent its own evolution in spelling and grammar. The above part of a pupil's exercise is written in hieratic of the period of about a century after Tut-ankh-amun. Schoolboys were set to copy the classics, in this case, two model letters, and often their garbled versions are the only copies now existing. The master has corrected the exercise by writing more correct versions of some words and dating the exercise in the upper margin.

40

Ostrakon, or flake of limestone, written in hieratic script, a cursive development of hieroglyphs, with part of a poem on the king in his panoply of war. Papyrus was too precious to be used for school exercises and potsherds or flakes of limestone were used instead. This ostrakon, written on both sides, is at Edinburgh and is continued on another ostrakon in Turin. It describes the royal war-chariot and abounds in Canaanite words and different puns on them. Since the chariot was an Asiatic import, however, the pupil would have learnt the foreign terms for the various parts by memorising this poem.

41
Serpentine statuette of a scribe reading under the inspiration of Thoth, the god of wisdom and learning. The scribe squats tailor-wise, his gown drawn tight across his thighs to form a table for his papyrus roll which is open at one end. On an altar squats the god, here in the form of one of his familiars, the baboon, who should bear on his head the crescent and disk of the moon which are his symbols as the reckoner of time, since the Egyptian calendar was primarily lunar.

6 Soldiers of the Pharaoh

The Egypt of Tut-ankh-amun had come to know the soldier as an important and permanent element in the society of the day, and the influential advisers of the king were nearly all high ranking officers of the chariotry and the infantry, though in earlier times the army had played a much more self-effacing role.

It was, however, in the New Kingdom, after the introduction of the horse-drawn chariot by the Asiatic Hyksos kings, that warfare became mobile again and the fortress, so characteristic of the strategy of the Feudal Age and the Middle Kingdom, became as much a depot as a bastion. With the chariot came new arms and armour, new methods of warfare and a military aristocracy, as we have mentioned earlier. The small standing army of the Old and Middle Kingdoms was expanded into a large professional organisation with squadrons of chariots, each manned by a driver and fighter, and armed with such new weapons as the composite bow, heavy bronze falchion and battle-axe. Military standards enabled units to be readily located on the field of battle and instructions could be signalled by means of the war-trumpet. Engagements became more than the shock of armed bodies meeting in a general mêlée. Strategy and tactics became the concern of the Pharaohs and their war-councils; and if we are to believe the official accounts it was, for instance, the plan of battle devised by Tuthmosis III that was responsible for his great victory at Megiddo over a confederation of Asiatic princes, though the indiscipline of his raw troops lost him the early fruits of victory.

The Egyptian forces, under the supreme command of the Pharaoh or his deputy, were divided into four armies named after the principal gods. There was an elaborate chain of field command from the generals and battalion commanders through the standard-bearers to the platoon leaders. In addition, staff duties were performed by a multitude of military scribes who attended to the commissariat and other logistical matters. Thus Haremhab, the Commander-in-Chief under Tut-ankh-amun, whose foot-steps on the battlefield he claimed to have guided, chose to have himself represented as a scribe reading a hymn to the god of writing in a granite statue now in New York. Haremhab subsequently became king on the death of Tut-ankh-amun's successor, Ay, another soldier who before his elevation to the throne had been in charge of the chariotry.

The reputations of such men lay in their ability to dispose of a great mass of manpower, for one of the main tasks of the army in time of peace was to act as a labour force for the quarrying of stone, the working of the gold and turquoise mines and the erection of great monuments.

In the earlier part of the XVIIIth Dynasty, the armies were manned by native Egyptians and Nubian auxiliaries who followed the family calling. But the pick of the young men called up for service in the general corvée were also conscripted particularly for the labour force. From the reign of Amenophis III, however, it became the practice to draft foreign captives into the Egyptian forces. After the end of our period the Egyptian armies were manned more and more by foreigners – Libyans, Sudanis and finally Carian and Greek mercenaries. The Wilbour papyrus lists a number of cultivators in Middle Egypt who bear foreign names and were evidently veteran soldiers settled on the land.

Despite what the satirist had to say about the miserable life of the soldier, its rewards were considerable. Warriors who had shown bravery in the field were promoted to officers, given prisoners as serfs and decorated with 'the gold of valour'. Such awards took the form of massive flies in gold, gold or silver weapons and jewellery of considerable intrinsic value.

Even the less distinguished soldier shared in the cattle, weapons, clothing, ornaments and other loot captured from luxurious Asiatic enemies. He was pensioned off with grants of livestock, serfs, and land, from the royal domains, on which he paid taxes but which continued to be held by his family as long as they had an able-bodied male available for military service. Such soldiers formed a privileged class, devoted to the tradition of service in the armed forces. In times of peace they dwelt in comfortable settlements.

Experienced military scribes and officers were appointed to positions in the foreign service as ambassadors or district commissioners, and to such court posts as stewards of the royal estates, butlers, fan-bearers, police-chiefs and instructors to the young princes or even major-domos to the king's daughters. Whenever the hereditary succession to the throne died out at the end of a dynasty, it was these warrior intimates of the king who stepped into his empty sandals.

---

42 (right)
Another detail from the painted box of Tut-ankh-amun (plate IV) showing Egyptian foot soldiers moving over the battlefield cutting off the hands of slain negroes for the final count of victory. The infantry, in contrast to the immaculate sun-king and his mounted escort, are painted with marked realism showing them with several days' growth of beard and unkempt hair, their cut-leather aprons and garments tarnished with the stains of battle, as though the artist had remembered the words of the satirist in recounting the lot of the infantryman – 'he is born only to be torn from the arms of his mother. He is battered and bruised with floggings.'

43
A relief at Bologna showing scenes of military life. On the left, a squad of soldiers is labouring under a great baulk of timber, while a mounted scout dashes into the camp. 'The infantryman marches to Syria,' continues the satirist, 'his bread and water borne on his back like the load of an ass.' But the aristocratic charioteer fared no better – 'When he has acquired a goodly span he is overjoyed and tears madly around his home town with them, but he does not know what is in store for him . . . . When he reaches the mountains he has to cast his expensive chariot into a thicket and go on foot . . . . When he reports back he is beaten with a hundred blows.'

44
Egyptian chariotry waiting to go into action against the Hittites, from the reliefs on the exterior walls of the temple of Ramesses II at Abydos. The Egyptian chariots were manned by two warriors, a groom and a fighter carrying a large round-topped shield. His weapons were the composite bow and a light javelin hurled with the aid of a spear-thrower. (These are carried in cases strapped to the side of the car.) The Hittite chariots held three men (plate 49). If we are to believe the same satirist again, the chariot officer got his position because he came of good family, 'he squanders his patrimony on an expensive chariot in which he drives furiously.'

45

Black granite statue of Amenophis-son-of-Hapu, the great minister of Amenophis III, who was noted for his wisdom and learning and later deified. He is shown in his capacity of a military scribe, i.e. a staff officer, the Scribe of the Recruits. In this capacity he was responsible for organising all the training, supply and manpower of the armed forces. The army was also used on great public works, such as the hewing, transport and erection of the so-called Colossi of Memnon in front of the now-vanished mortuary temple of Amenophis III at Western Thebes.

46

A relief, now at Leyden, showing another high-ranking military scribe, the General Haremhab, who claimed to have guided the footsteps of his King on the battlefields of Asia, being decorated with the Award of Gold at the accession of Tut-ankh-amun. He is in festal garb with a cone of perfumed unguent on his head. He raises his arms in the sign of jubilation as chamberlains hang the gold collars around his neck. It was such experienced soldiers who in the military state of Egypt during the New Kingdom were best able to ascend the throne when the royal line died out.

47

The Egyptian armies gradually came to be manned by foreign mercenaries, some of whom were defeated enemies who took service with their captors. Akhenaten had a bodyguard of Libyan, Asiatic and negro soldiers. This stela, also of his reign, shows a Syrian spearman with his wife, being waited upon by an Egyptian servant who helps him to drink wine through a reed syphon. This anticipates the boast of Ramesses III that, through his pacification, 'The bows and weapons [of the mercenaries] reposed in the armouries. Their wives and children were beside them as they ate and drank at ease.' Such soldiers were settled on the land and farmed it on favourable terms.

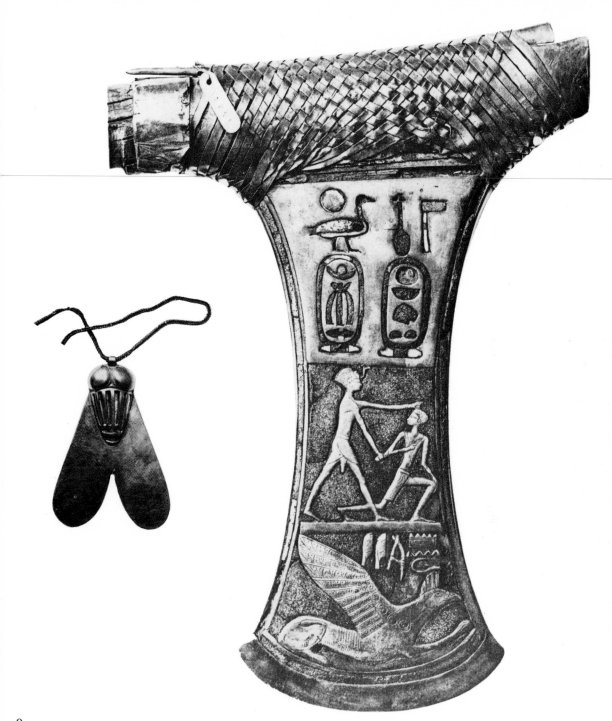

48

The massive gold fly of valour and the richly inlaid head of a parade axe from the treasure buried with Queen Ah-hotpe who rallied the Theban forces at a critical moment in their war of liberation against their Asiatic Hyksos overlords. It was appropriate, therefore, that such military decorations should have been awarded to her by her victorious son Ah-mose. He is shown on the axe-head wearing the new-fangled war-helmet and slaying one of the 'rebels' he had to defeat to secure the throne as the first Pharaoh of the XVIIIth Dynasty. Below, the Theban war-god, Mont, appears as a griffon.

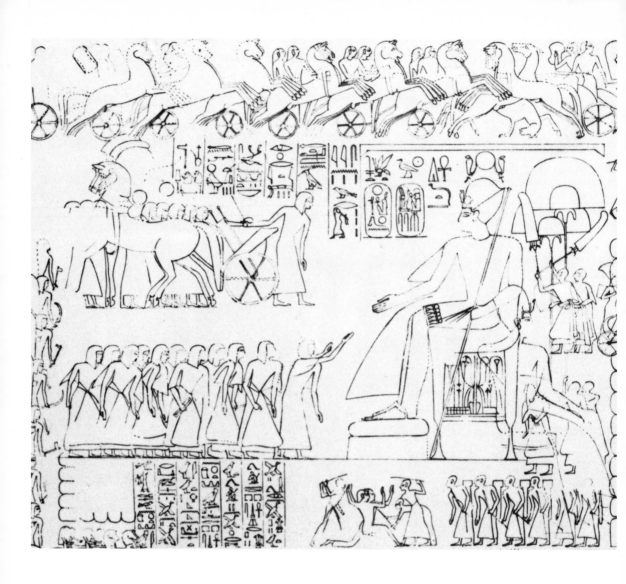

49

Line drawing of part of the scene of the Battle of Kadesh carved on the walls of several temples erected by Ramesses II. The extract shows the Egyptian advance guard encamping within a shield palisade. Two captured Hittite spies are being beaten to extort the news that the Hittite forces, far from being at Aleppo, are at hand and about to descend upon the Egyptian armies as they are strung out in columns of march. Ramesses II, on his throne, summons his war council consisting of a vizier and general officers to discuss what should best be done in this crisis. His chariot, in the charge of a groom, stands ready for him to mount. At the top, Hittite chariotry attack his camp.

7   Artists and Artisans

All the evidence suggests that the Pharaohs held their artists in high esteem. Parennefer, for instance, who filled the office of Chief Craftsman under Akhenaten, not only had a large sculptured tomb at Thebes but an equally important one at Amarna and was sufficiently intimate with his king to be appointed his butler.

Kings themselves did not disdain to be considered as artists. Bek, the chief sculptor of Akhenaten, claims that he was taught by his king; while there is a passing reference to the designing by Tuthmosis III of a set of metal vessels. If the names of only a mere handful of Ancient Egyptian artists are known and pictures of them are very rare, and above all if we are unable to accredit nearly all the surviving works of art to particular artists, that is only what we should expect. In Ancient Egypt the artist worked under the same anonymity that prevailed in the early Middle Ages. He was considered primarily as a craftsman; and sculptors and painters are often shown at work in the same studios as joiners, metal-workers, potters and other artisans.

The individuality of the artist was of no importance in Ancient Egypt; what mattered was his ability to render faultlessly the ageless conventions, which he had imbibed from his master and would impart in turn to his pupil. But despite all the forces that operated to ensure that a statue or painting should repeat only the primal pattern, Egyptian art did move. The wonder is that it should change so much; and it is often possible for the expert to date a specimen to within a few years by its stylistic features alone.

How could such artistic changes come about in the conservative and traditional milieu of the Egyptian craftsman? The answer lies in the qualities of the designers of Egyptian art. In the early days when the centre of Egyptian culture was at the capital of Memphis, it was Ptah, the god who had brought all things into being by his creative utterance, who was also the creator of all artistic enterprises. His high priest bore the title of 'Greatest of Craftsmen', and it was such literate men who designed the buildings, their decoration and their contents. They it was who guided the hands of the builders, stonemasons, painters, jewellers, joiners and other artisans who made and embellished the works that they conceived. Such humbler craftsmen were isolated in workshops attached to the palaces, the houses of the great feudal lords, or the temples of the gods to whom nearly all their lives were dedicated. Only in their leisure hours could they make something for themselves or for modest patrons.

No better example of such an institution exists than the community of workmen who hewed and decorated the tombs of the kings and their families at Thebes during the New Kingdom. The excavation of their walled village has recovered many articles and documents which tell us much of their lives and work. Generations of artisans and their families lived in this village, their employment being hereditary. They enjoyed a fair measure of independence and self-government, but the vizier or a king's butler visited the site from time to time to inspect progress and to listen to any requests or complaints. During the XXth Dynasty these were not infrequent and mostly concerned irregularities in the supply of their rations. When protests had no effect the workmen downed tools. A strike in the last years of Ramesses III caused especial consternation.

The workmen were paid in kind, though payments of silver are also recorded at the beginning of a new reign. Their rations consisted of emmer wheat and barley, for making the staple bread and beer. The manual workers were given more generous allowances than the clerks and porters. In addition they regularly received vegetables and fish and a supply of wood for fuel. Occasionally, certain bonuses in the form of salt, wine, sweet beer and other luxuries were distributed.

A considerable force of labourers was detailed to provide commodities and services for them. There was also a police force for guarding the tombs, particularly those under construction. The gangs worked a ten-day week, living and sleeping in roughly built huts near the tomb they were preparing. On their rest days and the many feast days they returned to their homes in the village. In view of the popular idea that the monuments of Ancient Egypt were built only by the blood and sweat of expendable slaves, it is disappointing to learn that these artisans worked for four hours in the morning before knocking off for a meal and a nap. The rest of their working day consisted of another four-hour stint in the afternoon. Even so, absentee-ism was common.

---

50 (right)
Quartzite stela of Bek and his wife Taheret, now in Berlin. Bek served Akhenaten as his chief sculptor, just as his father had served Amenophis III. He claims that he was taught by the king and was his favourite, by which he probably means that he carried out the peculiar ideas that Akhenaten held about the way he should be represented. Bek was almost certainly responsible for the impressively disturbing colossi that he carved for the temple that Akhenaten raised at Karnak (plate 56). Here he has carved his own figure with the fashionable distortion of his royal patron's pronounced paunch.

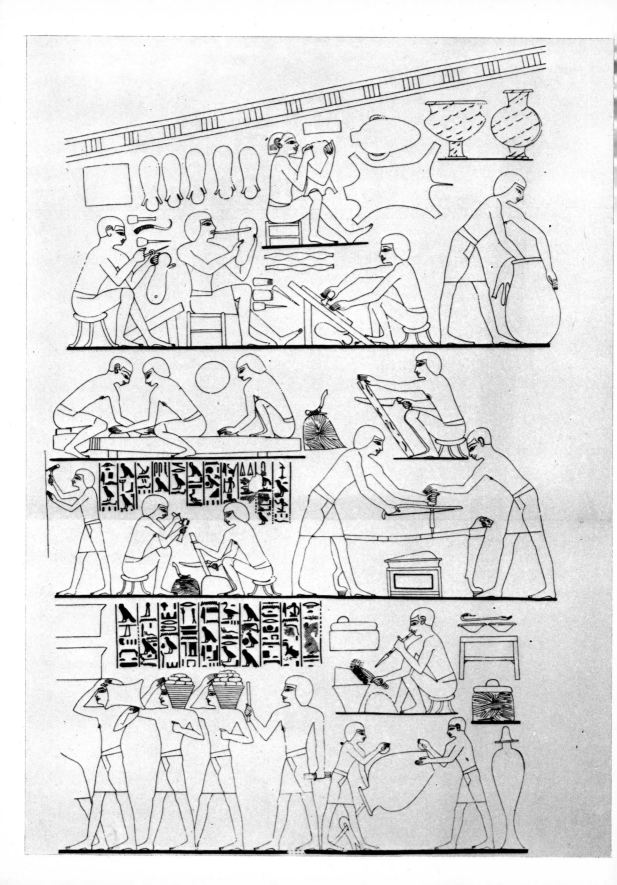

51 (above)
Part of the workshops of the King's sculptors Neb-amun and Ipuky from the painting in their tomb at Thebes. They were not only sculptors but scribes, well versed, like the earlier sculptor Iritisen in 'the sacred books' which may have been the pattern books preserving the canons stored in some of the temple libraries. They must have been familiar with, if not proficient in, all the techniques employed by the various craftsmen under their charge. Thus Neb-amun, not visible on the left, inspects a jewelled collar, armlets and bracelets brought to him on a tray for approval. Other jewels are being prepared by lapidaries who also inlay a casket. Metalworkers chase a gold vessel and sphinx, while others planish gold vessels on stakes. Above, a scribe weighs out an allocation of gold using a bronze bull's head weight, and joiners make and assemble a wooden shrine.

52 (left)
Line drawing of a painting in the tomb of the Vizier Rekh-mi-re showing part of the workshops of the temple of Amun at Thebes. In the top register leather-workers are preparing skins while others cut out and sew sandals. In the middle register joiners using adzes, saws, chisels, rubbers and a bow-drill are making a column, box and bed. In the bottom register metalsmiths are raising large vessels on a wooden stake using pebbles as hammers, while another squats at his furnace with blow-pipe and tongs. Three men under the supervision of a scribe carry bronze ingots captured in Asia by Tuth-mosis III for casting the leaves of two doors of the temple. All these different craftsmen are happily at work in the same studio.

53 (above)

Line drawing of a relief in the tomb of Huya at Tell el-Amarna showing Yuti, the chief sculptor of the dowager Queen Tiye, at work in his studios attached to the workshops of her palace. The care with which this small scene has been carved in the friable limestone, the over-large portrait head of Yuti and the repetition of his name, arouse the strong suspicion that this is the work of Yuti himself and the second occurrence of his name is his signature. He squats on a stool to put the finishing touches to the painting of a statue of Beket-aten, the Queen's daughter and a sister of Tut-ankh-amun. Other sculptors are at work shaping the leg of a chair with an adze, or carving heads with chisels, similar to the box-wood example in plate 55.

54 (right)

The men who directed the craftsmen and ensured that both the continuity and the innovations of Egyptian art were achieved under proper authority were the literate designers. In the earliest days when the centre of culture was at Memphis, it was the city god Ptah, 'the Creator who had made things with his two hands as solace for his mind', who was regarded as the patron of all artistic enterprises. His high priest bore the title of 'Greatest of Craftsmen' even as late as Roman times. One of a line of such men was Ranofer who was responsible for the making of this painted limestone statue carved about 2500 BC, which is among the masterpieces of Egyptian art.

55 and 56 (left)

This box-wood head in the realistic style of the last years of the reign of Amenophis III, with the eyes inlaid in coloured glass and the ear-ring in gold and lapis lazuli, is usually identified as Queen Tiye. It was therefore probably carved under the supervision of her chief sculptor, Yuti (plate 53). *Left*, Upper part of a colossal limestone statue of Akhenaten from the destroyed temple to the Aten at Karnak. This impressively distorted portrait could only have been carved at the instigation of the King himself, probably by his sculptor Bek (plate 50). Both pieces are rare examples in Egyptian art of work that can be credited with probability to particular artists.

57 (above)

The ruins of the workmen's village, 'The Place of Truth on the West of Thebes', where generations of craftsmen employed on making the royal tombs at Thebes lived from about 1500 to 1085 BC. The houses were built in groups and share party walls, the lower courses being of rough blocks of limestone. The upper parts and subsidiary walls were built of mud-brick and plastered with mud. The houses were one storey high and included a reception room leading into a higher living room lit by grilled openings, the ceiling supported by one or two columns resting on stone bases. From this room one door led into the bedroom and another into a passage giving access to the kitchen and to a staircase leading to the roof where so much of the daily life was spent.

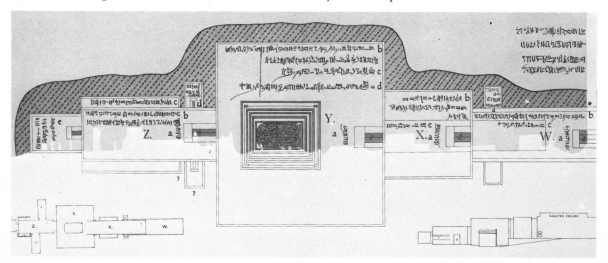

58 (above)

The workmen on the royal tombs followed a hereditary calling, the eldest son usually taking the place of his father. The post of secretary to the community, for instance, was in the hands of six successive members of the same family. The secretary had to keep a diary recording the amount of work done each day, the names of absentees and the reasons for their failure to report. His reports were submitted to the Vizier who was thus kept informed of progress during the intervals between his visits. Such a record is contained on the above ostrakon which has been put together from several fragments. It records entries in the last months of King Sethos II on the right and the first year of his successor, Siptah. The regnal year changes abruptly from Year 6, first month of Winter, day 29 to Year 1 of the new reign; when high officials come to report 'the falcon has flown to the horizon,' i.e., Sethos II is dead.

59 (left)

Part of a papyrus in the Turin Museum showing the architect's plan of the tomb of Ramesses IV, with a modern restoration and drawings of the plan and elevation of the actual tomb by Howard Carter. The entries name the various chambers and corridors of the tomb and report the state of work done in them. The red granite sarcophagus with a recumbent figure of the King on the lid is surrounded by shrines and a pall-support similar to the arrangements made for Tut-ankh-amun. It was the duty of the scribe to see that the architect's plan was followed according to his measurements and instructions and to enter on it the state of completion. In this he was assisted by the foremen of the two gangs into which the workmen were divided.

60

The most notable of the sculptors' studios excavated at Amarna is the workshop of Tuthmose, the chief sculptor and favourite of Akhenaten. The famous painted bust of Queen Nefertiti has been accredited to him, though it is perhaps more likely to have been made by her chief sculptor whose name is unknown to us. A number of plaster studies have also survived which are so realistic that they have been identified as life or death masks. This head of Akhenaten, however, is clearly a cast from a master statue, as the fragment of the Blue Crown in front of each ear shows, made to be sent as a pattern to the various sites where statues of the King were being carved.

Scientists
and Technologists

Science, as we understand it, is the study of basic principles from observed facts and their formulation into natural laws. This kind of scientific speculation would have seemed to the Ancient Egyptians to be presumptuously inquiring into the mysteries of the gods. They had, indeed, a kind of science but it differed markedly from that which is understood by the term today. They had collected a body of wisdom as the result of careful observation, the exercise of trial and the correction of error. With this knowledge they could solve the practical problems of everyday life.

As an example of Egyptian science we may instance mathematics. Various texts reveal that by the end of the third millennium BC the Egyptians had developed a respectable system of arithmetic and geometry, but since most of their learning was transmitted verbally from one adept to his pupil as a mystery, we have no means of assessing the full extent of their theoretical knowledge.

It is, however, extremely doubtful whether they were capable of doing more than solve problems connected with such matters as the distribution of rations or seed corn, the measurement of fields and the estimating of crop-yields for taxation purposes, the number of bricks required to build a given structure, and the number of men necessary to perform different kinds of labouring work. Nevertheless the inventiveness of the Ancient Egyptians produced effective results despite the absence of any spirit of scientific inquiry. The paper made from papyrus which they developed in the fourth millennium BC was still being produced in the eleventh century AD. Another substance that was greatly prized in the ancient world was lapis lazuli. The only source of the supply was centred in Afghanistan from whence it was exported all over the ancient Near East even as far as Egypt. At an early age, probably by about 2700 BC, the Ancient Egyptian had invented a calcium-copper silicate which closely imitated this most desirable but rare and expensive stone. He was able to mould this artificial substance into various objects. 'Egyptian Blue' as it is called was also powdered and used as a pigment, being exported to Italy as late as the seventh century AD.

His technology in fact, as distinct from his science, could accomplish enterprises that in recent times have fully challenged the ingenuity and resources of the modern world. As an example of this we may take the erection of large obelisks, which the Egyptians successfully achieved at least by the beginning of the second millennium BC. During the last century the French, British and Americans removed large obelisks from Egypt for erection elsewhere. The carrying out of these missions, using such modern devices as large compound shears, pulleys, capstans, hydraulic rams and jacks, was considered in each case as a notable achievement. A passage in an ancient papyrus, in which one scribe challenges another to calculate the number of men needed to transport a huge obelisk, 110 cubits long and 10 cubits thick, shows that such problems were well within the compass of the Egyptian Masters of Works.

The full technical achievement of the Ancient Egyptian is best appreciated, however, by examining one of his failures rather than his triumphs – the unfinished obelisk which still lies in the northern granite quarry at Aswan. It is 137 feet long and nearly 14 feet wide at its butt and if it had been extracted would have weighed nearly 1200 tons. Yet it was not because of an engineering miscalculation or a failure of nerve that it lies abandoned. The man who planned this colossal monument must have had every confidence that by his skill and calculations he could extract it from the quarry and erect it at Thebes or Memphis. It was a series of fissures in the lower bed of the granite matrix, which were only revealed as work progressed, that obliged the engineers to abandon their task. Their knowledge and experience were such that they knew that if they attempted to erect an obelisk of this size with such flaws, it would inevitably break in the middle.

The pounding of these great monuments from their beds of granite at Aswan, their removal on sleds to the banks of the Nile, their loading on great barges specially constructed for the purpose, their transport by river, their unloading, and finally their erection within a restricted space, all presented the Ancient Egyptian with formidable engineering problems which he triumphantly overcame with the help of his empirical technology.

It is true that the unfinished obelisk, weighing six times as much as Cleopatra's Needle on the Thames Embankment, was never moved from its quarry; but monuments just as heavy, such as the fallen colossus of Ramesses II in his mortuary temple, were successfully hewn and erected.

---

61 (right)
The red-granite obelisks of Tuthmosis I and Queen Hatshepsut still standing before the IVth and Vth Pylons in the temple of Amun at Karnak. Originally each obelisk had a partner. All four were erected within a narrow space by means of brick-ramps. The Queen's obelisk is 97½ feet high and weighs 323 tons. It is the tallest left standing in Egypt. An inscription on it declares that it and its companion were hewn 'from one block of hard red-granite without any patches or flaws'. The work in the quarry took seven months. The Queen adds, 'Let not him who hears this say, "It is a lie!" . . . but rather let him say, "How like her who is truthful in the sight of her father [Amun]!"'

62 (left)

The unfinished obelisk still recumbent in a quarry at Aswan. To find a suitable mass of granite the Ancient Egyptians had to go down to a considerable depth. The stone was worked by heating it between walls of mud brick, drenching it and pounding the fractured rock with dolerite balls which occur naturally in the adjacent desert. Not only was the upper surface levelled by this means but two separation trenches were pounded out on either side. Thereafter the obelisk had to be undercut, a laborious task, until it lay attached to its bed at a few points. The galleries beneath were then filled with suitable packing while the supports were bashed away, so that eventually it lay detached on a bed of rubble within its huge trench.

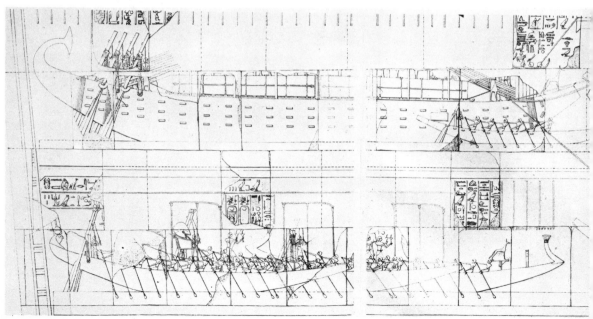

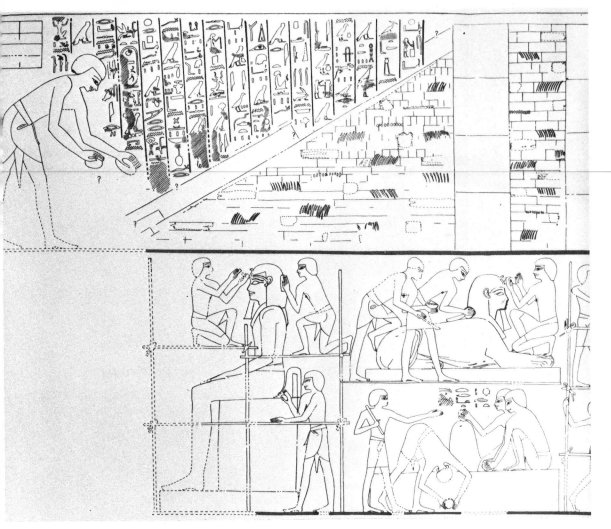

63 (above)

Line drawing of a painting in the tomb of the Vizier Rekh-mi-re showing the making of colossal monuments. In the lower register, sculptors are working on statues and an altar of Tuthmosis III. In the register above, what seems to be depicted is the building of a stone sanctuary, wall-blocks and the drums of columns being hauled up mud-brick ramps until each course is complete. The entire area is then levelled with rubble, wood, matting, stones and earth, ready for the ramp to be extended and the next course laid. When the 'topping out' blocks had been installed, the filling was removed and the stone dressed as it was exposed.

64 (left)

The obelisk had to be lowered down a sandbank by digging below its leading edge and using the levers to initiate a rolling motion like that of a cylinder. About forty ropes $7\frac{1}{4}$ inches in diameter pulled by six thousand men would have been required to control the descent. It then had to be manoeuvred on to a wooden sled and mounted on a transport barge. This drawing of a relief in the temple of Queen Hatshepsut (plate 24) shows two of her obelisks placed end to end on their barge, but is probably merely fanciful and it is more likely that they were stowed side by side. Even so this enormous barge was strengthened by three rows of cross-beams and towed downstream to Thebes by three rows of oared tugs, nine in a row, each row being led by a pilot boat.

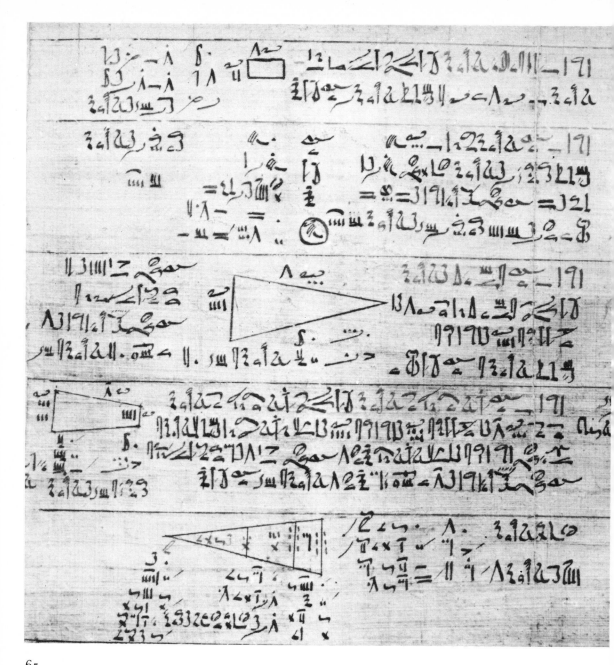

65

The Rhind Mathematical Papyrus in the British Museum written about 1600 BC, and other similar texts, reveal that by the end of the Third Millennium BC the Egyptians had developed a decimal system of numeration with which they could make arithmetical calculations involving complicated fractions with comparative ease and accuracy. They could solve problems involving two unknown quantities and had simple notions of geometrical and arithmetical progression using fractions. They were also familiar with elementary solid geometry and the properties of circles, cylinders, triangles and pyramids. Since they could find the area of a circle with tolerable accuracy by using a value of π of 3·16 they could also calculate the volume of a cylinder. They could also determine the volume of a pyramid or truncated pyramid. This page from the Rhind Papyrus deals with problems of triangles.

9   Man and the Gods

Every year the land of Egypt, parched with the summer heat, was submerged beneath the waters of the inundation. As the waters receded and the land emerged, first as a narrow spit of sand, the muddy wastes sprang into new life. Seeds in the ground germinated in the gentle heat of winter and soon an active population of tadpoles, insects and birds was inhabiting the vegetation growing on what had recently been an infertile hillock of earth sticking up above the water. This miracle of creation occurred each year in Egypt and profoundly influenced the imagination and thought of its people. This, they believed, was how the world began.

Egyptian creation myths all have in common this primordial ocean, the Nun, and the mound of earth that arose from it, but the other features of the story vary from place to place. This is hardly surprising. Egypt as a political and territorial entity did not arise suddenly but grew from very diverse human settlements on the banks of the river. Communities of hunters, herdsmen, cultivators and fishers, each with their local deity and beliefs, contributed their systems of thought, their explanations of the world around them. In step with political unification these ideas were assimilated into a theology which had nothing exclusive about it. One set of beliefs did not refute the others, since the ancient had a tolerant acceptance of all divine powers – even the gods of foreign peoples. In the great religious centres of Egypt, the prototypes of the universities of more modern cultures, thinkers formulated their doctrines and attempted a synthesis of the various ideas that were abroad; and this process was continuous in Egypt for the three thousand years of its life under the Pharaohs.

It was at Heliopolis, the centre of the sun-cult, however, that a theological system was developed which gained a wide and deep authority from the influence it exercised over the office of kingship. The primaeval mound at Heliopolis was a sand hill on which was a stone of pyramidal shape, the ben-ben. When the ben-ben was elevated upon a tree-pillar, the result was an obelisk on the top of which the demiurge Atum appeared on first emerging from the Nun. According to some beliefs, this manifestation was as a mythical bird, the Phoenix. The usual version of the doctrine taught that Atum, the Completed One, arose on the sand hill from Chaos and there copulated with himself as a result of which he spat out Shu the god of air and Tefnut the goddess of moisture, and from this pair descended two other divinities, Nut, the sky, and Geb, the earth, by normal processes of reproduction. Re, the active aspect of Atum, is represented not in the usual human form of the solar deities but as the disk of the sun. He early became associated with a sky-god Horus, who was manifest as a falcon and incarnate in the king. A composite deity Re-Herakhty, the Re-Horus of the Horizon, emerged from this fusion; and the Pharaoh, the living Horus, became first an incarnation of Re; but later the myth was sedulously cultivated that the Pharaoh had been begotten by Re upon the Chief Queen, and 'Son of Re' became an essential part of the royal titulary.

The close connections of royalty with the sun-cult led to its widespread influence over the whole spectrum of Egyptian religion and the identification of nearly every local god with Re. The sun-god traversed the sky by day in a special craft accompanied by a crew of gods. At sunset Re boarded another boat to sail on the waters that are under the earth.

There were other beliefs belonging to earlier strata of thought which were assimilated into the sun religion. Thus an earlier sky-cult concerned with star-worship was absorbed and the circumpolar stars 'which never rest' became the crew of the day-boat, while the stars that rise at various times in the east and are visible for part of the night before setting in the west, 'the unwearying ones', were the crew of the night-boat.

The position of man in this universe was clear. He shared it with the gods and was not there on sufferance. He had been fashioned by god in his own image.

'Well tended are men, the cattle of god. He created heaven and earth according to their desire. He made the breath of life for their nostrils. They are his images that have come forth from his body.'

The Egyptian universe, then, was created by a god whose manifold forms and activities kept it in a state of being. For the Egyptian view of creation was not that it had been completed when the universe came into existence but that it was a continuous process which had to be sustained by worship and cultic practices.

---

66 (right)
One of the three great ceremonial couches positioned in the ante-chamber of Tut-ankh-amun's tomb was in the form of a cow bearing the disk of the sun between her horns. She is Isis-Mehit, the great primordial ocean, the Nun, in which Creation began. It is in fact not a bed but a boat on which the dead King traverses the ocean of Mehit for his rebirth. To the prehistoric pastoralist roving over the North African savannahs as they dried up at the end of the Ice Age, the difference between life and death was water 'that begets all living things'. The illustration shows the head of the couch in the form of a cow, bearing the sun-disk between her horns.

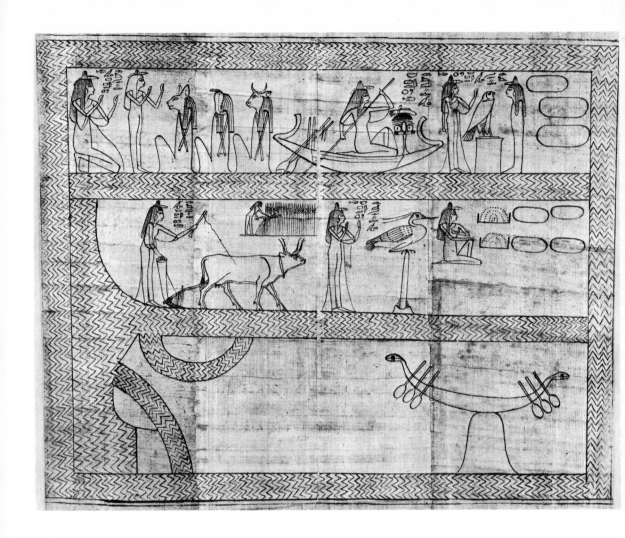

67

According to Egyptian belief, in the beginning was the inert water of the Nun containing all the germs of suspended creation within it. Something happened to begin the cycle of birth and as a result a mound arose out of the waters of Chaos which still surrounded the Egyptian universe. All the Egyptian creation myths have this feature in common but other aspects vary from place to place. At Heliopolis, the influential centre of ancient thought, it was believed that the Creator first manifested himself on this mound in the form of the Phoenix: and this vignette shows the bird alighting on the mound elevated on a pole, the obelisk.

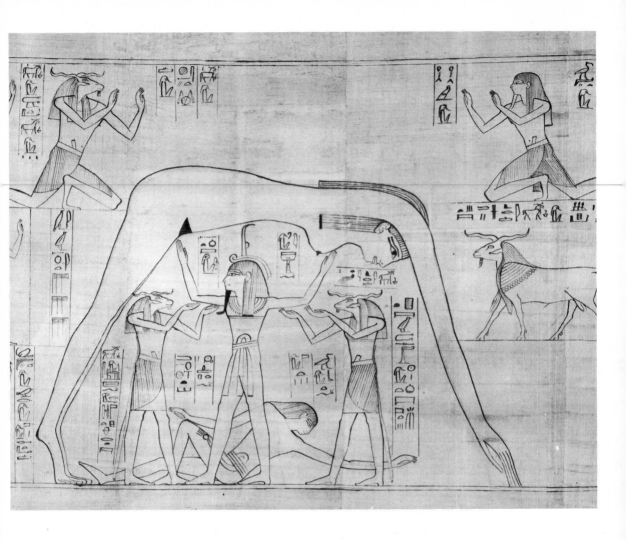

68

Another vignette from the same papyrus shows a further development in the Heliopolitan creation myth. The Creator, Atum, was the god of light who dispelled the darkness over Chaos and became a trinity with the first divine pair he formed from himself. These were Shu, the air, and Tefnut, moisture. From these descended another male and female pair, Nut, the sky, and Geb, the earth. Shu raised Nut from Geb and filled the vacancy between them. At night he lowered Nut upon Geb and from this coupling other gods were born including Isis and Osiris (plate 78). The scene shows Shu raising Nut from Geb assisted by ram-headed manifestations of the demiurge.

69

Re, the sun-god, reborn in the redness of dawn, traversed the sky by day in a special boat accompanied by manifestations of his power and by other gods. In this passage he had to contend with the cloud dragon Apophis (plate III), usually represented as a huge snake, but he always emerged triumphant even at an eclipse. This vignette, from the papyrus of another high-ranking Theban lady, shows the sky raising the day-boat with its crew to sail on the waters that are above the earth.

70

This neck ornament in gold and electrum, inlaid with semi-precious stones and coloured glass, is one which Tut-ankh-amun probably wore in life. The pectoral itself illustrates the universe as the Egyptian understood it. The moon in its aspects of a full disk, as well as a crescent, floats in a celestial skiff over the waters of the heavens in which grow lotus flowers similar to the one that opened from the Nun to disclose the sun-god (plate 15). They spring from the vault of heaven represented by a bar-like *pet*-sign supported upon the earth by sky-poles.

71 (above)

Another vignette from the papyrus illustrated in plate 69 showing, right, Osiris on his throne supported by his sister Nephthys and his wife Isis, all offspring of Geb and Nut. In origin, Osiris was probably a prehistoric fertility King who was ritually drowned in the rising Nile and buried beneath the primaeval mound where creation began and resurrection could follow. By historic times he was regarded as a former divinity ruling over Egypt who had been murdered by his evil brother Seth. Isis recovered the scattered members, reassembled them by surgical bandaging, revived the corpse and so posthumously conceived the son Horus who later assumed the throne. The appeal of this legend lay in the idea of a vulnerable god who had died like a mortal and been resurrected as a power in the hereafter. A promise was held out to all men who on death became Osiris (plate 78).

72 (below)

The manifestation of the dead man that could continue a ghostly life in the tomb was the *Ba*, represented as a bird with a human head as in this inlaid gold jewel from the mummy of Tut-ankh-amun. 'Thou shalt change into a living Ba and have power to obtain bread and water and air. Thou shalt take the form of a swallow or a falcon or a bittern whatever thou pleasest. Thou shalt cross in the ferry boat . . . thou shalt sail on the flood waters and thy life begin anew.' At nightfall the bird-soul, the Ba, returned to the tomb.

10   Death and Burial

Proper burial with due rites was considered by every Egyptian who could afford it as essential to the survival of his personality. The prehistoric Egyptian buried his dead in a crouching position in the dry sand of the desert as though awaiting rebirth. Above the grave was apparently heaped a hillock of sand and stones. By the early dynastic period such graves had become very much more elaborate, consisting of a complex of subterranean chambers and magazines lined with wooden planks and matting. The bench-like superstructure or 'mastaba' had developed into a large rectangular mass imitating the façade of a contemporary great house or palace. The idea of the grave as a place of rebirth was thus at an early date overlaid by the conception of the tomb as a kind of house, 'the mansion of eternity' as the Egyptians called it where, by magic, the deceased could continue a ghostly version of the life he had once enjoyed on earth.

From the belief that the *Ba*, or spirit, or soul, or ghost, could live on in the mansion of eternity like a twittering bird, there arose the vast elaboration of Egyptian funerary practices. When bodies came to be buried in sub-terranean chambers instead of simply in the desiccating sand, they had to be artificially preserved; and hence developed the practice of mummification, at first by dry-salting the body, in the same way as fish were preserved, after the internal organs had been removed and embalmed separately. With the embalmed dead were deposited the goods they had owned on earth and which they would require in their ghostly afterlife. Their chief need was for food and drink, and during the early dynasties a special niche was made in the superstructure of the tomb where food offerings could be laid by pious relatives of the deceased, who, like their modern descendants in Egypt, were accustomed to visit the tombs of the dead on feast days and there eat a meal in a kind of communion with the departed spirit of their ancestor. From this simple practice developed the great stone mastaba-chapels of the Old Kingdom with their courtyards, corridors, chambers and chapels decorated with painted reliefs of the deceased in all his worldly pursuits. The simple offering stela, with a picture of the owner seated before a table of food offerings, became a large false door through which he steps to partake of the daily meals. In periods of anarchy and transition, such as occurred at the end of the Old and Middle Kingdoms, the robbing of the tombs of former magnates or the lapse of their funerary endowments and a general impoverishment induced men to question the old tenets. On the return of new periods of high civilisation, however, the ruling classes revived with unquenchable optimism the belief that the tomb was the mansion of eternity. But after the New Kingdom, the tomb is often little better than a grave. The coffin with its scenes and texts became almost the owner's sole hope of immortality: the contents mattered less and less.

This change of view was not only the triumph of experience over centuries of wishful thinking. Other ideas of a more spiritualised existence after death belong originally to the cult of the dead king and manifest themselves particularly in two doctrines that steadily gained a wider recognition throughout the Old Kingdom. The first was that of the solar religion which under the influence of the priesthood at Heliopolis taught that the Pharaoh was the son of the sun-god who on death flew away as a falcon to the horizon to be assimilated to him who had begotten him on the Chief Queen. But there was also another cult which towards the end of the Old Kingdom began to spread with great rapidity and to influence the doctrines regarding the royal destiny. This was the religion of Osiris, a god who had died like a mortal and been resurrected as a power in the Hereafter, ruling over the dead, while his son stood in his place as the ruler of the living. Originally all such beliefs and practices belonged to the royal burial only; but they spread to an ever-widening circle of humanity until everyone who could afford a burial became as a king, an Osiris, on death.

But for all their apparent confidence the Egyptians really had very vague ideas of the next world and their views about it varied from age to age and place to place and were often in conflict. Death they regarded as a calamity which they hoped would not arrive until they had passed the ideal life-span of 110 years like that of the patriarchs of the Bible.

73

In this vignette from the papyrus of Hu-nefer in the British Museum the last rites are being performed. 'Invocation offerings shall be made for you and sacrifices made at your tomb stela.' The façade of the tomb is represented with its pyramidion above. Before the door is the round-topped stela. The mummy of the deceased is raised upright by a priest wearing the dog-headed mask of Anubis the god of embalming. The wife and daughter wail at the feet of the dead man despite his 'passing into bliss'. The ritual of Opening the Mouth (plate VIII), whereby all his faculties would be restored to the dead man, is performed by attendants under the guidance of a *setem*-priest wearing a leopard-skin robe. Below, a calf is sacrificed and the instruments of the rite are laid out on a table.

74 (left above)
A reconstructed predynastic burial in the British Museum. The dead man has been buried in the dry sands of the desert and his tissues have been preserved by natural desiccation. He lies crouched as though awaiting rebirth. Beside him are pots containing food and drink for his needs in the next world. Above the tomb there would have been raised a small mound of sand covered perhaps with pebbles, similar to grave-mounds made in Nubia until recent times.

75 (left below)
By early dynastic times such burials had become much more elaborate and enriched. The mound had developed into a bench-like 'mastaba' of mud-brick panelled with recesses to imitate the façade of a contemporary house. The deceased was laid out in an extended position, his shrunken tissues padded out with linen plastered and painted and dressed to imitate the appearance of a living person. He also acquired a coffin of stone or wood in the form of a house with doors and windows as in this sarcophagus of Ra-wer. The tomb has become the 'mansion of eternity'.

76 (above)
Despite the spiritualisation of the after-life in the Middle Kingdom, the monarchs of the New Kingdom and their high officials went to their eternal rest with even richer funerary equipment than before. This illustration shows the southern end of the ante-chamber of Tut-ankh-amun's tomb soon after its discovery. The material buried with these Kings was of two kinds—objects that they had used in their lifetimes and were therefore infused with their aura; and ritual objects designed to ensure their resurrection in the world of the sun-god as well as in the chthonian regions of Osiris.

77

The false door of Iteti in the Cairo Museum in which the deceased, carved three quarters in the round, steps into his tomb chapel to receive the funerary offerings. The deceased is shown in the essential scene of the relief seated before an altar, on which the ritual slices of bread are laid. A text above assures him of 'thousands of fowl, flesh, bread,' and other funerary offerings. The needs of the deceased are thus to be satisfied by magic also. Eventually magic in the form of prayer was to replace material goods in burial furnishings, and such prayers were to get even shorter. In this false door the invocation is still on behalf of the dead man; but a few centuries later, in the Middle Kingdom, the funeral offerings are petitioned for the *spirit* of the deceased.

78 (above left)

A wooden tray made in the form of the god Osiris, filled with earth sown with corn, and fitted with a perforated cover through which the seed could sprout. Such Osiris beds were put in some important tombs during the New Kingdom as a symbol of resurrection—the cycle of seed germinating to ripened head containing next season's seed. The Pharaoh, who in life had controlled the powers of nature for the benefit of his people, became indentified with those powers on his death. As Osiris he was present in the growing corn, as the star Orion, as the inundation and the waxing moon. Man and Nature were as one.

79 (above right)

This effigy represents Tut-ankh-amun recumbent on the lion-bier upon which he will traverse the primaeval waters to his resurrection as Osiris, the ruler of the dead. He is accompanied by a falcon and a human-headed Ba-bird, symbolising what is expressed as early as the Pyramid Texts, that the Ba, or external manifestation of the King, is in the tomb while his spirit flies in the heavens. This latter concept is expressed in the prayer to the sky-goddess Nut inscribed on the effigy – 'cause me to be as the imperishable stars that are within thee', referring to an ancient belief that the dead entered the great circuit of the sky.

Epilogue

In the foregoing chapters we have outlined the means by which the natural and human resources of the Nile Valley were employed in the fourteenth century BC according to a system which had been developed at the dawn of history and was gradually adapted to changing conditions with the passage of time. Only once in its long history was this system radically altered; and then for a brief interlude by King Akhenaten, the immediate predecessor of Tut-ankh-amun, who introduced an intolerant monotheism which upset the economic basis of Egyptian prosperity. Tut-ankh-amun, in a decree which he issued early in his reign, describes the condition of Egypt at his accession as being 'topsy-turvy' and promises to restore the morale and well-being of his people by returning to those age-old principles which had served them so well in the past, and which indeed were to prove equally viable for the next millennium.

80
Pendant in gold, lapis lazuli, green felspar and coloured calcite forming the rebus, 'Neb-kheperu-re', the Son-of-Re name of Tut-ankh-amun.

of related interest

Understanding Sensory Dysfunction
Learning, Development and Sensory Dysfunction in Autism
Spectrum Disorders, ADHD, Learning Disabilities and
Bipolar Disorder
Polly Godwin Emmons and Liz McKendry Anderson
ISBN 1 84310 806 2

Asperger's Syndrome
A Guide for Parents and Professionals
Tony Attwood
Foreword by Lorna Wing
ISBN 1 85302 577 1

Freaks, Geeks and Asperger Syndrome
A User Guide to Adolescence
Luke Jackson
Foreword by Tony Attwood
ISBN 1 84310 098 3
Winner of the NASEN & TES Special Educational Needs Children's
Book Award 2003

Parenting a Child with Asperger Syndrome
200 Tips and Strategies
Brenda Boyd
ISBN 1 84310 137 8

**Relationship Development Intervention with Children,
Adolescents and Adults**
Social and Emotional Development Activities for Asperger
Syndrome, Autism, PDD and NLD
Steven E. Gutstein and Rachelle K. Sheely
ISBN 1 84310 717 1

Raising NLD Superstars
What Families with Nonverbal Learning Disabilities Need to
Know about Nurturing Confident, Competent Kids
Marcia Brown Rubinstien
Foreword by Pamela B. Tanguay
ISBN 1 84310 770 8